Praise for Peter

NORTHERNMOST

"Peter Geye may well be the William Faulkner of the North Country." —William Kent Krueger, author of *This Tender Land*

"Peter Geye writes with an almost romantic passion about all things wintry." —*Minneapolis Star Tribune*

"A tremendously satisfying family saga about the tenacity of love amid the unpredictable, ungovernable forces that act on our lives." —Maggie Shipstead, author of *Great Circle*

"Elegant.... Satisfying.... Geye artfully spans 120 years of the Eide family's story." —*Kirkus Reviews* (starred review)

"A marvel of storytelling." —Tom Franklin, author of *Crooked Letter, Crooked Letter*

"Impressive.... A memorable, powerful tale of endurance and ancestral connection." —*Publishers Weekly*

"A study of marriage and family across time and geographies. . . . *Northernmost* is rich in history, adventure, and love." —Kao Kalia Yang, author of *The Song Poet*

"Evocative. . . . [A] literary yet action-packed novel that weaves together two stories, separated by a century." —Historical Novel Society

Peter Geye

NORTHERNMOST

Born and raised in Minneapolis, Peter Geye lives there with his family. His previous novels are *Safe from the Sea*, *The Lighthouse Road*, and *Wintering*.

www.petergeye.com

ALSO BY PETER GEYE

Safe from the Sea

The Lighthouse Road

Wintering

NORTHERNMOST

NORTHERNMOST

—

Peter Geye

VINTAGE BOOKS

A Division of Penguin Random House LLC

New York

The Library of Congress has cataloged the
Knopf edition as follows:
Name: Geye, Peter, author.
Title: Northernmost / by Peter Geye.
Description: First edition. | New York : Alfred A. Knopf, 2020.
Identifiers: LCCN 2019019921
Classification: LCC PS3607.E925 N67 2020 | DDC 813/.6—dc23
LC record available at https://lccn.loc.gov/2019019921

Vintage Books Trade Paperback ISBN: 978-0-525-56535-2
eBook ISBN: 978-0-525-65576-3

www.vintagebooks.com

Printed in the United States of America
10 9 8 7 6 5 4 3 2 1

For Eisa

and

For Emily

Oh that burning longing day and night were happiness!

—Fridtjof Nansen, *Farthest North*

The Eide Family

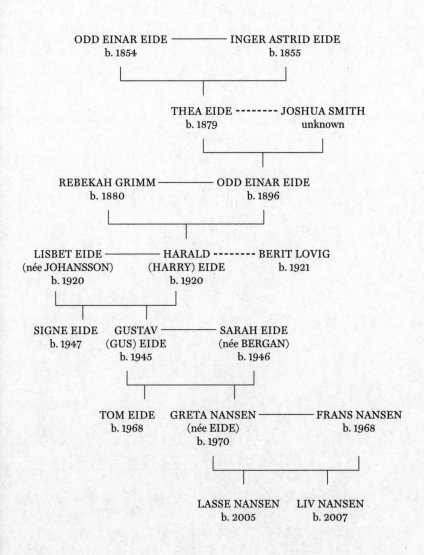

ODD EINAR EIDE ——————— INGER ASTRID EIDE
b. 1854   b. 1855

THEA EIDE - - - - - - - - JOSHUA SMITH
b. 1879   unknown

REBEKAH GRIMM ——————— ODD EINAR EIDE
b. 1880   b. 1896

LISBET EIDE ——————— HARALD - - - - - - - - BERIT LOVIG
(née JOHANSSON)   (HARRY) EIDE   b. 1921
b. 1920   b. 1920

SIGNE EIDE   GUSTAV ——————— SARAH EIDE
b. 1947   (GUS) EIDE   (née BERGAN)
                        b. 1945   b. 1946

TOM EIDE   GRETA NANSEN ——————— FRANS NANSEN
b. 1968   (née EIDE)   b. 1968
                      b. 1970

LASSE NANSEN   LIV NANSEN
b. 2005   b. 2007

NORTHERNMOST

Each night she leaves the light on in the front window and walks the cove shoreline out to the point and from across the water tries to believe she lives there, in the warm and quiet glow of the fish house. So many nights during the last year—the hardest of her life—after working all day on the house or at her desk, she's come out here to take comfort in the surging waves. My, how they keep coming. But for weeks the cove and even the lake out beyond the point have been frozen. The cold tonight will make the ice stronger. The snow will make it softer.

Her grandmother once painted the fish house from this vantage. Back in the 1940s, when she was first a bride and still in love with the idea of living here. That painting, along with five others, hangs in the historical society on the Lighthouse Road. It's titled *Fish House in Snow Squall,* and from where she stands now Greta can see it as she imagines her grandmother might have, even if she's standing in a blizzard, not a squall. The trees on the point sway in the gusts, their blackness a shifting smudge against the snowlit sky.

"You're doing it again, Mom," Liv says, her voice pinched on the wind.

Greta steps closer. "Doing what, love?"

"Talking out loud."

"I was thinking about my grandma." Greta brushes the snow from Liv's hat and sees its reflection in her daughter's eyes. "She was an artist. Her paintings are in the historical society. You've seen them."

"The one of the fish house," Liv says.

"That's the one I was thinking of."

"It's not the same fish house anymore."

Greta imagines some pride in her daughter's voice. "It certainly isn't."

Together they look back across the cove, the wind biting their faces. Usually the radiance from town a half mile across the isthmus comes up over the trees, but tonight the snow blots even that out. The only thing alight in any direction is the window.

"Axel!" Liv hollers as the dog chases a whorl of snow blown up off the ice. "Come here, boy!"

"He's okay," Greta says. "The snow's got him excited is all."

Now they watch him bound off. Liv's crazy about him, a giant mutt that looks as much like a bear as a dog. At two years old, he weighs a hundred and thirty pounds. His paws are as big as Liv's feet. Perfect for the snow.

"The wind's so quiet without the water," Liv says.

Greta's heard that before, and wonders whose expression it is. Her mother or father? Her grandfather? It can't be Frans, can it?

"If it wasn't snowing, would the wind sound the same?" Liv asks.

Greta puts her ear up to the night, as though listening for birdsong, and says, "I don't think so. If it weren't snowing, it would sound more like a scream. This is almost like someone whistling. Or humming."

Axel comes barreling out of the darkness, storming into Liv's legs and knocking her down. She laughs and bounces up and tries to tackle him but misses. Axel circles back and Liv gets up again and pushes her hat up off her eyes and together the two of them start toward the fish house. Greta watches them running, can hear Liv's laugh carried on the wind. Before they're halfway across the cove, the light in the window wavers and, on the ebb of another strong breeze, the house goes dark.

In the closet off the mudroom, Greta finds the lantern and a box of wooden matches and she lights up the mantle and they go into what she's now calling the great room. A fire still smolders in the fireplace and Greta rekindles it while Liv collapses on the leather chair. Axel shakes the snow from his coat and lies on the rug. The house is warm, but without power the new bedrooms up in the loft will soon get cold.

"We'd better sleep down here," Greta says.

"Like a slumber party."

"I'll go get blankets and pillows. You brush your teeth."

Greta goes upstairs for Liv's bedding and the stuffed polar bear she's lately been sleeping with again. She grabs her own comforter and another pillow and heads back downstairs. It's so quiet inside. Only the snap of the fire and the dog's heavy sighs and, out in the night, the wind through the darkness.

Before she'd done all the work on the house, the wind had flowed through it like water through a fishnet. But with the new fireplace and chimney and the loft, with the new windows and roof, the place has been trued and now the wind's kept outside. Greta arranges Liv's pillow and quilt on the big chair and spreads her comforter on the sofa.

Liv comes out of the bathroom and jumps in the chair. "Will it stay warm enough with just the fire?"

"I think so," Greta says.

Liv reaches down for the dog. "I can sleep on the floor with Axel if I get cold. He'd love that."

Greta smiles at her daughter's easiness. She hasn't seen much of it recently. Liv's only eleven years old. Eleven going on eighteen, what with all the mood swings and surliness, the back talk and pitting herself against the world, the unexplained tears and desperate hugs. Of course, Greta feels responsible for all of it. How many times each day does she agonize over Liv's mood? How much time does she spend wondering if her daughter will be all right? How much are her own choices going to cost her daughter? And her son, Lasse, too, who is staying the night up at his grandpa's house?

"I'll be up working for a while," Greta says. "I'll keep the fire going. Maybe the power'll come back on."

"Are you still writing the family story?"

Greta sits down and spreads Liv's quilt and kisses her forehead. "I'm almost done."

"Is it a true story?"

"Sort of."

"Are the people happy?"

"Are you okay, sweet pea?"

Liv rubs her eyes and looks like she's about to sulk. Instead she says, "It's tomorrow we go home, right? And Dad will be there?"

"That's right. We'll leave after breakfast. Dad's on his way home now."

Liv yawns deeply and when her eyes open again they catch the light from the fire. "I can't wait to see him."

"He's excited to see you too."

"Why's he gone so much?"

Greta smooths Liv's hair. "I think you should talk to him about that when you see him."

Liv yawns again.

"I love you, kiddo," Greta says.

Liv rolls on her side, facing the fire. "I love you back."

Greta gets up and takes the lantern off the coffee table and heads over to her desk.

She also built this. One day last fall, she'd gone up to a farm on County Road 7 to see about some old siding advertised on Craigslist. The unmoored barn had slipped from its foundation years earlier and seemed ready to collapse altogether, but the owner assured her it was safe to go inside, which they did. The same clapboard siding that covered the fish house was stacked in the haymow. It was a miracle, frankly, to have found it. She was about to start hauling boards out to her truck when she saw, in another corner of the barn, a workbench, the top of which was a chunk of white pine four inches thick and thirty square feet. When she asked about it, the man said, "Take everything. It'll be less to burn." Together they loaded the wood onto the trailer behind her truck. And on a warm day in October, after the loft had been sided, she'd stood outside and sanded and planed and varnished the top of the workbench. She built new legs from cedar posts and now it sat in the corner, up against the window.

Greta looks around the fish house at everything else she's done. The loft bedrooms are the most notable addition. Three small rooms up an open staircase, one each for her and the kids. There's the mudroom and closet beneath the staircase. She built the kitchen along the north wall and a small island where four barstools sit under the counter. The wall facing the lake is all window, divided into three floor-to-ceiling panes. The floors throughout have been refinished and shine beautifully. Especially against the fire in the hearth.

The fireplace is her favorite part of the renovation. She and the kids picked the rocks from the river up by her father's house and they cover a third of the wall opposite the kitchen. She had the hearth and flue installed but did the stonework herself, straight up to the tip of the chimney. Two solid weeks of backbreaking toil that had also been her best therapy.

She hears the fire snap, then a gust outside. She steps to the window. It still unsettles her to be here without the creaks and moans, especially on a howling night like this. She cups her hands around her eyes and peers out the window. The snow blows toward the lake, falling and dancing up off the ground at once. But Liv was right. Without the lake—without any waves—the wind in all its fierceness seems almost hushed.

That's it: her mother used to call a north wind a quieting wind, because it blows the water away from shore. God, she misses her mother. Greta supposes it's thanks to the many things she learned from her that she was capable of remodeling the fish house. And strong enough to have come back home to live in it. Strong enough to have found him, and to have insisted on him, despite the long odds against them.

He also spoke of the northern wind. In the first letter he sent, more than a year ago now, he wrote that she should think of it as a gift. That he'd send the breath of Boreas when he missed her most, up over the pole and on down to her. He wrote things like that, things that she read as both poetry and promises. He sent her other things too. A stone picked from the hills above Hammerfest. A bronze lighthouse figurine, small enough to wear on a charm necklace. A compass. A fountain pen. And his first and most amazing gift, that slight book and his translation of it, his penmanship so fine and precise it could have been typeset on some antique press. The original is leather-bound, with a polar bear from the shoulders up, its forepaws raised above its snarling face, embossed beneath the title: *Isbjørn i Nordligste Natt. The Polar Bear in the Northernmost Night.* Fifty-four pages chronicling a fortnight in her great-great-great-grandfather's life, published by some man named Marius Granerud in Tromsø, Norway, in the year 1898.

After reading it more times than she can count, she's still surprised by something she can only describe as being haunted each time she looks at it. That her family, as far back as it's known to her, has been suffering the cold and snow of this world as though these are the conditions of their natural and only habitat. It's like a confirmation of who she is. And that the stories of her father's and great-grandfather's bears should likewise have their provenance? This helps her believe in the manuscript pages stacked on the corner of her desk. She reaches over and flips through them.

It comes again, the quieting wind, and she feels the house heavy behind her. She thinks of the boats that have been built in here. First her great-grandfather's fishing boat, then her grandfather's and father's canoes. They all made their great discoveries on those boats. She knows the stories. Her father told them. Berit Lovig told them. So now she's telling one herself. They're as much a part of her as her own daughter, sleeping peacefully across the room.

And what will Greta do with the old place fitted out for her? Why, she'll just keep starting over again. She sits down and pushes the lantern over to the side of her desk. She waits for the wind to come over the house one more time, imagines he sent it, sends a thought back to him—that she misses him, and that she'll see him soon—and opens her computer.

Part One

—

DRAUGEN

I am not the first man who ever buttoned his coat and boarded a ship and followed his silence north. Nor am I the first made mouthy by what discovered him there. Indeed, how many stories have men like me lived to tell? If life is what I found on my return, among the wooden crosses and gravestones below the Hammerfest hillside.

I remember that wan early morning, the sun too low and faint to hold the fog at sea. The tender's oarlocks squawked in awful harmony with the gulls tilting above. The hills were scabrous gray, the scree poised as ever to bury the village. I remember all this. And old Magnus Moen on the oars, a man my age and one I'd known all my life, speaking no word to me. He only beat his oars against the harbor water while muttering into his coat.

I remember Bengt Bjornsen's horse and carriage, too, rolling along Grønnevoldsgaden. I could see his charge. A woman dressed in black seated beside him and the pastor in his frock standing on the back rail. I mouthed a prayer, that this meager procession was not for my daughter, gone two years. The thought of her turned my eyes to the mailbags sitting above the bilge on the deck of the tender. We'd not heard from Thea since we sent her off. Not one word, kind or otherwise. For all we knew she was drowned or buried.

By the time Magnus tied off on the wharf, the horse and carriage had disappeared. It wasn't yet eleven o'clock as I stepped ashore and turned to look from where I'd come. As though I could see those hundreds of miles behind me. But all was gone. Lost in the fog if not in my memory. The mailboat *Thor* out at anchor? The mountains of Sørø and the sea beyond? Even the birds and the sound of the birds? All was gone. Only North remained. I could point North and remember the snow and still believe in it. I *did* believe in it—and not much else.

Magnus tossed the mailbags at my feet, then climbed from the tender and stood beside me on the wharf. I felt in my pockets as though I had a krone to offer him. But all I found was my pipe and pouch, so I packed the bowl and Magnus offered me a light and we stood together and smoked.

"There's a bit of the Draugen about ja, Odd Einar." Magnus thumbed his hat and looked out from beneath his bushy eyebrows. He puffed on his pipe and shook his head. "It's a hell of a thing. Coming back here on a day such as this. Take a slow walk home, ja?" He pushed his hat back off his head and ran a knobby hand over his balding crown. "Give them a chance to see you." He snuffed out his pipe and tied a second line to a cleat on the wharf. "And God bless you, friend. God bless you and Inger."

I watched Magnus set his hat right. He put his reindeer hide gloves on and shouldered the mail sacks. He turned to leave but then set his load down once more, slipped a glove off, reached into his pocket, and pulled out a few coins. He picked from them two øre and offered them to me. I felt my face flush and tucked my cheeks into my coat's collar. "I'm all set, friend," I said.

"Odd Einar, stop at Bengt's bakery before you head home. Buy a loaf and some butter. I've known you since we were runts. I don't like the look of you now. A hungry man is a sad thing."

He pushed the money into my hand and put his glove on again, slung the mail sacks over his shoulder, and this time walked off. He didn't whistle, Old Magnus.

The Grønnevoldsgaden was swallowed by fog as I walked up it. The whole village was, as though it burned for the second time. On the corner of the Strandgaden, the electric streetlights flickered on and Inger's auntie was standing there on the cobbles with her cane and palsied foot. She looked up and saw me, turned and limped away. I tried to call out, but there was no voice in me.

As if mocking my dumbness, a pair of shrieking gulls banked low. I watched them wing back toward the harbor and then crossed the street and walked to the bakery. Its dark windows were filled with loaves covered by flour sacks. Baskets of Bengt's pepparkaka and kanelbolle were sitting on the far end of the counter. On the other, jars of butter and jams were stacked in small pyramids. I felt the coins in my pocket, and stepped to the door. It was locked, so I stepped back into the street and closed my eyes and felt the gnawing in my bowels.

I stood there long enough for what remained of me to notice its reflection in the bakery window: ugly and gaunt and tired as the pilings on the wharf. It would take a month of Inger's black pot to bring me back to life. With just that thought I went to the entry next to the bakery and opened it and climbed the narrow staircase and stood atop the landing and knocked on my door. How much time had I spent imagining this homecoming? Always it had been Inger answering the door, her hair down, the warmth of the stove and the brightness of the lamp glass falling from our room. If I'm being honest, I allowed myself Thea, too, sitting at the small table with a cup of tea and her knitting, humming some hymn or laughing. And in the darkest and coldest junctures of my northern straits, I saw her eyes turning up to meet mine and her smiling lips saying *Papa!* The thought of her saved me more than once.

I knocked again and stood leaning against my exhaustion, which was the only thing in this world as fierce as my hunger. How many moments such as this had passed since that boat came to rescue me from the fog? Moments when my weakness settled on me and my memories went back to the wastes of Spitzbergen, with nothing but blankness and distance before me. I was no more sated as I stood on the landing outside our door than I'd been on the Krossfjorden. My guts were tight as fiddle strings.

I put my rawboned and filthy hand on the doorknob, drew a breath, and heard the hinges screech as the door swung open. Dark-dark-dark. As dark as the *Lofoten's* coal bunker, but smelling faintly of potatoes. My stomach loosened and then turned and I poked my nose down into my collar, for I did not trust that sweet scent. If I had learned anything it was that a hungry man will smell his supper a hundred times before he gets a spoonful.

I stepped in and tried to blink the darkness into light. But it would not go and so I pulled the door shut behind me and crossed the room blindly and pulled back the curtain. I unlatched and opened the window, and the room was charged with the briny smell off the harbor. When I turned around to see my home again, my breath would not come. Not for a full half minute.

The pallet in the corner had been folded in half and tied with twine. Inger's rosmåling, which before had sat proudly on a shelf above the hearth, was gone. So, too, were the chairs around the table. In a tin bowl on the shelf I found a single potato, sprouting and black, then carried it over to the window to inspect it in the light. Against my better judgment I took a bite. It made me retch and I spit it out and threw the rest toward the stove, where it landed in Inger's cook pot and jiggled the handle of her wooden spoon. The promise of a meal set my teeth on edge, and I crossed the room in two long strides to look in the pot. A dead mouse lay on the bottom beside the potato. A fine soup for a starving man.

Across the room, in the chest of drawers beside the bed, I found a ball of yarn and her old needles and a half-finished mitten. The lamp atop the chest was empty of oil, though the matches still sat in the wooden box. I lit one and played it around the empty room. That place had never been a home, but to discover such emptiness and what came with it? Well, there were no words to describe it. I let the match burn out and closed the window and walked back down to the street.

A fresh wind came over the hills as I stood outside the bakery again. All this distance I had come. All this distance and with all my sorry hope. And for what? *Damn it all,* I thought. *Put me back on the wastes. Leave me for the ice bears.*

"Herr Eide?" Someone stood ten paces down the road with a basket hung over her arm. One of Thea's friends. Her father was a rope maker named Skjeggestad. I once bought my line from him.

"It's me?" I said. My voice came out hoarse, and I coughed and bent at the waist and swallowed as I righted myself. I turned away, my shame sharp. She didn't leave, though. When I looked at her face again, I could see she was amazed. "And you're Skjeggestad's daughter?"

"Hilde—"

"Of course. Hildegard Skjeggestad. Thea's friend. My daughter's friend."

Her eyes were wide and disbelieving.

"The bakery is closed," I said, as if to excuse my being there on the street.

Her mouth was open to speak, but no words came. Had she not heard me?

"Our room," I began, but then looked down at my garb, such as it was. My pants were threadbare and tattered at the cuff. My coat, a castoff from a stevedore in Vardø, was stained at the breast and missing every other button. My shirt had been on my back for weeks and smelled foul enough to prove it. And my socks, stiff with blood and worn through at the heels, would be the first things I'd burn. Only the boots on my feet, fine komager boots made from Spitzbergen reindeer hide, offered any proof that I wasn't a Draugen after all. "You've not seen Thea, then? Or heard news?"

"But Fru Eide and the pastor..." she finally said, turning to look up the Grønnevoldsgaden, even pointing there.

"Thea?" I asked, nudging my chin in the same direction.

Now she looked afraid. She might have even been crying. "Herr Bjornsen, he's also gone to the cemetery." She took a step back, making a wide berth for me.

I saw my reflection again. "I beg your pardon," I said. "I'm just home." Now I pointed at myself in the window as though it were explanation enough for my condition. "It was a long trip. I was in Vardø only two days ago. Five full days at sea before that. I was made to work for my passage, you see? Loading coal—"

"Excuse me, Herr Eide." She had in her basket a bunch of carrots and radishes. She took a carrot and handed it to me and said, "Fru Eide has gone to the cemetery."

And then, as if I were finally joining the conversation, I said, "But who has died?"

She stepped past me and said, "I must go, Herr Eide. My mother is waiting."

"Of course," I said. "Thank you. Give your mother and father my greetings."

I stood outside the bakery gnawing on the carrot, stem and all, as Hildegard hurried away.

I heard the pastor before I saw him, his voice starting and stopping on the wind. "Thou turnest man to destruction; and sayest, Return, ye children of men..." Rainwater streamed down the cemetery path, and I slipped on the rocks and muddied my hands and knees. I heard the horse neigh and stamp his hoof. "... Thou has set our iniquities before thee, our secret sins in the light of thy countenance. For all our days are passed away in thy wrath: we spend our years as a tale that is told." *What rot,* I thought, my intestines twisting around the carrot. I felt sickly but also charged. *We spend our lives in blind obedience. We pray for mercy and find only suffering.* "... And if by reason of strength they be fourscore years, yet is their labor and sorrow; for it is soon cut off, and we fly away." *But, we fly* home. *And not by the grace of God but by our wits and our own damn will. We are hungry, and you offer us nothing. We are cold, and you offer only wind and snow. We are lonesome, and you stow us in a coal bunker.*

It was not the first time since I'd been lost that I became furious thinking of the dreck I'd heard in church all my life, but the pastor's psalm stoked my anger afresh, and I bumped into the horse's ass. Inger's shabby handbag sat on the carriage's bench. The wind drew down. I patted the horse's withers and he neighed and swung his muscled neck around to meet my eyes. His own went wide and he snorted and then I heard Inger's sweet voice as I looked up to see her, a freshly turned grave between us.

"Kjære Gud. Kan det væredes?" she said.

"Inger." Did I say her name aloud? Did I say, "Is that you?"

I noticed Bengt and the pastor step back together as though startled. Inger's eyes widened as the horse's had, and she looked down at her Bible and closed it and then looked at me from bottom to top. I took my hat from my head and held it before me as if I was some gentleman. I could see her trembling hands and heaving chest. And, when stepping closer, her wet eyes now glaring at the gravestone at her feet.

"Inger, is that our daughter? Is that my Thea?"

She looked up and blinked the wetness away. "Thea?" she said and shook her head no. She said "Thea" again and finally came to me. She put a hand on my shoulder and then on my face, and said, her fingers still in my ratty beard, "But you're dead, Odd Einar."

"Dead?"

"That's what they said. On Spitzbergen. You and that man Birger Mikkelsen. At Krossfjorden. Killed by an ice bear." She kept her hand on my face, as though she could not otherwise believe I was there.

"Birger died on the Krossfjorden. But I didn't. I'm home, Inger."

When she dropped her hand I could see the softness of the inside of her wrist and the pink of her cold flesh. What trailed her hand was a fresh scent, nearly floral, something I'd never smelled before.

Bengt coughed and Inger looked over her shoulder, stuffed her hand into her pocket and, in the same motion, stepped back beside the gravestone. The pastor came forward and now he rested his hand on my shoulder and raised his gaze to the still-shrouded skies. "The waters saw thee, O God, the waters saw thee; they were afraid: the depths also were troubled." At this he looked at me. "I was but a man," he said softly before walking over to the carriage and climbing onto the seat.

Now I looked at Bengt, his thumbs hooked in his frock coat as he looked down his veiny nose. The grin of a fatted man spread across his face. He stepped to the gravestone and took Inger by the elbow, kicking at the ground with his leather boot. "Don't carve in stone what could be branded on birch board. I guess that's the moral of this story." He bent his thick neck and whispered something in Inger's ear before turning back to me. "But don't you worry, Odd Einar. I'll add the cost of this stone to what's already owed." Then he, too, walked to the carriage, where he handed Inger her purse and took his seat next to the pastor. The horse nickered and turned down the cemetery path.

Inger watched them go, the fog going with them, and I looked down on the gravestone. ODD EINAR EIDE, it read. B. 1854—TAPT PÅ ISEN I HERRANS ÅR 1897.

She turned to me, my wife did, and the look on her face left me to wish I *had* been lost on the ice, in this treacherous year of life.

S he might have been watching herself asleep at home, the soft rise and fall of her belly and the arch of her hip under the gray duvet made violet by winter's darkness. But she wasn't watching herself, and she certainly wasn't sleeping. She hadn't slept properly since she couldn't remember when. And so she wasn't dreaming herself into a hummock of snow. She knew the mounds and curves were buried gravestones taking light from the quivering aurora.

She followed the light skyward, up above the hillside, as it melded into the blues and greens and then an almost glaring orange the color of a Lake Superior sunrise. She could as easily have been standing back on the shoreline in Gunflint now, her evening behind her. But in fact she had never been so far from home, and all that stood behind her was the dark church and beyond that Sørø Sound and the islands distant across the water.

She resisted an inclination to turn around and stare seaward, moving instead to another grave marker and brushing off the snow. She'd arrived here—in the graveyard—with as little forethought as she'd used in flying north altogether. Upon landing in Hammerfest, she'd checked into a hotel and tried to sleep and then tried to eat. Failing at the last two tasks, she'd put her boots back on and stepped again into the darkness. On the Strandgata she looked left and right and saw in the latter snowy distance the church steeple. It seemed as fine a destination as any, and two blocks later she crossed into the cemetery with her mind suddenly on her ancestors who might be buried here. She cleared the first few markers of snow and played her iPhone's flashlight over the ground. She did this half a dozen times and then looked down the line of graves before scanning the graveyard altogether. Hundreds of stones were mounded under the snow. So instead of harvesting ghosts, she bunched her coat collar and gazed upward and studied the sky for what seemed a long time. If she missed Frans or the kids, she didn't feel it. Even as she conjured them sitting around the fire ring outside her father's fish house on a night such as this, the sky over Minnesota lit with its own phosphorescence, she felt only her own heart beating in time with the falling light of the polar sky above.

Was it really only a month ago they last gathered around that campfire? The kids roasted marshmallows. Frans had graham crackers and candy bars ready for s'mores. Because he was always vying for their attention, he moved opposite the kids and arranged his face so it was lit by the Halloween blaze. "You guys might not believe this," he said slowly, the last faint trace of his accent still on his voice some twenty years after she heard it for the first time, "but those auroras are not a natural phenomenon at all. No, sir. They're the wailing souls of all the dead women who never married." He looked at Liv, the only one young or smitten enough to be enchanted by this old saw, and added, "It might seem a wondrous thing, Liv-my-love, to live among the stars, but think of all that time and never touching the earth again!"

If Greta had been paying better attention, she might've realized these words were meant not for Liv but for her, might've noticed the look of sadness on her husband's face. But she didn't. She simply hadn't been paying attention. In this respect she was as culpable as Frans.

He was in Norway himself now. In Oslo, not Hammerfest. She'd traveled there thinking she was ready to confront him, to put to rights all that was wrong between them or finally end it trying. Yet when she deplaned in Oslo and saw the departures board in the terminal included a flight for Hammerfest she'd changed courses instinctively, the assurance of all the miles cross-country and up the coast dividing them suddenly urgent. Was that the point of being here, to find a new distance? A more difficult terrain? A foreign one at that? Surely this was on offer. And cold and snow of an otherworldly sort. The chill was duller and slower than she'd known in her life, the snow livelier. As she considered this, a gust off the hillside came up beneath her, lifting snow from the ground that twinkled and took shape before her, as if the ghosts of her ancestors were indeed there to meet her.

On the shoreline a few minutes later, she watched two boats emerge from the shadow of the islands across the water, moving slowly at first, gently rising and dipping. She could follow the slow-motion arc of their deck lights. As they got closer they moved faster and their lights steadied. She understood, while standing there with the wind at her back, that they'd come into the lee of the mainland. How long had it been since she watched a boat come back to harbor? It couldn't have been as long ago as she imagined, back in her childhood when her dad and grandpa used to motor out onto Lake Superior in their twenty-foot Lund looking for lake trout. Sportfishing, she was made to know, was as frivolous and jolly as quaffing aquavit.

But she'd imagined them differently back then, those men she loved. As though they were the ghosts of her great-grandfather and the men of his time, whose purpose on that lake was as serious and solemn as Christmas Eve mass. She often supposed that she was better suited for that epoch, or one even older, when people talked less and wanted less and loved quietly and less willfully. Maybe that's what she hoped she'd find here. Some quietude and an older way of life.

In a minute more the silhouette of the men on board came into view. As they did, the whine of the motors finally carried across the water. One of the boats steered right, toward the Rypefjord, and the other left, toward the Hammerfest harbor. Their falling wakes ran after them.

The church was quiet and dimly lit, the only light stuttering from a candle in a lysglober resting behind the pews. She paused and considered lighting a votive, but couldn't imagine what to pray for. Why had she come in here? She thought of turning right around, then started up the main aisle instead, drawn by the beautiful stained-glass window behind the altar.

Midway, three chandeliers flickered on and their light streamed past her and the glass blurred with the sudden luminescence. She felt chilled and turned to look at the back of the church. The towering pipes appeared burnished now. In the narthex, a man's blond hair followed him into a doorway, and seconds later he reappeared in the choir loft. He tucked his hair behind his ears and even from where she stood she could see his eyes widen and amusement play across his face as he sat down. What had been a chill only seconds before felt now like warmth that washed over her, and she turned again to face the window—Christ nailed to his cross in a thousand shards of blue and yellow, backlit by the green and blue harlequin of the northern lights out in the Arctic sky. When the first notes came from above she knew that she was not here for the silence. She had been wrong about that.

She hummed along even without knowing what song he was playing. Was it from childhood? One of the dirges her aunt used to play on her Steinway? Whatever the origin, it was beautiful. And it suited her mood. Wasn't it strange how music could rest in you for so long without being heard, but still be called up from old stores of memory? Pondering this, she sat at the end of one of the pews and listened with her eyes closed. This song played on the church organ was loosening some hardness in her. It wasn't unlike the warmth, which was now becoming almost too much. She took off her coat and hung it over her forearm and looked back up at the man on the balcony. He was wide-shouldered and lean and he wore a red sweater. His hair was shoulder length and straight and heavy as a bear's and it moved as he played. She could see the profile of his face when he occasionally turned to the deeper notes, and his calmness brought the same to her as well. She watched as he finished the song and started the same one again. Low and slow and holy and right. The song grew clearer in her memory and once he finished the second rendition she was positive it was a song from her life.

After he finished a third time she glanced back at the altar and noticed a woman moving boxes around. She was stooped and wore a gray wool sweater and had her hair up in a bun. In the absence of organ music, she could hear the old woman humming the song that had just been played three times. The sweetness of her voice reminded Greta of singing her own children to sleep. But this woman might have been sixty or eighty. Her shoes were the type nurses used to wear—thick rubbery soles, the color of Silly Putty— and the leggings beneath her heavy skirt were less stockings than sweaters for her legs. From the box she took a candlestick and candles, arranged them along the edge of the altar, and hung garland dotted with holly berries on what Greta now realized was an Advent calendar, and that Christmas would soon be here. *Christmas?* she wondered. Her favorite time of year, and yet it hadn't so much as crossed her mind. She hadn't thought of a single gift for the kids or Frans when usually she'd not only bought them all by now, but also have them wrapped and hidden in the garage. She'd have planned the Christmas feast and written and mailed her cards. She'd have strung lights in the evergreen shrubs around the house and hung her own Advent calendar in the kitchen and cued up the Christmas CDs. She would've dug out the old krumkake iron from the bowels of her cupboards and fetched the lefse grill from its storage place in the basement.

The organ began again, and Greta saw the old woman smiling toward the loft. Greta turned around herself. The man with the blond hair was playing faster now, yet still the same song. Behind her Greta could hear the woman singing quietly along, the choppy Norwegian words made beautiful by the music and her own lilting voice. When Greta spun around to study her, she was alarmed to see in the soft lines of her face an older, more wizened version of Greta Nansen, and she couldn't turn her gaze from her own future. Once upon a time she might've winced at such a vision, but instead she took comfort in imagining that in twenty or thirty years she might still be moved to sing. At this she closed her eyes and bowed her head and if she didn't pray, she imagined something new.

When the song finished, she opened her eyes and put her coat back on and, with the image of the old woman gazing upward so kindly, started back down the aisle. It was a small church—only twenty-odd rows of pews—and in five or six strides she was half-way gone before she ventured a last look at the balcony. He stood there, his big hands clenching the rail, his shoulders thrust for-ward to follow his stare, which as far as she could tell was set on the atmosphere as much as anything in particular. As if he could see the music reverberating in the air and was taking stock of his performance. In his face she could see all the qualities of the music: joy and sadness and longing. But there was something else, too, that had nothing to do with the music. He was alone, and lonely. She was sure of it.

He was handsome, absolutely. Even more than that. Beautiful. His eyes were dark and deeply set. His face round. His chin wide. The sweater he wore, which she'd noticed earlier, was heavy like his hair, which from where she stood appeared almost white. She could see his teeth were slightly crooked. And that his hands, grip-ping the balcony railing, were large and strong and weathered. Oh my, those hands, they put a knot in her stomach. When had she last taken stock of a man like this? She knew she shouldn't fix on those hands that had just played the song as though its purpose was to restore it in her. When finally she did look away it was to raise her gaze to meet his, now smiling down on her. She blushed, feeling it blaze up her neck and into her cheeks. Was she embar-rassed, maybe just shy, or was she simply as scattered and indefi-nite as the song still lingering in the air?

"Hallo," he said, his voice coming down from the choir loft like a snowflake.

Now Greta did smile, and she raised her hand to wave, and con-tinued out.

T*apt på isen*—lost on the ice. What trail of missteps led me to that latitude where I was indeed to become lost, if not found again?

The story of my going is much long and complicated. If truth be told, it began with the courage of another man—the great Fridtjof Nansen. I watched the *Fram* lay anchor on our waters in eighteen and ninety-three, on the eve of his great voyage. I heard him rile the crowd gathered in awe. I listened to the town band's tubas and trombones regale him. I watched children marvel at his crew of worthy men and that ship famous before she'd left Norwegian waters. I'd seen divers go under her hull to scrape clear the mussels, and saw, finally, her sails raised as she cruised up the sound and out to sea. And I thought it the *most* beautiful thing. Beautiful unto itself, as any ship at sail is, but also beautiful because of Nansen's courage. That a man could be so undaunted and fearless!

I knew as the world did that Nansen was to sail the *Fram* north and east until he found the currents that would take him and his crew right over the pole, with their vessel set in ice. By his reckoning, and an abundance of confidence, he believed his fame would arrive when the ice encasing the *Fram* set them free again in the North Atlantic. From there it would be a simple cruise home. Even now I shiver to think of his audacity. But back then, before my own travails and despair beset me much like my hero's ice? Well, it gave me hope. *A man should want a bigger life,* I thought. *He should want to make discoveries. To find a kind of happiness he could not find in his everyday lot.*

So I vowed that even if I could not drift away, as Nansen had, if I could not myself feel the same pull of the sea beneath the keel of my own boat, I would at least help my daughter to do so. I would set her free of this cold desolation, this rocky shore of hardened, desperate people living in poverty and gloom. I would usher her out the door of our lichen-chinked hut built into the cold earth out on Muolkot, would row her to the town quay, and put her aboard an outbound vessel, and call this a grand opportunity.

Inger saw it wise, even if it crippled her own happiness. What mother's daughter is not her own better self? My fair wife knew as much, and her countenance of our setting Thea on a better course was fresh proof of how much love could matter. Love all around, love sustaining us while we lived meagerly but with great anticipation. We fed our daughter twice what we ate ourselves. We sold what we could and worked endlessly. With our sheep and sorry garden and my faering and nets we labored so we might put our daughter on a boat bound for America.

And in the summer of eighteen and ninety-five—almost exactly two years after Nansen raised anchor and left our sight—I rowed her from Muolkot to Hammerfest harbor, where Thea boarded the schooner *Nordsjøen*. She was headed for Minnesota, to live with Auntie Hege and Uncle Rune. Almost exactly two years after Nansen raised anchor and left our sight, Thea did too. She departed with all she could carry, including a bag of pears I bought from Bengt with my last krone. She'd never eaten one before, and the first letter I wrote—the first of many, none of them, alas, answered—asked what she thought of its sweetness.

Now, two years later still, I would gladly trade all my remaining days for the answer to that question. As life goes, I might trade them all for another bag of pears.

———

Inger and I stood there above my grave, each grieving in our own fashion. Bengt surely had stabled the horse by the time I finally mustered any words. "No word from Thea, then?"

"None, Odd Einar."

"And none from your sister or Rune?"

"That there were."

I caught a glint in her eye, so I pressed. "I'm sorry, Inger. I thought, with all this time I've been gone…"

She wiped her eyes with her sleeve and then stared onto the village rooftops.

"All this damn time, and never a single word even from your sister. Is that too much to ask?"

She didn't answer, this argument about Hege being one of our oldest and most persistent, so I studied the cemetery path then said, after a while, "When I saw you and the pastor here, I feared it was Thea brought home. That's all I mean to say."

Now she looked at me as a killer would. "Thea and Hege are no doubt well. Even Rune. But *you* were dead, Odd Einar. Don't you understand? Dead for ten days. I waited this long." She pointed at the ground, and her look turned from anger to sadness. "Thea is saying prayers for me right this minute. She's singing God's praise in a church in Minnesota. She'll be boiling a fine kettle of fish for her husband this very night, and putting her young child to bed." Now she waved me away with the back of her hand. "Your dark thoughts, they're not for me."

"I only asked, Inger."

She covered her eyes and shook her head and for a long time I stood there watching my wife in much the same manner I'd stood on the Krossfjorden hoping for a ship to pass. My own thoughts had been this desperate, so wild that whenever I felt them coming to focus they blurred again. Like when staring too long on snow blowing across the fjord. Finally I could look at her no more, and turned again to my grave marker.

"What's buried there then, Inger?" The earth was freshly turned.

"Bengt thought to offer your hardingfele. We put it in the ground."

These words came as cold as a Spitzbergen night, and her gaze as bitter. No trace of tears. Nor any forthcoming, no doubt of that. "Your hardingfele and my memory of you."

I collapsed onto my rear end right there beside my grave, tugging at my beard as had now become habit. I fought the urge to shout or howl, and instead just sat there in my misery. Later, I rounded a ball of cold earth in my hands and said, "It's just as well. There's nary a song left in this godforsaken world."

Inger stood unmoving while I mourned myself. Through all of our silence beneath the hillside there presided a stubborn heaviness even greater than the weight of my own body as I crossed Spitzbergen. Or than the despair of my lost daughter.

I knew all this, yet would not allow it to grieve me as those earlier burdens had. Not until Inger said, "You tell me what happened, I will listen. I'll give you that." She brushed her hands together as though wiping away her own worry. "But not here. I want to go home. We have a new one. Let's walk there in silence."

So we walked through the village, past the quayside and the stream and up the shore of Gávpotjávri and into the valley. I was alone again with my memories, despite having Inger at my side.

Thea sailed in August of eighteen and ninety-five. One year later, I stood on the wharf myself. The summer evening rising as if from the water, which was still as ice and dark as a winter dawn. A boat called *Otaria* lay at anchor not more than a furlong offshore. It had been the most festive week in Hammerfest since Nansen and his crew sailed north on the *Fram* in 'ninety-three. It was lively again now because he had returned, a Draugen himself. He was aboard that well-appointed schooner with his beloved wife, Eva. The town had been draped with Norwegian flags and every living one of us lined the harbor. We waited like schoolchildren for the man to show his face, his story already known by all.

With his comrade Frederik Johansen, Nansen had been north of the eighty-sixth parallel. They had put their boot prints farther north than any man before, and news of their accomplishment granted their return a tidal holiness. And though I'd lately begun doubting my faith in God, Nansen's return helped me believe in *something*. I can't exaggerate how that relief washed over me, kindling a new hope that my Thea might be fine out there in the wilds of Minnesota.

On that particular night I watched the *Otaria* for a long time. She sat silent on the harbor. The cabin windows alight, softly, and reflected on the water softer yet, like a dozen portholes of promise. I fell to still more thoughts of Thea. Imagining her—healthy and happy and missing me—had, for so long, been the only thing that proved I was still alive. I pictured her with her aunt and uncle, living quietly in a log home on the shore of that river I'd heard so much about. It was said to run to a lake that was even colder than our own harbor. I saw her sitting quietly by the hearty fire. I heard the coo of a child. And when I imagined her looking at the face from which that coo came, I believed she might love me all the more. If these were foolish dreams, if they were untethered or imprudent, Nansen's safe return made them less so. He had suffered his years of Arctic winds and utter dark and ice. He had done it honorably, and with such magnificent purpose. And now he was sitting in the light behind one of those shining windows, right before my eyes.

As if my thinking of him had the power of a summons, his dark form emerged on deck. He seemed to be looking out to sea, up the sound toward Sørø and beyond. I saw the flare of a match and thought he must be lighting his pipe. In his honor, I lit my own.

"Our national hero," came a voice. A man stood next to me as though he'd materialized from the weathered boards of the quay itself. I flinched but was quick to compose myself. I didn't recognize him, but when his own pipe was packed I offered a match and together we smoked.

"I wonder how he could spend a single minute on deck with a wife so beautiful below," I said, as if I'd been thinking of anything except my daughter.

"That man, he's got his nose to the north no matter where he is." He puffed his pipe thoughtfully. "Three years, ja? Three years apart, those two. Husband and wife."

I stole a sidelong glance in time to see my companion flatten his mustache.

"You've a wife?" he asked.

"A fine and loving one."

"Then you can understand how long those three years must have been. Like ten for Eva, no doubt. I too would be shy in the company of my wife after such a long absence."

This man seemed notably sturdy. His beard was long and strangely shaped, but his hair beneath his hat shorn above the ears. He was well dressed and appeared at peace with himself. Like nothing could rankle him. Like he was heavy of keel indeed.

We stood there smoking silently until I said, "Me, I'd point my own nose west."

"West?"

"Two years ago, on this very day, we sent our daughter to America."

"That takes another kind of daring."

I studied him once more. "You're not from here."

"Born in Helgeland, but just arrived last night from Tromsø."

"Come to see Herr Nansen?"

"The one and only."

"It's because of him I sent my daughter off."

Now this man turned to me and raised an eyebrow.

"I watched the *Fram* leave here in 'ninety-three. I was inspired by his courage."

"His courage is epic."

I squared up and looked at him directly while he turned his eyes back onto the harbor and the *Otaria* out at anchor. After we finished our pipes we pocketed them together.

"How is your daughter?" he asked.

"We've had no word from her."

"That's a bitter thing, friend."

"The bitterest."

"How can it be?"

"Her boat from Christiania landed in New York. We know that much. But as for her trip to Minnesota, where her aunt and uncle have settled, we've no news. Nor any since she might have arrived with them."

Now he turned again to me. I could see he felt sorry. And that he measured his words before saying, "Three years the world waited for Fridtjof Nansen. Three years and now here he is. There's a lesson there."

"I've been thinking the same."

Now a tender came knocking against the quay, a lantern lit against the gloaming. The man on the dock with me raised his chin toward Nansen, who had just ducked back belowdecks. "Another man's courage is a fine start. And if Nansen's buoyed you once, it can do so again." He jumped down into the tender and grabbed hold of the gunwale to steady himself. "But I will pray for you to find your own courage. I truly will. Tell me your name?"

I was by turns taken with his garrulousness—this steady man minding me, his suit a fine worsted wool, his kindness something I was actually measuring as he spoke—and curious about his audacity. To pray for my courage? What a thing! Before thinking better of it I said, "My name's Odd Einar Eide. Born in this very town. I make my living from my faering."

"It's a pleasure to know you, Odd Einar."

"Where are you going?" I asked, suddenly desperate to hold his attention.

"Nansen is expecting me."

"Expecting you?"

He reached his hand up and offered it to me. I knelt and took it. "My name is Otto Sverdrup. Captain of the *Fram*. I'll call on you when next I visit this fair town."

He let go of my hand and pushed the tender from the quay.

"When will that be, Herr Sverdrup?"

Already, the tender man had taken a turn on the oars. Sverdrup removed his hat and shouted, "Soon!"

Greta and Frans had lunch the Friday after Thanksgiving at the Burnt Wood Tavern. Lasse and Liv and Greta's father had as well, but now the kids and Gus were walking up Wisconsin Street toward the bookshop. Greta watched as the snow fell slowly around them.

Frans set his newspaper on his knee and checked his phone for the fifth time since they'd sat down an hour ago. He closed his eyes for a second and slipped his phone back in his breast pocket. The sandwich Greta had ordered sat on the table mostly untouched alongside a beer she'd hardly tasted. She could tell by how Frans sighed that he was looking at her. Imploring her, really. But she kept her eyes on the kids and her father as they crossed the street.

Frans picked up the newspaper again. "Says here highs in the thirties tomorrow," he said. "All this snow'll melt. You guys should have a great weekend."

He said this more to himself, she knew, than to her. And she knew it would be better to keep her thoughts to herself. But the tone of his voice put her on edge, like it so often did. As if reading the weather report in the paper made him an expert? As if she hadn't been able to judge the weather up here since she was a little girl? "There'll be plenty more snow. Plenty more winter."

She could see his grip tighten on the newspaper. His voice tightened too. "It's always winter with you, Greta."

"Please be quiet. Please."

He again laid the newspaper on his knee and took measure of her. She could feel the little quiver of anger on her lip and sensed the slight pulsing of her eyes under the interrogation of his stare. She hated her tics, and his calmness in response to his own anger. In a voice he'd often used on the children when they were babies and toddlers, he said, "You should finish your sandwich. You haven't eaten anything all week."

"You have it." She slid the plate across the table, then picked up her lukewarm beer and took a long swig.

Frans folded the newspaper and finally set it beside the uneaten sandwich. He shifted his eyes out onto the harbor and studied it for a long time. She watched him as she sipped the beer. She could tell he was trying. She knew she should be glad of that.

His gaze was still on the water when he said, "I was only talking about the weather, Greta. The snow and the weekend you guys might have. That's all."

"I know."

He reached across the table for her hand, which she gave him without thinking.

"I thought, after last night—"

"No," she said.

"Greta."

"Don't." And now she withdrew her hand as quickly as she'd offered it.

"There was a time, you know, when it *was* always winter," he said. "A hundred thousand years ago. Ten thousand years ago. A whole age. A hundred millennia."

Now *that* was an idea she could take pleasure in contemplating. An ice age. The thought of it stilled her anger. Her breathing grew more natural.

A minute might have passed. Or five, she didn't know. When she turned her attention to Frans she spoke as though she'd been deep in thought. "It'll come again. That's what you always say. Another ice age. Sooner than we know."

How quickly he could regain his posture, the one full of confidence and expertise, that look that preceded one of his exegeses on the ill fate of the world and all mankind. As though he were still a practicing scientist, not just a subscriber to *National Geographic* and philanthropist for the cause. She knew what was coming, so before he could muster his sermon, Greta interrupted him. "Not now, Frans. Let me just watch the snow fall." She reached across the table and touched the cuff of his cashmere sweater. This loosened him and she moved her fingertips from his sweater to his wrist and the skin there as soft as the wool. Still she didn't look at him. She would take this silence, however it was given.

After a minute, she turned her own wrist up and looked at her watch, a beautiful stainless-steel Omega he'd given her for her fortieth birthday. "It's almost one," she said. He had a flight out of Minneapolis at nine, and with the snow it would be a five-hour drive. He would need to leave soon.

He had a sip of water and wiped his mouth and finally said, "Are you okay? Are we?"

Greta didn't say anything.

"I could cancel this trip," he continued. "We could stay here for another week. Keep the kids out of school. Or maybe your dad could take them home, get them off to school next week, and we could hunker down? You could do some more work on the fish house. We could go ski at Misquah. All this snow and we'd have the place to ourselves."

Why would he put such a plan to words? Was he completely blind to her mood? Or was he trying to trick her?

He smiled. "What do you say?"

She couldn't think of anything, and did not smile back. She rarely smiled anymore unless she was being cruel, and despite her frustration she didn't wish to be so now. She knew he deserved an answer of some kind. But the best she could do was a nod, and not one intended to mean much. How many of their talks ended up in a ditch like this? In this baffling silence, inspired by her amazement and wild ambivalence? Sometimes the hush lasted for days, only to be broken by a quieter resignation that announced a false truce. She trusted none of it. Not the resignation, not the bogus truces, not the resentment that attended both.

"You might say something, Greta."

"Such as? That keeping the kids out of school for a week's a good idea? That spending another week up here with you is exactly what I need? Just what *we* need? That you're right, the weather will turn beautiful and the snow'll melt right away?"

"All I said is that it was going to warm up. I was just reading the goddamn weather report."

"I don't care about the weather, Frans. I don't care if it's hot or cold or snowy or not and I certainly don't care about the fucking ice age. See?" She took another drink of beer and spoke before he could get a word in. "Of course you should go. I'm fine. I'll be fine. Go now and you can get home for most of the ski season. That would make the kids happy. Maybe we can come back up at Christmas. I can work on the fish house then."

He reached for her hand. "Do you regret taking me down there last night?"

As if she had no control over it, her hand recoiled again. Could he possibly understand this otherwise? That regret was the best thing she could say about it?

Over the few days before Thanksgiving, there'd been the usual round of stories about the hallowed fish house. All the trysts and secrets and solid things built in there. The livelihoods made. The loneliness kept. And because Greta had just started clearing it out, she asked if Frans wanted to go have a look after Thanksgiving dinner.

She unlocked the door and shouldered it open and they stepped into something still rooted so firmly against the wind off the lake, so quiet in the manner of unvisited places. In this it reminded her of her father. And of the other men who'd also haunted it. She was starting to feel more and more like them, more like the structure itself: silent and reserved and immovable against the wind. Certainly she felt calm in the hours she'd spent working there. She felt, too, that it was the only place left where she could track herself down. In her solemn hours of cleaning and sorting and imagining what it might become, she found herself stronger and more purposeful. On the occasions she'd brought the kids along, she discovered the kindness and patience she'd had for them as newborns. She rarely thought of Frans while she was there, a thing she realized only as she walked in with him.

It was a mistake, she was sure of that. Once Frans lit the lantern and started pointing it into corners and babbling about things that required no intelligence whatsoever—*They didn't make those windows to catch daylight, did they? Sure this place has withstood the lake winds for a hundred years, since half of it comes right through. Ah, but those trusses will hold a winter's worth of snow on the roof*—she could hardly stand the noise. When he said, "Whoever laid this floor had in mind centuries of work"—as if it had been some stranger and not her great-grandfather who'd pounded those boards together, as if the feet of anyone outside her family had ever smoothed them, as if it were not *she* who'd spent the last season of weekends working to uncover them—she'd finally had enough and told him to just look.

It wasn't that he was mistaken about any of it. The place was sturdy and rough and worth commenting on. It was, after all, the reason she'd brought him there in the first place. And of course he was trying to be part of something with her. And though she wanted none of it, she said "Follow me" and brought him to the counter along the northern wall. It spanned the fish house from east to west and on one end of the counter old fish boxes were stacked eight or ten high, each branded with the EIDE LAKE FISH logo. There were some tools on the pegboard above the counter and half a dozen vises clamped along its edge. The whole deal was shadowed by a cedar-strip canoe hanging above. "I was thinking I could plumb this corner. Put a sink here. Box this corner and put a toilet in," she said. "This is where I'll write, under this window. It has the best view of the lake. The best morning sun."

He tried to be agreeable in the wake of her voice's openness. He set the lantern down and leaned against the counter and looked around. "Well, it looks great." There passed between them a moment of kindness.

Until recently, unkindness had never been their problem. Even now, it was Greta who lashed out. Never him. It was almost as if he were incapable of meanness. That his ancestry forbade it, insisting instead on decorum in every situation. It was a quality she'd once found attractive. He had other attractive aspects, too, then as now. He was intelligent. He'd earned his degrees from the universities of Bergen and Exeter, even if he hadn't put them to much use lately. He read voraciously, a trait they shared. But he could be pedantic. And he still signed most of his correspondence *F. Nansen,* as though he might be confused with his great-great-great-uncle. There was a time in their marriage when this irked Greta, but she no longer cared. Loneliness, that was the only feeling she had anymore. She was lonely all the time.

The first casualty of this loneliness had been their sexual life together. It must have been a year since they'd last been intimate, so when she stepped toward him as he leaned against the counter in the fish house, when she turned down the lantern and looked up at him, the moonlight falling through the window and onto his face showed perfect surprise.

"Don't say anything, do you understand?" she said. "If you talk, if you say one word, I'll walk right out of here."

She kissed him hard, almost violently. Their teeth met and she kissed him harder yet, then stepped back and lifted her sweater over her head. She reached behind her back and unclasped her bra. It was cold in the fish house and she felt her skin go taut. When Frans whispered her name, she twisted in his arms and grabbed for her sweater. But he raised a finger to his lips and pulled her back to him.

And so she unbuckled his belt and unbuttoned and unzipped his pants and pushed them to his knees, and as fast as she could kicked off her boots and took her own pants off. She pulled herself up onto the counter and in the next motion pulled him to her. Even though she was ready and wanting, it hurt. It hurt and then felt good. She watched him, his head thrown back, his eyes clenched shut even as they were turned up to the ceiling. She noticed the gray hair at his temples, the lines around his eyes. She noticed also that he was thinner than the last time she'd held him like this. His legs were muscled and the arms around her were those of his younger self.

And he was ecstatic, she could see. He looked almost pained. As he moved and clinched his eyes tighter, she realized he wasn't making love to her but to that woman in Norway. The one he worked with, or used to, she wasn't even sure anymore. Her name, she remembered, as her husband rolled his hips into her, was Alena. She was one of those long-armed, long-legged Nordic types with downy hair and hard eyes and heavy breasts. She was beautiful. Greta had met her twice and could understand why Frans had gone to her, and it was a relief that he had. A fantastic relief, actually, because it had spared her this part of their life together.

He was not long inside her. After a few minutes he threw his chin down on his chest and she saw the veins in his temples and felt him pulsing inside her. He went from his tiptoes to his heels and slid out of her and only then did he put his lips to hers. He kissed her and tried to wrap his arms around her but she pushed him away. Now his shoulders slumped and he folded his hands in front of his cock.

"Would you light the lantern again?" she said.

He stumbled back as though he'd been punched in the stomach. She put her bra and sweater back on and felt their warmth against the iciness of their lovemaking. She slid off the bench and pulled her underwear and jeans back on, she slipped her feet back into her boots. The moonlight made his pale and thin legs and his sunken belly appear almost malnourished.

She lit the lantern herself and when he finally looked up tears were welling in his eyes.

"My God, look at us," she said.

She leaned back against the counter and watched him pull his pants up and hitch his belt. He would not meet her gaze. Would not so much as raise his eyes for her to see them. She wished to undo what had just happened, to have stayed up at her father's house on the Burnt Wood River. To have let Frans adjourn for the night with his iPhone and what he thought were his secrets. She wanted that desperately now, would have waited for the whole house to fall asleep before sneaking outside for a cigarette with which to inaugurate another sleepless night. All of that would have been a thousand times preferable to this debacle. She reached into her purse and dug through to its bottom and removed her pack of cigarettes and her lighter and unthinkably lit one in front of him.

He finally looked up, his eyes flashing wet in the lantern light. He had beautiful eyes, blue like ice behind his tears. But she could not read them, and this infuriated her. They looked at each other for a full minute before she said, "I wonder if Fridtjof Nansen ever fucked his wife and then cried about it."

The gloss on his eyes disappeared all at once, yet he said nothing. How often had she asked for quiet lately? But now that she had it she wanted something else. So she smiled, even if she didn't mean to.

"You have no kindness left in you. Not one bit," he said. "You could've come back to me. You know that, right? I love you and would take you back any time. I would forgive you right now." He pulled his own shirt back on and walked halfway to the door.

That awful smile still hung on her face. She could feel it there. So she put her cigarette to her lips, hoping it would give her mouth something else to do.

"You decided it would be like this," he said, and then crossed the fish house to stand at the door with his hand on the knob.

How could she tell him this wasn't true? She no sooner chose for things to be like this than she did for the weather to behave one way or another. What she longed for was not some former version of themselves—when they were younger, with laughter in their lives, when she looked at him and felt happiness—but rather for something it had *never* been. Never *could* be. And though she knew this was true, and why it was, she could not explain it. She had learned, during these endless sleepless nights, that there weren't words for everything the heart harbored. He took one last look at her, shook his head, and went to wait in the car.

Later that night she lay unsleeping. He snored beside her and she felt shame and sadness looking down the bed at his naked legs. That fuck in the fish house, it was a betrayal. She tried to remember how it felt to have him inside her. Tried so she might have the pleasure of forgetting again. And then she played the same trick for the first time they made love, a month or so after they'd met. He was such a gentleman, so earnest and proper. It had been as unerotic as a glacier, which is what he'd spent so much time talking about on their first dates together. And mostly it had remained like that.

Frans said, "I'm sorry. I shouldn't have brought up last night." He put his hand on the table. A lame offering. "You're going to stare yourself blind, looking out at that harbor."

She answered him softly. "Where else should I look, Frans? Should I watch you reading your newspaper? Checking your phone every minute? Or stare at the television over there?" She pointed toward the bar. "I hate basketball." Now she looked around the Burnt Wood Tavern. "Maybe I should watch that old couple down from Canada and admire their smiling faces, wishing we could be so happy? Should I lie to you? Should I stare longingly into *your* eyes instead of out at the harbor? Would that make you feel better?"

"If we're being honest, you haven't looked at me except to scold me or mock me in a very long time." Now he leaned toward her. "I try to reach you all the time. And you know what? You never answer. So you bet I'm reading the paper and checking my phone."

She wanted to tell him to be quiet again. She wanted him to leave. To take his newspaper and phone and walk out the door. Did she want him never to return? Did she want for their life together never to have happened? Should she say those things? No. Even in all her coldness, those words would be too much. So she turned to him and said, "You have a plane to catch."

He sat there, staring at her with that expectant look. What was he waiting for? Where had his self-assuredness gone? She'd made it vanish. Or at any rate it had vanished.

Now he spoke in almost a whisper. "All I've wanted is for us to be a family. For us to talk like we used to."

"What have you wanted to talk about, Frans?" She could feel the snow falling harder outside even though the afternoon was brightening.

"My God, you're cruel." He buttoned his coat. "I've been thinking," he said, and she could tell his temper had changed. "About fixing up the fish house. You've got a real knack for improving things. You always have. I know why you've been working on that place."

"I'm sure you do."

"Now you be quiet." He pulled his hands into his calfskin gloves. "No matter what you do to that place, it will remain what it's always been."

"And what's that, Frans?"

"A place for wayward boats and heartache."

"That's very poetic," she said.

"You have no idea how hard I've tried, Greta."

If she stared at *him* long enough, would she go blind? Frans with his fine hair and square jaw. His big right hand raised in a fist and pressed to his lips.

"I'm sure it's been hard," she finally said. "I'm sure that woman in Størdal makes it *very* hard."

His breath escaped him instantly and, as if in answer to his suffocation, the door to the tavern swung open and Lasse and Liv came back in ahead of their grandfather, all three of them carrying paper bags under their arms. They stomped the snow from their boots and Lasse brushed snow from his grandfather's coat and Liv went to stand by Frans.

"Papa, where are you going?" she said.

Frans lifted his daughter onto his lap and hugged her. "I have a flight to catch. It's time for me to go."

"Don't leave, Papa! Stay here and look at this!"

"I suppose you bought them books?" Greta asked her father.

"I suppose I did."

"You spoil them, Gus," Frans said.

"Yes, I do. But I spoil you too." Gus handed him a bag from under his arm. It was a rock-pickers' guide to Lake Superior, a book he'd given Frans at least twice before, the last for his birthday just two months earlier. Frans slid the book back in the bag and said thanks.

"I'm sure there's not much to learn in there you don't already know, but the pictures at least are beautiful," Gus said. "You'll have something pretty to look at on the plane."

"Oh, I don't know much," Frans said, darting a glance at Greta. To Lasse and Liv he said, "What did you guys get?" Lasse held up a book of moose photographs. Liv had a book about wildflowers. "Those are fine choices. I hope you thanked Grandpa."

"We did," Liv said.

"Of course they did," Gus said. "These two goofballs are as good as that snowfall out there."

Praise always made the kids uneasy, and rather than face their blushing, Greta looked again out the window. Axel was tied to the streetlamp. He was covered in snow and even sitting on his haunches better than three feet tall. Not even full grown yet, and as wide in the shoulders as Liv.

"Can I have kisses and hugs?" Frans said, going to each of the kids and saying goodbye.

"It's always good to see you, son," Gus said. "Have a safe trip, eh?"

Franz held up the bag with his guidebook and said, "Greta was just saying this snow will stick. I hope she's wrong. It'd be fun to put this to use next month. We could do a study of some Eide Cove agates."

"Why, that beach hasn't been picked in years," Gus said, as though they might really spend an afternoon hunting for rocks outside the fish house. "We'll get after them together. You and me and the kids."

"You bet we will, Gus. Kids, will you wait for me outside with Grandpa?"

Lasse and Liv moved out the door in unison, dropping to their knees next to the dog and brushing the snow off of his long coat.

Now Frans and Greta were alone again. The waitress and bartender had stepped into the kitchen. Even the old Canadian couple had disappeared somewhere.

"Do you actually expect me to leave in the middle of this?" he asked her, gesturing vaguely out the window.

"It stopped snowing."

He looked out at the kids. She could see the sadness overwhelm him. His whole body went limp.

"You think you've got it all figured out, but you don't." He took a deep breath. "Neither do I. Jesus, how I can love you so much? How did we get here?"

This scorned and weak side of him was one she'd not seen often. She knew he was holding back tears, which made her want to tell him they'd talked enough already. That what needed to be said could wait until he returned. Or more likely be forgotten altogether. But he kept on, persistence being a side she saw at nearly every turn.

"How long have you hated me?"

"I don't hate you."

"But you don't love me."

No, she thought. *I don't.*

He must have read her conclusion now because he let out a groan, sounding like something you might hear unexpectedly up in the muskeg on a hot summer afternoon.

"Please, Frans."

"Please *what*?"

"Don't cause a scene." She twisted the beer glass on its coaster and took a deep breath. "I don't hate you. I'm angry and I'm tired and cold and I want you to go."

"You think I'm going to see some woman."

"You'd be smarter not to mention her. I don't like it that you think I'm a fool. I'm many things, but I'm not one of those."

Frans checked the time on his phone, leaned halfway across the table, and spoke plainly. "You make it seem like I had a choice. All your hatefulness—you think this is the first time I've felt it? I live under its bombardment, Greta. You're relentless. But you know what? It's your unhappiness that's the cause of all this. I've done nothing except try to reach you. To talk to you. All I do—all I've done for God knows how long—is try to save us."

"Alena," she whispered. "That's her name. She's proof of how hard you're trying?" She couldn't imagine why she brought this woman up again. She didn't care about Alena from Størdal any more than she cared about whether the snow would melt or stay. But now she couldn't stop. She leaned forward just as he had. "Last night, in the fish house, right before you finished, right when you threw your head back and moaned, I could practically see her there with us. Alena with her big tits and her long blond hair and flat stomach. You can't even fuck *me*. How can you save *us*?"

"Go to hell."

"Go to hell? That's priceless."

"You're cru—"

"Oh, Frans, you *asked* for this. You keep pushing and pushing."

He stared at her but didn't speak, though his sadness and anger and guilt were all plain to see. What was he waiting for? She was done talking. She was sorry she'd said a goddamn thing.

"I'll call you when I get there," he finally said.

"Don't bother." The thought that this was what she truly wanted occurred to her only as she said it. "Just go do your business. Let me have some quiet. I'll be here when you get back. Here, I mean." She pointed outside. "Right here."

He took a last hard look at her and then walked out onto the sidewalk, where the snow came up again in the wind as he hugged Gus and Lasse and kissed Liv on the forehead. Before he reached the street corner, he was invisible to her. Now she was gazing onto the Hammerfest harbor, willing the memory of her husband farther into that hoary Minnesota winter. On the wharf outside the Hotel Thon, there was a sculpture of a sailboat beset in ice, its sails furled, its bow pointed out to sea. If she focused on her reflection in the window, she almost appeared to be a passenger aboard that boat. Was it a ketch or a yawl or some other type she couldn't name properly? It didn't matter, she guessed. Any boat would do just fine.

———

She might have felt lonesome or heartsick—probably should've, given the quarrel she was trying to forget—but the pleasure in having disappeared to this tiny Arctic town, in sipping a second aquavit from the cordial glass with the thought of that man playing the church organ coming over her like the tide, well, it all left her feeling flustered instead. Maybe even a bit reckless. She wondered if the sculpture were in fact a real boat, and ready to sail out to sea, would she go? Who would she want on board with her?

She looked at the sculpture again. It seemed to be made of steel, since she could see the patina of rust in the glow of the streetlamps. At least the triangles of ice were white. Wood, maybe. Or painted steel. The boat was as seaworthy as she was to captain it. Had she ever once been on a sailboat? Could she even imagine a place to go?

She finished her drink and said good night to the woman behind the reception counter and took the elevator up to the seventh floor. It was afternoon, early or late she wasn't even sure, but for as tired as she'd been since landing in Oslo, she was now wide awake. The drinks. All the thinking. Outside her room's window, across the town's rooftops, she saw the church and the music came back to her and roiled her even more. She went to the bathroom and brushed her teeth and started humming the song. For a second she believed she knew the words, though this was impossible. She rinsed her mouth, washed her face, and rubbed cream into the lines around her eyes, then went back out to the bed—pillowy and sleek and made for two—and sat on the edge and had a spontaneous memory of Christmas Eve mass at home in Gunflint. Of course. That's where she knew the song from. The eight-person choir performed a handful of Norwegian carols each season and that man had played one of them here.

She was still humming as she undressed, laying her clothes over the chair in the corner. He had played it beautifully.

His hair. She could picture it, and his welcoming look down to her, and his aspect as he watched the invisible lineaments of his performance. Only someone who'd lost something could play like that. And his hands, Jesus.

She folded down the comforter on the side of the bed closest to the window and turned off the lamp. Now there was just a strip of faint light in the middle of the window where the curtains didn't quite meet.

She hummed. And sighed at the strangeness of it all coming together and thought of him again. She pulled the comforter up and fluffed the pillow and turned on her side and then closed her eyes and saw him holding the railing. She could well imagine him reefing a sail, his gaze fixed on the horizon. He probably could look at the sculpture on the harbor and know exactly where a boat like that should be headed, know exactly how to grip the wheel and steer its course.

She didn't even realize that her own hands were searching herself out. One on her breast, the other on her lower belly. Now she heard the halyard lines whistling on the real sailboats docked in the harbor. Such a sweet, sweet sound. Why did she feel so easy? Was it because no one on earth knew where she was? This thought didn't startle her, as it might've once upon a time, but rather set her very much at peace.

She closed her eyes and rolled onto her stomach now, raising herself just enough to slide her fingers farther down her body. The hand down there was not her own anymore. No, it was not.

Bengt's farm was built along one of the streams that fed Gávpotjávri. A stately three-story of cog-jointed birch logs built before the fire of eighteen and ninety, and so one of the oldest buildings in Hammerfest. He kept his fjord horse in his own stable and his Dala sheep on his dekar of land, where he put the sheep up at night in a hillside barn. He also had a shanty for his carriage, cog-jointed to match the barn and house.

Inger and I stood at his fencerow, the sheep flowing toward us.

"I don't understand," I said again.

"You were dead, Odd Einar. I hope if I were dead you'd take care of yourself."

"But to be *more* fettered to this man?" I spread my hands before Bengt's estate.

"Where else would I go? I have nothing. No money. No hope. You'd rather I froze to death in that room above the bakery? Bengt's charity—Herr Bjornsen's charity—is all that's saved me."

The sheep gathered at the fence, stopping and starting again in unison, dispersing like a cloud breaking up. Our old Steigar sheep, the one we'd sold to Bengt before Thea left, came limping up apart from the others. Ever since Bengt had him castrated, he'd been a hobbling thing. I'd seen the Dala rams come after him more than once. I dropped my hand over the fence and let him take my scent. He sniffed twice and gave a little buck.

"You're keeping his house, then?"

"He's given me the maid's quarters, but I'm not his house servant."

The Steigar sheep trotted back up the fencerow. I watched him climb the hill and pause at the knoll atop it. "Then what are you?"

"I'm alive, Odd Einar." She sounded exhausted, possibly even more so than I did. "If I'm anything, I'm still alive. I cook their dinners. Sometimes breakfast. I tend the bakery twice a week. I help the lady Bjornsen with her trips to market. When her spells come on, I play nursemaid."

It seemed a rotten lot, that. I knew Gerd Bjornsen to be a difficult, mean woman whom I never could imagine caring for. I wanted to tell Inger that we would get back on our own feet, but the distant and troubled expression still hanging on her face gave me pause.

"You seem little joyful I'm home, Inger."

"I prayed most nights, Odd Einar."

"That's something."

"It's what I could do."

"Should I thank you?" I squatted and picked a stone and threw it down the hill, toward the Dala sheep. "It wasn't your prayers that carried me those nights." I threw another stone. "Not those many miles, either."

She would not so much as glance at me.

"And now I find you living with this man? And standing over my own grave? Find you colder than any wind I ever felt on Spitzbergen?"

Now she did look at me. "Our life was so warm before, Odd Einar? All this coldness is why you left in the first place. The only thing changed since you got aboard that ship is that we have even less. If I've found a warm place to lay my head, if I've found a chunk of bread and a regular cup of coffee, you'll have to forgive me."

"There were days I would have traded my life for a cup of coffee."

Inger put her hands together as if in supplication. "First I prayed that no harm would come to you. After you died, I prayed you went without suffering." She unclasped them and turned to me and very suddenly put them on my cheeks. "And now? What do I pray for now?"

Everything about her—the tone of her voice, her hands limp on my cheeks, her tearless eyes as she gazed out at the sheep—told me what I must have feared all along: my cherished wife was sad to see me home. I picked another stone and tossed it from one hand to the other. Finally I said, "Well, I suppose now there's a cup of coffee to be had that we needn't even pray for. What say we share a cup?"

So we did. We crossed Bengt's rocky land and entered his house and walked down a long, dark passageway. I'd been in his home many times, though never beyond the kitchen. In a room new to me, a window overlooking the hill was open to the afternoon light. A coal stove stood in one corner, Inger's dyeing pot next to it along with a batt of sheep wool in a basket and a large bucket of water. There was a shelf beside the stove with basic foodstuffs and a plate and a cup and saucer, one of each. A chair and her spinning wheel sat under the window opposite a rocking chair. Another basket sat next to the wheel, overflowing with yarn and needles. A single bed and a chest of drawers and an armoire with a mirror on its door completed the furnishings. Atop the chest on a stand was Thea's portrait, taken by my friend Toralv Hagen two days before she left. It had been a gift to us, so we could always picture her.

But to see her face stunned me now. She was different in the portrait than she was in my memory and it chilled me to think I'd misplaced her. I stared at her for a long time, righting her in my mind, recalling her lilting voice and quiet laughter. I saw her bobbing head on Friday nights, her hand tapping out the time as I ran the bow up and down my hardingfele. I saw her easy stride as she walked ahead of me up the Grønnevoldsgaden with her mother on Sunday morning, going to church. Great Christ did this almost bowl me over. How I missed my sweet child. I would gladly suffer all of my indignities a thousand times over could I but see her standing next to me, the golden down of her hair under my chin. I would gladly suffer them again to simply know she was well.

"Put that down," Inger said. "Come sit."

I turned and saw her at the stove. I could tell she'd been studying me while I gazed upon the portrait. Her arms were crossed and her chin jutted out as it did when she was angry.

"How is it possible she's not sent word?" I asked.

"It's what happens," she said, and took the kettle from the stove and filled a teacup.

"Not with my daughter," I said, holding Thea's portrait up as evidence of a greater benevolence.

"Oh, Odd Einar." Her tone changed abruptly and was, if not kind, at least singed with resignation. "People go off. The world gets bigger. They forget where they come from. They forget who they are. They change. They change all the time." She put the teacup on the saucer, stepped away, said "Please," and gestured at the rocking chair.

I started over with the portrait but Inger said, "Leave that. Come, this will warm you up."

I sat in the rocking chair and Inger handed me the coffee. She went back to the stove, cut a chunk of grovbrød from a loaf, then laid it on the plate and brought it to me. "I haven't anything else to give you. No butter, even."

I put the cup down and lifted the bread to my nose. If it had been honey on the Queen's breath as she bent to kiss my hand, it wouldn't have smelled so sweet. Before taking a bite, I set the plate beside the coffee on the floor and, despite the chill in the room, removed my coat and unbuttoned the collar of my threadbare shirt. I sat back down, took up the bread, and looked at it anew.

"Eat, for goodness' sake. Drink." Yet again she went back to the stove. "I'll warm more water so you might wash."

I already should have apologized for the state I was in. But I thought any energy taken to win her favor would be better spent regaining Thea instead. So I closed my eyes and dreamt of her. It might have been five minutes or an hour that I remembered my daughter. When I opened my eyes, Inger was sitting beside me on the floor, holding a cloth. Her dyeing pot had been filled with steaming water as though my dream had softened her. She said, "Wash yourself. I'll warm your coffee."

She then stepped away, poured it from the cup into the kettle, placed that on the stove, and finally came back. "Will you tell me what happened?" She gathered her dress beneath her and sat at my feet. It was only then that she noticed my boots, fine komagers made of the sturdiest reindeer hide. "You come home penniless, but sporting these?" She stood and crossed her arms over her bosom and stepped back. "You'll explain yourself."

"These boots once belonged to a better man than me, Inger."

"You've said that about most men you ever knew."

"Ay, but Mikkelsen, he was a true one. Strong and ready with a laugh to stay the cold. He knew where the seals were, too."

Inger looked at me from across the room. I could see fog creeping down the hillside again. Was this day determined to conceal itself from me? I bent to untie the boots and slid them one at a time from my feet.

"How was it these boots came to be yours, then?"

"I'm reluctant to tell you, Inger. It's not a story fit for a woman's ears."

She shook her head and walked to the bed and around it and came back with my duffle, which she dropped at my feet. I could see the sealskin coat and the woolen mitten liners tucked in the bag. What I wouldn't have given for that sack and all it held as I traversed the perilous glaciers and landkall of the Krossfjorden. "A man came to me on Svene Solvang's behalf and delivered these goods. I had no idea you had changed your employer. I had no idea you wouldn't show up when the *Lofoten* next called in Hammerfest." She returned to her seat and took her needles up and said, "You rise from the dead to tell me I can't hear where your fine komagers have come from? Nonsense. I'm not only fit to hear it, Odd Einar, but I'm well deserving of the story. Now get on with it."

She was right, of course. I had never been one to keep secrets from Inger. Our lives depended on each other. They always had. And I knew as soon as I thought about it that my reluctance was born not of wishing to start with secrets now, but from an intuition that what I'd endured could not be expressed in words. At least not words that I possessed. I took the plate from the floor and ate the bread under her watchful eye, then sipped the steaming coffee, which she'd returned to me. And though I felt anchored, I also felt queasy. The fog had come down full, and between it and the hour the view outside dimmed considerably.

The collar of Inger's funeral dress pinched her neck. When I met her eyes, she seemed emboldened and her impatience disarmed me. So I looked into my lap and spoke softly. "A man named Svene Solvang hired me on his sealer. This was up in Hotellneset. On Spitzbergen. We were hunting, Mikkelsen and I, on the ice up there. And then came an ice bear."

Even from half a thousand miles away, that beast bedeviled me. The fog might have been its long shadow, so much did the memory of him haunt me. When I looked up to see if my story was satisfying Inger, I could see it wasn't. She plied her needles, her eyes flitting between me and her work, and I knew from her pursed lips that she was holding her tongue. I suspected, now, that any softness in her might be harder to find than my salvation on that distant fjord.

And what should a husband say to his wife at a moment such as this? What words will one day be invented to describe her distance? Or how it feels to be unwanted, to be thought better of dead? I felt the dread iciness creeping up my back and it took some kind of courage to say, "If you'd rather not hear more—"

"Rather not hear?" she interrupted. "You were going to speak of those boots. Surely part of your story will explain how they went from his feet to yours."

"You're in a hurry, then? You have other obligations this evening? Is Bengt wanting his dinner? Is that it?"

Now she looked up from her knitting. "I was alone for some four months, Husband. And a widow for ten days. Now I find myself with a ghost."

"You're no widow, Inger. And I'm no damn ghost."

She tossed her needles and knitting back into the basket and stormed into the same corner of the room where she'd fetched my duffle. From beneath her bed she pulled a glass jar and came and stood before me and uncapped it. "We'll be ghosts soon enough," she said, and dumped the few coins in the jar onto my lap. "That's what we have. All of it. That and whatever charity Bengt bestows on us."

I dropped the kroner—seven of them—back into the jar one at a time. "Bengt doesn't pay you for your labor, then?"

"Where do you think those are from?"

If she'd asked I would have admitted it was a meager fortune, and that its threat of hard times was something to worry over. Quickly enough, I started to scheme for what new money I might find. "Svene owes me," I said, though I thought it unlikely I'd ever see him again, or any of what he owed me for the seals I'd clubbed to death. "And I'll find work myself. I'll take the faering tomorrow and bring in a haul. Some to eat and some to sell."

She only shook her head.

The darkness came swiftly now, and if not for the warmth of the stove across the room I might've been staring at that swath of land out there on the Krossfjorden. The lonesomeness of that view out the window kindled in me a feeling that was already becoming familiar, but the mere thought of trying to explain this to her filled me with dread. Yet her expression, that persistent look, suggested I had better try.

"Okay, Inger. Here, then: The bear got Mikkelsen. I didn't know right away because we'd been separated. I would know soon enough, though." I looked at her expressionless face. Thought of giving up, but continued instead. "Oh, Inger. I was alone in a way I cannot describe to you. I could spend the rest of my life trying and never get it right." I drank the rest of the coffee and set the cup down on the floor. "After the bear had gone, after Mikkelsen disappeared, I came to a rocky shoreline below a glacier. I remember the sound of the wind. This was all that could be heard. It would've taken me another hour to get to the jut of land I saw down the shore, or a different hour to walk to the base of the mountains rising up from the glacier's edge. It might have been a lovely sight if not for all that troubled me. Foremost in that thinking was that I would die. But you asked about the boots. And you want me to tell you plainly.

"I turned away from the shore. Headed away from the fjord up toward the mountain. I walked slowly. Fearfully. With no true plan in mind. What I was going in search of I could not imagine. But then I found it, not a quarter mile distant. First one boot, below the bloody stump of a knee. Then some paces more the other komager, still on the foot of a leg torn off just above the ankle. There was no sign of struggle. No blood but for that knee. No human claw marks. There weren't even many bear tracks, though those that I saw in the permafrost were more than a foot from end to end. It was as if those boots and the feet still in them had been dropped by a passing bird." I pointed at the boots. "A gift? Or taunt?"

I risked another peek at Inger, who finally seemed moved.

"I looked into the gloaming and fog and I thought, *I was never alone before now.* Except for the wind screeching up the fjord, no sound wanted to be heard." I kept my gaze on her, and she didn't avert it. "No cry of pain. No slavering bear. No ripping flesh. Just the wind and, behind it, that long and vacant land.

"Inger, what I saw was desolation in every direction, and *miles* of it. On my feet, alone in the darkness. I thought of how slowly it would go, and in unimaginable pain, given my own boots practically didn't have soles. I saw myself hiking up that glacier's edge and over the mountains behind it, or down the landkall ashore. I was so afraid, Inger."

Now she spoke, with much solemnity. "Hereunto were ye called: because Christ also suffered for us, leaving us an example, that ye should follow His steps," she said, quoting some scripture.

It took me a moment to catch her point. "You're right," I said. "If a time had ever come to take comfort in the Lord's suffering, it was then. But I'll tell you, Inger, that when I turned to Him I found not a fellow sojourner but a man I didn't much believe in anymore."

"Blasphemy, Odd Einar."

"Ja," I admitted, "it's blasphemy of a sort. But I was less concerned with my soul than my feet, which is why I took Mikkelsen's boots one at a time."

"That's why they said you were killed by the bear. You and Birger Mikkelsen both."

"Who said that?"

"Solvang's man. They searched for you. They went up that fjord the next morning and found your boots by Mikkelsen's feet. They found him and his rifle on the glacier."

"They found Mikkelsen?"

"What was left of him. Much else of him was also missing."

I reached down and rubbed my ankles and then my toes. They were right where they should be. "You say they looked the next morning?"

"The killing boat was floating on the Krossfjorden. With your duffle. They knew where you were hunting and they looked. That's when they found you."

"Solvang's man, he came here? He brought you my bag?"

"I already told you that, Odd Einar. Yes, he came and brought me your bag."

Now she blanched, which hinted at some admission if she was still the wife I'd left in the springtime.

"What is it, Inger?"

She fixed her gaze on the window. "Solvang's man, he also paid me your share. I used it for your lot in the cemetery."

"That's rich," I said, and would have laughed if my anger weren't on me as suddenly as that bear had been. "And so you hate me for the folly of it? As though I summoned the bear? That it was a lark for me to wander that island wondering if I'd ever be found? Christ, Inger, do you think I'm some man you've never known or ever seen?"

As if she hadn't heard me at all, she said, "So that was all, then? You took his boots and started walking?"

"Ja."

What more was there to say? I would not tell her what it was like to remove those boots from the severed feet of my friend, that his leg and ankle were like bowls of some meaty soup, that what I'd found of him, apart from the boots, weighed no more than a dog-fish, and felt much the same slathered as they were in his blood. I would not, I decided just then, Inger's head now bowed as if in prayer, speak again of the boots or how they came to be sitting on our floor. I would keep the darkest parts to myself.

As if my memory and my resolve had coupled in me and rendered me harsh—more than I'd ever been toward her—I said, "Tell me how it is I could have walked where I have walked, could've trundled through that darkness wanting for all that I did, as *afraid* as I've ever been, Inger, only to sit here in the warmth of this fire with a hearty crust of bread in my belly and be more fearful now, in your company, than I ever was at the top of the world."

I waited and when she said not a single word I simply rose from my chair and rewarmed the water for a bath. It took as long for her to speak as it did for the pot to steam, and then I heard her coolest words yet.

"You think you're the only one who's grown tired or been afraid? Hardly, Husband. Hardly at all." She stood up and came to my side at the stove. "First I watched Thea go. My only child. To a place I could never see. Then my husband disappeared. Or was killed and eaten by a bear, in another impossible place. I've also been alone and afraid." She took her apron off a hook and hung it around her neck and tied it behind her back. Then she put on her mobcap and tucked her hair up under it and lit a small lamp. "And now I will go make my master and his wife their supper." She stepped to the door. "I will learn to be here with you again. I suppose that's true. But when I woke this morning you were dead. I might need some time to find my bearings, too."

With those words she unlatched the door, walked out, and left me to my bath.

———

I stood over the simmering pot on the stove, letting the steam rise across my face. One minute, then two minutes, my hair and beard growing damp and droplets already trickling back into the pot. After the third minute, I stepped away and undressed. What foulness. What filth. I strummed my ribs and took measure of the umber tint of my feet. My toenails were half of them missing. I could feel the ache of my feet up my back and into my shoulders.

I dipped a cloth into the scalding water and wrung it out and started washing myself, first my face and then on down. It felt more like a skinning. By the time I reached my feet the cloth was mottled gray. When I finished, I poured the brown water out the window and filled the pot from the bucket and washed my hair in merely warm water and then rinsed my whole body again. Last, I emptied the pot again and set it aside to be washed in the kitchen, then snuffed the lamp and stepped over my pile of clothes and walked through the darkness to lie down in my wife's new bed.

How long had I slept before waking to the sound of Inger hanging my trousers and shirt from a hook beside the bed? I could smell the lye she'd used to launder them, and could also smell the tea sitting in a cup on the table next to the bed. Tea and a cake made of lavender and lemon. Seeing me awake, she stepped bedside and handed me the teacup.

It was warm, and I drank half of it in a long, tight-lipped gulp.

"The cake will please you, Odd Einar. Here. It's Bengt's favorite, but I thought of you while I turned the batter." When she handed me the plate, I took a bite and my mouth began to seep because I'd never tasted anything so delicious. I finished the cake in three bites and drank the rest of the tea and collapsed again.

She sat there the whole time, and as I lay back she put her hand on my ribs, her palm warm against my cold skin, and said, "You'll need many cakes. You're as thin as Thea was the day she left." Her eyes were damp and she held her gaze on me while she stood up, removed her apron, and reached back to unbutton the long string of eyelets running down her spine. "I'll not wear this dress again."

"It suits you," I said.

I could tell she was appraising her own mood.

Finally, the corner of her lip turned up and she said, "Well, you were a long time without seeing any women."

Now she removed her stockings and her legs glowed in the darkness. Crossing the room to the basin, she combed her hair out, washed her face, rinsed her mouth, removed her knickers and camisole, and then donned her linen shift. When she reached the bed, she slid under the eiderdown and lay very still, her eyes closed. I could feel her warmth, as I earlier had the stove. She whispered, "I have been faithful to you and to my love for you, Odd Einar." She opened her eyes but was looking only at the ceiling. "I missed you all summer. I waited for word from you. I wondered where you were. And how you were." She turned to look at me now and I could see her eyes wet again, this time with tears. "I prayed for you every day. I prayed for you and longed for you and, oh, I missed you dearly."

"Inger—"

"Shush," she said softly, then continued. "I can't describe what happened when they said you were dead. And how you'd died. I don't remember how it felt. But I was scared, too. Just like you must have been with that bear. I was scared because I couldn't imagine you gone." She took my hand under the eiderdown. "When you came back today—when I saw you walk up the cemetery path—I didn't know what to do. You were *alive*. Imagine it." Now she wept quietly. She squeezed my rough hand with her soft one and cried just like she did on the night we said goodbye to Thea. "And here you are," she managed. "Here you are in my hand again."

I rolled onto my side and laid my arm between her breasts so my fingertips rested in the curve of her neck. Her tears shed onto the back of my hand and I held her until she began to settle. Outside, the moon came over the hill and shone through the window. It filtered through her hair and pooled in the soft valleys of her shoulders as though it had risen just for her—never mind the tides, never mind the howling wolves. I felt myself warming against her. I measured my contentment with the slowing of her heartbeat.

The moon over Spitzbergen illuminated only its desolation. The fog had gone out to sea as I traversed the landkall along the shoreline, feeling nothing save the vacancy of my sorry life. Well, and terror too. The shadows and the fact of all this cold and snow and ice already in October, and of the bear, its appetite surely whetted. Where was that beast? Each glance back, at the behest of any tiny sound, brought an eclipse of the rising moon. Was it the ice bear? The shadow of the bear? The bear's ghost? How could I know? How could I do anything but walk into the night? And so I did. But as the moon rose higher, my own shadow grew strangely longer before me.

By the time the moon outside Inger's window set at night, she would ask again about the ice bear and all that came after, yet the simplicity of her questions did not make the answers easier. That's not how it works. No, the more direct the question, the less certain its answer. Would I be wise in keeping to myself the profundities those days offered? Would I admit to my wife that I was still trying to step into the shadow of *myself*? Or that this was the best I could hope to do in what life I had left?

No man ever dreamt who wasn't fast asleep. But how else to explain what it was like to lie there with Inger beside me? The moon was gone to shine into some other window, but through ours fell the incandescence of stars, and in their light the curve of her hip and the peak of her shoulder showed faintly through her linen shift. Her face was nestled into the pillow we shared but I could hear her soft breaths.

I closed my eyes tightly and thought of the faraway places I'd been and reminded myself that I'd not slept much lately and so might be dreaming of myself in that bed, yet when I opened my eyes and rolled over Inger was still beside me. I ran my hand down the slope of her shoulder and arm while I sent one foot burrowing through the covers and found her leg and touched her gently with my aching toes. She stirred and found my hip with her hand. I watched her eyes open and take measure of me, no doubt dubious herself.

"It's you, Odd Einar."

"Is it?"

She stretched her legs and arched her back and then settled closer and said, "I wasn't dreaming, then?"

I pointed at the window. "Look, Inger. Those stars high up? They're shining on the Krossfjorden even as they're shining on us. I looked for you among them. I chased after you. And you brought me home."

She turned and pressed against me, her hand playing up my bare back and resting on my cheek. "You sweet man," she said. She kissed my face and tugged the eiderdown from between us and let it fall on the floor before reaching down for me. "You certainly *are* here." Now she rose to her knees and lifted her nightdress and sat astride me.

She put her arms on my chest and took my face in her hands and whispered my name and moved slowly, her breasts lolling in the falling collar of her shift, my own skin thrilling at her touch. When I let out a small groan she said, "Shhh," and held a finger to my lips. She went slower and let out her own gasp and shook her head and said, "We must be quiet," and then closed her eyes and lips.

I strummed my fingers down her sides and scooped the folds of her nightdress into my hands and lifted it over her head and dropped it on the bed beside us. I let the backs of my hands graze her nipples before sliding my palms around her. What I felt was not the stock of the Krag-Jørgensen or the hakapik or a coal shovel, but the lissome curve of her hips as she rolled them into me.

She untied her hair and it fell in a veil as she whispered that she loved me. Gentle Inger. She whispered it a hundred times. I closed my eyes and tried to wake myself once more. When I looked up she was still there, her head thrown back now, the starlight glazing her throat. She moved faster, her hands gripping my knees, her body like a wave coming ashore. I held her fiercely and moved my own hips to meet hers and good lord it was not long before she folded over me again, her hair splashing across my face and her breath heavy in my ear. Sweat pooled in my belly as we softened, holding each other, before she collapsed onto her side.

Out the window I could see the valley across the lake. The luster of starlight appeared as snow on the hillside, which meant clear skies above. I thought of the pleasure of studying the night through a glass window, and of all the nights I'd spent with nothing between my eyes and the heavens except the bitterest cold.

I felt myself settling too, my eyelids growing heavy, and realized that I had slept and woken and made love to my wife. I knew it hadn't been a dream. And I knew that sleep would come again and with a new kind of weight. I felt gluttonous and ready. And then I noticed a new light in the window, dull and sputtering, and saw in it a face that at first I mistook as being outside. It was a face I recognized as surely as I'd known Skjeggestad's daughter on the street just the day before. If I didn't flinch, it was only because I was too tired. But then I put a name to the face and turned to the doorway, where Gerd Bjornsen, Bengt's wife, stood, a candle guttering before her, her hair wisping from under a nightcap. I again glanced at her reflection in the window and then back at her face in the door.

Though apparently not realizing I was awake, she kept her body hidden in the darkness of the hallway, but I could see the hem of her nightdress swaying as she rocked from her heels to her toes. If my guess was right, she seemed to be focusing on Inger's backside. I wanted to ask what had brought her to this corner of the house, yet when opening my mouth I found I had no voice. So instead I lifted the eiderdown from the floor and spread it over Inger. Only then did Gerd look at me. Her hollow, bespectacled eyes darting across my own for just a second before she turned to leave. I watched as the candlelight went down the passageway with her.

I had finally roused myself from bed and first dug in my duffle to retrieve the Krossfjorden chart and then to the window to study it.

Some combination of fog and snow had slunk down the valley and laced the shore of Gávpotjávri in white. I listened to the baaing of sheep somewhere in the brume, a sound that brought me happiness.

At the stove I put more water on for tea. While waiting for it to warm, I unfolded Mikkelsen's old chart and tried to locate the spot where I'd spent my first morning. Shivering and hungry, the loneliest man alive. Just the thought of that spit of land made me uneasy. Yet I couldn't put the map down. Even when the kettle blew, I just stood there guessing at where I'd been.

It was Inger who finally rescued me from that reverie.

"You'll burn the place down, Odd Einar," she said, grabbing a mitt and removing the teakettle from the stove. "And what's this?" She took the chart from my hands and inspected it and, when she realized what it was, folded it quickly and stowed it in a basket on the counter. "I suppose you have better things to do than woolgather over that old map." She was already busy making me a cup of tea.

"I suppose I do."

"You might start by getting dressed. But here's your tea." She handed me the cup and hurried across the room to the wardrobe, from which she pulled a new pair of trousers and a shirt and waistcoat. She brought the trousers back to where I stood and held them up to my waist. "I believe these are cut right. Why don't you freshen up and try them on?"

"What's the hurry, Inger?"

"There's a man wants to meet you."

"What man?"

"A man Herr Bjornsen sent for. A Herr Granerud. Marius Granerud. He came up from Tromsø, a newspaperman from *Aftenposten.*"

"What could he want with me?"

She had crossed the room and back and now held the shirt up before me. "This might be a little long in the sleeves, but it will work."

"Where are these clothes from, Inger?"

She was now heading for the waistcoat. "Herr Bjornsen sent me to get them this morning. He wants you presentable."

"Presentable? And when did you get down to the village for all of this?"

Now she stopped and, with my new outfit hung over her arm, said, "Herr Granerud would like to hear about what happened to you. He thinks your story might sell some newspapers." She took the teacup from my hand. "We're having dinner in one half hour with the Bjornsens and the newspaperman. You must get dressed."

Without waiting for a response, she handed me the soft clothes and nodded toward the wardrobe. "I have to go help prepare the food. Come down to the dining room when you're ready. There will be lamb and potatoes to eat, and butter for your bread." She took my face in her hands and kissed me on my whiskery chin before turning to leave as suddenly as she'd surprised me.

Lamb and potatoes? The mere thought of this set my mouth watering. I could picture the butter shining on the bread, the lamb soaking in its blood. On Spitzbergen and my return home hunger had become an essential fact of my existence. Just yesterday morning, I tried to eat a rotten potato. And now mutton and bread and butter and sweet warm wine were soon to fill my cup.

G reta slept and woke and slept again and woke the second time from a dream of this small Norwegian village more than a hundred years ago. The streets were hazed with fog, and the voice of a man she surely knew called her name. In the dream she walked toward him, his face as ghostly as the fog. Only tripping on a cobblestone saved her from meeting him, and she bolted upright in bed in the dark hotel room, breathless and completely disoriented. She tried to go back to sleep, but found herself in another kind of dream instead, recalling the Saturday after Thanksgiving.

At her father's house, she'd made leftovers—shredded turkey, mashed potatoes, stuffing, corn, asparagus, and gravy all baked into puff pastry and served with more gravy over the top. They ate at his kitchen counter, the same place she'd had breakfast nearly every morning until she left for college. After dinner, the kids played three-handed cribbage with Gus until bedtime. They went off and brushed their teeth and came back to the great room to kiss her and their grandpa good night and trundled up to read, both of them, before falling asleep. It was only eight o'clock, and she asked her father if he'd mind if she went down to the fish house. He of course didn't, so she drove the snowy trail to town and through it and to the lake and parked right outside. The waves on the lake boomed through the darkness and she felt better before she even lit both the lantern and a cigarette with the same match.

She found her bottle of Maker's Mark in one of the fish boxes and grabbed a coffee cup, stepped outside and filled the cup with new snow and then poured in a little whiskey and sipped while she smoked. Grandma Eide had once said the only good thing that ever came of a North Shore winter was a Whiskey and Snow, and sitting there in the dim light with only the waves for company, she might have agreed. Not that the winters at home were much better.

Frans had called three times before his plane departed at nine, when he sent her a text: *Really? You won't even take my call?* She didn't answer his text, either. Instead she put a new piece of sandpaper on a rubber block and started with the gunwale on the bow of the old canoe, slowly and steadily sanding it smooth. She wanted not to think, and this was a perfect job for that. After a few minutes, she paused and tuned the battery-powered transistor radio on the windowsill to WTIP and listened to an Erik Koskinen song while the smell of old cedar rose from the dust.

Lying in the dark in the Hotel Thon, she was as much back at home as she was here under a warm duvet.

She'd sanded the whole gunwale smooth, up and down the port and starboard sides, changing the paper twice. Sawdust had settled on her arms and hands like a second skin, and she brushed it off before deciding to make herself another drink. When she stepped out for a second cup of snow she noticed the sky had cleared in the east and with the stars came an even more raucous sea.

Back inside, after a sip of her drink, she held the lantern right beside the canoe and studied the fine grain of the wood. She thought back to what it must've been like for her dad to stand in this place working silently beside his own father. It was a thought that filled her with a comfort she couldn't articulate exactly, neither on that night over Thanksgiving nor even now, more awake with each new breath, but it came as an enormous relief on both occasions. Maybe it was because all the jobs she'd undertaken thus far in the fish house had come with unforeseen troubles. Whether it was replacing panes of broken glass in the windows or tuck-pointing the foundation or hammering new shingles on the roof, everything had been more difficult than she'd expected. Her father might have said that was how things went, and she supposed he was right.

By the time she finished her second drink she'd made another pass around the gunwale with a finer piece of sandpaper. "Girl from the North Country" was playing. Her father's favorite song, *her* song, he always insisted. She figured he'd be asleep by now, nestled on his side of the bed, the side his wife had occupied for forty-odd years still reserved for her. Greta often checked in on him late at night, as though he were one of her children. Now that it was turning winter, he wore a stocking cap to bed just as her grandfather had. Lately, she'd wondered more than once what it would be like to love someone as much as her parents loved each other. What it would be like to lose someone after such a long life together. Though she ought to have taken comfort from this speculation, it only made her own loneliness more profound.

What had she expected, really? If she was being honest with herself—and those hours alone in the fish house were fertile times for honesty—she should've seen how little she trusted her feelings for Frans from the outset. They'd met at a fund-raiser he was attending at the Sons of Norway, when she was writing features for a Minneapolis weekly. After his talk about climate change in the Arctic and how the apocalyptic, long-term effects of melting ice caps and glaciers would wreak havoc on coastal areas all around the world—standard rhetoric, but delivered with panache and an old-world authority by a descendant of a polar hero and patron saint of Norway—she introduced herself and asked a few questions.

She could still remember how he'd answered them, seriously, thoughtfully, and in an academic manner, passionately. In this, he was like most of the people she met and talked to about this science, their vehemence measured and calculated. The only thing notable about Frans was his inflection, for which he apologized at least three times. Finally she said, "Please, don't. You speak better English than anyone I know." This was true, even if his accent was unmistakable. After her brief interview, she said thank you and good luck and good night and thought nothing more about him. Not until the next evening, when she was having a drink with a friend at a place downtown called the Times. She might not even have recognized him in his corduroy pants and leather jacket if he hadn't come up and introduced himself.

Greta's friend, whom she worked with at the weekly, excused herself soon after Frans joined them. They ended up ordering something to eat and had a couple drinks and everything about him that had been formal the night before was now easy. He had a deep laugh he was quick to use, and a powerful curiosity. He asked many more questions than she did, and by the end of the evening he said he was sad to be leaving, that she was the most interesting person he'd met in the week he'd been there. And that he hoped someday to get up to Lake Superior, it sounded so beautiful.

"Next time you're in town, I'll take you up there," she said, figuring that this would be the last time she'd ever see him. "Come in winter, though, okay? It's the best season by far."

That had been in October, and right after New Year's the phone rang on her desk at the weekly. She couldn't say she'd thought much about him but he had crossed her mind, and when she heard his voice she felt a surprising thrill.

"I'm here in Minneapolis," he said.

"Spreading more doom and gloom?" she teased.

He laughed and said it must've been a false alarm, given the cold and snow that greeted his return to Minnesota.

"So what are you doing here, then?" she asked. "How long will you be staying?"

In her years as a journalist she'd developed the ability to tell when people were lying, and even on the phone she could hear untruth in his story about meeting with climatologists at the university. Then he said, "I'd love to have dinner."

This, too, sounded like a lie, though why else would he call her? So she agreed, and they met that evening at a place in Uptown near her apartment. It would take most of that winter before he admitted he was here, and kept coming back, not for climatology but simply to spend time with her. Not knowing whether to feel flattered or just embarrassed for him, she mostly laughed it off. He'd stayed four days the first visit and by early March had returned three times. For the last they made plans to drive up to the North Shore so he could finally see the big water and—why not, she figured—meet her parents.

Naturally, up in Gunflint, Frans charmed them with his intelligence and manners and stoicism. He'd done his research on the glacial history of Lake Superior and the North Shore and was soon telling Gus and Sarah about Lake Agassiz, the river Warren, dire wolves, and the Holocene. He did this without arrogance or condescension and even realized, halfway through their first meal together, that perhaps he was talking too much. He checked himself and by the end of the weekend was fast friends with Greta's mother and father.

They ventured north a couple more times in the coming months and on Thanksgiving, after dinner but before pie, Frans announced their engagement. As she sat in her usual seat at the big dining room table, watching him raise his wineglass and declare his happiness in knowing them all and having the chance to become part of their family, she felt—and there was only one word for it— unmovable. Here was this steady, handsome, considerate, quiet man. Who liked to laugh. Who wanted children. Who was worldly, with an air of nobility, especially in Norway, which she'd seen firsthand that summer. But there was no arrogance in him. He was a good man, a very good man indeed.

Yet why had Greta's mother asked, while they were washing the Thanksgiving dishes later that night, if she was happy?

"Of course I'm happy, Mom. Don't I seem happy?"

Sarah had put her hands back in the dishwater to scrub another plate. In answer, she said, "When your father asked me to marry him, I cried for ten minutes before I could say yes. I cried because I loved him so much and couldn't wait to be his wife." She paused, rinsed the plate, and handed it to Greta, who started wiping it dry. "But that was a long time ago. In a different era. A different place."

Feeling defensive, Greta said, "The times aren't all that different. And our life in Minneapolis isn't very far away."

"Oh, I know that, sweetheart. That's not what I'm saying."

"What *are* you saying?"

Now Sarah paused again and dried her hands and pushed a wisp of soft gray hair off her forehead. "He's a very nice man, Frans is. And handsome. Oh, *my*. We love him already, because it's hard not to. But we don't have to love him the same way as you."

Greta might have been furious, but her mother's observation instead made her feel relieved. Hadn't she wondered about the fidelity of her love for him from the moment she'd accepted his proposal? A moment, incidentally, that required no tears whatsoever. In fact, she couldn't remember any emotions accompanying her rather direct "Of course I'll marry you."

And she had, with not much trepidation but without enough exuberance, either. That was almost twenty years ago. She had been curious at the start, anxious if not exactly excited to see how their lives together would evolve. She wondered almost philosophically about the phases of their relationship, and gave them a thorough accounting as they passed. He worked. She worked, too, now at the *StarTribune*. They bought their first house, near her old apartment, and then five years later traded up to a much nicer house a block off of Lake Harriet. A beautiful home, large enough to raise a family in, large enough for her to finally have a home office, and Frans a suite of connected and finished rooms in the basement for his own work and assortment of Arctic collectibles. He traveled often and ambiguously, but he was devoted and she never doubted his faithfulness, nor did she doubt her own. They had Lasse and, two years later, Liv, and through the kids' infancy and toddlerhood she kept waiting for other big changes to come. Despite the fact that Frans was a wonderful father and a doting husband when his heart was in it, she never felt her life moving as she'd expected it would, and by the time Liv was in preschool Greta realized that she was unhappy and probably depressed. Parenthood could not be life. Not *her* life. And her marriage to Frans, well, it hadn't changed much since they'd had kids, a truth she woke up with one morning as though it were a racing heart. Was this going to be the sum total of the rest of life? It was a question she resisted asking too often, for fear of its answer. And she'd avoided it with astonishing success, until the day her mother died three years earlier.

On that morning, as Greta sat bedside at the hospital, Sarah looking better and feeling spry, she'd held her mother's hand and they'd talked about Lasse and Liv, about springtime and making pickles and fishing the steelhead run on the Burnt Wood River, and when Greta was getting ready to leave, Sarah said, "I'm glad that you found your life. I didn't know if you would, but you seem so happy and that makes *me* happy."

Greta smiled and felt a tear come to her eye but then, a few minutes later, as she left to pick up Liv at a friend's house, her stomach dropped out of her all at once. She rushed to her car through a drizzling rain and cried in the parking lot for twenty minutes. She was late picking Liv up. Her mother died that afternoon in the same hospital bed.

Greta got out of the hotel bed, went to the bathroom, and poured a glass of water. In the mirror above the sink, her silhouette took form in the dark. She couldn't help thinking that this was just how she must appear to people. The shape of herself. Maybe that's why she'd taken so much pleasure in working on the fish house, where rarely was anyone there to see her. She could simply be herself, sanding the canoe, listening to music, remembering to forget. What would her mother have said about that? That it was no way to live. And she'd have been right.

Greta went back to bed and distracted herself by returning to the fish house and her father's canoe, on which he'd traveled the most perilous miles of his life back when he was just a teenager. He'd built it himself. Beautiful cedar strips, the thwarts hewn of white pine, the cane seat still tightly drawn some fifty years after it had last been used. Gus said many times over the years that he'd never put another canoe in the water and, once Greta started refurbishing the fish house, even told her that she should sell it if she could find a buyer. Looking at it that night after Thanksgiving, she was beyond glad it was there. As if it were proof of the quality of work that could be done in this place.

The thought of work had buoyed her then, and she'd pushed the canoe into the corner by the barn door. Last she turned out the lantern, as she had the night before, and crossed the dark room to walk out into the wind. The horizon over the lake was clouded again, its surface lit by the stars above. And even fifty feet from the shore, she could feel the spray of the waves on her bare cheeks.

When she got back to her father's house it was after eleven. All the lights were out inside, but from the driveway she could tell a fire was still burning in the grate. Her father was sitting in his old leather chair, his chin on his chest, his eyes closed in peaceful sleep, a book open on his lap. He startled awake as she closed the door behind her, then looked at his watch and marked his page and closed the book and sat up, yawning.

"What are you still doing up, Dad?" She hung her coat by the door and stomped the snow from her boots. Six or seven inches had fallen since lunchtime.

"How are the roads?"

"The plow's been up the trail and it stopped snowing." She crossed the great room and sat on the couch opposite him.

When the wind quieted, she could hear the river in the distance. It sounded lovely with the snapping fire. "Listen," she said, and cocked her ear.

Gus turned his own ear toward the sound and waited for the wind to pass.

"Hear it?" Greta said.

"Naw, I can't. Christ, I can barely hear the phone ringing nowadays."

"It's rushing. The lake was up, too."

"Rain and snow and rain and snow again. Almost every day since Halloween. The river's just about topped off."

She sat back in the couch and watched the fire.

"Speaking of the phone ringing, Frans called while you were in town. Said he couldn't reach you."

"No, he couldn't."

"All right. Well, I told him you'd call him back in the morning."

"Thanks, Papa."

Gus wrestled himself up out of the chair and went into the kitchen. She heard the cupboard door open and the faucet run and the ice-cube tray crack. Then the lid of a bottle being unscrewed and two faint splashes. He brought back a glass in each hand and she took hers and looked up at him.

"Is it that plain to see?" she asked.

"Not much is obvious in this world, kid. But I like to think I know my daughter."

"So you waited up for me?"

"Like when you were in high school," he said, and stoked the fire before he sat down and switched on the lamp beside his chair. "You used to sneak in past curfew all the time. You and your brother both. I always wondered what the hell there was to get into that late at night around here." He took a sip of his drink.

"But now that I'm as old as this, I find the hours late at night or early in the morning to be the most productive. Why, the newspaper's better read alone at night than in the morning at the Blue Sky Café. At least here my complaints go unheard. Don't have to listen to those old fellas sticking up for our dipshit president. The other day—"

"You don't have to talk to fill the air, Dad," she interrupted. "We can just sit here. I'd like that."

He took another sip of bourbon and settled back into his chair. After a minute he said, "I'll be damned, I can hear the river after all."

Greta counted to ten—a trick from childhood that her mother taught her to use when she knew she was about to say something she might regret—and then did it once more. "I think my marriage is over," she said, though she wasn't sure it was loud enough for her father to hear. Was he counting to ten himself?

"Does Frans know this?"

She turned her eyes from the fire to her father. "Are you kidding? Frans knows everything."

Gus made a mirthless smile. "It's a hard thing to do, ending a marriage. I had a front-row seat for my parents' coming apart."

"I'm so lonely, Dad."

"Is that all?"

"We don't love each other anymore."

"Oh, Frans still loves you, sweetheart. Any ninny can see that."

"Well, I don't love him." She took a long sip and added, "He's having an affair. I don't even care."

Gus tilted his head up and looked at her through his glasses.

"I can't believe it's come to this. I feel like a failure. I look around here. I see my childhood. I see your perfect marriage with Mom. How could I screw it up so bad?"

"Your mom and I, we didn't have a perfect marriage. I don't think such a thing exists."

"It seemed perfect from my vantage."

"I suppose Lasse and Liv think the same thing about you and Frans."

At the mention of them, she lost her breath. She sat up and set her empty glass on the big coffee table.

"It took me about twenty years to learn how to be married," he said. She could tell he was trying to help. Trying to carry the conversation until she got her bearings again. "Your mother had patience enough to wait all that time."

"Mom knew he was wrong. She knew it from the beginning."

"Your mother knew an awful damn lot, that's for sure."

Was that an admission? She looked at him hopefully. "She must've talked to you about it. Back then, I mean. Did you agree with her?"

"I like Frans. I did from the word go. He's a good man. A tremendous father. He's steady."

She waited.

He looked down into the bottom of his drink before he said, "But he's not running for office, is he?"

"I said the most horrible things to him. Before he left."

"You're not the first person to dress down their spouse."

"The next time I talk to him, he'll be four thousand miles away."

He wedged himself up in his chair, looked hard at her. "Do you have any hope, Greta?"

"I don't know." She thought of the anger on Frans's face as he walked out of the Burnt Wood Tavern. Of her own seething resentment. And their shameful fuck in the fish house. She thought of the kids. Of that woman, Alena. She pictured knocking on his hotel door in Oslo, thought of going that far to tell him it was all over. That he had to come home with her so they could take care of finishing it. And then without thinking she said, "Can I ask you a favor?"

"You know you can ask me for anything."

"Will you take the kids home tomorrow? Get them off to school next week? I think I need to go over there."

"To Norway?"

"Yes. I have to go see him."

Gus shook his head slowly. Not approvingly, but as if to say he would. Of course he would.

"I won't be gone long, Dad. Four or five days. Long enough to get over there and find Frans and…"

Her voice trailed off, and in its absence Gus spoke up. "And see what happens, right, kid?"

"Right. And see what happens."

Well, she had gotten this far. Too far, she supposed. Into a country that seemed full of ghosts and dreams and memories. She curled onto her side in the down of the hotel bed, closing her eyes against all of it, and decided that the next day would come. She would see herself in the mirror. She would call Frans then.

Even on the darkest nights, when the only proof I had against death was the wind and the distant booms of calving glaciers, when I stumbled on that gale-scoured scruff of land spongy beneath my feet where it wasn't strewn with rocks or snow, when all I had was the thought of my wife and daughter to keep me from abandoning myself to the icy seas, I would sometimes see before me, at a distance I could never quite fathom, a sudden blossoming of light. It rose from the ground all golden and soft as smoke, and put before me someplace to go. It might linger for a second or a minute and in this span I hurried as if in that light I might find the warmth I so desperately imagined. Of course the light was only ever swallowed up, and the following darkness only ever more profound.

I can't say why I was thinking of this as I walked down the hall to the Bjornsen dining room. The light spilling from the entryway proved to be entirely of fire—from the chandelier, from the candelabras, from the enormous hearth, all of it reflected in the blackened windows and reaching into the night beyond. As I walked into the room in my overlarge trousers and shirt, I hardly knew which of my senses to indulge first. The warmth of the fireplace? The sound of cheerful laughter? The bouquet of stewing meat and heady fish free for me to whiff? Or the sight of my beautiful wife, standing beside the hearth? She greeted me with a kind glance and turned down a hallway.

From the corner of the room a short man with a monocle and the belly of a fat seal wobbled over to me. Pocketing his eyepiece and looking me up and down, he said, "Well now, Herr Bjornsen, you said he was wasted to naught. What I see here is a man hale and hearty." He winked at Bengt, then turned back to me and said, "The fish is fresh and the mutton's been stewed in wine and sweet cabbage, my friend, but first, here—" And he gestured to a sideboard in the corner he'd come from, where on a silver platter sat heaping bowls of caviar and black bread and gherkins.

Bengt himself was spooning the fish eggs onto a piece of bread. He took a stein of beer from another silver-plated tray, handed it to this man, took a second and set it on the sideboard, and then offered me a third, as though I were one of his bosom friends and this our regular Saturday night social. "Odd Einar Eide," he said, raising his own stein, "meet Marius Granerud, here from Tromsø to hear your story of coming back from the dead." He now addressed Marius. "If our friend looks hale and hearty, it's because he's full of spirit." And then, to both of us: "Gentlemen, it's my pleasure to bring you together. We shall feast and parley and—before our supper's done—have a plan to tell your tale, Herr Eide. But first, to your safe return, and to the happiness of your comely wife, and to settling old accounts. Skål!"

"Skål," Granerud echoed.

I merely tipped my stein.

Granerud wiped the suds from his upper lip with the back of his hand. "I grew up with the makers of this fine ale down in Sigdal. The Ringnes brothers. It's a beautiful part of Norway, Sigdal is. Nestled in the mountains just this side of Christiania." He took me by the arm and crossed the room and stood before a painting on the far side of the fireplace. "Christian Skredsvig—the man who painted this—was one of our mates, too."

I looked at the painting hanging in a gilt frame above a bookshelf. Two candle sconces flanked it, their fluttering light casting shadowy waves over a flock of sheep, some white, some black, scattered on a field of turf with trees barren of leaves and hills on the horizon. Two farmers, indistinct well beyond them, tended to their rakes.

I looked down from the painting and saw that Bengt now stood with us.

"From the time I was a boy," he said, "all I ever wanted was a field of sheep. Sheep and a wife. I never cared to have children, even when I was still a child myself." He seemed in love with this memory of himself as a boy, as if he wanted to walk into the painting and rake the hay. After a spell, he roused himself from his reverie and looked at me and said, "Most people, they have no idea how to make their lives what they wish. Most people, if you told them they could have anything, would ask only for the simplest things. A few more potatoes, a lump of sugar for their tea, a pair of mittens. The most imaginative might ask for a new faering, in order to cast their lines in deeper seas." He took a long drink of his beer before setting it on the bookshelf and removing a pipe from his waistcoat pocket. He packed it and lit it and puffed and fingered his stein again, then finally said, "What would you ask for, Odd Einar? If you could have anything?"

"Why, the chance to see my daughter again," I said without a moment's breath. "A whole Sunday with her laughter and sweetness."

"You see?" Bengt said, to Marius Granerud. "He makes my case for me. You, man, have been to the polar seas and back. You have outfoxed the ice bears. Why, indeed you have risen from the dead!" He took another puff of his pipe. "Why not ask for what might come of that? Fame. Wealth. Immortality."

What odd and quizzical remarks from a man who had always considered me insignificant at best. I hardly knew what to think, let alone how I might respond. I could have said, *I've never cared for any of that.*

But Marius spoke on my behalf. "A father's love of a child is a powerful—"

"My own father," Bengt interrupted, "was an irascible gambler and drinker. He lost everything and ended up dead before I was twelve years old. My mother would not abide us living in squalor, so she moved here the year he died. That was some thirty years ago, and do you know what has happened since?"

Of course I knew. Everyone in Hammerfest did.

He relit his pipe and continued. "I own the bakery and the dry goods. I have a share in eighteen fishing vessels out of this harbor. I brought the village its electric streetlights. I brought them the first electric ovens the world has ever used. I own forty-nine percent of Tora Jansen's hotel. I paid for the bell in the church tower." Now he stepped to the window, drew aside the curtain, and gestured outside. "And my flock is some forty sheep strong." He let the curtain fall and took another pull off his pipe and rested a thumb in the pocket of his sealskin waistcoat. With one long draw he emptied his stein of beer. "Why? Because of my *ambition*." He tapped his temple with the mouthpiece of his pipe. "Because I knew to pursue these things while others did not."

We crossed back to the fish eggs and bread in grave silence, as though I had just been made to see the lever long enough to move the world. Bengt said he would now check on the feast and stepped into the kitchen, leaving Marius Granerud and me alone at the sideboard.

"Even if he's a braggart," he told me, "Bengt can speak with authority on rising up. I knew his mother. He got no help from her."

"I also knew his mother. She was a sickly thing."

"Sickly and overmatched. But also mean as a shark."

"My father used to bring her fish and reindeer. She came to church twice a week."

Granerud craned his fat neck to peer toward the kitchen. Satisfied that he might now speak freely, he whispered, "You have something he never had."

Bengt suddenly called for him to come.

"More on that another time, Herr Eide. I'll go see if his feast is ready."

And now he, too, left. I took a gherkin from the bowl, and my mouth gushed around the flavor. Next I reached my fingers into the caviar and ate a fistful. After another, I took a long draft of beer. I might have wolfed all the caviar down had my wife and Gerd Bjornsen not stepped into the dining room arm in arm, like old childhood friends. Inger wore a dress I'd not seen before. Her hair was pulled up on her head, and I could see the suppleness of her neck and the delicacy of her small ears. She told me where to sit at the table while Gerd called the men to dinner.

When everyone was gathered around the table, Bengt offered a speech. "Just yesterday I stood in the churchyard, listening to the pastor intone the holy words meant to ease your passage. My God, we even buried your hardingfele, Odd Einar. And now"—he spread his arms expansively—"here we sit in the warmth of this fire, ready to sup, to pass an easy evening among friends. Fru Bjornsen, bless our celebration."

Gerd lowered her chin and closed her eyes and began by asking the Lord to consecrate our table. She thanked Him for His everlasting love and for the great good fortune of her name and kin. She asked for a blessing on the King and Queen. Finally, she said, "And we thank You for bringing Herr Eide back into our fold. Let him forsake wantonness and lust. Let him give thanks for Your leniency and love. And give him the strength to look on this reprieve as a chance to atone for his failures in his service to You." She looked up and unclasped her hands and rang a bell, whether to call for the food or for hosannas from on high, I wasn't sure.

But soon enough two young servant girls hurried into the dining room with plates of tørrfisk and rutabaga. A pot of glogg was brought around the table and poured steaming into our mugs, and before I knew it, I was feasting with the wealthiest man in Finnmark and a scrivener from *Aftenposten*.

I didn't know which was more astonishing, the plate of food before me or Fru Bjornsen's peculiar blessing. I studied her from the corner of my eye. Her hair was plaited down her back and her bangs pulled from her face by a kerchief, making her look even more severe and unpleasant. But for all her hardness, she was not unpretty. She had soft cheeks and svelte hands. The ruffles of her gown went over her, up and down, front and back, like frothy waves. She held her chin high and canted toward her husband, who had tucked his napkin into his shirt collar and ate like a bosun in the mess aboard the *Lofoten*. His wife was a study in contrasts. She cut her food into minuscule pieces and ate them without seeming to chew at all. Her eyes flitted about the table and then paused on my wife, who apparently had no appetite and whose gaze was cast down.

What did Gerd mean about wantonness and lust? I thought of her shadow appearing in our doorway the night before. Had she deliberately set out to find us? It occurred to me that I didn't even know where she slept. Surely in a bed beside her husband, but where in the house? Was it perhaps logical she would pass our chamber? No sooner did I wonder this than she turned to me. The firelight glowed on her face, which looked much as it had in the dark hallway.

"I hope our dinner is to your liking, Herr Eide. Inger told me you were fond of this dish, so I added it to our menu."

"It's very good," I said.

"Because if the fish doesn't please you," she continued, as though I hadn't said a word, "there's a pot of mutton and cabbage for our next course."

Feeling scolded, I immediately cut off a hunk of fish and scooped it into my mouth. I could tell without looking up that her gaze was still fixed on me.

"Well?" she said.

"I'm afraid I've been too long removed from respectable company." I had another bite of fish. "It's delicious, a godsend. I thank you, Fru Bjornsen, for all this kindness."

Now I looked at Inger, who had about her an air of exhaustion. I wondered how hard she had labored in preparing this meal, and what else besides her toil this dinner might be costing her. Despite this worry, I was still able to conjure the simple joy I felt in resting my eyes on her. It felt like a miracle, and I smiled shyly.

A servant came around with a bowl of barley rolls veiled by a square of fine linen. Bengt snatched one and slathered it with butter and had eaten half of it before the girl stood beside me, offering the bowl. The bread smelled divine, and in my hand its softness made me blush.

"I myself find the fish exquisite," Marius Granerud said. "Same with the glogg. Same, too, with the bread." He let a winning grin fill his rosy, glistening cheeks. "Tell me, Odd Einar, what it's like to have the story you do?"

"Beg your pardon?" I said.

I saw Inger shift her gaze onto that fat, strange fellow.

"Why, a man doesn't spend a fortnight alone on Spitzbergen and come back the same as he left." He looked around the table as though to ensure no one would dispute this claim.

"Of course he doesn't," I said.

"And isn't the story of what happened to him up there chiefly about the change he feels inside?"

"I never considered it like that."

"Certainly there are also outward signs," Granerud said. "A little less flesh on his face, the scars that biting cold leaves behind, a vague but strident weariness. But all that's just his body, and what does a man need his body for except to sleep and eat and dance a halling?" He winked at me. "What you have is your story, and that's better than flesh on your bones or a song for your feet." He took an excited drink from his mug.

"Each night out there, I would have traded that story for a bowl of black pot and a bed to sleep in. Never mind a dance."

"And what man wouldn't?" Granerud said. "Anyone who's cold wishes he was warm, and when tired wants a bed. But now that the coldness and fatigue are behind you, well, now you have the bounty of your *experience*. You can look back with pride at what you did."

Everyone else was staring between Marius Granerud and myself as though in that space our riddling might come to life. Of those fourteen nights, I recalled mainly fear. "I find no pride in my surviving. None. When I look back, sir, I see only darkness and terror."

"That's just the thing, Herr Eide. We ought to strike now, while that feeling still lingers. While it's still fresh and fierce. Wait too long and time will muddle it. Before long it won't be a story at all."

"I'm not sure I understand," I said.

"I'm speaking now of the story you lived. The one I want to tell. The tale of your survival."

"Who would want to read a story full of foolishness and cowardice?"

Bengt set his mug harshly on the table. "The world loathes a coward!" he said. The glogg was getting the better of him.

"But you are no coward, Herr Eide," Granerud said. "Why, if you let me, I can make you into a legend. I can tell your story so people all across the world will read it." He fixed me in his gaze and said, very seriously, "Perhaps in places like Minnesota. Provided we get it all down before you lose the edge of it, before the terror you speak of becomes little more than the wind passing through the garden outside."

"I don't see how time will dull what happened," I said, though I wasn't certain of that. Yet I *knew* I didn't believe that what happened to me was worth the time it would take to tell Inger, much less this man from Tromsø.

Marius Granerud still spoke with great deliberation and thoughtfulness. "But it *will* dull, Herr Eide, I promise you. The first thing I noticed about you was the scar on your hand." He gestured at it, resting there on the table with a fork pinched between my thumb and forefinger. "I'd venture to guess that mark goes back half your life, maybe more. Am I right?"

"I was twenty years old. A hatchet wound."

"I imagine the pain was something awful."

"Of course."

"The first couple days were the worst, no doubt?"

"Naturally."

"But then the pain lessened. The wound began to heal. And a month later, I'd guess you hardly remembered it. And now?" He looked at me from under his brows.

"Your point is well taken, Herr Granerud." This was Inger speaking, suddenly and firmly. I looked at her, thankful, but not at all clear myself about the point he intended to make. If he was saying that the hatchet wound had healed, of course he was right. But if he meant to further imply that the incident was forgotten, well, he was wrong about that. What's more, if Marius Granerud ever had to haul nets in frigid water with this battered old stump, then he'd know what pain I carried with me daily.

Now Inger continued, emboldened I'm not quite sure by what. "My husband has had a harrowing experience. Most men would have perished the first night. But he didn't. And, as you say, in exchange for all his trouble he has a story to tell. Our question, sir, would be why you're the best man to tell it."

Gerd sat up. "Fru Eide," she scolded her. "Herr Granerud is one of the most important men in the Norwegian press. And beyond that, he's a guest at my table." Her lip twitched in anger as she gulped for more to say.

But Granerud was quick to raise his hand. "It's a fair question, Fru Bjornsen. Why, after all, would these fine people trust their story to anyone, much less a man they've only just met?"

"I meant no disrespect," Inger said.

Granerud took another long sip of his glogg. "None taken. As I say, it's a fair question. Perhaps I can offer an anecdote in answer. Two years ago, do you know who first was offered an audience with Nansen?"

Inger and I both looked at him, his smooth confidence obvious but not ostentatious.

"I was. Now, there was a man worse for wear. He was slack of cheek, himself. Not unlike you, Herr Eide. His eyes were sunken, too. His aspect had taken on the very hue of the place he'd just escaped. Ashen, I'd say. Scoured. But somehow vibrant. Somehow"—here he paused and glanced at the chandelier, considering his memory—"*immortal.* That's what I thought. You could see, from how his suit hung loose over his shoulders and long at the cuff, that here was a man not all of who he once had been. But do you know what else I saw?" He looked around the table, from one face to the next. "A man more alive than any I'd *ever* seen before. Alive with the magnitude of his accomplishment." He paused again before slipping his fork under the last bit of tørrfisk, chewing it carefully, then setting his silverware down and dabbing at the corners of his mouth with his napkin. We all sat there staring at him.

He turned his attention to me once more. "Some men seek their destiny. Some have it thrust on them. We revere the former, but do you know what we see in the other, Herr Eide?"

I shook my head, afraid to look away for fear I would miss something important.

"We see *ourselves*. When people read your story, they will already *know it.*"

"Why—" I began.

"Because who among us has not been lost in the night? Who has not ever been frightened? Or stood on some distant shore and counted the miles home? Who among us has not fought the ice bears of our imagination, of our own worst fears?"

At that moment the servants came into the dining room and began removing our plates. As quickly as they left they were back again with new place settings, and as soon again with a platter of mutton and cabbage.

"I think that's where we ought to start," Marius Granerud said.

Now I was the one who glanced around the table, the four of them peering intently as if expecting me to divulge some great secret. But of course I had no secret simple enough for these story-telling purposes. "With the bear?" I said.

"Ja, sure, with the bear. On that very day. But how did you get there? Who was your employer?"

"Svene Solvang, captain of the *Sindigstjerna*, a sealer out of Tromsø."

"And how many were in his crew?"

"There were six of us, including Solvang himself. Two men each for two killing boats. Solvang stayed aboard the *Sindigstjerna* while we hunted."

"That fateful morning," Marius Granerud said, his voice hypnotic, "you were in one of those killing boats?"

I nodded.

"And your partner, what was his name?"

"Birger Mikkelsen."

"Birger Mikkelsen," he repeated, as though our tablemates might not have made out my faint voice. "So, tell us where you were."

"Up the eastern tooth of the Kross."

"The Kross?"

"The Krossfjorden, sir. In Spizbergen."

Marius Granerud wiped his glistening lips and again picked up his fork and knife, but then paused and pronounced, once more surveying each face around the table, "The mere mention of that barren place stirs the imagination, does it not?" He settled his gaze on me. "Now, about that day. Could you tell us about the bear?"

I felt as I imagine a criminal might while being questioned by a keen and persuasive inspector—that is to say, compelled to tell the truth.

The autumn ice was forming again and the glaciers were calving and the seals would be plentiful. This would be our last hunt before steaming back south to Norway. On that morning, an easterly wind boasted and I hauled my hakapik and duffle and a Krag-Jørgensen rifle into the killing boat and took the oars while Mikkelsen manned the tiller. We doffed our hats and steered for the shore, where floes clogged the rising tide.

We carried with us a cask of fresh water and a sack of biscuits and after an hour Mikkelsen and I switched spots and I took my breakfast at the tiller. And what a fine desolation I saw from my post. The water had the appearance of quicksilver where it wasn't clotted with ice. The dimming sky above the glaciers and mountains cast a hoary light. Everywhere was gray. All distance was inestimable.

Two times I saw an ice bear picking among the floes. On the second I raised my rifle and aimed at him for sport, but the boat was unsteady and so was my shot and he only startled at the report from my rifle and ambled silently ashore to disappear among the ice. Another half hour passed before Mikkelsen and I beached the boat and threw our anchor onto the ice.

Within three hours of landing we were flush with eight bludgeoned seals. Though the bilge was swamped with blood, we again took measure of the ice. Mikkelsen thought we might profit another seal or two. The *Sindigstjerna* was to meet us at Kapp Guissez an hour before sunset, which was still three hours away. Given Mikkelsen's seniority, I demurred and together we set out with our rifles and hakapiks for one more round of slaughter.

Already the ice was smeared crimson. The rich tang of death hung on the air like the gulls that had been jeering us all day. A man could not find bloodier occupation. Nor harder work. We sweat on those bergs like fiends, and by the time we finished lunch had drained that cask of water.

If I was exhausted and worn to a nub, Mikkelsen was a man made for such labor. He was tactical and careful and he knew the habits of seal and gull and bear alike. All day he regaled me with tales of hunts past. He took pleasure in his work, both its lustiness and its rich reward. I took none myself. With each blow of the hakapik, each strike on the blubbered head, each stab of the pick, I felt myself recoil, and longed only to be back aboard my faering, hauling fish instead of seals.

But I was not, and as Mikkelsen and I hefted that last seal over the gunwale we saw our killing boat go keel side up, as though a rogue wave had shot toward us through the fjord. But none of the other bergs yawed. When the boat found her level again I could see the bear's nose and eyes just above the opposite gunwale, its claws gripping the old wood like garden rakes. Can you imagine how sweet was the smell that had drawn him there? Nine dead seals, and not one of them with an inkling to swim away.

Mikkelsen instantly jumped onto the berg and shouldered his rifle in the same movement, hurrying into position for a clean shot. The bear raised his paws and pulled down on the boat again, reaching in this time to swipe at the heap of seal carcasses. But there was enough freeboard to hold the boat upright and even this beast couldn't quite pull himself out of the water. His forelegs must have measured eight feet from claw tip to claw tip, his neck three feet long and as big around as a foremast. He bobbed twice more and then was gone.

"He'll come aboard our berg," Mikkelsen said, his eyes alert and searching. "I'd put a round into the barrel of that fine rifle you use, Odd Einar."

No sooner had he said this than the bear burst from the slurry onto our berg, his coat as slick as a seal's. How fast and beautifully that ice bear moved! As smooth out of the water as the animals he hunted. I aimed and fired but missed, even as he rose there on his hind legs, twice my height. He roared his protest, and from my stance thirty feet away I swear I could feel the warmth of his breath.

Now Birger, who'd hurried to shore and stood apace me, aimed and fired and winged the bear. If his anger had been roused by my shot that missed, he was now crazed. His eyes went wide above his gaping black mouth and his teeth showed like icicles, and I felt the roar that came from his belly in my tightening scrotum.

"You damn devil!" Mikkelsen hollered. "Leave our haul alone!"

As if the bear had the intelligence to heed Birger's request, he did just that, but not before scrawling the ice with a massive paw, slicing the line that held the anchor. Mikkelsen fired another shot, which missed the bear but blasted into the killing boat now floating away. "Drit og dra," he cursed, as the bear howled again, dropped to all fours, and started toward us. "Pluck him one. Now! Right in his goddamn cock!" I fired once more, and the bear heaved right and bounded up the shore.

"Have you got your hakapik, Odd Einar?" Mikkelsen asked, his eyes sharp on the shore.

It sat ten paces behind me, and I told him as much.

"Grab hold of it. Do you have another shot in that gun of yours?"

"Yes." I patted the pocket of my coat to see if I had more cartridges. "But none more."

It was a fearful business. Made so as much by Mikkelsen's darting eyes as by the sight of our killing boat getting sucked out into the fjord. It wouldn't have moved so damn well under sail. The colony of gulls escorting us all along sent up a mighty cheer as they settled upon it from bow to stern.

"We are right fucked, Odd Einar," Mikkelsen said. "That's thirty or forty kroner worth of sealskin floating away."

"The *Sindigstjerna* will catch her, though."

"Likely she will." He scanned the waters from boat to shore. "But that's an angry bear. He got a nose full of that rich seal blood. His appetite is excited, you can be sure of that. And he's vexed by that bullet in his shoulder."

"Where did that fiend go?"

"Not far. He's hunting *us* now." He marked the falling sun. "Great Christ, is this worrisome." From his pocket he removed the spyglass he'd earlier used to spot seals, ran it over the shoreline to the south, and handed it to me. "We can try to jump those bergs, ja? Hope our boat runs aground on that jutting land down there? Have a look."

I did, as though I might have a nice opinion on this matter. But of course I knew nothing of these currents and eddies and tides up here and couldn't begin to guess where the killing boat might end up. The only thing plain to me was that it drifted farther away with each gust of wind. When I turned back to Mikkelsen, he had his ear tilted landward, his gun raised again to his shoulder.

"Is that our bear?" I whispered.

He didn't answer, only walked slowly up the shore while studying the shadows among the ice. I readied my own gun and watched as he skittered up a wedge of vindskavler. When he got to the top he lowered his gun.

"Faen ta dag," he said, more, I thought, to the wastes than to the bear. "He'll track us, Odd Einar, unless we track him first."

"Why track him at all? And with what—two bullets and a hakapik?" I checked the barrel of my Krag-Jørgensen again. "We need our boat, not that bear."

Mikkelsen stood atop the drift, surveying the land and ice. "You're lame now," he called. "I can see your trail of blood. I'm going to find you." He checked quickly the horizon to the south, the angle of the sun. "Find you and put one right in your brain." He turned to me. "From his blood"—he pointed with his gun barrel—"I can tell he's moving inland. You make a wide sweep down the shore. A hundred yards. Then cut across the ice. Be careful. We'll kill this hellion and then get our boat back."

"Flush him out, then?" I scuttled up the ice. What I saw was a world of crags and crevices and shadows. An eerie fog emanating from the glacier's ragged surface. Darkness in the east. "He's disappeared, right? Gone off somewhere to lick his wounds. So why not just march down the shore in hopes of finding our boat? Or even hail Captain Solvang and the *Sindigstjerna* from that open coast?"

"He's offended. He'll mark us every step. Let's keep him in front of us, not behind."

This thinking seemed dubious. The bear had been lamed. He was gone. Why we'd persist in hunting him while our boat floated down the fjord was beyond me. But there was such a thing as rank, even in a two-man crew, and I was in Birger Mikkelsen's service, despite being ten years his elder.

Now, what I knew of him at the time didn't amount to much. He came of age in the village of Røst, a third-generation fisherman, a fact that impressed me. But Birger had a touch of the nomad about him, and at the age of fifteen went off on a whaling ship. He'd been as far as the South Sea and came home eight years later a harpooner in Svend Foyn's fleet sailing out of Iceland. After three years he joined Solvang's crew, preferring sealing to whaling because the killing was more regular. If that makes him sound simple, it shouldn't. His appetites were not base, and he sought the pleasure of hunting as a man of God might seek divine inspiration. At least that's how I'd come to understand him.

And when he said, "We won't rest until we've cut the heart out of that thief," I could only follow.

So it was that Mikkelsen debouched onto the glacier, following the bear's blood, while I wandered down the water's edge to flank the beast should it turn south. It couldn't have been a minute or two before his paws emerged from the sea onto our gunwale, and maybe ten between our decision to keep hunting and this desperate situation. But isn't that how these things happen? One moment happily counting the kroner those skins would bring, the next deserted as the drifting boat carried them away?

I'd never see Mikkelsen again. Not as a whole man, anyway.

It seemed impossible that I should find myself standing alone there, given how our day had started. We'd taken our breakfast in the *Sindigstjerna*'s mess, same as any other day. Cold cod and lingonberries and tea. Mikkelsen sat at the board, fish bones stuck in his beard, and showed me the chart of the Krossfjorden.

"Imagine some hand what's been hammered once or twice. Put it palm down and that's the Kross. But, see, the little finger's the biggest fjord. Lilliehøøkfjorden, we call it. But we'll start on the middle finger"—he pointed at a smaller inlet, the middle one indeed—"where the fattest seals will be gathered like church ladies." He took a big bite of fish. "That'll make twenty miles back down to Kapp Guissez after we do our clubbing. A hell of a row. So, eat more fish, and quaff that tea. Bellies full."

I heeded his instructions while studying the chart, which seemed inadequate to the place I'd been watching off our port bow all night, the ice packing up in the Forlandsundet, the light resolutely low.

"The current makes its own streams in these waters. Might drive us up, might drive us back down. Either way, we'll be working. Bring a change of clothes. Your hakapik and rifle. A sharp knife, too. And memorize that map. When I get eaten by an ice bear, you'll want to know where you are!" He guffawed and slapped the board and drained his tea. "You find yourself land-bound, keep your eyes on the water. The last thing you want is to get up in the glaciers and snow. That's all the same place. North is south and east is west as soon as you blink. You'll be dead on the first night." He stood up, checked his pocket watch, and said, "We'll be in the water by seven. Don't be late. And bring the chart."

I stuffed the last of the cod in my mouth and hustled to our quarters, packed my duffel, and had a smoke. It wasn't my first hunt, but if Spitzbergen had taught me anything yet, it was to be humble in its midst. Each night, down in the bunks, it was one story after another of the crushing cold or darkness or wind or fog or snow or ice bears, any one of which could drive you crazy or kill you. Usually one right after the other. And though I never knew a hunter or fisherman prone to telling the truth, something in these storytellers' hard eyes and expressions was reverential if not downright nervy.

Our quarters weren't much for sleeping. Between the tossing of the ship and the blood-reek of our coats and trousers hanging bunk-side, to say nothing of a persistent uneasiness about our general whereabouts, I was lucky for a few hours most nights. And even those were fretful slumbers. My bunk was hung rudely between two bulkheads in the forecastle, with two others above and below. What a godless ruckus we snoring hunters sent up! It might have done the job of convening with the whales somewhere beneath our hull. But who ever put a crew of men like that in such close quarters and expected a nursery full of sleeping babes? The condition of our bunk room bears mentioning only as it compares to the fourteen shivering nights I spent alone on Spitzbergen. This is what I meant to get to.

I remember the first night best. What a thing it was to watch the moon over the wide and cold fjord and know the bitter odds that I would be dead before it finished its arc. What a thing to see death in its slow and deliberate march toward you. How many times in those initial hours of darkness did I aim my cocked Krag-Jørgensen at the night and think to fire, to offer myself up to that same undead night? To meet my Maker and accept my fate not like a beggar, but like a man finished with his evening prayers and ready for sleep? How many times did I conjure Inger and Thea in my delirious fear and wave them goodbye?

But instead of lying down I walked in circles, the mountains all around me growing taller with the settling dark, their snow-covered caps aglow, lit like distant fires by the light of the brilliant moon. I had heeded Mikkelsen's advice and packed the chart, but instead it now rode in my duffel aboard the killing boat, down those tricky currents and tides toward Kapp Guissez. And try as I might to recall the five hammered fingers, I couldn't imagine a route to get to where the boat might be going. In the crux of each fjord between where I circled and where I needed to be loomed an immense glacier, calving its blue ice. While rowing up we'd seen four or five or six of them on the starboard side, each guarded by towering mountains. To walk the twenty miles Mikkelsen had earlier mentioned would have required not only crossing each glacier with their deadly crevasses but also climbing and descending ten or twelve mortal peaks.

To the west, a more difficult route promised both the same treachery and an even more remote chance of rescue. The *Sindigstjerna* wouldn't search those waters. And anyway, such a passage dictated a nigh impossible march across the mountains and glaciers without providing any view of the water, which Mikkelsen had specifically warned against. At least the shelf of land I circled was relatively flat and full of ancient rocks that I might stack against the wind. So that is what I did. I made a shelter of stone and called it my camp for those sleepless hours.

I returned to myself at Bengt's table. All eyes were on me, including Granerud's, one behind his monocle. The only sound was the rasp of flames in the great fireplace. I felt as if I'd emerged from a dream, and I looked to Inger, whose gaze just then was gentle and proud.

I didn't let go of her attention. "And even as I lay there with nothing to do but die, do you know what thought I settled into?" I asked. "I thought of you, Inger, who had sanctioned my plan to go with Sverdrup last June, who had believed in me as you had once believed in our daughter. And even though I didn't pray, I thought of God and of what a fool my life of faith had made of me. If I slept it was only for a minute at a time, and when the morning light came, it was shrouded in fog. A fog which by noon had become snow."

The other three at the table also turned their focus on Inger, who held a hand up to her blushing cheek.

Everyone but Bengt Bjornsen, that is, who swirled his mug of glogg under his nose, cleared his throat, and interrupted the calm that had descended over the room. "What you say there, about that bear and your first night up north, it sounds like a folktale my mother might've told me."

At this Granerud now stared at Bengt and said, "Herr Eide's story sounds exactly the sort that the whole world wants to read."

Now it was Inger's turn to speak. "Perhaps my husband can take a break from that night and finish his dinner. He nearly starved up there. That plate of mutton must look heavenly to him."

"Of course!" Bengt agreed. "Let him fill his belly!" He raised his mug and offered a wordless cheer before taking a swig while surveying the table. Then his eyebrows shot up and he slammed the mug down and shouted, "Fru Bjornsen!" as if the mutton had caught fire. "Why!" And without another word he rose and hurried into the kitchen.

So fast did all this happen that the rest of us sat merely wide-eyed. A knowing expression softened Gerd's face. She put her hands together, almost in a gesture of applause, as Bengt returned mere seconds after leaving, another platter raised above his shoulder on a flat palm, as though he were a waiter in a city café. He rearranged the candles and the mutton and with a flourish set the new platter on the table, right before me. "That Ruth is no replacement for you, Inger! She forgot to serve the smalahove!"

The boiled sheep's head sat with its snout toward me, its sockets paired hollows that, for all the world, seemed like my own eyes reflected in a mirror. Startled by its gaze, I lost all at once what was left of my appetite.

Bengt, again at the head of the table, beyond the twin candles flickering in their holders, plopped down and regarded me closely. His pink face, flush from dashing about, appeared both drunk and suddenly menacing. "It's no small thing to slaughter a sheep." His words were meant for me, though he glanced around the table as the platters passed by one person to the next. The aroma of all that fresh meat being spooned caused my stomach to coil so urgently that I felt I might have to excuse myself.

"Why, just this morning I was out in the lambing shed. An old Steigar sheep, out of step with the rest of my flock and of no particular use to me, was leaning against the wall. I wanted him. I knew it when I went out there." He spoke almost like he was making a criminal confession. "I had whetted the knife and it glinted in my hand, and do you know what? That old sheep just stood there. His eyes were no more concerned as I walked toward him than they are right now!" He waved at the smalahove with his fork, a piece of mutton hung dripping from its tines. "God's creatures," he said, as though two words spoke volumes.

Marius Granerud was quick to change the subject. "There's a café at the harbor hotel in Tromsø that serves a fine plate of mutton, but it's nothing like this, Fru Bjornsen."

She nodded her thanks.

"I bet you could get used to someone providing your supper every day, couldn't you, Herr Eide. Get some ballast back in your tank. What if you allowed me to arrange for a visit?"

"To Tromsø?" I said.

"We'd wait until you had time to reacquaint yourself with Fru Eide, of course. But yes. We might transcribe the story there—if you're willing, of course. We'd also arrange the best accommodations. And great stores of mutton and warm glogg! You might think of it as a holiday."

"Why Tromsø?" Inger said, her soft voice barely rising above the hum in the room.

Granerud gazed at my wife and said, slowly and thoughtfully, "I'd need the resources of my office, naturally. And we'll require portraits of Herr Eide to run beside his story. In all, I'd intrude on your lives only for a week or two."

"The resources of your office?"

He set his fork down. "Fru Eide, this story can't be told in a day. It likely can't be told in a week. I'll need my assistant and secretary.

The typist. The portraitist. All of those people live in Tromsø. You have my word we'll take good care of him. We'll also make sure he returns as quickly as possible."

He waited for Inger's response. I was less patient myself. "Herr Granerud," I said. "I'm still unclear why anyone would want to know the first thing about what happened to me."

Again he considered his words carefully before saying, "Did you not hear your own words just now? Because *we* all did." He swept an arm around the table. "What we learned after Nansen's triumphant return is that there's no limit to people's eagerness for stories of survival. Especially in the polar climes. The mere *idea* of all that cold and ice, the darkness and danger—why, it stirs our souls. You've got the impetus of that frightful bear on top of it all."

"The adventure!" Bengt added, more sotted now than even a minute earlier.

"The adventure is part of it, to be sure," Granerud conceded. "But people aren't as interested in accomplishments as one might think."

"You mean to say that Nansen's achievement is that he went to a cold place?" Bengt scoffed, slurping the end of his glogg in one sloppy pull. These windy men—they want to be heard no matter what they're shouting.

"Nansen is no ordinary person," Granerud said. "He's even more popular than the King."

"But I'm a common man," I said, hoping that might put the matter to rest.

"Less than that, I'd say!" Bengt was quick to chortle.

All eyes turned to him, whether to scold him or to laugh along I couldn't tell. But he was right, so I echoed him, "Less than that."

"*This* is why your story's important," Granerud whispered. "Why people will love to hear it. Precisely because you're exactly what you say."

I must have looked flummoxed.

"And yet *here... you... are*," he said, with an urgency in his voice that I recognized as pleading.

Inger must've heard the same thing, because she said, "Herr Granerud, please. You know that my husband has had but one night home. Look at him, he's as lean as a schoolboy. He could hardly be expected to make the trip to Tromsø, or to recount his story before regaining his strength." She paused, daintily wiped her lips, and laid her napkin beside her plate. "And I could hardly be expected, after so long an absence, to be without him."

At this Gerd shot her a piercing look, which Inger pretended not to notice.

"I know just the thing!" Granerud said. "You'll join your husband, Fru Eide. Both of you will come to Tromsø. You must! You can comfort him there as well as here!"

"I'm not sure," she said.

Undeterred, he went on. "People are now calling Tromsø the 'Paris of the North.' It's a *very* sophisticated place. Theaters, cafés, museums. I've already mentioned the fine hotel. Just the sort of place for a woman of your intelligence."

Then Inger did something I'd never seen her do before: she blushed and played coy. "It *does* sound lovely."

"Ruth!" Bengt shouted, giving the table a hard slap. "Ruth, bring the aquavit!" He pushed his empty plate away. "I believe we have an agreement," he told his guests.

His servant appeared with a decanter and filled tiny glasses around the table. Once the digestifs were poured, Marius Granerud raised his glass for yet another toast. "It will be my honor to bring your story to the world," he said, taking a sip. Then he sat back and loosened his tight collar around his neck. He took another, longer drink and said, "Now all I need to know is how much it's going to cost me."

Inger set her glass down and reached over to touch my hand. "The question isn't how much the story will cost *you*, Herr Granerud, but what will it cost my husband to relive it. Please do remember that."

Part Two

—

THE FONN

True to his word, Otto Sverdrup sought me out when next he called in Hammerfest. The last week in June, it was. Late morning. I rowed in from Muolkot, where I'd gone to fish, and saw a stately vessel at the dock. I'd never seen the *Lofoten* before, and I marveled at her lines and, once again, at the audacity of shipbuilders.

I tied my faering off and brought my catch ashore: three ugly wolffish, hooked from the bottom of the sound, that had cost me six hours of miserable chill. Out in the darkest morning hours to fetch only that pittance. As I walked up the Grønnevoldsgaden, I saw him striding toward me as if the entire world was his fiefdom. The wings of his beard fluttered up as he raised a hand in greeting.

"Herr Sverdrup?"

"I asked around the village for you. I went to your place above the bakery and Fru Eide told me I might find you coming in." He peeked into my fish box and waved a hand under his nose. "My, aren't those wolffish ugly."

Looking down in the box myself, I saw three meals. Or two meals and a loaf of bread, should I trade one of the fish. "Ja, but with a little butter and a pinch of salt they'll do for supper." I shifted the box to my other arm. "What brings you back?"

"You must have seen the *Lofoten*?" Sverdrup said.

"She looks ready for whatever might come."

"I hope so. I'm her captain."

"Headed where?" I asked.

He pointed skyward. "Far north. Spitzbergen. I'll be making regular runs this summer."

"Spitzbergen," I said, as though it were a fairyland.

"Halfway to the pole." He took the fish box from my arm and set it between us. "Tell me, have you heard yet from your daughter?"

"Not a word."

"For all that is holy, I'm sorry."

I thanked him, and was strangely relieved that the enormous weight of her absence had not lessened since our last, our only, conversation about her. "Tell me, Herr Sverdrup, how does a man like you remember me, much less my daughter?"

He looked at me, genuinely surprised. Perhaps even insulted. "There are few people in this part of the world, Herr Eide. You made an impression when we met. It was a memorable evening. It's hard to forget decent people. It's harder yet to forget brave ones. You qualify on both accounts."

I waved a hand at him, brushing that remark away.

"Modesty. Another righteous quality."

Perplexed by his affection, I couldn't help suspecting I was the fool of some ruse. This thought caused me to look for jesters up and down the street, which was empty but for one man walking toward the church.

"In point of fact, Herr Eide, I come with a question for you."

I turned back to him.

"You're acquainted with the sea?"

I toed the box. "I'm partial to these waters. My faering isn't much beyond Sørøsundet."

"But you know port from starboard, and how the wind blows and shifts?" He nudged the fish box himself. "You clearly know how to drop a line."

"You'd have to travel some distance from here to find a man who didn't know all that."

"And a sense of humor, too!"

"I haven't laughed in a long time, Herr Sverdrup."

"But you remember how?"

"Beg your pardon?"

"To laugh, my friend. You remember how to laugh?"

I allowed myself a smile.

"That's a start. I'm a man short for the season, Herr Eide. My bosun needs a hand. Lots of odd jobs, but if you can tie a knot and shovel coal, I could use you aboard my ship. The pay's twelve kroner a month, plus board. I could advance your first month's worth to leave with Fru Eide. And I'd outfit you, at no charge, for the weather and the job. She's a worthy ship." He nodded toward her. "And I know worthy ships."

For the first time since I watched my daughter sail off, I felt an honest thrill. Then I tallied the numbers quickly in my head. A season of this and I'd have us out from under Bengt. And possibly enough to buy passage to America so I could go find Thea. Never mind the sheer excitement of venturing north—with Otto Sverdrup, no less. The chance to see the storied shores of Spitzbergen, to feel the magnetism of that last northern outpost.

"Herr Eide," he said, gripping my shoulder. "You look about to faint."

"I feel so," I said.

"What say you?"

I gathered myself, and spoke slowly. "I'm confounded by your offer, Herr Sverdrup. Of all the men you must know—"

"I sought you out," he interrupted. "I stopped here expressly for *you*."

"Why should you do that?"

Now his eyes softened. "Some men spend their whole lives with strong beliefs. In *possibility*. In *hope*. In other things, too. When one of those men meets another, well, he can't help feeling an affinity."

"There are twenty men in this village better suited to your needs, sir."

"Yet I stand here with you."

I took my pipe out of my pocket, thumbed a pinch of tobacco

into the bowl, and lit it, then looked across the square at the *Lofoten,* unmoving beside the wharf. "I'd need a word with my wife, of course. And with Herr Bjornsen."

"Herr Bjornsen?"

"My employer, you might call him. And my landlord, too."

"What work do you do for him?"

"Oh, whatever he wishes. I muck his barns. I chop his wood and shovel his coal. Last month I put new shingles on his carriage house. I might better call myself his drudge."

"Then sailing with me will be both liberation *and* adventure."

No offer as overwhelming had ever come to me. I was so stupefied that when Sverdrup started toward the bakery, he had to wait for me to follow. As we walked, he said, "We'll sail after the supper hour. I hope that will give you time to gather your things and say farewell to Fru Eide. And to arrange your affairs with Herr Bjornsen."

"My goodness."

"We'll call again in Hammerfest in eighteen days, depending on the weather, and again eighteen days anon, and so forth, until some time in September. If the season cooperates, you should be back home for good no later than the end of September. Have you any concerns?"

"I reckon my concerns have most to do with my wife, sir. It's possible she'd like better my declining your offer."

"Of course. But otherwise?"

I shifted the fish box from one arm to the other. "I suppose Herr Bjornsen, too, might have an opinion about my departure."

Sverdrup waited for me to say more. We had almost reached the bakery before I continued. "Not once have I been separated from Inger, never more, that is, than a few days on my faering."

We stopped at the door, and he said, "It takes a woman with conviction to see her husband off."

"Her conviction I do not worry about."

He put a reassuring hand on my shoulder. "Go up and talk to Fru Eide. The *Lofoten* will steam at seven o'clock. If you decide yes, come see me at Gunnar Hagen's tourist office on Oscar's Plads before three. We'll sign you up and see to your wife's advance. After three I'll already be aboard my ship." Then he looked toward the harbor, where the *Lofoten*'s two mastheads stood above her single amidships stack. "It's no small choice, Odd Einar. And a season apart from your wife is hardly a trifle. But I will tell you that once the wind is in our face and we're riding the cold waters north, once you feel the pull of the place we'll be heading—why, time itself will disappear. You'll be a new man before we make Bjørnøya. And once we sail up the Isfjorden, you'll forget you ever owed that man a krone." He bowed toward the door, as though urging me to hurry to Inger's side. "The currents flow north in these seas. Men were made to follow them. What do you say to coming along?"

With that he was off, back toward his ship or Gunnar Hagen's office or to speak to some other unsuspecting soul, how could I know? And how could I do anything to dispel his charms? Even walking up the narrow staircase to our humble room with my misgivings, I was certain that any man would accept his offer. As I would, for many reasons large and small, not least the money that could set us free. But I was also going to go for another kind of freedom, one I couldn't name but surely felt. Now that Sverdrup's destination was on offer, I realized why men lined up to risk their lives to get there. It had nothing to do with fame or fortune, neither of which was mentioned in his promise, only with how this journey tugged at my *spirit*. Why shouldn't I feel drawn to those ocean waters, to a new and an unseen horizon? Even if I'd never known it, these questions were inside me. And now that I'd asked them, I knew I had to seek answers. And if these proved to be simple or worse, so long as they came with the midnight sun or an Arctic summer storm, they would be mine to call wisdom. Even more than money, those were the thoughts that spurred me to go with him.

My new prospects had put me in mind of older ones, and with Inger already toiling away on Bjornsen's behalf, once in our room, I went to the small dresser, shuffled through the top drawer, and found the pamphlets and brochures and broadsides that Hege and Rune had sent from Minnesota. On one, a map of that place was rendered, the northeastern corner amputated from the rest of the state and set apart in its separate box as though that little triangle might belong to Canada. No towns dotted this box, only rivers spilling into a lake labeled Superior. The town our kin called Gunflint, nearby acres they'd cleared of pine, the log house in which we imagined Thea lived, the bed where she slept—was any of it real?

I'd by now stopped asking myself why neither our daughter nor her aunt and uncle had answered my letters. I had made it my practice to believe that Thea was simply too busy living on a farm to be bothered. This made the silence roaring from America easier to bear. But every time I pulled out this old map, I had the momentary sense that she'd simply gone to a place that did not in fact exist. That this was why none of them had written in such a long time. Again I dug through the dresser drawer, for the most recent one, from my brother-in-law, which was dated six months before Thea left home. He described a persistent winter colder and longer even than ours in Hammerfest. He described a wolf pack that harassed his livestock. He described the inhospitable soil. The onslaught of mosquitoes and blackflies after the snowmelt. How could we still have been excited to send Thea to a place that existed only as a series of complaints from our ornery Rune?

It was a risky business, rooting around in this drawer, so I stuffed all the papers back inside and shut it tight against my now sharper fears and thought instead about my new prospects. I would sail away with Otto Sverdrup. He would be my captain. He knew the uncharted places where he himself had made his fortune and fame.

As I stared down on my faering—caked in the shit of the harbor gulls, so plentiful they made their own, forever-dark sky—I wondered if I would ever make sense of this life, much less find any wisdom.

There had been a time when I'd stand above my little boat and ponder simpler things. Where could fish be found this morning?

Was the wind suitable for raising my mast? Did those clouds over Sørø threaten snow? But those questions seemed meager now, so paltry beside the one that plagued me this morning. Should we go to Tromsø with Marius Granerud? Again, there was but a single response: yes, of course.

But Inger had a gift for gauging new prospects more clearly than I ever did. The day Otto Sverdrup asked me to join his crew, she said only "Have you ever seen a whale who thought he was a tern?"

When I cocked my head quizzically, she just pursed her lips and said she guessed we did need his money.

Then again, last night. Back in our little room above the bakery, I said, "I'll have to tell the story somehow, whether to you or to this Marius fellow. But those hundred kroner do make his a different proposition." She studied the reflection of the candle in the window for a long time before saying, "Why do we keep having to move our lives around in order to live them? First we send our daughter to America, then you go up to Spitzbergen, now we're being summoned to Tromsø. Why can't we make our lives here, at *home*? Where do we go next, Odd Einar? What happens after you give everything to Marius and people start mistaking you for someone you're not?"

"Better for me to decline his offer? For us to stay here, living in this drudgery?"

She stared at the window for another long while. When finally she faced me again she said, "If you tell that man your story, you'll no longer have it to tell to me. And then I know you less. Much as any man or woman in any village from here to Trondheim would. And then what? Then who *are we*?"

She blew out the candle. And tucked her hair into her nightcap. And went to sleep without so much as a glance.

Though I knew she would sleep in peace without me answering her questions, for half the night I had no rest at all. And once I at last got there, it was to an uneasy dozing fraught with bad dreams. Near dawn I woke to an empty bed, but forced myself back to sleep by thinking it was better to lose Inger in a dream than wide awake. When I awoke again, in full light, she was still gone, no doubt off to

Bjornsen's for work, though her nightcap sat there neatly. I arose and rinsed my mouth, then dressed and walked down here to the docks, befuddled by my riotous thoughts and great fatigue.

Two empty fish boxes were wedged beneath my faering's middle thwart, atop which I'd coiled some rotten line. There was only one oar—the other gone missing—and my ten-foot mast showed cracks at its top end. Brackish water sloshed in the bilge. My God, what a sorry mess. I could see the hull beneath the waterline, and all the mussels that had attached themselves to my little vessel. It would take a week's work and several kroner just to get her ready to cast my first line. How many kroner were in that jar beneath our bed? Not enough. There never would be.

"I might've taken better care of her," Inger said.

I turned, surprised, to see her there in her old house clothes again, her sweater buttoned up to her chin, the hems of her skirts speckled with mud from the long walk along Gávpotjávri.

"What to do first?" I said.

"It's just, how could I get her out of the water? And where to keep her? Where to put the oars and mast? The sail at least is stowed above the bakery."

All at once the weight of my failure beset me. In the raw shine of my wife's eyes I saw only that once more I had let her down.

"It'll take some getting ready," she said.

"Ja."

"And some money, no doubt."

I nodded.

"Is it worth it, Odd Einar? Fixing her up? Will we make it back in fish?"

"How long has it been since fish bought us anything besides just another day?"

"I almost set it free." She pointed at the boat. "It looks sad and tired there."

"I guess we're all tired," I said. "Inger, where did you go last night?"

She kept looking at the boat while fooling with the top clasp of her sweater. And just when I thought I'd get no answer, she said, "The glogg didn't sit well. I needed to take in some night air."

I didn't see it so much as feel it. Her lie, that is. As I gazed at her blue eyes now cast down, I knew she wasn't telling the truth. "How were the stars, then?"

She glanced up at me with the expression that I know meant I couldn't possibly understand, but instead of answering my question merely said, "How much would it cost to get the boat ready?"

Was that how it would be? Would we start feigning honesty? I didn't like the feel of it, but since I wasn't yet certain that she would have me back, I answered. "An oar. Some tackle. I could do without the mast for a while, and hope against wind. In truth I don't know how much. Certainly more than we have."

Inger gathered her skirts about her and sat on a crate there on the wharf. "Should we sell it and pack our things and move to Tromsø? Maybe we need to make a fresh start."

This idea wasn't without intrigue, and no small part of me wanted to say yes. But what of our daughter? Imagine that, Thea coming home without us here to greet her. And anyway, what would be easier in Tromsø, where we didn't know a soul? "Do you suppose the fish are more plentiful down there? The winter less bitter and their prayers closer to God?"

She didn't say anything for a long time. Just stared out over the harbor as if some other ship were about to sail in with a new cargo of opportunity. She must have read my thoughts because she said, "Odd Einar, if Otto Sverdrup returned in the *Lofoten* this minute and offered you that same job would you—knowing everything you've been through—accept it all over again? And if you had another chance with Thea, would you still put her on the *Nordsjøen*?"

"Next you'll ask if I'd take you as my wife again."

"Well?"

I took a step toward her. "Of course I would, Inger. And I'd send Thea to follow her wishes. And I'd say yes to Sverdrup, too. And finally, because I have to, I'll take Marius Granerud's offer as well.

Better to give something to get something than to give everything and get nothing, which is what my faering promises."

She steeled herself against a harbor breeze. "You speak of Thea as though she were on a lark, Odd Einar."

How many times in my life had I been out on the sound with my faering, racing on the wind, the fish boxes stowed with my catch, only to feel the wind die or shift and watch my sail hang slack? That was the feeling I got now—my spirit the sail, and my wife's words the dying wind. "Christ, Inger. My own sick worries about her aren't enough? I need your doom?" I jumped from the dock into my boat and lifted the masthead off the bottom. It was splintered clear through. My line might as well have been kelp, so I tossed the stringy coil overboard, and the dark water swallowed it whole before the ripples stopped circling.

"She's my daughter too. You are hardly the only one who misses her."

"But I'll wait for her," I muttered, almost hoping that Inger hadn't heard me.

"You would be forgiven if you'd gone straight to Tromsø and stayed there." Her voice was low. "It would be as if you hadn't survived. The good Lord God would know the truth, but no one else would need to." Then she glanced over at the suddenly clear Håja plateau, its emerald grass now lit up by the white sun and clouds. I climbed back onto the dock and moved to her side, and together we looked out across the water.

"Do you remember the summer days we used to take her out there?" I said. "How she'd scramble up that slope like a sheep, through grass taller than she was. And her soft blond curls!"

Inger's breath caught, and for a long minute we stood there with our memories, more colorful in the past but surely still alive on this day. Inger believed they'd have to be enough. I could accept that now, even as I should've admitted it a year ago. Yet I would never rest until I knew it with complete certainty. Telling my story to Marius Granerud—and more important than the hundred kroner this would bring—would be a first step toward that prospect. But I already knew I would not go Tromsø without Inger.

"Those summer days, Inger, and the sound of her laughter… the sound of *your* laughter. Why, those days alone have made my life worth living."

Now she looked at me.

"I'm not about to quit them yet. I fought those nights up north because I wanted more of you. And more of our daughter." I took her hand, there on the dock above my faering. "I'll go see Marius Granerud now, to tell him I'll go. That *we'll* go, I beg you. Then, the minute that's done we'll come back home and get the boat ready. To make a new life here. I want all of that, but I only want it with you."

She shifted her gaze back to Håja as a new bank of clouds lowered over it. "You're a good man, Odd Einar. A good, gentle man." The island disappeared under the sky. "And I love you," she added softly. "All I ask is that you let me grieve for my daughter, even if you won't. So please let's not speak of her."

The phone vibrated on the nightstand, pulling her from sleep and into an alien hotel room. It was dark but for the sheen of streetlights through the curtains and the glow of her phone's screen. She propped herself up on an elbow to look: a photograph of Liv kissing Frans's cheek with an exaggerated pucker that was displayed every time he called. The picture had been taken at a concert at the Lake Harriet band shell the August before. Later that night, Greta remembered, a hailstorm had struck and a big branch from a linden tree snapped onto the boulevard, narrowly missing her truck. Axel, just a puppy but already as big as a Lab, had pissed in his crate and cried all night after the storm passed. She knew because she'd been awake with him.

When the phone stopped pulsing she got up, went to the bathroom, and brushed her teeth. Even in the dark mirror she could see how drawn and tired her face was. And angry. How had she become this person, day after day?

She was practiced at the art of not taking his calls. But this time felt more deceitful. Sure, it was the middle of the night—3:07 according to her phone—but factoring in the time difference it was just after eight in the evening at home, where Frans thought she was; so lateness of the hour was no excuse. There was also the matter of where she now stood, so much closer to him than he was to her. She felt like an intruder in their marriage, and wondered if this was how he felt, whenever he went to Alena and had to find the proper time to call home.

Back at the window, she parted the curtains and felt a wash of something like vertigo as the lights in the square came rushing up at her. She was surprised to see so many people in the square itself, bathed by the lights from the stores and streetlamps in quiet snowfall.

Her phone buzzed again, with a text this time: *Why aren't you answering my calls?*

As she pulled on a T-shirt and her underwear she remembered her fantasy from hours earlier. Her neck flushed and she felt another kind of light-headedness; her hands went warm and damp, and she sat on the edge of the bed and for a full minute conjured that man again. Then, as if waking for a second time, she shook her head and wondered what sort of woman sat in a foreign hotel room dreaming about a stranger.

As though to remove this new temptation, she put jeans and a sweater on, slumped in the small chair under the window, and picked up her phone.

"Mom!"

Liv's voice sounded like it was next door, and Greta missed her suddenly and fiercely.

"Hi, sweet pea."

"Where are you?"

"Far away, Liv. I'm in Norway."

"Are you with Dad?"

"No," she said. "Not yet."

"With Grandma and Grandpa?"

"I'm not with them, either."

Liv let out something like a laugh, then said, "What *are* you doing there?"

Greta looked over at the church tower and told her daughter that she was just visiting. "Anyway, you must be getting ready for bed?"

"More like getting *out* of bed," she said. "It's morning, Mom. Duh."

Liv and Lasse had both made half a dozen trips to Norway to visit their grandparents, marveling anew each crossing about the loss or gain of hours. After the last visit, Liv had asked what happened to those hours. Greta wondered herself now. "I guess I slept a lot longer than I wanted to, kiddo. I thought it was the middle of the night. Because it's dark out."

"Grandpa Gus made apple pancakes this morning and now it's snowing again. It snowed all day yesterday, and at recess I made a snowman with Claudia and we put her scarf around his neck. Then we forgot to take it off when we went back inside."

"I hope she doesn't catch a cold."

"Lasse's gonna catch one."

"Oh?"

"He took Axel out skijoring and didn't wear his hat."

Greta started to say that she'd have a word with Lasse, but Liv had apparently handed the phone to Gus, whose voice came low into her phone. "How's the motherland?"

"Hi, Dad."

"I heard Liv tell you Lasse was skiing without his hat. Don't believe her."

"I hope she's not making too much trouble."

"Trouble's the last thing she is. But that boy of yours is bound and determined to teach that dog how to ski. He was up in the dark harnessing him. Been gone for almost an hour now. His pancakes are stone cold."

"Well, he's Frans's son, too."

"There are worse fates. How was the flight?"

"Longer than usual."

"Oslo's pretty dreary this time of year, eh?"

"I'm not in Oslo."

"Oh?"

"I made a detour. To Hammerfest."

"Hammerfest?"

"And yes, it's dreary and dark. I thought it was the middle of the night here."

"Greta, what're you doing in Hammerfest?"

In fact, she was on the phone looking out the window at the snowfall. "It's snowing here. Big, heavy snow."

"Does Frans know where you are?"

"No."

He was silent for a beat, then said, "Well, I'll be. If I'd known you were going, I might've sent some letters along with you."

She could see the bundle of letters he was talking about, sitting in a glass-topped wooden box on his coffee table, letters written by Greta's great-great-grandmother—Thea Eide, who'd been the first of her family to immigrate, a hundred and twenty-odd years ago—to her mother and father back home. And half a dozen letters they'd written to her, too. Not a single one of them ever delivered. They sat there like a strange homage to the stories that never got told in her family.

"I went to the cemetery to see if I could find their graves," Greta said.

"And?"

"Everything was covered with snow. And it was dark. Maybe I'll go back again today."

"Hammerfest," he said again, as though the idea was just starting to sink in. "What else is there?"

Greta pushed the curtains wide open. "A couple hotels. Lots of boats in the harbor. A pretty square with a few stores and restaurants. A church, of course. I went in there yesterday. Not much else. At least not that I've seen yet." She counted the hours again. "I think I just slept for eighteen hours."

"That sounds like more than jet lag."

The residue of all that sleep came up in a big yawn. She stretched and felt her toes and the soles of her feet on the cool tile floor. "It's the first time I've slept like that since Lasse was born." She yawned again and felt suddenly alive. "What day is it?"

"It's Tuesday, here and there."

"Everything's all right at home? The kids are being good?"

"You already know the answers to those questions."

On the far side of the square she saw an awning and a lighted window and thought, *Café*. Her stomach somersaulted. "I don't think I've eaten since I left Minneapolis."

"There must be a damn good plate of fish to be had in that town."

"I bet there is." She pulled a pair of socks from her bag beside the bed and sat down. "You'll be okay with them for a couple more days?"

"Are you kidding? Between the kids and your fancy digs, I'm in paradise. Anyway, I saw in the paper this morning that it'll only be sixteen up in Gunflint today. The older I get, the less this season agrees with me. It'll be twice that temperature down here today."

"Huh, Tuesday. Lasse has guitar lessons after school."

"He already told me that."

"And Liv gets a homework packet today. She won't want to do it, but Frans tells her that unless she wants to fish for her dinner, she'd better study hard."

"Hey, there's no shame in fishing for your dinner."

"That's what I say. Anyway, you'll see to it she does it?"

"Of course."

"Thanks, Dad. Really. I'll call again when I'm headed home. Is that all right?"

"You bet. But, Greta?"

She waited for her scolding.

"Call Frans. It's not right he can't reach you."

"I'll call him right now. I love you, Dad. Give the kids hugs for me."

She kept her phone right next to her plate of king crab, just below her glass of wine, as if it were a part of the place setting at the restaurant in the Scandic Hotel, which the concierge at the Hotel Thon had recommended. Frans hadn't called or texted since he woke her up this afternoon. She'd ordered the crab because she liked how "Kongekrabbe" looked on the menu, softer than the other Norwegian words. She was in a mood for softness. For lightness, which was why she'd got the chardonnay, something she couldn't remember ever ordering before, and also the reason she was taking such pleasure in the quiet restaurant and the light shimmering beneath the clearing sky outside the window.

Fine as the crab smelled, she had no appetite. She'd brought along a novel she got at the airport, read the first page, and then closed it and taken another sip of wine. There was only one other customer in the restaurant—a middle-aged woman sitting by the entrance and having coffee after her dinner.

The waitress—who, as far as Greta could tell, had also prepared the crab and poured the wine—came by her table. "One minute, the snow and clouds," she said with a smile, then waved her hand like a magician, "now this—what, this starlight?"

Greta looked up at her. "It's like snowfall, illuminated, isn't it?"

The woman, who might've been her cousin given how much they resembled each other, sighed in exhaustion. "And now this is our only light for months. You are Canadian?"

Greta smiled herself. "American. But my hometown's only fifty miles from Canada."

The woman looked down at her and said, "No Americans visit Hammerfest unless they come on the cruise ships."

"Do the Canadians?"

"No." She shook her head. "No Norwegians, even. No one comes until summer. Why are you here?"

Greta looked down and twirled the stem of the wineglass between her thumb and forefinger. "I don't know."

"Then another glass of wine?"

"Okay."

Stepping behind the bar to open a fresh bottle, the waitress also turned a stereo system on low, and soft piano notes filled the small dining room. A dirgeful sound that made Greta's stomach catch. She took a deep breath and felt the long night of sleep seeping out of her.

"Is something wrong with your food?" the waitress asked, trading her empty glass for the full one.

"No. I guess I'm just not hungry after all."

"Or too much wine and no food." The woman tsk-tsked.

"You're right." So Greta took a bite of the buttery crab, which was delicious. More than delicious. She had several more bites, and listened to music so slow that it seemed not to be moving at all, with low, breve notes—as her mother had called them—interrupted by higher, trembling ones. The same repetition over and over for a full minute, then shifting into an even lower scale. It struck her that it sounded like something beyond longing. But there was playfulness in it, too, as though the darkness was searching for a little light.

Greta herself had never learned to play, despite her mother's wishes. Sarah had taken lessons all through college, from an English woman who, by her account, was ninety years old when she'd first taught her in kindergarten. Sarah could play anything. Classical, of course, but also jazz and country and anything in between. Greta could remember her parents performing Christmas carols together—Sarah on piano, Gus on guitar—and making their happiness seem like the easiest thing in the world.

The song ended and another began, still melancholic but with more pace.

"It is lovely, yes?" the waitress said, startling her. "The music." She set a basket of warm brown bread and a ramekin of butter next to the crab.

"Very," Greta said.

"It is winter music."

"Chopin?"

"Stig Hjalmarson," she said, pointing to a small balcony hidden by the fireplace.

He sat at a baby grand piano that Greta hadn't noticed when she walked in, drawn as she was by the table overlooking the sound. Behind her, a short glass-brick wall flanked the fireplace, and on the far side was the piano with him sitting on the bench. He wore the same sweater as the night before, but his hair was pulled under a knit hat and his eyes were behind stylish glasses. He was facing the dining room, so she couldn't see his hands, but the second she thought of them she warmed again and picked up her glass of wine.

"When he's in town he plays every night. Just comes in and plays even if no one is here."

"I thought it was the radio at first," Greta said. "But I should have known better. He plays at the church, too."

The waitress cocked her head and glanced at the wedding ring on Greta's left hand.

"I stopped in there last night," she said quickly. "He was playing a Christmas song I know."

Now the waitress looked her in the eyes before turning to listen intently. "He's been working on that same fugue for two winters already."

Greta, too, swung her gaze over. He seemed almost to reabsorb the music as he played it, only to play it again, slower, until it reminded her of waves breaking in a dying wind.

"It's the saddest thing I've ever heard," Greta said.

"He's not a sad man," the waitress told her.

"He's got to be *something*, to write music like that." She regarded him as though he were a curiosity. Some strange nocturnal animal that only lived in the Arctic.

The waitress sat down in the chair opposite her. "I'm Ava," she said.

"And I'm Greta."

The man began from the start again.

"Do you know what he told me when he came in tonight?" Ava asked.

"What?"

"That tonight he would finally play it right. That in church last night he understood why it was different in his mind than in his fingers."

Greta blushed. But why? As if she'd been caught staring, she turned away and said, "It sounds wonderful to me."

"I think he was ready to quit this one."

"Do you know him well?"

"Ever since we were kids." She was looking at Greta. "We are not kids anymore."

"I guess none of us are," Greta said.

Ava looked around the restaurant. "You are the only customer left. I will clean up and then take a drink with you?"

"That would be nice."

Ava stood and tucked hair behind both ears. "Enjoy the rest of your crab. I will tell him to play another song. Less sad. He knows every song in the world."

"Please ask him to play that one again."

Ava said she would, then walked toward the kitchen.

Greta swiveled around, her back now to the piano, her king crab cold before her. She buttered a piece of bread and ate it and took a long drink of water, the ice tinkling against the glass.

There were other songs in her life. Summer songs and songs that reminded her of her kids. She decided, as she called Frans, that she would keep them to herself, and count them among the happy memories. But some others she would have to renounce altogether. She'd start making a list.

"I didn't think you'd call," Frans said, his voice distant, the background noise boisterous. A restaurant or bar or party.

"I didn't either."

"You're not at home. I spoke with your dad twice today."

"You don't need to keep calling him."

"Where are you, Greta? What's that music in the background?"

"I'm in a church," she lied.

"A church?"

She glanced over her shoulder at Stig Hjalmarson. "I should ask you the same question. It sounds like you're at a party."

"I'm with colleagues."

"Colleagues? You mean Alena Braaten?"

"No, I'm *not* with her."

"I don't care if you are." She turned back to the view out the window. "It doesn't matter."

In the background of wherever he was, a woman's voice came garbled and closer. "Fine. That's fine," he told her, or someone else, she couldn't say. But the tone of his voice was suddenly detached.

"She's there," Greta said. "How in the world could I feel guilty about not calling you sooner?"

"Just a moment," he said, and in only a few seconds the background noise was replaced by the sound of wind.

"You've left her inside," Greta said. "Now you're standing outside the bar. It's cold in Oslo, isn't it? I can see you."

"Will you stop that? Can we talk sensibly for once?"

"What sensible things do you have in mind?"

"I'm sorry about the holiday. I know it wasn't good for you."

"They never are, Frans. But that's not why you should be sorry."

"And I'm sorry about what happened in the fish house. That's not how it should be between us."

"How should it be, then?"

He didn't answer right away, so they sat with only the background sounds between them. Stig Hjalmarson played on. She took a sip of wine and set the glass back down by the candle burning on her table.

Finally he said, "I don't know how it should be. I'm sorry for that, too."

"I'm so unhappy," she said, knowing it would quiet him and give her a moment to think.

Stig finished the piece yet again, and she could feel the last note hanging in the air. Every part of her wanted to cut off the call and just listen to the music, let it comfort her. But she knew it would be better to get this conversation over and done with. "I'm not at home. I'm—" And she paused, deciding what to tell him.

"You're where?"

"Dad's with the kids. I needed to get away."

"Get away to *where*, Greta? And it's not your dad's job to raise Lasse and Liv."

"Not my dad's job to raise them? That's the sensible advice you're giving me?"

"Your unhappiness, it's like a fucking anchor we hand off back and forth."

"I knew it was a horrible idea to call you."

"Oh, for God's sake. Not this again."

"You're right. The same thing all over again."

What would happen if she just hung up? Was it possible for him to somehow track her call? Would he catch a flight himself if he knew she was here? "I should go," she said. "It's not as if we're even talking to each other."

"I'm trying to." It sounded like he was whining, and she wanted to tell him to shut up.

"That's what you said when we were in Gunflint. That you're trying."

"I am."

"No you're not. You're wanting to feel less guilty. You want the kids to be safe. You want your life exactly the way you like it. You want to go to the gym in the morning and have dinner ready when you get home in the evening. And you want to go to Norway and fuck Alena without me saying anything about it."

His voice rose in pitch and volume. "I'm in Norway raising money. I just left a table full of donors sitting there without their host. All so I can listen to you tell me how busy you are being unhappy. A full-time job, apparently."

"*You* called *me*, Frans. You called my dad. You keep texting. Tell me, what do you want?"

"When are you going home? That's what I want to know. And where are you?"

"Are you afraid I'm in Oslo? What if I'm in that church right across the street? Can't you see me?"

"Stop it."

"The stars came out only an hour ago. Before that it was snowing."

"There's no church across the street," he said. "What a fucking mess."

Well, he was right about that. Again they fell silent.

She thought of a run she'd taken just a month or so ago. It was a warm October morning in Minneapolis and she ran a ten-mile loop around the city's lakes. Her legs were strong but her lungs were aching when she came up the western shore of Lake Harriet, then felt her breath go all at once. Her heart rate spiked, and she still ran. It felt like someone was squeezing her chest, but she kept going. Harder, faster, even as her vision narrowed. At Beard's

Plaisance, only a quarter mile from home, she crossed the parkway onto the grass and lengthened her stride to run up the hill that in winter they sledded down. She and the kids and now the puppy. Frans, too, when he wasn't somewhere else. Under the best of circumstances taking that hill would've put her at her limit, but with her chest tightening more with each gasping breath, she stopped halfway up and put her hands on her knees and vomited in the grass. When she stood upright, her vision blurred and her knees buckled and she fell over. She thought she'd die on the spot. Was *certain* she would. Even welcomed the idea of it. Her thoughts went to Lasse and Liv, to the sound of their laughter and the feel of their soft, soft skin when they were babies. She lay down on her side and tried to vomit again but only heaved, fighting for breaths that wouldn't come. She closed her eyes and rolled onto her back and vowed to hold the image of her children behind her eyelids as she died.

No one came to rescue her. A woman dying in the park on a warm October morning. She didn't know how long she lay there, but when she opened her eyes and sat up her breath came easy and her heart and chest felt loose. She might have been relieved to be alive.

"Greta, are you still there?"

"What?" she said.

"What are we going to do?"

She thought of standing up on that hillside, the backs of her legs covered in mud, her shorts grass-stained. She thought of walking home like a drunkard, her vision focusing and blurring with every other step.

"Do you remember last month, when I came home from that run all muddy?"

"That day you tripped?"

"I didn't trip. I was running up the hill at Beard's Plaisance and just collapsed. I thought I was going to die."

"Jesus Christ, Greta. Why didn't you tell me? Why did you *lie* to me?"

"I lie to you all the time," she said.

Now it was his turn to go silent.

"I'm so tired of it. Lying. Keeping things from you." She took a long pull of wine. "I felt like I was having a heart attack. Couldn't breathe, my chest was so tight. My pulse must have been two hundred-plus. And still I kept going up that goddamn hill."

"Why?"

"Why what?"

"Why did you keep running? Do you hate our life that much?"

"Hate is the wrong word."

"And I suppose you know the right one?"

"No, but I might figure it out."

"I'm going to catch a flight tomorrow morning," he announced.

"I won't be home."

"Okay."

"Should I tell my dad to expect you?"

"Yes. If I can get the first flight, I'll be home by bedtime."

"I'll tell him."

Another long lull filled the connection. She could hear the piano again. She saw the waitress standing at the cash register counting receipts. Outside the window, what was called Sørøsundet on the little hotel map lay drunk with starlight.

"When will you get home, Greta?"

"Soon. I don't know."

"How'd you know it was snowing in Oslo? And starry now?"

"My phone told me."

"Greta?"

"What?"

"Can we see a counselor?"

"Let's talk about it later. I'm going now." She looked over and saw the waitress smiling from across the restaurant, raising a bottle of wine. "I'll let you know when I'm coming home."

"Okay," he said, then hung up.

She sat there with the phone still at her ear. There was no more piano music. No sound at all. She felt liberated, and also that she might be honest now. When she lowered the phone from her ear, the picture of Liv kissing Frans popped up. She held it back to her ear and rehearsed the words twice before mouthing them, with not even a whisper, though she felt like she was screaming them: *I'm supposed to love you.*

She stood up, walked past the fireplace, and pulled a chair from a table by the small platform on which the baby grand sat. The grin on his downturned face erased everything. She sat back and crossed her legs and gestured with her hand as though to say, *Keep playing.* He shook his head and closed his eyes, then started on some ragtimey number.

"No," she said, loud enough for him to hear. "Play the one you've been practicing."

"'Vannhimmel'? It is no church hymn."

"No, it's not."

"You like the sad music?"

"I do."

"Close your eyes," he said. "Only listen. I will play it with the calvings and all the blue."

"What does that mean?"

"Just listen. But first…" He passed his hand across his eyes. When he revealed himself, his eyes were closed and that grin played on his lips again. Toothy and full-lipped and as genuine as the starlight outside. "Ava!" he shouted. "Dim the lights, would you?" Then he laughed, looked at her once more, and started playing.

She kept her eyes closed through the first notes, which seemed to come from her own mind. But after a moment, she realized that it didn't sound the same. This performance was more classical, the tempo perhaps even slower. When she looked at him—eyes still clenched shut, his head drooped, his expression exulted, his shoulders rolling as his hands moved up and down the keys—she instantly felt scandalized. A sudden warmth rose from the small of her belly up her chest and neck and cheeks.

She glanced around as if she might be discovered. But no one else was in the restaurant except Ava, who was switching off the kitchen lights with a bottle of wine under her arm. Greta turned back to him, and almost impossibly the music came slower still. Her frustrated piano teacher had preached posture and composure, but Stig Hjalmarson played with a stoop in his wide shoulders, his head hung so low that his long hair fell like a curtain around his face. She brushed her own hair back off her damp forehead and watched him. His head and shoulders trundled faster now as the tempo built, as if he and the music were one, which she supposed was true.

Her own sensibilities had not given music like this much credence. Or music played like this, anyway. Until this evening, music had mostly been something to allay grief. Even the saddest songs brought her peace. As he played—the song was changing movements, the clattering of high notes adding other dimensions, she thought, like a sun shower does—everything changed. The room became warmer, quieter. It was as if the simplicity of her life was finding its voice again.

Stig struck the bass notes with his left hand, his right hovering, fingers limp, above the treble keys. One second, two. In a motion that seemed choreographed, he lifted both hands and swept off his wool sweater. It fell on the bench beside him and as though it were all part of the performance, a crashing and totally inharmonious sound came thundering from the piano.

He opened his eyes like he'd been stabbed in the back and sought out her own. "A calving," he said.

As simply as that she understood what he'd meant. She closed her eyes against the feeling and just listened. By the time he finished, she was stripped and open wide and no longer despairing.

And then he was walking toward the table she sat at. He was pulling the red sweater over his head and sliding his arms through the sleeves and, once it was on, tucked his heavy hair back behind his ears. He gestured to Ava at the bar for a glass to sip from and then was standing right across the table from her.

He must have been six-foot-three, and his chest and shoulders eclipsed the window behind him. The candlelight flitted into his eyes and they speckled blue and gray like mica-flecked granite.

"I'm Stig." He reached his hand out and she could see the tufts of hair on each knuckle.

"I know," she said as she gave it a shake.

"May I sit down?"

She pulled out the chair next to her.

He rearranged the three candles guttering on the table and looked at her through their flames.

"I keep showing up to listen to you play," she said.

"I saw you at the church last night."

"Yes, you did."

"'No koma Guds englar.'"

"It's a Christmas song," she said.

"It is. We are getting ready for the season at church."

"And tonight? 'Vannhimmel,' you said? What kind of song is that?"

"That is one of my own songs."

"What does 'Vannhimmel' mean?"

Ava came to the table carrying a bottle of red wine under one arm and a glass of whiskey in the other. "Don't ask him about his songs," she said, sitting down. "He will say something dreary now, you can believe it. But I knew him when he used to ride his bike to school from the Rypefjord. His legs were so skinny he had to wear a rope around his waist just to hold his pants up."

Stig waved his hand as though to contradict her.

"He wasn't always such a serious man," she concluded.

"I am not serious even now."

They both spoke near-perfect English, only a slight lilt to their accents.

"Answer her question, then," Ava said.

Stig looked at Ava and then switched his gaze to Greta, who stared right back. He rolled his whiskey around his glass. "Oh, I don't know," he said. "Maybe it means something about all the ice melting."

Ava reached across the table to touch Greta's hand. "See? With this one it is always about the world ending. He quit his job on the oil fields because he has a philosophy."

"The world *is* ending," Stig said, his eyes arched. "Arctic sea ice levels—"

"A *very* good paying job," Ava interrupted.

"I want the world not to end."

"This is not how to romance two beautiful women!" Ava told him.

He let out a throaty laugh, mouth open wide, head thrown back. The glasses resting atop his head fell to the floor. "Okay," he said, reaching down to pick them up. "I will not make the night darker." His eyes narrowed on each of them once, and then he took another sip of his whiskey. "Tell me," he continued, "why are you in Hammerfest? Certainly not to follow the sad songs around town?"

"I'm just visiting," she said, though of course this was a lie. "My people are from here. Five generations ago." That was true, but it wasn't the answer to his question. She could tell by his eyes that he understood she didn't know why she was there. They looked at each other for a full five seconds.

"What's your name?" he asked.

"Did I not introduce you?" Ava asked. "This is Greta from America. She knows your name."

"I told her my name," he said, his voice sounding softer, as if he wasn't really sure about that. "Didn't I?"

"You did," Greta said. "Stig Hjalmarson."

"What's your family name?" he asked.

"Nansen," she said.

"Not like Fridtjof Nansen?"

"A distant relative, in fact." As soon as she said it, she wished she hadn't, that this was the last thing she wanted to get into. But the silence was so awkward that she added, "Cousins several times removed. And several generations, of course. It doesn't matter. I can't keep track." That was not a lie, except these weren't *her* distant relatives, they were her husband's. Noticing how her fingers were pinching the stem of her glass, she casually lowered her hand beneath the table onto her lap.

Ava poured herself more wine and said, "Men and boats and adventure," needing to say no more.

"We're not all so simple," Stig said.

Ava rolled her eyes. "Stig *lives* on a boat."

For an instant, Greta felt as if she had been caught. "You really do?" she nearly blurted.

"Sort of," Stig said.

"When you go home tonight," Ava asked, "where will you sleep?"

"On my bed, of course."

"And where is your bed?"

"On my boat."

"I think that means you live on a boat."

"What kind of boat?" Greta asked.

"A sailboat. A forty-five-foot Hutting."

"Wait! You live *here* on a boat?"

"I live *now* on a boat." He took another sip. "It's not just any boat. It's fitted out for Arctic latitudes. This is only my second winter on her. I was thinking of heading down to San Sebastián after Christmas."

"What kind of a man can just sail off to San Sebastián?" Greta asked.

Ava's tone—until then teasing, almost sisterly—now turned solemn. "If Stig wants to go to San Sebastián, it is okay. Anywhere he wants to go it is okay."

Stig peered into his glass again, sighed, and glanced up, as though he'd seen a ghost in the amber whirl of whiskey. "I am a lucky man, yes," he said. "To sail around without a care."

His voice belied a storm his eyes gave away. They went wet and pensive, and behind them Greta could see a kind of bareness. She knew the look well from studying her own sleep-deprived reflection in the bathroom mirror almost every morning. It took her breath away to recognize it so clearly in someone else.

"Why is it fitted for the Arctic?" she asked, not even realizing she was appraising him.

Now the faraway look came closer, and he said, "Because I like the North. I like the ice. And I like to see it when I am alone."

"He also likes to be among the living," Ava added. "But I'm going to go outside to smoke." She flipped open the box of cigarettes and offered them as she stood. "I only smoke in the twenty-four-hour dark. I wish I could stop."

Greta shook her head, and Stig said, "I'm going to steal another whiskey while you're gone."

Ava closed her eyes tight, miming that she'd see no evil, and Stig got up and followed her to the bar. Ava continued out into the lobby, and Stig scooped ice into a cocktail glass and poured a splash. Greta watched him, the easiness of his stride, the wave of his hair. Before he returned, he reached up to the stereo receiver and dialed the knob. He twisted another and the radio moved to a different station, and a song she recognized filled the restaurant.

She watched him walk back as she'd watched him walk off, the drink in his upturned hand. "I should have offered you one," he said.

Greta lifted her wineglass. "I'm okay. I've probably had enough."

"Ava," he said, as though she needed no further explanation, but then quickly added, "She is a bad influence. When I am here, she sits and listens to me and pours me drinks. We are old friends."

"I wish I had a friend like her," Greta said, raising her voice and her eyebrows at the same time, hoping to glean what sort of friend Ava was, exactly. When he offered nothing, she asked, "Your boat, what's her name?"

"Like the song I played for you. *Vannhimmel.*"

"Yes, but what does it mean?"

He pointed out the window into the dark night. "In the Arctic, when ships or men are caught in ice, they can use the sky to find open water. The water's reflection in the sky is brighter than the ice's. That is *Vannhimmel.* Water-sky."

Yes was all she could think.

They traded long looks and though she'd never admit it to anyone—not even him, in the months to come—in that instant she felt that a water-sky was shining down on her and that under its light she herself brightened.

She took a deep breath and said, "Well, it's one of the most beautiful things I've ever heard, that song."

"Music is only as beautiful as the ear that hears it."

"Seems to me that it takes two," Greta said, not sure what she meant.

"A song is nothing without someone to listen to it." He appeared to be thinking something through, his head bobbing slowly. "I have been trying to make that song right for a long time. Since I sailed the *Vannhimmel* up to Svalbard when I first got her." He paused again. "Tonight is the first time it sounded right."

The bottom of Greta's stomach dropped.

"It was nice to have you listening," he said.

What sounds do I recall?" I asked.

Marius Granerud nodded, his hands folded over his belly, his eyes heavy in their folds. Here in his office he appeared much older than he had at Bengt's feast, and perhaps it was my perception of his agedness that made me ponder his questions as though they might reacquaint me with the power of belief. It was only the second morning of our interviews, and already I realized that my powers of description were inadequate to the memories themselves. He also knew this, and waited patiently in his chair while I attempted to conjure the echoes of my first morning as a castaway.

After a moment I said, "I might better tell you about the sounds I *didn't* hear."

"What?"

"Birds. The birds were gone that morning. All their cawing and whistling. I had grown so used to their racket that its absence alarmed me." I paused to consider this. "Their sound was like life, and without it, well..."

Granerud dipped his nib in an inkwell and scribbled a note, then looked back up at me.

"I'd never known such a strange morning," I continued. "I woke nestled into that pile of rocks as though I were some gnarly old post planted into the tundra. The Krag-Jørgensen lay across my lap, and as I sat there in the dark—mind you, a darkness so complete I couldn't see the nose beneath my eyes—praying for the dawn, all I had were my other senses. Touch and sound and smell. Which is why I noted there were no birds. Now that I think on it, the silence was as powerful as the blackness. Or so I told myself, to prove I hadn't died in that long night before."

There appeared on Granerud's face a look of satisfaction. Like that of a father proud to have taught his son how to raise a sail. I might have felt condescended to, but in truth I felt much as that son might've, and so I kept on.

"It was something else to wake with even fewer prospects than I'd had the night before, but there I was. As the first light of day rose, I was a blind man. You've never seen fog the likes of this. And a cold fog it was. The snow was melting, I could hear it, which meant it had warmed overnight. But the fog, why, it gave the air an icy clutch. And it lingered, I think for hours, its smell like a fresh snow up on the fjeld." I paused again, and in my mind could see that whiteness. "It was of a thickness I'd never witnessed before. Indeed I had never even imagined such a thing. And persistent. I'd always known fog to come and go, like steam from a kettle. But this, it was more like a tub full of cold milk."

Granerud's eyes widened and he jotted another note, then removed his monocle to study me from behind his desk. "Yesterday, you mentioned how afraid you were that first night. Trying to sleep. Worrying about the bear. And about who would find you. Well, I wonder if that fear lingered there in the fog that first morning?"

"What man wouldn't be afraid?"

"Herr Eide, I make no judgments regarding your fortitude. I only ask because your state of mind is a part of the story here, and I want to be careful to get it down right." He leaned over his desk as much as his belly would allow, and spoke as though we were conspirators. "I myself would've been terrified. You can believe that. As you say, any man would be."

I lifted my teacup and sipped. My chair was covered with a plush cushion, crushed green velvet with a frill of golden silk. Never had

I sat on a finer piece of furniture. I took another sip of tea and set the cup back down.

"As I sit here, it seems that where I found myself that first morning was like the journey's end of all my foolishness. Or perhaps failure is putting it better."

Granerud's expression was different now, as if I were an orphan on the streets of a mean city. He lay his pen down and laced his fingers behind his head and leaned back. His belly spilled out from under his vest.

"My people came to Finnmark during the time of Napoleon."

"Your people?"

"My grandfather, Vegard Eide. My father, Olav, was born in the same hut I was. This out on an island called Muolkot a half hour's row from Hammerfest. It's where Inger and I had our daughter. Where we lived until she left. It was our home. My *family's* home."

"May I ask what your father and grandfather have to do with your sense of foolishness and failure?"

"They were good men, and taught me well. How to fish. How to handle a mallet and a saw and an adze. They were good providers. Their families were strong. As my father's eldest son—I had two sisters—our home on Muolkot was mine. So were the sheep. The faering. The same resources my father and grandfather had, those too I was given. Yet I squandered them. Thea, my daughter..." And here I paused, realizing that even to call her name was to be back on Spitzbergen, alone in the fog.

"I was told of your daughter, Herr Eide."

I sat up. "Told of her?"

"Only that she has not been heard from. Gerd Bjornsen has, as I understand it, been quite like a sister to your own wife in this respect."

"Like a sister, sir?"

"They pray together. And Fru Bjornsen has become a confidante."

"What do you mean, a confidante?"

Granerud sat forward and leaned on his elbows. "I see you've turned the tables, Herr Eide, and are now the one asking questions." Though his tone was lighthearted, still I felt reprimanded.

Even put in my place. But he must have sensed my discomfort. "It's a good thing Fru Eide has come with you to Tromsø. You can clear this up with her over supper."

I only stared at him, benumbed. So Gerd and Inger were intimates—and on the subject of our daughter, no less? That seemed more sensational and unlikely than the story Marius Granerud was coaxing from me.

"You were saying, about your daughter?"

"I was?"

"About Muolkot and your father and grandfather."

"Would you excuse me, sir?"

"Of course." He stood, and I did too. "Herr Eide?"

"Yes?"

"You needn't be so formal. Please, call me Marius."

I nodded, left his office, and by some instinct found myself in the midmorning bustle on the avenue outside. I packed my pipe and lit it and looked out on the passersby. My ignorance had betrayed me again. First Inger had told me she did not wish to speak of our daughter. If I'd abided by her wishes, it was only because I didn't know how to deny my wife. But it was she who was denying me, preferring her whispers to God and—as I now understood it—the counsel of Gerd Bjornsen.

I smoked and watched a woman and her daughter stroll by, their dresses grand, their bonnets fine. It would rain today, I could tell that much. I thought of marching back up to Marius Granerud's office and returning the kroner he'd advanced me, half of the total. I'd thank him and walk out. And I'd disappear among the shadows of these people on the avenue. I had all but resolved to do it, being of no use to anyone.

Yet when pocketing my pipe I felt the bladder of fresh tobacco there, and remembered how on that foggy morning at the Krossfjorden I would surely have traded my last bullet for such a luxury. It wasn't my first thought up there that morning, but it couldn't have been more than my third.

Now I was looking up and down the street in this strange city. Only a block away, high above the rooftops, the gulls were wing-ing and calling and arched in mocking elegance over the harbor. Instead of disappearing among the throng on that Tromsø street, I flew back up to Granerud's office.

He asked an assistant to fetch me another cup of tea, and for two hours I sat opposite that odd and charismatic man and told him about the first morning.

If on the interminable night previous I'd longed for my family, if my chief concern was that I would never lay eyes on them again or tell them one last time what a proud father and husband I was, if I cataloged and scolded and cursed myself for my shortcomings, if I then cursed that wicked scree and ice and sea, if I went from sadness to regret to anger and then action, it was because I knew as sure as I stood on that snow-caked slope of land that I would survive only by saving my own hide. So, once my blood found my feet and hands, I shouldered my rifle and went where I somehow knew I had to go.

My boots still sat beside Birger Mikkelsen's feet. His were still on mine. In the light of that new day, this sight had a ferlie air about it—as though I'd once dreamt it and was now seeing that dream come to life. Whereas the night before I saw no sign of the ice bear, now there was evidence of him in abundance. I could see the contrast between the undisturbed snow—shimmering like a halo— and the trodden patches where whatever struggle Mikkelsen had offered had packed it all down and tinged it pink with his blood. The imprints of the bear's paws marked the snow as if he'd measured off a proper slaughtering pen. Each track was the size of an oar blade, and I knew in an instant that if his thirst for human blood had been excited, he would get mine no matter how careful I was. This realization came as a relief, frankly, for it toggled my outlook from fear to fascination, and for the rest of my time on Spitzbergen I considered the bear as a moral animal, not some deranged murderer.

Another thing occurred to me and was instrumental to my survival: he was native to that savage place, and his intelligence and instinct were qualities to mimic as much as dread. Though I had

no claws or woolly coat, was no great swimmer, and couldn't smell
blood from a mile's distance, and had neither a powerful jaw nor
sharp teeth, I could—indeed *must*—simplify my thinking. That
was why I found myself at the scene of Mikkelsen's death again,
despite all the fear that place inspired. I needed concern myself
only with the sorts of things the bear would. Hunger. Thirst. The
instinct to *live*. Perhaps Mikkelsen had left me an inheritance.

Thirty paces beyond the red rainbow of trodden snow, I found
his hakapik and his mittens. My own gloves had gone down the
sound with the killing boat, so I was mightily glad to have his. I
also found his shoulder pack, sliced open as with a sharp boning
knife, but an outer pocket still held his flint and steel and a pouch
of tinder, a box of soaked-through matches, his eyeglasses, and his
pipe. There was, too, a small leather sack for tobacco, empty except
for its heady scent.

Each of these discoveries proved essential, though none matched
my last unearthing. After I'd pocketed the booty, I returned to the
edge of the fjord and stood on rocks cleared of snow by the tide.
Fog still shrouded the eastern view, but to the west the three-mile-
long spit of towering and snow-covered mountains shone brightly
under a white sun. Possibly, I thought, if I could get to the end
of that land, where the Krossfjorden met the wider waters of its
main artery, I might signal a passing boat. That spot would be like
the palm of the hammered, five-fingered hand fabled by the late
Birger himself.

I looked out to sea and considered the ice, more of which had
flowed into the fjord overnight. Much more and no boats would
be able to break through. I wondered how persistently it would
come, that ice. How soon before I'd be able to simply march across
the sea. Mikkelsen, one night on board the *Sindigstjerna*, had
described how suddenly the waters changed up there. Like the
winds and the weather. Having spent plenty of hard seasons in all
of it, he had a story for every occasion. I lifted his tobacco pouch to
my nose and sniffed.

The only sensible thing to do was to cross the plain and attempt to traverse the moraine at the base of the glacier. Once across, I would trek to the foot of the mountain along the sea line until I reached the headland, where I would await my fate.

Once more I passed the site of Birger's death. This time I didn't stop, just continued on across that snowy mile headed for the base of the glacier. I might have missed it altogether if not for a flash of the sun, which caused me to look down and shield my eyes. There at my feet was Mikkelsen's knife.

Most of those nights, after our evening tea Birger would unsheathe his knife from his belt, wet his stone, and sharpen the blade. It had a whalebone handle, the head of which was scrimshawed into the blunted face of an ice bear, and a blade of thick, hard steel he claimed had been forged from a retired ship's anchor. He spoke lovingly to it there in the mess, and when finished with his sharpening, he'd slide it gently back in the sheath and say that a sharp knife and the love of God are all a man really needs.

I picked the knife from the snow, wiped it clean on my pants, and held it up to the shimmering sun, which seemed in a hurry to cross the sky: already it had moved several degrees. That knife would prove one of my most vital finds. Even standing there on the plain, the sun growing almost warm up off the snow, I felt for the first time that I might actually make it. Such was the power of that handful of bone and steel. Its weight in my palm renewed me and put a purpose in my stride.

This feeling was short in lasting, though. The glacier there didn't meet the water. Instead it crumbled, and together with the melting snow it became a slurried river between myself and the cape I'd planned to traverse. I might as well have been standing along the edge of Gávpotjávri during the spring melt. Yet that rushing water was no harbinger of longer, warmer days.

I knelt on the shore of the unfortunate slough and scooped handfuls of water into my mouth. It was good for that much. After a final drink, I stood and tramped north along the glacier's edge, thinking there might be firmer ice closer to the snout. But all I found for the trouble of that amble were two enormous tunnels in the head of its craggy face, each of them thirty feet above my head and pouring meltwater in waterfalls. At least I would not die of thirst.

During our long row up the Krossfjorden the prior morning, Mikkelsen spoke with authority and childlike wonder about the shrinking hours of daylight this time of year. As the season of darkness drew nearer, so did the rate at which each new day grew shorter. But the sun was here for now, racing toward an ominous southwestern sky. I reckoned I had four hours more of passable light, and again looked at that godforsaken watercourse now spread out before me, almost equal to the plain I'd crossed to get here. It would take me an hour to get back to where I started, which suddenly seemed my only course of action. There was simply no hope of crossing that water. I took a few last, long drinks and retraced my steps back to the place I'd woken on that same cursed day.

Marius Granerud had been writing as I spoke, dipping his pen in his well so often that even from where I sat, the ink splatters on his blotter were plain as day. When he caught up to my story, he glanced at me and sighed and flipped through his notes. "You mentioned Herr Mikkelsen's knife, and how it was the most essential of his belongings you recovered that morning. Why was that?"

"I'd lost my own knife somehow," I replied.

He leaned forward, expecting more, I reckon. But it struck me as too obvious a question to require elaboration. When I only sat there looking back at him, he cocked his head and again went through his notes and then pondered a new phrasing. "You quoted Herr Mikkelsen as saying all a man needs is"—and here he read from his papers—"'a sharp knife and the love of God.' Have you given any credence to such a thought?"

"I may as well tell you that by the time I was rescued, my use for God was much outweighed by my uses for that knife."

"Who ever cut off a hunk of animal flesh with a prayer, right?"

"Indeed."

He looked across his desk appraisingly, then pulled his pocket watch from his sealskin vest and eyed the time. "I suppose you'll tell me how you employed that knife soon enough?"

"I can explain that in detail anytime you like."

He raised a hand as though to quiet me. "I prefer my stories from start to finish, Herr Eide. Old-fashioned, I know, but I'll wait. Just as you had to." He tidied his papers and put them in his valise and then planted his hands on the blotter and looked at me. "I don't know if it matters to you or not, but I find your honesty noble and your resourcefulness admirable. I've spent most of my life sitting behind a desk, living vicariously through the stories I've been lucky enough to report on. Through all the years of doing this, I've met any number of charlatans and cheats. You strike me as neither." He stood. "I'm glad of that. It's invigorating. And so far, your story is living up to its billing."

Now I stood, too, ready to adjourn with him. He donned his bowler, shouldered his long coat, and checked his watch once more. "I've an appointment I cannot miss this afternoon, I'm sorry to say. What say we meet back here tomorrow morning at the same time?"

"Of course," I said.

He ushered me to the door and held it open. In the antechamber, his secretary stood and handed him his cane and two envelopes that he deftly slipped into his valise.

"There've also been two telegraphs for you this morning, Herr Granerud," his secretary said, handing them over his desk.

Granerud glanced at me. "All things in pairs today, ja?"

Holding the first telegram at arm's length, he read it without reaction, upon glancing at the second he raised the monocle to his eye and read it slowly, carefully. A quizzical expression passed over his face as he folded the sheet in half. "Herr Eide," he said. For the first time since I'd met him, his voice sounded uncertain. He tapped the paper on his chin and took off his monocle. "I'll need to take your leave now. You can see yourself out?"

"Of course."

"Very good." He doffed his hat and then said to his secretary, "Herr Rudd, please step into my office." Then he turned back to me while the man picked up his stenographer's notebook. "It seems our dear Bjornsen is arriving on tomorrow's boat."

"Here? Why in the world?"

"He says he's got business to attend to." He shrugged, then added, "He *is* a man with diverse interests. In any case he won't disrupt our interview, you can rest assured of that. Until tomorrow, Herr Eide."

We shook hands before he stepped back into his office with his secretary.

I stood on the quay listening to the ruckus of gulls as they harassed a trawler coming to dock. Two men in coveralls were atop her decks, gazing across the water. Their aspect reminded me of the solemn work of pulling fish from the sea, and I felt a tug from my forgotten self. I would be very happy to get back home and put my faering to rights so that one day soon I might be sculling home with my fish boxes full.

Other boats were moored in the harbor, and across the sound, burrowed beneath the mountains and tufted by the green and gray scrub of the forest, a single farm and its fields lay ready for winter. A chill was in the air that the midday sun could not absorb, and I felt its faint galvanic force. This was a sense I hadn't had before Spitzbergen, but understood now as though I'd conjured it myself. I knew that by dinnertime snow would be falling. There were other things like this, too, I was now attuned to, but the habits of my companions in life were not among them. The thought of Inger awaiting me at the hotel, of the conversation we'd need have about her confidence in Gerd Bjornsen, why, it gave me no pleasure to anticipate this.

We had planned to have lunch together following my meeting with Granerud, but when I returned to the hotel she wasn't in the café. I checked our chamber and, finding it empty, went back downstairs to wait for her. A half hour later she still hadn't joined me, so I stepped outside. Was this my new fate, to stand in a strange place and not know where to wander? At least here there were no glaciers to cross. No obliviating darkness.

At the end of the street a church spire rose above the rooftops, and I walked toward it. By the time I stood before the grand entry, peering up at the bell tower and clock, I was well beyond salvation of the sort the good book evangelized. But I was not without my hunches, so I opened the doors and walked in. Even from the last row in the church I could tell it was Inger in the front pew. She believed much in prayer, and usually whispered hers into her hands folded at her heart. But I was surprised to see her head tilted up, as if studying the cross above the altar. She wore her shawl and her bonnet and there was something about the quietude and the image she cut up there that gave me to think she was atoning.

I stood and watched her for some minutes before she suddenly looked around and stood quickly and came down the aisle carrying a parcel. Not until she'd nearly reached me did she notice my presence, which seemed to almost frighten her. She had to catch her breath, then said, "I lost track of the hour, Odd Einar. I was just coming to meet you."

"When you weren't at the hotel, I thought to find you here."

She looked as though she'd been caught. How else to describe it?

"What's in the package?" I asked.

She held it up. "I know I shouldn't have," she said. "But it's been so long since I indulged in any pleasure, no matter how small."

I wish I could describe how proud it made me to know that my wife had coddled herself, and that it was my own earnings enabling her to. My expression must have conveyed that happiness and pride, because now she took my arm and ushered me out into the churchyard.

We took our lunch in the hotel café, where she unwrapped the parcel and showed me a hairbrush and mirror, pewter handled and porcelain backed and painted with peach-colored cloudberries and their soft-lobed leaves. She presented them to me as if she'd stolen them, and when I said they were beautiful and she deserved such pretty things, she responded, "I can't remember the last time I bought something for myself. And now that you're home"—here she looked suspiciously around the café before reaching across the table to touch my hand—"I'd like to look my most charming for you. I hope it pleases you."

"Of course it does, elskede."

We ate cheese and bread and preserves and drank tea and chatted away, as though time and money were of no concern. I believe the easiness and ease of that afternoon was unmatched in our lives together, and I could nigh see her love for me retaking shape, like her affection had a physical essence that I could trace as it crossed the table. Akin to smoke or fog.

Toward the end of our repast, I risked mentioning the news that Bengt would be arriving the next day.

"That means Fru Bjornsen too, then."

"Why?" I asked.

She paused, finished the last sip of her tea. "The marriage of Bengt and Gerd is complicated."

"How are you privy to this?"

"I see it in the bakery. I see it in their home," she said quickly. Perhaps even defensively. "Gerd confides in me. I confide in her."

"She's your friend now?"

"She is my friend. And Bengt my employer."

"Not anymore he isn't."

She was still looking at me, her expression as changeable as the daylight on Spitzbergen. "These kroner Marius Granerud is paying you, they keep us afloat, Odd Einar. But they don't excuse us from work."

"I'll work, Inger. You know that. When have I not? But I won't have us indentured to that impostor any longer. That's why we're here."

"And what will you do? When we get back home. Where will we live?"

"I'll fish, of course. I'll make the boat ready and climb back in it. We can see about a room in Iver Hauan's place and save for something more. If the fish aren't biting, I can apply for work in his lumberyard. We can make do." I paused, rotten with the feeling of pleading again.

"Okay, Odd Einar. Okay."

I finished my tea. Already the midday gloaming filtered out the light: it would be full dark in an hour. And how the onset of the polar night triggered in me some new dread.

I must have stared out for a long time, before Inger brought me back. "You're watching ghosts dance out there, Husband."

"It's fair to doubt me. I know that. I deserve it. But this time I'll make good."

"Okay," she said again.

Later that night, as we readied for sleep, Inger sat at the foot of the bed with her new brush, pulling it through her just-washed hair. She smelled like flowers from the shampoo and if the crew's quarters on the *Sindigstjerna* was the foulest place I ever slept, this hotel was the freshest, not least because of that scent emanating from her hair. She wore her old nightdress but somehow even that seemed elegant in the light of the oil lamp flickering on the bureau. We hadn't talked much since lunch, and I wondered if we'd finished our conversation or if Inger yet had more to say.

The brush. All day I'd been trying to recall why it seemed so special, and only when sitting there on the bed did it come to me. Inger had sent her hairbrush to America with our daughter. The night she left—it was in August, and the hut on Muolkot had been overwarm from an unseasonably balmy day and Inger's urge to finish putting up the beets—Inger sat at the foot of our bed at home, her hair sticking to her neck and forehead. It was her habit then to brush it out before getting under the covers, but on that night and all of them ever since, she'd been reduced to using a wooden comb. As she sat there in Tromsø, I wondered if she was thinking of our daughter.

Of course I dared not ask. So while Inger finished her hair, I let my mind wander back to Thea. The next morning, I would ask the concierge for stationery and write her a letter about all these goings-on. I imagined her growing into a woman like her mother, possessing the same wisdom and verve. I hadn't exactly known how much I admired those qualities in my wife, but the last couple of days had shown me.

I studied Inger again. Now holding the mirror, she was gazing at her reflection. I could see the left side of her face from where I sat, her eye and cheek and the corner of her soft lips. My goodness, never was there such a beautiful woman. She had the complexion of butter and eyes that still were, after all she'd seen, kind in daylight and suggestive at bedtime. I'd memorized her shape in three distinct ways: as it lay against me sleeping, as it looked from across the room, and how it felt in my own unworthy hands. There in the hotel room, I was taking all this in at once when I noticed that she was not staring at her reflection in the mirror but at *me*.

"It's been a long time since you watched me brush my hair."

"Too long."

She put the mirror down and turned to me and ran the brush through her hair once more. "Tell me," she said, "if it's still nice to look at me?"

"I can think of nothing nicer."

She lay the brush on her lap. "It makes me happy to have your tender eyes on me. I've missed the looks you give me."

"I promise I'll keep my eyes on you until the day I die, Inger."

Her skin flushed, but she kept her gaze on me. "And what about the rest of you?" She stood and put the brush and mirror on the chest of drawers across the room and turned out the lamp there, then came back to the bed and lay down beside me.

"The rest of me?"

"Your eyes will be attentive, but what about your hands? Your lips?" She kissed me softly, then more passionately.

"Every bit of myself," I said, pressing up against her. I could feel her lips curl in a smile as she kissed me.

They hadn't spoken for several minutes, not since Greta had commented on the cold and Stig offered her his sweater. The starlight had gathered in his eyes, which were upturned and smiling. Was she being as distant as those stars? Was that why he wasn't talking? Had she gone too far away, lost in temptation as she was? She'd thought of declining his invitation to sit for a while on the shore of the sound. She certainly had practice in telling men no. But here she was, the water lapping on the rocks below them.

"What do you see up there?" she said.

His eyes fluttered, as if he were averting the sun's glare. "It is funny, how the stars need the dark to be seen. Yes? There are not very many things that need the night."

"I've never thought of it like that."

"I have been reading books about the cosmos"—he looked at her and shrugged—"Yes? 'Cosmos' is the word?"

Greta spread her hands toward the sky. "The stars and everything?"

"Yes. I have been reading about how big it is. It is one way to find calm, I think."

He looked down, like he was embarrassed, so she glanced up and felt the starlight fill her own eyes.

"How big is it?" she said.

"Oh. Well, it is too big to understand. And getting bigger all the time. This is what they say."

"Why does that make you feel calm?"

He thought for a moment. "Maybe I like how small I am. All of us." Now he was clearly embarrassed. "I do not know all the words in English. *Vi er så ubetydelige. Våre menneskelige feil og dårskap har konsekvenser. Men de er færre hvis vi holder dem opp til universet. Samme med vår smerte og tristhet.*"

Greta couldn't understand a word of it, but felt herself inching toward him.

"But they are beautiful to see, also. Yes? And we will have nothing but stars until January. No sun or daylight. I am only one happy for this."

"I suppose the stars are different in San Sebastián." She wasn't even sure what this meant. "Maybe fewer stars. And less night to see them."

"This is why I am not already there. Maybe I do not go."

Now clouds rose above the island across the sound. She watched as the crest fell into milky light.

"Sometimes I think I will live here forever. Just waiting. I have no idea what it is I am waiting for," he said softly.

She understood this, too, and felt the pull of his modesty. She tilted her wrist up to the starlight and checked her watch. Just past eleven. They had been out there for an hour and said so little. Now she almost panicked. What if he got up and left? There were things she wanted to ask him. And other things she wanted, too, things she was afraid to admit. So she scanned through the obvious questions, none of which held up. Maybe she should just take his hand and ask him more about the stars. Maybe—probably— just get up and say good night. But she could no sooner stand up and walk off than she could swim across the inky sea.

"I used to sit here with my daughter," he said. "Not so late, of course. But in the dark. She loved the stars."

"Where is she now?" Greta asked. It was the first she'd heard of a daughter, and it made her think of the girl's mother.

"Her name was Kjersti Anne," he said, and now she knew this awful truth, too.

"I'm sorry," she said, so softly she wasn't sure he even heard.

For a long time he just gazed up at the sky. After a minute or two or three he took a pack of cigarettes from his pocket, offered her one, lit it and then another for himself. After two long drags he said, "Only three years ago. Now Jorunn lives with her family by Bodø."

"Jorunn?"

He took another pull on his cigarette. "Kjersti Anne's mom. My wife."

A strong wind came up off the sound, smacking her.

"A north wind," he said, as though to announce it was to say everything about it. "It means the same thing here as it does where you come from, yes? Winter. Snow, maybe."

"Mainly cold."

"This wind brings the clouds too, yes? See?" And he pointed out to where she'd already looked. "And probably more cold. Like for you."

She could no longer understand anything he was saying. She could no longer see the clouds or feel the chill of the wind. She didn't know where she was. She had a drag off the cigarette and held the smoke in her lungs until she had to breathe, then blew it out all at once and took a deep, catching breath.

"I do not talk to Jorunn anymore. She drinks to have no feelings. Sometimes she drinks a lot. And then she blames me."

Greta shook her head as though she already knew all this.

"But I do not blame her. Jorunn. It makes no sense. Kjersti Anne. Like the cosmos." He appeared ready to weep, but then he shrugged again and rose and took a last pull from his cigarette.

"Are you still married?" The wrong question, she knew. The right one—the only question—was to ask what happened to Kjersti Anne, but this wasn't a question she could ask. No, she needed to know about this woman named Jorunn in a town called Bodø.

He rubbed the cigarette out on a rock and put the butt on the edge of the bench. "Yes."

"Where is Bodø?"

"Nordland County. Maybe seven hundred miles down the coast? It is a nice city."

Now Greta thought of her husband, another seven hundred miles beyond Bodø. Or was it even farther? She thought of Alena, too. Of the perfidy. The *sinning*. She looked at Stig, whose face offered nothing. Was he thinking of his daughter or his wife?

She should leave. She even scooted to the edge of the bench and started to pull his sweater from her shoulders.

"Jorunn, she is not happy, but she is a good Christian, so she does not want to divorce…"

And again she was left wondering about this woman. She settled back on the bench and watched as more clouds gathered over the sound and the islands, then turned toward the steep hills above Hammerfest and saw clouds on that horizon too. "I wish these clouds would bring snow," she said.

"Sometimes the snow comes off the fjeld," he said. "Even when the stars are out over Sørø."

"Like a sun shower," Greta said, "only snow."

"A sun shower?"

"When the sun is shining and it's raining at the same time."

"Ah, yes. Soldusj." He appeared delighted by learning this new English word. "Yes. Like that. It is possible for snow."

For too long he hadn't looked at her, so she touched his arm and said, "How long have you lived apart?"

"Now it is two years. Almost. When I bought my boat, she moved home to Bodø. With her mother."

His face was framed with the stars that then started falling all around him, landing on his wild hair and his big hands. He leapt from the bench and craned up his head and opened his mouth to catch them on his tongue. An enormous laugh barreled from his wide-open mouth, and it took all of Greta's self-control not to rise and join his frolic.

Feeling them land like needle pricks on her own hands and face, she felt charged and couldn't help laughing herself. But it wasn't her laugh, not as she knew it now. Instead, it was her laugh from childhood.

"It is perfect!" he said. "You have made it snow!"

Snow? Had she really mistaken these flakes for stars? Should she be embarrassed or delighted? After all, how long had it been since such a whimsical notion crossed her mind? Was this possibility really still inside her? She held his eyes and felt a thousand things—none so pronounced as wonder—and realized she was already making this man into something permanent. Fated. She hadn't understood anything so simply since Lasse and Liv were born and she knew she loved them.

"I mistook the snow for falling stars," she said, standing up and laughing. He laughed too, and together they stood on the beach unable to gather themselves.

When finally she stopped gasping, she said, "You'd better walk me back to my hotel."

"May I buy you a drink when we get there?" he asked, wiping his cheeks with the cuff of his shirt.

"I'd like that," she said, and they walked up the narrow staircase to the street below the church and then on through town.

What happened in the next hour she would later think of much as if the stars *had* turned into snow, something chimerical and beautiful that she'd called into existence. The two of them now drank aquavit sitting at the hotel bar, overlooking the harbor. He told her more about his boat and the fugue he was writing, but nothing else about Jorunn or Kjersti Anne. Nor did Greta ask. She told him about Lake Superior and the winters there, and the fish house. She'd decided over that first aquavit that she wouldn't bring Frans or Lasse or Liv into the discussion.

When last call came, she got up and ordered another round. They grew quieter, more serious. They talked about their mothers. About the persistence of grief. They both admitted feeling too sober given how much they'd drunk. They could hardly look at each other for what was happening between them.

At half past one, Greta excused herself and went to the bathroom. As she washed her hands she asked her reflection in the mirror a very simple question: *You know what this will mean, right?* She shook her head, then took a mint from her purse and tousled her hair and walked back across the bar telling herself, *People will judge you differently than they judge Frans. I hope you know that.* But she'd never felt so aloof and so certain.

Stig was looking out the window, his back to her, his empty glass still in his hand. When she touched him on his shoulder, he turned to her and said he'd walk her to her room. They rode the elevator up and turned down the narrow hallway.

"It was so nice talking with you," he said when they reached her room. Then he appeared nervous, unsure of himself. "I have never met someone who can make it snow." She could smell the aquavit like licorice on his breath.

She put the key card next to the lock on her door, then pushed when it clicked. "The snow follows me everywhere," she said, meaning this as a joke, but it came out sounding grim.

He seemed boyish standing there. Lost, perhaps even scared.

"Good night," she said. "Maybe I'll see you at the church." And with that she stepped into her room and heard the door bump closed behind her.

His sudden absence was dizzying, so she rested her head on the doorframe and listened for the sound of his feet padding back down the hallway. A second, two, three, but no footsteps. And then a soft knock. She opened the door at once and before it closed behind them he had taken her face in his hands and pressed his lips into hers. Her hands went to his hips, seizing him there. They parted and came together twice more, only their lips and fingertips touching each other. And even lost in the clamor of desire, she knew this: finally her private universe was expanding, as magnificent and mysterious as the cosmos swelling beyond the stars they'd witnessed and, farther away still, the stars that were not yet born.

She wanted to take him in and undress him. She pressed herself against him and felt the broadness of his firm body against hers. She was overwhelmed, and could tell he was too. And his want alongside her own made her catch her breath. She clenched her legs to stop their quivering, and felt an ache and wetness between them, every part of her warming and loosening.

How long did they stand inside her doorway? Long enough to

imagine seeing his face as he made love to her. Long enough to feel herself hollowing out. Long enough to realize that she had not been mistaken about this man.

She pulled back, put her hands on his chest, looked up at his eyes in the dark room. He appeared dazed, almost injured. And before she could go further, she opened the door and pushed him out.

Again she rested her head on the inside of the door, waiting for another knock. She stood there for a minute or two and then hurried across the room and saw him down in the square, his hair like a lion's mane in the street light, looking up at the hotel.

His sweater still hung over her shoulders and she could smell him on it. She lifted her hand to wave, but he was turning and walking off, then gone around the corner.

The stars were still falling.

Every second or third evening, Svene Solvang—the *Sindig-stjerna's* captain—would join his crew in the galley for dinner, his long hair slicked back with bear grease, matching the sealskin vest he wore for such occasions. His arms were colossal, and two of the fingers on his starboard hand a knuckle short. He wore his beard long and unkempt and if the rest of us carried the fetor of our rotten boots, or worse, Svene was meticulous in his personal hygiene and left a sweet smell behind. But most notable about him were his eyes, which flitted around as he spoke but were piercing while he worked, whether at the wheel of his boat, shooting his gun, or inspecting a sealskin. More than once we gathered in the mess and speculated on their milkiness—in hushed tones, mind you, never knowing when he might join us for one of his sermons. Mikkelsen speculated that the captain's proclivity for taking the overnight watch was because the brightness of day offended him. Another at our table, Terje Andreassen, a God-fearing young man from Skerjvøy who'd recently lost his wife and infant in childbirth and was a gleeful killer of seals, likened Svene's eyes to the foxes on Spitzbergen, whose pelage morphed from season to season: mottled brown and gray for summer, and pure white for winter. "Except the captain's eyes stay white all year, what with staring out at ice all the damn time." When I first laid my own eyes on his, I thought he was blind.

Now, Svene was a sober man who had been on the polar seas for most of his life. He had no wife. No children. No home. His only concerns were his boat, which he owned outright and had helped build, and his wealth, which was rumored to be considerable. The *Sindigstjerna* was unlike most vessels in the Arctic fleet. The sealers around Greenland—largely up from Newfoundland and the Maritimes—were often proper ships, some as long as two hundred feet and powered by steam engines. Whereas the Norwegian boats that stayed close to home were wooden schooners used for both seal and herring. The *Sindigstjerna* fell in between, some eighty feet long and twenty feet abeam. High up on the foremast was a glassed-in crow's nest where he stationed a barrel man whenever ice was near, and this was a vessel well acquainted with the floes. Svene had been as far east as Severny Island and the Kara Sea, as far north as Kapp Flora in Franz Josef Land, and as far west as Disko Island on Baffin Bay, where he had wintered in eighteen ninety-two. All of those travels—more than thirty years of them, the last ten aboard the *Sindigstjerna*—had been spent hunting seals. Svene estimated that under his charge the *Sindigstjerna* had brought more than twenty thousand skins to market.

When he appeared in the galley, it was often to take measure of his crew. Were we hale? Were our guns oiled? Were the killing boats—a term he invented and employed with relish—shipshape and ready to launch? Was the tea strong and hot enough? But sometimes, especially as the days shortened, he became more contemplative, and he instead would expound on more ethereal topics. He'd give whole hours over to the cause of the tides, infinity, or his belief in suicide, if it meant an end to suffering either physical or spiritual. He seemed, in the throes of these sessions, like a preacher of impossible things.

The sermon I remember most clearly came two nights before I was lost. We were steaming north toward the Isfjorden and Hotellneset, where we would rendezvous with a coal supplier before continuing to the Krossfjorden for our last hunt of the season. By that night I had already been in Svene's employ for more than a month. We'd circumnavigated Spitzbergen and had over four hundred pelts in the hold, despite our share of fearsome weather. Off the coast of Nordaustlandet we'd met a gale that stirred the seas some thirty feet above us and left the killing boats empty for two days and nights. We sheltered in a bay protected on three sides, yet still found ourselves rocked as though in open seas. When finally the storm passed, we discovered that passage over the top of Spitzbergen would be impossible thanks to the ice pack, so we reversed course and headed south and west, between Edgeøya and the Spitzbergen mainland, where we were then stalled by an unrelenting fog that lasted half again as long as the gale. Those three days passed in a silence so eerie that one of the men, Eivind Hushovd, went on deck with his rifle and threatened to shoot himself. Svene spent an hour sitting there on the shrouded deck, coaxing him to live, fog evidently inadequate grounds for taking your life.

But our most treacherous delay came soon after we weighed anchor off Edgeøya. Though remnants of the fog remained, we'd been able to steam south for six hours when, near the Kapp, the skies took an ominous turn, and by the time we were passing Point Lookout a tempest of otherworldly might came straight out of the west across the Greenland Sea. For two days further it snowed with such spirit we were again stranded, in the shelter we'd found in the last bay on the bottom of Spitzbergen. By midnight of the first day, a foot had fallen. Enough water had lapped onto our decks that fangs of ice hung sharp from every line and railing, and the mainmast shroud, and the bowsprit.

Svene had been fine with the gale and unworried by the fog, but the blizzard and its steady western wind made him both uneasy and downhearted. The snow he took personally and I often saw him staring into its teeth from his spot in the wheelhouse. As though he might divine from its whiteness the source of all malevolence.

On the evening I speak of he entered the galley with his hair coiffed and his skin ripe with that floral bouquet. "Gentlemen," he said, then ladled himself a bowl of stewed seal meat and took his seat at the board. He stirred the steam up out of the crock, scanned the faces around the table, and settled his milky gaze on

Birger. "Mikkelsen, you were with me last year this time, ja? On the Greenland coast?"

"There was a blizzard."

"Indeed there was," Svene said, now blowing on a spoonful. "Six days and nights." He took his first bite of supper. "It was the longest storm I've ever beheld. Lashing winds. Bounteous snow." He took another bite, so now both cheeks were filled. "For many years I'd wondered what drew me to these places. I mean, a man might choose any labor. He might choose a wife and family. He might choose a church to pray in. Why had I neglected the domestic life in order to wait out a six-day snow on the cold waters of the Greenland Sea?" He took yet another bite. "Why didn't I choose a wife and a church? Surely there were easier paths to riches. Why didn't I work in a Tromsø packing house?" He set his spoon down and knuckled the sauce from the corners of his mouth.

"You," he said to me. I'd been sitting there, studying his missing fingers, hoping to escape his attention.

"Sir?" I said.

"You're from Hammerfest, ja?"

"I am, sir."

"A fisherman, I was told."

"You were told true."

"Why have you chosen to be here? Why are you not sitting on the Sørøsundet hauling your nets?"

He might as well have asked me to explain the stars and where they slept, for all I knew about how I'd ended up at that table, and my expression must have betrayed my ignorance. But he would not relent, and soon the others turned to me, all of them awaiting my answer. "As you know, Herr Sverdrup recommended me—"

"That's not the question! I know when I took you on. I even recall what Otto said in his recommendation. But a man doesn't end up on this northern edge of the world without having looked first into the very depth of his *soul*. You, man, what did you see there?"

In the greasy light of the lamp swaying above the table, our eyes met. He grinned, but not kindly. Or perhaps it was the vacancy of his gaze, of its whiteness, that made him seem unkind. In any case, I saw in the absence of any reflection one thing that *had* led me there, and I admitted it at once. "Why, I was failing to provide for my family. It's true. And though I don't think I ever looked into the bottom of my soul, sir, the fact of my failure weighs heavily on me, and were I able to see down there I suspect I'd discover shame."

"Yes!" he said, pounding his fist on the table.

"And so I've come here to make right not only my purse but also my pride."

He raised his hands as though offering a blessing. "Our purse and our pride," he whispered, and then looked around the table. "My purse and my pride," he said again, his gaze shifting from man to man. Once it got back to me, he nodded and took another spoon of stew. "When I was a boy in Trondheim, my father was a pastor. And an ardent one at that. I used to spend my Sunday mornings in a prayer so earnest and searching that I was often accused of absentmindedness. To this day I can still recall my urgent pleas. I wanted God to shine on me. I wanted to know that He loved me. I wanted to know that salvation would be my reward. Yet I never felt it. All my life, I prayed for the wisdom to understand. I prayed for the touch of God's love." He took the last bite from his bowl, ran his fingers around inside it, licked them clean, and then looked up into the lamplight with his snowy eyes. "I prayed in churches and in taverns. I prayed in schools and in shipyards. I prayed in bunks on twenty different boats, and until that storm off the Greenland coast I prayed without answer. But there! During that six-day storm! There I found my answer."

Now he stepped to the porthole and cupped his hands around his eyes as he peered out into the darkness. Though we had found a fine lee from that storm, the *Sindigstjerna* still rocked, so did Svene's body. He stood at the window as if adjusting a load on his shoulders, then turned and pulled out his pipe. "Smoke, gentlemen." And so we took out our pipes and in solemn unity packed them and lit one another's and the aroma of stewed seal was soon replaced by the sweetness of tobacco.

"Why have we made these seas our dwelling, gentlemen? Why have we chosen these floes of ice and snow, these temperatures and gales? Why have we ventured so far away from our fellow men?" He drew a puff. "Some of you have come here thinking you might leave your past behind. Find respite from your conscience. Have you committed crimes and done misdeeds? Are you punishing yourself? Odd Einar here is restocking his pride. He's making things right for his family again. What about you?" And here he stabbed the tip of his pipe toward Mikkelsen and Andreassen and Hushovd, one-two-three. "Whatever your reason, whatever your aim, let me tell you what I learned there in Greenland."

He walked back to the table and stood above us. "It was the *Fonn* I saw in that storm." He bent at the waist so as to be closer to us all. *"The eternal snow,"* he whispered, smoke issuing from his mouth and his nostrils. "It was the answer to my lifetime of prayers."

He took another puff and turned to Eivind Hushovd. "Have you been paying attention, man? Did you see the pack at Nordaustlandet? When was the last time you looked out that porthole"—he aimed his pipe over his shoulder at the window—"and saw a world that wasn't snow and ice?"

"It's where the fattest seals live, sir," Hushovd said.

"It's also where the *truth* will be found, Eivind. Don't you see? It's all there is. Stand up, man! Stand up and have a look." He shook Hushovd by the shoulder, guiding him toward the window. "Birger, dim that lamp so Eivind here might see what I just saw." Mikkelsen reached up and dimmed the lamp until the galley was almost as dark as the night outside. Hushovd went and gazed blankly out the porthole.

"What do you see?" Svene nearly hissed, then turned back to us at the table. "Close your eyes, lads, and think about what Eivind is seeing. Listen to him tell you about it."

"I see the snow," he said, as though making a grave admission.

"What else do you see?"

"The night."

"You are preaching, friend!" Svene said. "That is the Fonn. That is the answer!" He turned yet again toward us. "Birger, bring that lamp flame up again." He did, and Svene ushered Hushovd back to his seat. "This storm will pass. We will get back to killing seals, to replenishing our purse and our pride. But that snow out there now, that snow is eternal. Hold the Fonn up as a mirror. That snow is God's answer."

He tapped his pipe empty and slipped it back in his pocket and went around the table once more, marking each of us with a look of uncommon gentleness.

We all sat in the stunned silence of his conviction until Hushovd ventured a word. "I don't recall the gospel preaching thus."

Svene raised his hand as though to bless him, or perhaps to forgive him, or merely to suggest he understood his misgivings. "Eivind, that's merely the gospel of my own experience. But let me ask: Why would you put faith in any god when this is all around you? Heaven or hell, what's the difference?"

"My second morning as a castaway, I woke to the Fonn. Or I might better say that I opened my eyes to it, as sleep eluded me."

Marius Granerud sat hunched behind his desk, scribbling. I'd been telling him about Svene Solvang's sermon in answer to his question about whether or not I thought to pray up there.

For breakfast Inger and I had sipped strong coffee with cream and sugar, had eaten roe and crackers and Danish cheese, had reveled in our simple contentment. As we stood to go, she asked whether the thought of spending more time with Granerud, dredging up the memories he meant to shape and immortalize, filled me with any sort of feeling. I told her no, and meant it, but I must admit that once sitting there across from him I *did* feel something. A cross between regret and fortitude. Regret because I understood now that my decision to accept the offer to join Svene's crew had ultimately meant the end of my faith. And fortitude because I possessed a resolve I never could've mustered with faith as a yoke.

"Of course I thought to pray, and did, you can believe," I said. "At many different times and with shifting hope, over and over. But on that morning, I can see now, I was already beginning to doubt. Even if I didn't understand why. You see, my first thoughts on that morning were not to ask God for guidance or salvation—salvation of any sort—or even forgiveness. No. My first thoughts were of the Fonn."

"The eternal snow?" Granerud clarified.

"Yes," I said. "I held myself up against it, used it as a mirror, as Svene Solvang had commanded. And the truth is, I saw myself. I understood his meaning. Even if I hadn't that night in the galley, I did that morning in the snow."

"What a terrible loss," he said.

"Beg your pardon?"

"To abandon God, in a place like that. You might have found such comfort."

"Herr Granerud, I understand your sentiment, but I must tell you it was no loss. It might have been humbling, even humiliating, to give up my belief. And it might sound like lunacy to make a covenant with that wild, falling snow. I might even have hesitated. Might have looked once behind me at what I was abandoning. But the truth is, absolving myself from the clutches of His almighty grip, forsaking the notion that all my days on earth were only an audition for the next, everlasting life, giving myself the freedom to rail against the forces of nature and my own ineptitude—all of that was a true gift."

When Granerud finished making his copious notes he glanced across his desk at me and said, "So, having forsaken God, and having found comfort in your own"—and here he double-checked his notes—"*ineptitude,* what did you do next, that snowy morn on Krossfjorden?"

"I remember this well, sir: The snow fell straight down, there was hardly a breeze, it must have been late morning because now a diffuse daylight was illuminating the snow. I unburied myself, took stock of all my belongings, and started slogging through the snow. A foot had fallen, maybe more. Everywhere I looked the world was banked in it. I thought of what Svene had said. Accepted it almost casually. And as I walked I hummed a song I used to play on my hardingfele. A song for Thea. 'Draumkvedet,' I'm sure you know it. And that simple song carried me along."

"Where were you going?" From the tone of his voice I could tell he was rapt, and I thought this was because we were getting to a part of the story he couldn't possibly have foretold. He appeared almost embarrassed, whether for himself or for me I couldn't say.

"I followed the shore of the fjord, through the snow to the base of the glacier. It was hard to tell where the sky ended and the ground began. I tell you, Herr Granerud, that while hiking up the valley of ice, searching for a passable section not rutted with crevasses or pocked with moulins, I felt a great *lightness*. As if, unencumbered by my faith, I might make haste of my situation. And indeed I did that first glacier in the Fonn. Was I sheltered from its hazards? Was the snow my salvation? Certainly it carried me that day."

I closed my eyes, hoping to draw the memory of that trek closer. I wanted to convey to my scribe the beauty and treachery of it. I wanted, I see now, to proselytize. But he was unmoved, perhaps even upset. When I opened my eyes, he set his pen down and reclined in his chair and fixed me in a blue-eyed stare that mimicked Svene's. But Granerud's eyes were penetrating, not bottomless, and we stared at each other before he raised his meaty fist and pointed at the crucifix hanging on the wall of his office. He began to speak, but only stammered and then lowered his finger and then his face.

So, still trying to conjure that morning, to make Granerud *see*, I began to sing in a voice calm and uncharacteristically clear. *"Will you hark to me, I can sing / Of a good young man / About Olav Åsteson / Who had been asleep for so long."*

He looked up as I sang on, right through the refrain that was for me then, and remains even now, a great comfort, because it reminded me that, for all of my desolation, I wandered same as any other man. *"For the moon shines / And the paths disperse so wide."*

"You sing a lovely song, Herr Eide. And I suppose it's true our paths disperse. And widely at that. But I believe those paths converge again. Do you not?"

"Some paths do. But my path goes on. I am happy to be on it."

"And Fru Eide? How does she see it?"

"You'd have to ask her."

"She strikes me as a pious woman."

"You can be sure of it."

"And she's content with a husband who believes in what... *snow*?"

"It's not a religion, Herr Granerud."

"What would you call it, then, this worshipping of snow?"

"I don't worship the snow."

He leaned forward again and consulted his notes. "You said your first thoughts were not of God—whom you had forsaken—but of the Fonn."

"Yes, but I only took comfort in how the snow obliterated me. How it made me meaningless. How, when measured against it, I was *nothing*."

"And this is still the reflection you see?"

"Yes."

"But here you are, telling me about the snow. About crossing the glacier. You seem very much alive. Very much *not* obliterated."

I looked at him for a long time before responding. "In the flesh, I *am* here. Of course. Just as I was on Spitzbergen. What I'm attempting to describe is how my spirit left me. Or rather, how I found new peace in that bleakness. It was as if I'd been pardoned from worry and guilt." I paused, and thought deeply. "Had I put my faith in God, had I trusted in His guidance, I would've perished on Krossfjorden. Instead I trusted that my death would not matter. That I myself did not matter. And I did that by seeing the hereafter not as a time spent in heaven or hell, but as time I'd spend in the eternal snow."

"A most pious heterodoxy, Herr Eide."

"You asked me if I thought to pray up there."

"And? It sounds as if you'd prayed to *snow*. What foolishness is that?"

"I did not pray to the snow. I communed with it. And in answer, the snow saved me. As you will see."

When I took leave of Marius Granerud that morning, I was unmoored. Outside his office, the gulls skimmed the rooftops, cawing their pleas, and with them I felt more kinship.

I had never considered myself an apostate, but Granerud's reaction to my description of the Fonn left me doubtful. Was it possible to renounce God yet still have some devotion to the *divine*? My revelation—if I dare call it that—had certainly changed me. I felt more holy, and closer to salvation, than I ever had before. But I also knew that others—even thoughtful people like Marius Granerud—would be scandalized by my thinking. His wondering what Inger would make of it chilled me.

She had already rebuked me. Back in Hammerfest, when I first spoke of relinquishing my faith, she had even called me blasphemous. Would her own piety and love of God supersede her love of me? *Did* she love me anymore? What thoughts these were, for a fisherman from Hammerfest. A man who, before the Fonn, had bowed his head every day of his life.

I walked back toward the hotel. Inger and I had made no plans for that day, but I assumed she'd be in our chamber. We might have lunch and then take a walk through Tromsø. If she hadn't already, she'd likely visit the church again for another hour's prayer. Granerud, no doubt changing the subject, had suggested on parting that I should take Inger to the University Museum or the opera house. Such bourgeois extravagances seemed unthinkable. But then, what else could we do? My meetings with Granerud had so far not lasted more than three or four hours, leaving so many idle hours in this foreign city that I had no clue what to do with them.

When I got to the hotel I found no sign of my wife in our quarters, other than a few strands of golden hair in her new brush sitting atop the bureau. It thrilled me to see them there, and to have Inger with me on this peculiar adventure. Given how few weeks had passed between that moment standing over her brush and the morning of the Fonn, I might've been excused for not compre-hending my whereabouts. But with each hour that passed, I felt closer and closer to being the sort of man who would regain his wits.

So off I went again, up to the church. It was now midday and snow was falling on the mountains across the sound. I paused and watched the squall line pass up the valley between two peaks, shimmering like the sea on a cloudy afternoon.

The door was locked so I walked around the church and then two blocks more to the harbor. Now the snow had engulfed the nearest peak and seemed to be shining differently. Dozens of faer-ings were tied to the wharf, and I studied them in turn until I saw one that resembled my old girl, and I stood before her overcome by nostalgia. I resolved that I would fix her up, and that together we would get back on the water and start hauling in fish again. Feel-ing strong, I walked still farther up the quay to where a schooner was tied off before the cooper. A crew of four men was loading barrels across the gangplank. On deck, a blacksmith hammered against an anvil, his forge smoking behind him.

Now the squall advanced on the city side of the sound like a cur-tain, hanging so close and thick I thought I could reach out and touch it. Beyond the end of the wharf, a fishmonger stood between two warehouse buildings. Everywhere, folks were making their liv-ings. Fishermen sold their catch, stevedores unloaded boats, ten-der men rowed out to moored frigates and barques. There were riggers and welders and wagon drivers, even a fellow mucking the horse shit around with a shovel. I stood and watched the com-motion as the snow finally reached the docks. But still the men worked, their breath steaming, their busy boots making a slurry of the muddy lane. I fingered the few øre still in my pocket, once more determined that as soon as the foolishness of telling this story was behind me, I would return home with Inger, get back among my own people, and earn an honest wage in the village where I was born. Together she and I would prosper.

Around the corner, I came upon a group of men wrestling still other barrels onto a flatbed wagon. A team of two horses—they must've stood fifteen hands—stomped their hooves and whinnied as I passed, their eyes peering at me from the shadows of their blinders. One of the laborers stopped to light a cigarette, and I asked him what they were loading.

"Mack's brygge. Taking it to the tavern."

"What tavern?" I asked.

"The cellar at the Grand Hotel, friend." He bent with his partner to heft another keg. After they'd hoisted it onto the flatbed, he removed his gloves, took a pull off his cigarette, and waved it around. "Best beer in Troms." Now he patted a barrel as though it were his horse.

I thanked him and moved on. *Why shouldn't I have a beer?* I thought. After all, things were now going well and I ought to relish my good fortune. So I walked back toward the hotel, damn well alive.

But our chamber was still empty. I thought Inger might've read Granerud's mind and gone to visit the museum. Or perhaps she was enjoying a late lunch at a café somewhere. Maybe she went for a walk out of the town center, up onto the hillside. Whatever the case, I found myself somewhere close to worried.

It bears mentioning that I was then forty-four years old. Tromsø, at some hundred and sixty miles down the sounds and fjords of Finnmark and Troms, was as far from Hammerfest as I'd ever been, excepting my voyage to Spitzbergen. Inger had never ventured farther than Alta, and that before she gave birth to Thea. The village of Hammerfest might have fit into Tromsø three or four times over. Which is to say that this new place daunted me, as I'm sure it did my wife. The thought of her lost in the hurly-burly unsettled me, and I stood there in our vacant room wondering what to do before I remembered just how savvy Inger was, and that no doubt my worries were pointless. So, I went in search of the Grand Hotel's cellar, figuring to wait for her there.

My experience in taverns was on that day original. After all, when had I ever had two øre to rub together, much less to pay for a tankard of beer?

A man with a handlebar mustache stood behind the counter,

before which were aligned stools and brass spittoons. I took a seat, asked for a beer, and, while he drew from a tap behind him, surveyed the rest of the cellar. On either side of the entryway, ice-bear skins draped the wall. Several reindeer antlers hung above the door. The whole place glowed with the guttering light of oil lamps.

I paid for the beer and swiveled around and looked off into the corners. All around the hall, stout tables carved of birch with matching chairs stood like bulwarks to sobriety. All the tables but one were unoccupied, and that by a lone man with his back to me. A candle burned in front of him, and in the wobbly light I could see a bottle and a fluted glass at his right hand.

"You're not a sporting man," the bartender said.

"True enough," I said, turning back to him.

"And you're not from Troms."

"Down from Hammerfest."

"What's your business here?"

"I'm here to conduct interviews with Marius Granerud."

He glanced at the man in the corner, then leaned across the bar and whispered, "The drittstøvel. He might try writing the truth once in a while."

The look on my face must have conveyed my surprise.

"And he's a goddamn sot. Look at him over there." Now he nodded toward the same man sitting there with the bottle.

"That's Herr Granerud?"

"The chronicler of our every misstep."

"He seems affable enough to me."

"Most liars are. Never mind the drunk ones."

I turned again in time to see Granerud pouring another ounce into his glass. "A drunk? Truly?"

"Every day after lunch, he brings his work in here. Usually I freshen his glass five or six times of an afternoon. Today he just asked for the bottle. He's been over there for two hours, scribbling away on his papers."

Now Granerud held his glass directly in the candlelight, his head tilted as though the job of conjuring my travails fell exclusively to his imagination. I watched him for several minutes, contemplating what liberties he might take with my story. Would he do such a thing? Did it matter if he did? All of the bloodletting I'd done in his office only hours ago, should I have saved that part for Inger? Or kept those bits to myself?

It's one thing to measure the fathoms of the sea, and altogether another to plumb the depths of your own lonely soul. Sometimes the wiser course is to seek the silent company of a draft of Mack's brygge, which is what I did. First one, and then another. By the time I sprouted from that cellar staircase, the world had gone dark above the spitting snow. It fell like an affirmation and so I strode along, sanguine in my newfound faith that fell through the night all around me.

But this day, which had already offered so many beguiling questions, had yet one more to ask. I checked our lodging for the third time, finding neither Inger nor any trace of her. So I walked back downstairs and asked the proprietress—a young widow named Andrea Jensen—if she had a message for me. Shaking her head, she offered the same list of possibilities that I'd already considered. She also suggested that perhaps my wife had grown weary of waiting for me while I'd wasted the afternoon in the tavern, and gone off for dinner at the café on the Strandgaten. She even insinuated that I might benefit from a square meal myself. I suppose she thought me drunk, and perhaps I was.

In any case I thanked her, then asked that if she saw Inger, she let her know I'd return after dinner myself. And with that I ventured back out into the snow, down toward the quay and a café I'd seen there on my ramblings. I ate reindeer stew and a heel of bread and paid my tab before again walking back to the hotel. Now the streets were deserted and the snow blowing as much as falling. The widow Jensen was not behind the desk, nor did she appear when I dinged the bell, so I reached across and took the key from its slot and walked back up the stairs.

The hallway was carpeted and dimly lit and I was pushing our door open just as a different door opened at the far end and out stepped Inger. There must have been thirty paces between us, but I could see a blank look on her face.

What can I say? I wouldn't have been more flummoxed if she'd appeared before me on Spitzbergen. She was wearing the same dress she'd had on for dinner at the Bjornsens' house the night I met Marius Granerud. Her long hair caught the lamplight and veiled her face like a whiteout moving along with her. She usually wore it up or in a single braid, and to see it mussed like that gave me a moment's excitement before I wondered why.

She seemed not to even notice me standing by our door as she drifted down the hallway. At least not until halfway, when she looked up and stopped suddenly where she stood. After gathering her wild locks and smoothing them behind her ears, she continued toward me and, without so much as a word, stepped right by me into our room. I followed the sweet scent of her hair, lit a lamp, and stood there looking at my wife.

She sat on the edge of the bed, unlaced her boots and took them off, then tried again to tame her hair.

"You might explain where you've been all day," I said.

"Not sitting in the tavern drinking beer," she snapped. "I can smell it from over here."

"I came looking for you several times today, Inger. It's now past nine o'clock." I crossed the room and sat on the end of the bed, our shoulders almost touching. "Yes, I had a beer in the tavern, and another with my dinner. That hardly seems profligate."

"Nor noble."

"Whose room were you visiting?"

Now she turned to face me. "The Bjornsens have arrived," she said.

I scooted closer, our knees touching now as well. "Granerud told me that you and Gerd have become friends. Confidantes, he said."

"It's true."

"You and Gerd, you were in her quarters there?" I gestured down the hall, then looked at her and brushed her hair with the back of my hand.

"Yes," she whispered. "That's right."

"And Bengt?"

"I'd have thought he was at the tavern with you."

"This is foolishness. What were you doing with Gerd so late at night?"

But instead of answering Inger rushed past me to the bureau and changed into her nightdress. She picked up her new brush and worked it through her hair until she was satisfied, then pinned it up and got under the covers.

"Should I not wonder?" I asked.

"If you must know, I was getting ready for bed—having no idea where my husband was, I might add—when Gerd knocked. Night-time is the worst for her. She gets headaches. I helped her. I waited for her to fall asleep. And now I'm here, and I'm going to sleep myself."

"I was worried," I said. But she had already turned on her side, and again gave no answer. So I, too, got ready for bed and slipped in beside her. The warmth of her body gave as little comfort as the stone cairns I'd built up against the Spitzbergen night.

When, by four a.m., she still couldn't fall asleep, she got out of bed and went to that now familiar spot at the window overlooking the town square. She would've sworn she could still see his footprints in the snow.

In the hours since Stig had left those tracks, Greta had tried to reason with herself. Why had she kissed him? Did that count as unfaithfulness? Would she do it again? The answer to each of these questions—and the countless others strafing through her mind— did not come in words, but rather in the commotion of her desire, now reverberating in her like one of the notes in "Vannhimmel." Much as his footprints were still there in the snow, the skin where he'd touched her still held the impression of his hands. Her lips were still thrilled by the memory of his own. These palimpsests paused in her mind, but then funneled like a maelstrom into her belly. A flood of need that was sexual, but also something more. She wanted to kiss him again, she wanted him to undress her, to make love to her—but she also wanted the possibility of emotional deliverance, and this man had somehow offered it.

These thoughts made her feel foolish. Wanting him, believing in her yearning, her deranged notion that he could offer her a kind of salvation—it occurred to her that she was behaving like those people who visit Paris for a weekend and suddenly decide it's their destiny to live in the shadow of the Eiffel Tower. She was a grown woman, for crying out loud. With a family and a respectable life.

She doubted she would ever even see him again. Which meant that she'd have to live with the longings of a single night. A single kiss. This notion—inevitable as it seemed—left her feeling more pathetic than ten years of a failing marriage had.

Her marriage, she thought. *Her children.*

The thought of Lasse and Liv roused hopelessness in her. Her love for them was fathomless. She could see them this very minute, as if they were asleep on the bed behind her. She could smell the sweetness of their hair. Could see Lasse's T-shirt riding up his sleeping body, and Liv's arms resting on the pillow above her head. It would be too much to disrupt that peace, wouldn't it?

The answer to that last question was unambiguous. She spun away from the window, sat down at the desk, and picked up her phone. Within minutes she'd bought a ticket on the first flight to Oslo—going through Tromsø—later that morning. She called the front desk and asked them to arrange a taxi to pick her up in three hours, took a shower and readied herself, then packed her few belongings. It was not yet five o'clock.

She took the elevator down to the lobby and stepped outside. It was warmer than it had been, and the melting snow sent up a ghostly vapor that smelled briny. Or perhaps that was the breeze off the harbor. She walked up Kirkegata to the cemetery and passed through the gate for the second time since she'd arrived. Somehow, she'd lost track of exactly how long ago that was. Two or three days? Maybe even four?

In any case, much of the snow that had greeted her then had melted, and as she walked down the lanes with her phone's flashlight on, she now could read most of the names on the headstones. The longer she walked, the greater the kinship she felt for this place. Hansen and Johnsen and Berg, Larsen and Wahl and Bergdahl. There were people buried under those same names back in Gunflint. Why this calmed her, she couldn't say. Perhaps it was merely the thought of her childhood home. Or maybe it was how quickly the world seemed to shrink with any sense of recognition. She paused in front of a bronze cross in one grouping and brought her light closer. ANNA OLAVA KNOBLOCK, it read. The only date she could make out was the year of this woman's birth, 1832. The markers on either side, she saw, were for more of the Knoblock family. In the plot in front of them, in the row closest to the fence, were several other bronze crosses. She waded through the snow and stopped, disbelieving, before one of them.

ELSKEDE

INGER ASTRID EIDE

FADT 6 NOVEMBER 1855

DSD 30 APRIL 1900

Elskede? She used her phone to translate the word: *beloved.* And only forty-four years old. Younger than Greta was now. She stepped close enough to the cross to touch Inger's name, and traced it with the tip of her finger, bringing this Inger more to life. She counted back the names. Inger begat Thea begat Odd, then Harry and then her own father, Gus. Then her. Finally, Lasse and Liv. Families were like seasons. Each built on the others.

She stared at Inger's grave. Studied the scrollwork on the cross, which looked as medieval as a Viking sword. Then, as abruptly as she'd discovered the grave, she wondered about Inger's husband, Odd Einar. She checked the other graves nearby, but there was no sign of him. As soon as she realized this, the story of what might have happened to him started to vaguely take shape in her mind. His feet would have been the last of her kin's to walk these village streets. His eyes the last to look out across the sound. That was more than a hundred years ago, and now here she was, in the polar night, almost having forgotten the kiss that had catapulted her out onto this snowy lawn at this ungodly hour.

She read Inger Astrid Eide's name and numbers with her fingers again, as though she were blind and the markings in braille. She felt a sudden and profound connection with this woman. What suffering had she endured? What poverty? What loneliness and longing? To have lost her daughter—Thea, Greta's own twice-great-grandmother—that alone was sorrow enough. She knew this part of the story. But as she stood in the cemetery, the fog rising off the snow, her own heart rent from her body, Greta could feel not only the suffering and sorrow and longing, but, she imagined, the thrill of an *elskede*. A man like Stig.

She stayed over the grave for an hour, absorbing all she could. She even heard herself talking out loud, telling herself the story of this woman and her husband. Of their intimacies and their illnesses. Of the disease that took her life. Of the grief that gave him freedom. Before she left, she took a picture of Inger's grave. And as she walked away, she could hear Inger saying goodbye.

Walking back to the hotel, she practiced mimicking Inger's voice. Greta knew that to any passerby she would seem crazy, but she hardly cared. By imagining their lives, she was already feeling more connected to herself. She would live vicariously through their ghosts. She would let herself be haunted. And that would be enough.

She had to let that be enough.

She went up to her room and washed her hands and looked around for anything she might've missed. Stig's red sweater was folded over the back of the chair, and she pondered whether or not to bring it along. How could she explain this well-worn wool? She couldn't bring it home. Or could she fold it up and put it in one of her boxes of extraneous clothes in her closet? She could let it be the memory she allowed herself. Hidden away, taken out only when she was alone and needed a reminder of how beautiful life could be. Shaking that thought from her head, she left the sweater draped over the chair.

In the lobby there were bananas in a wooden bowl next to the coffee machine. She poured herself a cup and peeled a banana and set her things in front of the same window she and Stig had drunk aquavit at only hours before. The same sleepy-eyed receptionist was still behind the desk, and when Greta asked, the woman handed her a few sheets of hotel letterhead and a ballpoint pen. Greta went back to the table by the window and started making notes about the Norwegian husband and wife who would save her.

Two hours later, at eight, Greta folded the letterhead—by then four full sheets covered with her handwriting—and put them in her purse and gave the pen back to the receptionist.

"We don't have very many visitors this time of year," she said. "And now you are leaving so soon. What was your business, if I may ask?"

"My family came from here. Part of it did, anyway. I guess I just wanted to see."

"What is your family name?"

"Eide."

"Yes, of course," she said.

Of course? Greta wondered.

"So you see where your family is from and also meet the most handsome man in Finnmark." She raised her eyebrows. "Too bad you have to leave now."

"Yes," Greta said. "It really is too bad."

"But there's your taxi." She pointed out the window.

Greta slung her bag over her shoulder and glanced at the receptionist. She wanted to say that, yes, Stig was handsome, but also much more than that. He was divine. He had, in one night, changed how she understood her life. This conclusion gave Greta pause—enough to realize that, to anyone, such a proclamation would sound like the stuff of a high school crush—and she wondered if she'd inflated the entirety of the experience. Instead of saying anything about him, Greta simply thanked the woman for her stay and walked out to the taxi.

The driver got out and put Greta's bag in the trunk, then opened the back door and closed it behind her. "To the airport?" he asked over his shoulder.

"Yes, please."

He put the car in gear, turned on the meter, and started up Kirkegata.

"Could you drive by the church on the way?"

"Of course." At the church, he rolled slowly to a stop and Greta lowered her window. Fog rested atop the bell tower. She closed her eyes and listened in her mind to the song he'd played on the organ, letting it come alive, and it still sounded sublime. She snapped a picture of the church with her phone, then opened the door, stepped out to have a last look at the cemetery, and took a shot of that too. Finally, she whispered goodbye and got back into the cab.

The driver turned right past the church and then right again on Sørøygata, toward the harbor and the bench they'd sat on the night before. He drove past the Scandic Hotel, where she'd heard him play the piano and first learned his name. And just as Greta was putting Stig in the right compartment of her heart, there he was, walking quickly toward her hotel at a few minutes past eight in the morning, his feet crossing the same tracks he'd made when leaving. The sight of him stole her breath. He must've heard the taxi because he turned to look, and then froze when his eyes fell on her. He raised his hand—to say goodbye? to stop the taxi?—as the driver turned the corner, and only ten minutes later she was stepping through the airport's only entrance.

In how many ways would she be undone? During the course of the last week, she'd admitted she didn't love her husband and followed her impulse to chase Frans over here, only to end up in Hammerfest. She'd met Stig and decided, for the sake of her children, to leave him there in the Arctic night, despite her gaping hunger. She'd tracked down the ghosts of her ancestors and given her imagination the license to spirit her off. All of it seemed to happen without her registering these tectonic shifts in the balance of her life. But none of them had shaken her like the look on Stig's face as her taxi drove on. That look would be her final undoing.

Now, sitting at the airport, another cup of coffee trembling in her hands, she tried to picture the scene on the quay in Hammerfest a hundred and twenty-odd years ago, Inger and Odd Einar taking turns saying goodbye to their daughter, not knowing if they'd ever see her again. What was the look on Thea's face that day? Did it resemble Stig's? And what had Greta's face told him in return?

Had it seemed thankless, or regretful? What if he would never know how much meeting him—hearing him play his music, talking and laughing with him, conjuring the snowfall, kissing him, all of it—had meant to her?

Now the same woman who had sold her a cup of coffee in the café upstairs was poised by the door that led onto the tarmac, testing the microphone. Then she spoke in garbled Norwegian and a few of the other passengers gathered their belongings and queued up, presented their tickets, and went outside to the plane. Greta checked the boarding pass on her phone, as though it might offer some sign or instructions.

Another announcement came over the waiting area, and now everyone else stood up and moved toward the gate. Greta went to the back of the line—there were only twenty or so passengers—and clenched her eyes shut. Now she *did* see Thea Eide standing on the quay saying goodbye to her life in this inhospitable and magical place. She saw the expressions of love and sadness on Inger's and Odd Einar's faces. She saw the ocean of opportunity and the fear of a new land in Thea's imagination. She saw a woman a third her age, embarking on the voyage of a lifetime without benefit of the language she would need, without money, without friendship or even a familiar face. She saw a bravery she'd never possessed herself, because, why would she? What sort of courage had ever been required of her? In herself she saw a moral failure, or an ineptitude, at living. If she were being honest, she saw cowardice. Her eyes were still shut, and now she put the heels of her palms against her eyelids and pressed. There was darkness ahead—the husband she did not love, but instead of being angry at him she felt something more like sadness. For both of them, because she could not stay with him. She could no longer be fainthearted. She couldn't live the rest of her life feigning devotion and pretending to return his love. Because he *did* love *her*. She knew that. Despite his dalliances with Alena Braaten, despite his own aloofness. And he would fight for her. She was sure of that too. All of this taken together meant that she was going to hurt him, if not ruin him. Despite her deep resentment, that prospect brought her no satisfaction. On the contrary, it felt like an enormous onus that she immediately cast from her thoughts.

Then she saw Lasse and Liv again and again and again. She saw both her children and the aura of love she kept in her vision of them. What would happen to this sacred love? Or was it better to ask: What would happen to their love for her? Would they feel the shroud of its protection vanish? Would they abandon her? Hate her? Would they choose their father? She saw herself—there in the darkest part of her vision—without their love, and knew that she could never allow that to occur. She would never countenance any of those losses. She would make loving them the most important thing in her life. She would preserve it. She would make it even stronger. She'd become a better mother by becoming a better person. She would laugh with them and play with them and romp through the woods with them like she hadn't done for years now. She would show them how a woman could remake herself, in her own image. She would become, Greta would, more like her own beautiful mother.

"*Hallo?*"

Greta opened her eyes. She had not moved since she closed them. The last person before her in line was passing through the door onto the runway.

"*Er du ombordstigning?*" The agent raised her eyebrows, then added, "Time to board."

"No," Greta said. Simply. Declaratively. The light in the airport hall was shining from above and below, reflecting off all the tile floors. "I've changed my mind." She reached down for her bag. "I've changed my mind," she said again. "I won't be leaving today."

The woman didn't say anything in response, just turned toward the door, stepped out onto the tarmac, and disappeared.

Greta took a deep breath, then slowly exited the airport. Outside, she rubbed her eyes and opened them wide and looked up at the stars and moon, shining like daylight. She saw his face—Stig's—as if he were standing in the choir loft in the church. So easily did he occupy her mind. She glanced around, to make sure she was alone, and whispered, "Are you sure?"

In answer, she went across the parking lot and knocked on the window of the same cab that had dropped her off. She told the driver to return to the Hotel Thon, and five minutes later she hurried back into the lobby. The same woman who had bidden her goodbye remained behind the counter. When she saw Greta, she smiled, and held up her finger for a moment before bending down to reach under the counter, then she held Stig's red sweater out before her. "You left something," she said, to which Greta said, "Yes, I did."

All night a wild wind came down Grøt Sund, rattling the windows at the Grand Hotel and stirring snow and grit up off the Storgata to spit against the panes. In the morning, it roused me from my wayward sleep. Inger woke, too, and together we got ready for breakfast with hardly a word between us. The café was empty but for the maid setting the tables. She showed us a seat by the window and brought us strong tea and brown bread with butter and a boiled egg and we ate in silence. It was hard to tell which appealed less to Inger's appetites, the food or my company. Indeed, she would nary look at me, and only as we sipped the last of our tea did she say anything at all.

"You'll be going to Marius Granerud's again this morning, then?"

"Of course."

"First thing?"

"After breakfast. He's eager to continue. No doubt he'd like to be finished as much as I would myself."

"When will that be?"

"Who can say? I've spoken with him only about the first two days."

"At that rate we'll be here until the start of Advent."

I'd never known Inger to embroider the facts, and it did not become her. "The meetings with Granerud might as well be counted as mornings spent at the oars and nets."

She took a drink of tea and then pursed her lips. "You had trouble sleeping last night."

I glanced at her.

"I saw you up, sitting at the desk in the middle of the night. What were you doing?"

I touched my pocket under the table, to feel that my letter for Thea was still there. "I made a list of things to tell Herr Granerud. The memories, sometimes they wake me and I'll lay there thinking about them. But when I get to his office, they've left my mind altogether."

Inger rarely exaggerated, and I rarely told a lie. It felt unnatural to keep the truth tucked into my pocket. The fact was, I'd spent my sleepless hours contemplating things I would never tell Granerud, not if we had a lifetime of interviews.

Another gust rocked the window, this one startling my wife. "Will this wind bring more snow?" she asked. Though she knew as well as I did what kind of wind portended snow, what shadows at midday meant thunder by sundown, what chill on the evening air meant frost on the windows by morning, I could tell from the inflection of her voice that this wind reminded her of a very particular season of storms, one neither of us would ever be able to forget.

I knew all this, but still I said, "Hard to say." Then I dabbed the corners of my mouth with the napkin. "Should I plan on taking lunch with you?"

"If you can avoid stopping at the tavern, I don't see why not."

I fixed her with a hard gaze and then got up to leave.

"I've never know you as a drinking man, Odd Einar."

I turned back to her. "I'm no more a drinking man than I am a member of the King's court, and you damn well know it." I thought to rage more, but in truth I didn't even know what I was angry about, so I put on my coat and walked out of the café. On the Storgata the wind came with sharp sleet. I didn't need to glance skyward to know more snow would come hard on its heels.

Even from a block away, I could hear the water tossing in the sound and followed its noise until I stood at a piling on the wharf. There was a schooner coming down from the north, her sails down, her exhaust harried into the gale the instant it coughed out of the stack. The boat looked like a larger version of the *Sindigstjerna* as I watched it navigate the treacherous seas. The captain was attempting to bring her portside to a dock in front of the brewery, though the waves allowed little progress, and she was soon coming astern for another approach. That's when I noticed her Danish ensign. I looked closer, and sure enough the schooner attempting to dock was the very boat that had washed ashore in Hammerfest during the storms of 'eighty-two. The *Tifældighed*. How could I forget her? Half of her hundred feet had lain aground at the foot of the church, so you could nearly have walked off the bowsprit right into the narthex.

Having glimpsed that memory, I fell headlong into recollection. Thea was not yet three years old when the first hurricane struck in January. My God, I can still hear the wind and see the seas breaking on land that had forever been dry. Two days it rained and snowed and blew a tempest and when finally on the third morning we woke to calm, our stock of awe was long spent. Whole docks were rent from shore in the village, two warehouses on the water reduced to rubble. I believe the first shock of those storms destroyed eighteen fishing boats and ten townsfolk in Hammerfest. In villages out on the open sea, in Sørvær and Hasvik and Loppen and countless others, whole houses vanished, along with the families who lived in them.

Our own hovel was a simple sod-covered hut out on Muolkot. The northern half of our home was carved into the earth, and the half facing the village was built out of logs. The onslaught brought ankle-deep floodwaters into our dwelling, but it was otherwise valiant against the storm—my sweet young daughter less so. Goodness, how the wind scared her. Having never been much for fussing or crying, she spent those two nights in sleepless terror. Neither my lullabies nor my hardingfele could calm her, and her keening harmonized with the weather outside.

In the following two weeks, we put our place back together. We helped our neighbors in the village—fetching lost nets or buoys, mending houses, washing laundry, cooking fiskesuppe and lefse for those who'd lost everything. Those days showed us the best of each other, and as January turned to February, Thea regained her childish spirit. She played in the snow. Sang alongside me. Went to sleep without holding my hand.

But bitterer weather lay ahead, and in the shortest month our skies began to turn three days before the second hurricane fell upon us. This one also from the north, bearing even more elemental force. The wind in this round came hardest the first night, as if it had been born in the bowels of hell and used for its fuel all the hate of the demons dwelling down there. Even Inger lost that night's sleep.

I remember holding Thea, walking with her between her bed and our own, making promises I could never deliver—ones I had to believe myself so as to survive this pitch-black ordeal. The second night brought with it the cold, and the next morning, after a few hours of lucky sleep, we woke to a world hard as steel. We dressed in all we had and rowed to town. The sea itself was proof of the storm's wrath. The mast of an unlucky ship, its halyards trailing like the tentacles of a Kraken, its sail unfurled and nothing more than a shadow in the depths. A flock of exhausted sheep, their long coats a certain death knell, swimming in circles a hundred yards off, their baaing an unholy testimony. There were uncountable oars and barrels and unmanned skiffs, countless boards and planks and doors. Gulls circled above the flotsam like accountants, calling out an inventory of loss, one atop a bobbing chest with its left wing broken and wavering in what gale remained.

I knew the words I'd consoled Thea with the night before might as well have vanished in that wind. What good was I to her in a world capable of such devastation? I looked at her there in Inger's lap, feeling certain we would be swallowed up. Later that morning, as stragglers filled the church pews, I prayed that I was wrong. What others prayed for I might've guessed, given our congregation's solemnity.

Yet for another two weeks we all worked together, replacing

windows and roof shingles, cooking and cleaning and salvaging wood for fireplaces and stoves. Inger's sister, Hege, broke her arm in the storm, and her husband, Rune, swore they would leave this godforsaken country the next summer, which they did. But before that summer came, before they could liquidate their lives on this icy shore to make a new one nigh four thousand miles westward, they had to endure the worst of the three hurricanes that winter's season.

Later in my life I would remember this last as the cruelest, without knowing if that was actually true. We were in awe of the first round, in terror of the second, and furious with the finale. Perhaps it was fatigue. Maybe the challenge of surviving three in such close proximity felt like God was taunting us. Or possibly it merely inconvenienced us beyond any measure, taking as it had my faering and lying it atop the hillside on Håja—four miles across the sound—as though it were a kite. In fairness to the Lord or the wind it was set down upon that grass with such a gentleness that it had no need of repair. I had all but given her up for lost when Magnus Moen came rowing up to check on us in the town tender.

"Odd Einar, Inger, sweet child," he said, pulling ashore on Muolkot, our first visitor since the storm passed two days earlier. He brought with him a basket of fresh bread and cheese, a jar of milk.

"How are things in the village?" I asked.

"There's a Danish ship aground," he said. "At the door of the church, which is about the only building still standing."

I remember wiping my eyes, trying to conjure what he'd just described.

"I figured you must've lost your boat, else we'd have seen you in town with a hammer to help."

"Ja," I said, and could say no more. Without my boat, we were as good as dead.

"Well, my friend, grab your mitts and a length of rope, if you have one left, and come with me."

Under any other circumstances I'd have asked why, but I only had to glance at Inger to know that I must follow. We rowed out to Håja and spent a half hour scaling that mighty hill. There she sat, my boat.

"How in God's name did you know she was here?" I asked Magnus.

"I saw it in a dream," Magnus said, "and I mean that true. Toralv Hagen and I came out to check his flock earlier this morning, and I went for a look. She sat then just as she does now. You'll need new oars and a mast, and you'll have to visit Skjeggestad to see about new lines too. But a luckier boat I've never seen."

I believed him. How many died we never did learn, but the storms assaulted Norway from the Lofoten Islands to Vardø. In the end, it took the largesse of a German Kaiser, an English Queen, and a Russian Tsar to rebuild Hammerfest, right down to oars and rope for our boats.

As I reached Granerud's office that day in Tromsø, the wind still rising, I'd replayed that storm right up to when Magnus had reminded me of how lucky I was. I wondered, as I stamped the snow from my boots and brushed my shoulders clear of it, whether he'd been right back then and if that luck had held. In any case, when I was finished with Granerud on this day, I vowed to rewrite Thea's letter. I would ask if she remembered those hurricane nights and the songs I sang and played for her. I would state simply that my love for her had anchored me then, and it still did.

"I'm happy to see you this morning, Herr Eide!" Granerud stood as his secretary led me into his office, and hustled around his desk wiping the crumbs of breakfast from his waistcoat. "Please, have a seat. That's one hell of a blow out there, ja?" I'd never seen him so animated. "Please bring us a pot of tea, Herr Rudd." He spun back to face me. "Is there anything else I can get you? Have you had breakfast?"

"Thank you. But I don't need anything else. Inger and I had our breakfast at the hotel this morning." Though curious about his great excitement, I didn't ask what had brought it on.

"Sit down, sit down." Now he hurried back to his side of the desk and quickly organized his papers. Then taking his seat, he said, "I've been thinking over what you said yesterday. In fact, I haven't stopped thinking about it since." He spoke rapidly, even as he readied his pen and ink. "After we adjourned, I went off to lunch and—"

Now his man carried in a tray of tea. Granerud motioned for him to set it on the sideboard and then waved him out of the room.

"Anyway, I couldn't help wondering the sequence of thoughts that would have to pass through a man's mind . . ." He suddenly stopped speaking, and looked at me directly for the first time since I'd arrived. Sitting back and removing his monocle, he said, "Is everything all right, Herr Eide? You look as if you've seen a ghost."

I got up and poured a cup of tea, then sat back down. "Do you remember the hurricanes of 'eighty-two, Herr Granerud?"

"How could anyone forget?" Now he made himself a cup as well. "I was working for the *Morgenbladet* then, with an office in Trondheim, but as luck—if that's the word—would have it, I was in Narvik when the third wave crashed in. I wrote a story about the Bjerkeengen family. Perhaps you remember those people? Their story caused quite a sensation back then."

I shook my head.

"Well, they lived out in Svolvær, on the Vestfjorden. A fisherman he was. Six children. Married to a second wife. Good Christians all. The second youngest child was a girl named Margrit, who I believe was nine or ten years old." He took a sip of tea. "Dear Lord," he said "the day after the storm passed, another fisherman from Leines was out recovering what he could of his nets when he saw a skiff across the water. Mind you, this was not uncommon in the days following the storms. No doubt you know this firsthand. But he saw the skiff and he went to retrieve it. And do you know who he found inside?"

I shook my head again.

"Little Margrit Bjerkeengen. She was all alone. Dressed warmly, it's true. But alone. She'd spent a full day and night on the sea. Adrift in her father's boat. When that old fisherman found her in there and asked her where she was from, and what she was doing in the boat all by herself, she simply told him her name and that she came from Svolvær.

"Bear in mind, this child was thirty or forty miles from Svolvær. The storm had passed, but do you remember the cold that followed? And that poor child alone in the boat." He paused here, and I noted the change in his demeanor. He'd gone from bustling to moribund in the space of half a cup of tea, but he wasn't done with this story. He sat back in his chair and folded his hands over his paunch.

"When they returned the girl to her home, nothing was left of it but the stones of its footings. Every board used to build it, every plate the family ate from, every doll Margrit ever played with, every one of her five siblings, both of her parents—vanished, all of it. All of *them*."

He paused again, transfixed by the glow of his desk lamp. Outside his windows, the sleet of a half hour ago had turned to driving snow. "Margrit went to live with an aunt in Narvik." He shook his head, as if to lose this painful memory. "Yet I saw her again. I went to see a performance of *A Doll's House* in Christiania, and do you know who played Nora Helmer?"

"Margrit?"

"I like to think I'd have recognized her, but in truth she only looked vaguely familiar. I opened the playbill though, and with God as my witness, there was her name. Margrit Bjerkeengen." He raised his eyes from the lamp flame and set them on me. "As I recall she gave a fine performance. A few times after, I read her name in the paper. Usually it was followed by some small praise, and I wondered what the critics might say if they'd seen the face of that little girl on the boat."

Now he caught himself. "I beg your pardon, Herr Eide. You asked if I remembered the hurricanes and here I am at the Christiania Theater ten years later."

I pointed at the windows behind his desk, where snow made the wind visible by falling slantwise. "Weather of this sort puts me in mind of those hurricanes. In Hammerfest, during the storm a boat called *Tifœldighed* ran aground. Right in the middle of town. If you can believe it, I saw the very same vessel attempting to dock this morning."

"Men and ships—both persevere."

"And daughters," I said. "My Thea was two years old in 'eighty-two. But she knew enough to be terrified of those storms." Now I paused to consider the lamp flame. "I guess it's the storms we keep in our memories."

"Yes, you'd asked if I kept them in mine."

"And your answer was yes. Why is it we harbor those recollections?"

"I reckon ease and pleasure don't go far in marking our constitution."

"Yet, isn't ease and pleasure what we strive for?"

"Do we?"

"Give me the choice, and I'll take them every time."

"So you could be a man like Bengt Bjornsen?"

"With a spacious home, with bounteous food, with money he'll never even need?"

"But also a man without conscience, without integrity, without children. Without love." He paused, weighing the rightness, it seemed, of what he'd say next. "Without any experience of loss or travail?"

"You overestimate the benefit of loss, I think."

"Perhaps."

"To say nothing of travail."

"Suffering makes a man. My father taught me that, and I believe it to this day."

"Then I'd be happy to think myself made by now."

He gave me that segue grin of his, the one I'd already learned meant the time had come to return to our occupation. Without waiting for his prompting, I brought us back to Spitzbergen. "Now I will try your tactic, Herr Granerud. You said yesterday that you think our paths—however widely they disperse—converge again. I believe you're likely right. How else to explain my sitting here with you?"

"So I've convinced you of *something*, then."

Now I grinned. "Oh, I was far afield. As far as a man can get, I think. Then *and* now. So, let me tell you about the rest of my time up there without further digression. I'm a simple man, and I ought to let the story speak for itself. God, the Fonn, these things are like the weather or the polar night. I'll now stick to putting one foot in front of the other."

"I rather appreciate your digressions."

"I don't trust myself to make sense, sir. Besides, once I took my first step onto that inscrutable glacier, when I felt its great firmness beneath those komagers even as I looked across its jagged and crevassed shell, when I felt the strange, cold wind that seemed to come up from the ground as much as down from the sky, when I caught that otherworldly scent, one I can only describe as *blue*... why, then I gave *all* my thoughts to the path right before me. Or rather, what would become the path. You can believe I did."

He started to speak, but I raised my hand before a word came out of his mouth. "I will tell you," I said, "about crossing the glaciers. About those days of harrowing blindness."

You might have thought, given my time on and around Spitzbergen—in the fog and in the snow; plying waters as far off as Nordaustlandet and Kvitøyjøkulen, closer to Franz Josef Land than to the Isfjorden; on the everlasting floes, where even the blue glacial ice had grown into something hoary and gray—that I'd been trained to have a second sight, one that comprehended and categorized the laws of polar whiteness, and saw through it. But that was not the case.

From a distance, the glaciers seemed little more than gentle fields of new fallen snow. But the first thing you should know about my maiden steps into the slud is that I was instantly cast into an invisible realm. It was one thing to witness the blankness of that snow-shrouded land from a ship at anchor or a killing boat or even a cairn of sheltering stone, and quite another to stand upon it. The mountain above me, whose base I'd traversed on the glacier line for a mile or more before venturing onto the ice, had disappeared as if it had never existed, or that some mix of fog and mist and snow and cloud had swallowed it altogether. So suddenly did this happen that I staked my hakapik in the ground before me just to know which way was forward. For each step I took, that planted stick guided me.

Oh, that godforsaken slog. I went along like this for an hour or more, stumbling in the deep snow, pitching down into troughs invisible in the gloom, rising again on the steel head of the hakapik. Sometimes even that bloodstained thing was invisible before me, at only an arm's length. In the absence of sight, I attuned my other senses instead.

Do you know what it's like to hear the exhalation of your breath or your weary grunts as you fall waist-deep into a skavl of snow, knowing those lamentable sounds will never meet the ear of friend or foe? Or, worse, to hear the echoes of the men from decades past likewise lost in the Fonn and know—to be almost certain—that your own grunts and gasps were merely joining the chorus of such lost souls? Why would you walk on? Why not lie down right there and welcome the inevitability of your fate? Why would you not seize what little dignity and control you had left?

My own thoughts ran this treacherous course as I plodded on. The only change in the atmosphere was that the smell of the sea, which had accompanied me since I'd first left Hammerfest under Otto Sverdrup's command, now vanished. I had gone that far from shore. I wondered if ever in my life I'd been so distant from it, and probably I hadn't.

Another hour, and still the murkiness would not relent. I moved on—hakapik, foot, foot—with my face upturned to the snow and drizzle, welcoming the cold sting on my face, for it served as solid proof I was still alive. And because I could not tolerate being so alone, I thought of my sweet Thea. I convinced myself that this ice and snow was the conveyance of her prayers for me. For as sure as I toiled upon that glacier, so would my daughter toil upon her faith; she was Inger's daughter on that account, through and through.

I thought that if I could recall her voice singing along with my hardingfele, I might be spared the awful ruminations about my solitude.

So I did. And for another hour, I moved along—hakapik, foot, foot, over and over—into my daughter's voice guiding me, certain that I had found the middle of the Fonn and that here I would meet my end. Oh yes, I would die thirsty. Without having eaten a morsel in some three days. Without a single thought of my grace and salvation, or of the peace that might've attended it. But I was untroubled. Indeed, I might have already been lying down, the snow entombing me on that wondrous glacier. And this was its own kind of peace—that I could be dead without even noticing. Without pain or trouble. With only the memory of Thea as my parting vision.

But the Fonn wasn't ready for me. Or perhaps I wasn't ready for it. By then, I had paused in my drift across that old ice cosseted in new snow. Whether to rest my feet or take my death slowly, who can say? But I *had* stopped, of that I'm sure. And was sucking on a mittenful of snow. When in the brume above me I glimpsed four black smudges eddying in the whiteness, at first there seemed no logic to this movement. But the longer I watched, the more clearly I detected a pattern. Almost as if the specks were drawing a circle around me. What pleasure this thought brought me, that I would be granted this final respect. *Here* sits Odd Einar Eide! These are the bounds of his final rest! I was now more sure than ever that I would soon close my eyes and never open them again. I even made a small ceremony of this last act, bidding an eternal farewell to Inger and Thea and tearing up at my love for them.

But just as I was giving myself over I heard the unmistakable cry of the krykkje, so close it seemed like a kiss on my cheek. Again and again it called. I opened my eyes and saw, above the bird's gray wings, a halo: the sun, relieving the Fonn. It called again. A familiar sound imploring, *Get up! Get up!*

Now the krykkje circled low enough that I might've reached up and touched it. Low enough that I could see its black eyes and the gray shadow running along the tops of its wings. How often had these birds harassed my fishing boat? How often had I scorned this nuisance? A thousand times? Never once had I regarded this bird's loveliness. Never once heard that cry and thought it a melody to the song of my life.

My life!

Unfolding myself from the snow, I picked up the hakapik and again planted it ahead of me and took another step. Then the krykkje did something I'd never seen one do before. It pulled its wings up and landed about ten paces before me. I fell toward its beckoning call, then rose, and fell again. When I got close enough to pet its little head, it took wing, circled, cried for me, and landed again another ten strides apace.

That bird led me to the far edge of the glacier. When my feet found the purchase of the mountain's scree, my guide alighted on a ledge of rock just out of reach. Its yellow beak opened as if to loose another cry, but none came. It cocked its head, its tiny eyes prying. I lowered my head—in thanks and exhaustion—and looked up to the gentle whoosh of my bird taking flight. Its work complete.

I had crossed the first glacier. In a blinding fog, no less. Without food in my belly or water on my tongue. I closed my eyes again, longer this time, until I felt a warmth on my lids. When I opened them, the sun had come through the fog. I looked down the bay on which, three days afore, I'd merrily been slaughtering seals with Birger Mikkelsen. It was clogged with floes, all of them snow tufted. Slowly, the farthest shore came into the light of the sun. A white field broken only by the stone cairn under which I'd pretended sleep for two nights.

Now I looked at the shoreline I'd next have to travel. I knew a formidable mountain towered at the end of the headland, but the route before it—at least from where I stood—appeared passable, and not such an endless distance. I removed my mitten and held my thumb at arm's length. I measured first the distance between the sun and the mountaintop toward which it fell. There might have been two hours of daylight left, which made the time somewhere near two o'clock. Ideal for afternoon tea. But the closest I could get was to suck more snow and sweat from my mitten, so I put it back on and did exactly that.

I took a last look around for my friend the krykkje. But again I was standing alone. I checked my gear and hefted the hakapik over my shoulder and went toward the flats, uncertain of everything except that I had not died on the glacier. And this thought itself spurred me on. I reached that evening's resting spot with an hour of daylight left. An hour I used to build a mound of snow to sleep under.

Later that day, she found Stig back at the Scandic Hotel. He was playing the piano again, but once Greta walked in he took his hands from the keys, lowered the fallboard, and steadied his gaze on her. He wore a different sweater. A gray and cable-knit turtleneck whose collar broke like a wave in the tangle of his beard, accentuating his strong jaw. She stood there as though waiting for a table, half of which were full and all of them flickering with candlelight even at lunchtime.

He stopped and spoke briefly to the waitress—not Ava, an older, almost matronly woman, kind-eyed, Greta could tell, even from a distance—who kissed him on the cheek and touched his forearm before letting him go.

When he reached Greta, he took her by the arm and kissed her on the cheek like the waitress had just kissed him. "Hello," he whispered. "Thank God."

He picked up her bag and led her out into the noonday darkness, under the streetlights, and stopped at his car. An old Audi wagon. He opened the passenger door, shut it behind her, and put her suitcase in the backseat. In the time it took him to walk around and get in himself, she'd noted two CDs on the dash, First Aid Kit's *The Lion's Roar* and Shostakovich's *Preludes and Fugues for Piano;* a pack of mint gum in a nook below the stereo; an empty but stained coffee cup wedged between his seat and the parking brake; a pair of leather gloves; one of those hand grip exercisers; a handheld tape recorder. The car smelled of all these things. Her breath was visible in the cold.

He turned on the ignition before shifting toward her. She was already looking at his beautiful profile, and when he faced her she took a deep, catching breath. She wanted him to kiss her, but he only reached over and took her hand. She had still not spoken a word and found no desire to do so. She was more than happy just to sit there with him. To be in his company and set aside the thoughts that had been spinning in her like a windmill for several weeks. She felt easy. She felt ready. If he'd said he was going to drive her to Paris, she would've nodded and smiled.

Instead he said, "Can I show you my boat?"

"Hi," she said. "Stig," she said, then took a very deep breath. "After I saw you in the church, I went back to the hotel and had a drink sitting at the window. You know that sculpture on the harbor?"

"Of course," he said.

"I imagined you on a boat. I thought you had good hands for a boat."

"Good hands for a boat?"

She took one of his in hers, looked at it, and said, "Yes, show me your boat."

He still didn't kiss her, simply put the car in gear and looked over his outside shoulder and pulled onto the street. He drove ahead for two blocks and turned right and drove by the square—she saw the Hotel Thon, where she'd checked back in, and got the same room at the corner on the seventh floor—and then past the church and cemetery and out of town. She had no idea how much of a drive she was settling into, but when he didn't switch the stereo on, she guessed it wasn't long.

And she was right. Rypefjord was only a couple of miles over the hill, quiet and seeming almost deserted. He parked in front of a small, two-story house with a deck on the second floor and a gravel driveway and came around and opened her door and took her hand.

"Whose house is this?" The windows were dark.

"It is my mom's house. Or it was her house. I guess it is my house now."

"Is there something wrong with it?"

He looked at her, confused.

"Since you live on your boat," she said.

"I am happy on my boat. I am trying to sell this." He gestured at the house. "She did not leave me much. But this is at least something."

Greta turned to scan the water and then back to him. "Well?"

They walked down to a dock where the *Vannhimmel* bobbed against fenders tied to pilings. There was another boat docked beyond Stig's, a fishing boat with its cabin lit up and its engine idling.

Stig jumped down onto the deck, then held his hand up for her. She jumped, too, and he was quick to put an arm around her waist. "This is her," he said, as if there might be some confusion.

He motioned toward the stern and she walked along the railing, holding the rigging to steady herself. As she stepped down into the companionway, the boat's white decking caught the pearlescent reflection of the noon sky. She stumbled, and he caught her by the elbow. From behind, he used his other hand to unlatch the cabin door, his body pressing into her, a minty scent on his breath. And warmth. Even in the chill air, she could feel it exuding from him.

He lit a small lamp and the tidy cabin came into view: a galley and a sitting area, an electronic keyboard on a shelf above the settee, and a loo off the bedroom cabin. She sat at the table and surveyed everything again. For such a large boat, belowdecks it seemed awfully small. Especially given the size of Stig, who had to cock his head to stand at the counter.

Now she watched him take two glasses from a shelf above the sink and a bottle of aquavit from a cabinet. For all his bulk, he moved gracefully. Like he could perform any task aboard that boat with his eyes closed. My God, his eyes seemed to fill the two glasses with warmth even before he tilted the bottle, which he did then, holding it first in her direction to make sure she'd like one.

"Yes," she said, and then, "I was going to leave."

"I know this."

"I went to the airport this morning. I was in line to fly back to Oslo."

He poured them each a finger of aquavit and brought the glasses to the table, handing one to her and offering a silent toast with his. She felt the almost imperceptible undulations here on the water, and could see, out the porthole window behind him, the boat seeking its level.

"Why did you not leave?"

Taken aback by the question, she picked up her drink and took a sip, then another. "How could I?"

He must have been embarrassed, because he put his own drink up to his lips.

"I'm married," she said. "And I have two children."

"What are their names?" he said from behind the glass, as easy as if he'd already heard about them.

"Lasse and Liv." Just saying their names made everything more complicated.

"How old are they?"

"Thirteen and eleven."

"How old are you?"

"Old enough to know better," she said, and heard in this answer her mother's voice. For an instant she regretted saying it, but then felt, as if her whole body wanted to come clean, that she was in fact *herself*. "That sounded glib and silly."

"Glib?"

"Sarcastic. Or something. I'm forty-eight."

"I do not believe you."

She took another small sip of her drink. "Let's not do that."

"What?"

"Act like we're supposed to. Say the things we're supposed to say. Joke and make compliments."

"I thought you were thirty-five. Maybe thirty-eight." He sounded wounded.

"I bet you're younger," she said. "Forty-two."

"I am forty-two."

She drank the rest of her aquavit and handed him the glass. While he poured her another she glanced around the cabin again. Books on a shelf. Cushions on the settee. Cabinets. Windows. And a cork-board with photographs: polar bears, walruses, icebergs, reindeer, glaciers, kittiwakes and gulls, and one of a little girl. Greta walked over and bent closer to look.

"That's Kjersti Anne," he said.

"What a beautiful girl." She took one more look and stood up straight. "She looks just like you."

Stig handed her the aquavit. "She died almost three years ago."

"Oh, Stig."

"Cystic fibrosis. Seven years old." He got lost looking down at the little, braided girl in the photograph. She sat on a toboggan in the snow, her cheeks wind-kissed, her eyes as brilliant as the sky through the skylight on his boat. When Stig turned back to Greta, he said, "She was so beautiful."

"I can see that. I'm so sorry. I can't imagine."

"You have two children. You can very well imagine."

She moved to the settee now and sat down, and Stig sat across from her on a leather chair.

He crossed his legs and took a sip of his drink. "She died when I was gone. For work. This is why Jorunn blames me."

The burden of being apart from Liv and Lasse settled on her then, and she had to take a deep breath. Her children were fine, of course. Neither of them had cystic fibrosis or anything at all wrong with them. They were with her father or her husband. Perhaps even both. They would soon be getting ready for school, coming messy-haired and sleepy-eyed down the staircase, stopping at the bottom to lay their arms around the dog before stepping into the kitchen for cereal and strawberries.

It was her job to get them breakfast, yet here she sat, on a strange man's boat, some three hundred miles north of the Arctic Circle.

"I used to work for Statoil. I was on a platform in the Snorre oil field in Tampen. That is the whole story. Jorunn called me on the telephone. 'Kjersti Anne,' she said. I knew as soon as she said her name. It was before Christmas. Three years ago."

Greta went to him and put her hand in his hair and held it there. It was how she greeted her children as she poured milk over their cereal.

Stig looked up at her and smiled and said, "It is very sad. I am still very sad, naturally. But now I am better, too." He took her hand in his and held it and then said, "Your husband?"

Greta sat back on the settee. "His name is Frans."

"Nansen?"

"Yes. A distant cousin or something. But related."

"What is your maiden name?" he asked.

"Eide."

"How do you spell that?"

She spelled it for him, and he said it differently. Eid-ee. The Norwegian pronunciation, she assumed.

"Yes," she said.

Now a much broader expression came across his face. "This is a very famous name here. Do you know?"

"Know what?"

"There was a man named Odd Einar Eide—"

"My great- and great-great-great-grandfathers were both named Odd Einar."

"He is like a folk hero. Is that the name, folk hero?"

"What do you mean?"

"In the 1890s this Odd Einar Eide worked on a seal-hunting boat and was stranded on Spitzbergen. He survived for many days. In snowstorms. Without food. All alone. His partner was killed by a polar bear. They wrote a book about him. Ever since he has always been a story we tell. To make us feel strong and clever."

As soon as Stig said this, Greta felt something dislodge inside— like a calving glacier, it came to mind—and she understood that a whole part of her family's history had been kept secret by the lack of this knowledge. Thea Eide, dead in childbirth. Odd Einar Eide, drowned on Lake Superior. Harald Eide, her grandpa, suicide in the Devil's Maw. These deaths had, she now realized, created the sense of impending doom she'd felt her entire life. Like it was only a matter of time before some weird and crushing fate befell her, one she was powerless to change. And she'd lived accordingly.

She looked at Stig, sitting there with his drink, looking at her as if he'd searched *his* entire life—sailing the northern seas, studying the starry skies—in order to discover *her*. No one had ever looked at her like this before. And no one had ever given her such gifts, and simply by existing.

Twelve hours. That's how long she'd known him. And already she believed in both the gifts and the hours and *them*. So much so that she put her aquavit down on the counter, stepped to him again, put both of her hands in his hair, tilted his head back, and bent to kiss him. The taste of licorice. Still a trace of mint. The heat of his lips. The reach of his hands around her waist, and the ease with which he pulled her onto his lap.

She spoke with her lips still brushing his. "I want this."

He pulled back, looked at her, took a tremulous breath. "Yes."

"I want to know you. I want to know why we found each other."

He kissed her again, deeper.

She kept her hands in his hair, trying to pull him closer, and spoke again, their lips still together. "I had no idea you existed."

He pulled back again, only to settle his face into the small arch of her neck. "I thought exactly the same thing," he whispered. "I cannot believe it. I think I must be dreaming. *Du er som et skip for å redde meg.*"

"What does that mean?" she asked, her voice almost panicking.

"You are like a rescue ship."

"Yes. Exactly. I am a ship to rescue you." And she kissed him again, reaching this time for his chest, which filled her hands. She ran them up over his shoulders and down his arms and found his own hands, which she lifted to her breasts. She shivered as the warmth of his touch coursed through her body.

She'd felt desire before. Of course she had. But this was different:

she felt herself *thawing*. All of her iciness melted into the bottom of her belly and was radiant there. She held him close. And as if he understood what was happening to her body, he made a bowl of his arms and scooped her up and carried her to his berth. He set her down on the bed and she felt herself dispersing. She felt herself spilled.

He bent and rested his knees on the edge of the bunk and took hold of her. She watched as his hands engulfed her feet, then ran up her calves and around to her knees, which she parted just slightly. Even in the wan light of that boat's sleeping quarters, she could read his eyes. They were doubtful, even afraid. But also fierce, and she could see him staring into a hurricane on the Barents Sea, his hands on the *Vannhimmel*'s wheel, his sails reefed.

The thought of a storm made her realize suddenly how cold the boat was. In her hands, stretched out on either side, she clenched down and cotton and pulled the comforter back and then over her, leaving a corner turned for him.

Stig reached down to remove his shoes and then with one hand pulled his sweater over his head and off. He balled the sweater and stuffed it into a cubby on the bulkhead by the foot of the bed. His baby-blue oxford shirt hung wrinkled and slightly too large, and when he stood upright again she could see what she hadn't yet noticed, that he had a small paunch to go along with his booming hands and chest and shoulders. In the time it took her to register this, she also noted that he must outweigh Frans by a hundred pounds. The thought of her husband crossing her mind did not trouble her, though. She knew that being here was a violation of those long-ago vows. But what did distress her was the realization that she'd gone so long without feeling this urge. Like years of her life had been laid to waste. And now she was thrilled to discover she had only gone dormant, not dead.

And it thrilled her again to see him crawling toward her on the bed, to feel him burrow under the comforter, to herself awaken still more under the gravity of his hands, to be devoured by the gentleness of his eyes. "I do not want to make love to you?" he said. And then, as though to contradict himself, he kissed her more fiercely than he had yet, his left hand tracing the length of her from shoulder to knee.

In answer, she pressed herself against him as her whole body flushed, like a fever had broken. And almost as if he knew what she was feeling, he leaned back and brought his hand to her forehead, where he brushed the now-damp tendrils of her hair back over her ear.

"I mean, I want to very much. You"—he lost himself searching, she thought, for the right words—"are the most unexpected thing. When I saw you in the church, I thought, *That woman!* But then I could not think more. Only dream you would come back. And then I saw you in the taxi and I—"

"I had to come back," she said, reaching to touch his face.

As though he hadn't heard her, he said, "How would I have found you?"

Now she kissed him, her fingers playing with his beard. The boat rolled, knocking against the fenders on the dock, and she broke away.

"Another boat has passed on the sound. It is okay. That is the waves behind the other boat."

"The wake," she said, then covered her eyes in embarrassment.

"Yes," he said, running his hand down her arm now.

And so the passing of another boat had brought them back above water. She peeked at him from between her hands and laughed lightly. Stig brushed her hair back off her forehead again and then did the same to his own, pinning the loose strands behind his ears. He rolled onto his back and pulled her into the shelter of his arms.

"I have never done this," he said.

"Done what?"

"Brought any woman to my boat, much less a married American. Drunk aquavit at noon. Climbed into bed."

"Are you feeling regretful?"

"I am feeling very happy."

"Me too."

"What about your husband?"

Now she rolled onto her back so they lay shoulder to shoulder, both staring up at the skylight in the deck above his berth. She had an instinct to lie about Frans. To say that she hated him and wished she'd never met him. That he was cruel, or worse. But instead she simply told the truth. "I have been married for a long time. Almost twenty years. Everyone thinks we're happy. We have every reason to be. But I don't love him. I think I used to."

"Why don't you love him?"

"Whenever I'm with him—and I try to be as little as possible—my overwhelming feeling is loneliness. It's like he's made me less than I used to be, instead of more. Isn't the opposite supposed to happen? Isn't your partner supposed to make you better?" She said all this before she'd thought it out, and it occurred to her that it might be more information than Stig wanted, so she changed course. "He has a lover. A Norwegian woman, actually. Alena is her name. Frans is down in Oslo with her now. Or *was* in Oslo. I think he went home yesterday."

"And now you are on the other end of Norway. Is this... what is the word for 'hevn'? Getting even?"

"I don't think so."

"But maybe?"

"No," she said. "No, I'm not. I don't like it that he lies to me, but I guess people lie all the time."

"I don't want to lie."

She turned to rest a hand on his wrinkled shirt. "I'm not lying. I won't. Not about anything. Let's just not do that."

"Okay."

"I'm not here to get even with Frans. I'm here"—and she pointed her finger into Stig's chest—"because I had to know what this felt like. When I saw you in the church... I don't know, I had to meet you. And then I did, and I was so smitten. And I had to know you better."

"Smitten?"

"Charmed, captivated. I think you're beautiful."

"So you are happy to be here?"

"'Happy' doesn't begin to describe it."

He pulled her closer. Relieved, she thought.

"What about Jorunn? Did I say that right?"

"Yes. Jorunn. I have not even seen her in six weeks. I told her we should divorce, but she does not give me an answer."

"Do you still love her?"

"I love that she was Kjersti Anne's mom. She loved our daughter very much and that made me happy." Now he rolled onto his side, their faces only a foot apart. "I married her because I thought it is what every man does. She is an interesting woman. She likes music and art and having fun. She has a good job. We have traveled all over. But I always wondered if I loved her. Just for myself, I mean. Or if I only loved her for Kjersti Anne."

When he said his daughter's name, his pupils enlarged and she could see the lines around his eyes twitch. "I bet she loves you," Greta said, and then thought, *How could she not?*

"I have been thinking lately, if I have to wonder if I ever loved her, probably I did not."

That rang true, especially when Greta held her feelings for Frans up to her own reflections over the last few days.

"Anyway, I think she has a new man too. In Bodø. She is living with her mother there. Her mother tells me things. I do not care. I hope she is happy."

Greta tried to imagine what Jorunn looked like. And also this man's mother-in-law, and the house where she lived in a place called Bodø. She'd never heard of it before today. She tried to imagine Jorunn's lover, and wondered if she even had one, or if Stig had conjured him up to make himself feel better for her. Less responsible for her. She tried to imagine the loss of a child. A seven-year-old child. And how slowly three years could pass.

Then she looked ahead, and wondered how fast time really did move. In the space of the last thirty minutes, her life had become impossibly large. She nestled her head onto his chest and lay there listening to the muffled beat of his sweet heart. She knew with certainty that she wanted this man. And not just to fuck. Not just to fill a spot in her left empty for years. No, she wanted to know him. She wanted to love him. She wanted to someday stand on the deck of this boat while he hoisted the mainsail to catch the wind that would bear them off. That's how she now wanted to move through time.

"You'll be happy too," she said, undoing the top button of his shirt.

He touched her hand, as if to ask her to stop.

"It's okay," she said. "I also want to go slow. I just want to feel you beside me."

He shook his head slowly, and she unbuttoned the rest of his shirt and then unpeeled it from his left shoulder, which she beheld in awe—and nearly laughed that it could stir so much desire. She put her teeth to his flesh and then her tongue between her teeth and tasted him. A tremor ran the length of his body and in its aftermath he seemed to relax. With his hand on her lower back, he lifted her on top of him, pulling the bunched comforter from between them in the same motion.

Now she sat astride him and rolled her hips into him. She had to break from kissing him to swallow twice, and the ache between her legs was astonishing. The only relief she found came when she rode against his prick, but after each pass the ache grew worse. She'd never felt this kind of insatiable wanting or suffered the inability to do something about it. So she abandoned herself to it entirely. To his hands. To the spreading of her fucking *want*.

Then she sat up and the weight of her body funneled into his center, and it was him rolling his head back into the pillow. She slid his shirt from the other shoulder and tossed it aside, never moving her eyes from his own. He appeared as helpless as she herself felt. But without any awareness at all. As though he were stunned or even shocked. To help him, she kissed him again, her hands running up his arms as he'd run his up her legs, starting at his wrists and then slowly, slowly up and around his forearms and elbows and around the fleshy part of his upper arms and finally to his shoulders, which she used to press herself up again.

With her back to the door, she shadowed the light from the main cabin, so only the midday stars speckled him with light. But even so she could see the contours of his hairless chest, the undefined strength of his body, the wanting in it, how his skin had grown taut without the comforter to warm him. His lips moved almost as if he were attempting to speak, but he'd either found no words or was keeping them to himself. Rather than speak, he fixed her in a new gaze—one she read as questioning—and ran his hands under her shirt so they held her bare waist. Those hands on her flesh brought with them something like the beauty and longing of the songs he played on the piano, and, in much the same way she'd wanted to hear that song over and over again, she wanted also to remain in his grasp.

The thought must have come out in her expression because he ran his hands farther up her body, her shirt rising with them, her arms lifting as though pulled by strings from above, until she felt the newness of her skin under the same starlight that freckled him. He didn't breathe. Didn't blink. And only when he reached behind her with his left hand and unclasped her bra did she realize she was breathless herself. With his pinkies under the straps of her bra, he peeled it from her body. And when her breasts came free, he finally took a gulping breath. But for all that his eyes questioned, they never so much as twitched. His steadiness was stunning.

And when his hands came around her ribs and cupped her breasts, when his heavy thumb tips glanced across her nipples, when each of his fingers followed, one by one, each softer than the last, each finding a quieter key, she felt a relief she hadn't known from another's hands in years. But this also aroused a new, more urgent need, so she slid away and unzipped his jeans and tugged them down until they were off his hips and then, with less confidence or more shyness, she reached under the waistband of his boxers and took hold of him. He tilted his head back, exposing the soft flesh of his neck beneath his beard, where she could see his thumping pulse. She wanted to put her legs around him, to slide him into her, to feel this hard cock with its soft skin in her hand fill her up inside. But she didn't, and not only because they'd agreed not to. No. She also wanted to preserve the possibility of what that act would have in store for them. To hold this anticipation, to have longing become a part of her daily life. She wanted, she realized already, the semblance of a romance. She wanted to fall in love.

If this thought should have embarrassed her, it didn't. She knew the slim likelihood of love coming of all this. But even the idea of it, the hope of it, the notion that such a thing might still exist for her, this electrified her. "You're so handsome," she whispered, as though people were eavesdropping. She still had her hand in his underwear, caressing him, the wires running from the tips of her fingers to the palm of her hand and then through her body to that spot just above her clit, all of it was burning. To calm herself, she let go of him.

"I only care that you think so," he said. He bunched the pillow under his head and ran his hand gently across her back, his fingers still playing her flesh. "I cannot believe we are lying here. When I saw you in the church I..."

She waited to see if he had the words she lacked, but when he remained silent she said, "I know. Me too."

"What will I do?" he asked.

"About what?"

"About you."

"I don't know, Stig." The feel of his name on her lips was like another kiss. "Stig Hjalmarson."

She thought she could feel his body lighten upon him hearing his name. His shoulders rose, his belly sank. His hand on her back came to rest, and wanted to hold her there.

"You will go home. And I will still be here," he said. "I do not think that one night is enough."

His voice delighted her as much as what he said. It was like they were continuing a conversation they'd been having for years. The intimacy. The lulls. The inexactness that was no barrier to understanding what they meant to say. It aroused her as much as his flesh did.

"One night that will last now for one or two months or more," he said. "After I kissed you last night, I said to myself, *That will have to be enough.* But I was wrong."

"I thought something like that, too. Which is why I went to the airport."

"But you did not leave."

"No, I didn't."

"Am I supposed to make this night everything I need?"

She knew exactly what he was asking, and exactly how impossible the answer. The silence between them was amplified by water lapping against the hull of his boat. He pulled the comforter up over them, and drew her close to him. Her appetite was resting now, and she took a different kind of pleasure in the warmth of his nearly naked body next to hers. She closed her eyes and tried to memorize what he felt like. She breathed in the fresh smell of him. And somehow she fell asleep to the gentle rocking of his boat.

Before leaving Granerud's office, I stopped by his secretary's desk. Herr Rudd possessed the countenance of a man beholden to the drudgery of office work: ashen, pudgy, even sickly. But his voice carried almost birdlike, and he happily obliged me when I asked for a pencil and stationery. He even offered me a table beneath a window overlooking the harbor to write my letter.

The wind had not relented, and the bustle I'd grown to associate with the quayside had vanished that afternoon, replaced by the forlornness of vacant boats tied to docks. The view from that pane of glass was the perfect vantage for composing the missive I intended for my daughter. I licked the tip of the pencil and wrote her thus:

Min Kjære Datter,

If I told you the circumstances under which I find myself writing this letter, I doubt you'd believe me. But since I last wrote to tell you of my great adventure, much has changed. Or, maybe I am changed.

Your mother—who sends her best wishes and regrets that it has been so long since her last letter—and I find ourselves in Tromsø, at the behest of a man named Marius Granerud. A newspaperman, you see, intent on capturing the story of

*my unlikely survival on Spitzbergen, which is an island
archipelago due north of Hammerfest and halfway to the Pole.
When I have more time I will tell you of my tribulations, but
on this storm-tossed day suffice it to say that I have weathered
a most harrowing ordeal, the experience of which has caused
me to take new measure of my life.*

*Much of what I once believed has been altered, and if I find
myself adrift as never before, then it is on such uncharted
seas that I have rediscovered something very important that
I wish to tell you: For all the inconstancy of my life I have
not been dissuaded from knowing that my love for you has
withstood every bit of my suffering and is the one sure thing,
on stormy days such as this one, that spares me from despair.
If in America you have found yourself similarly altered, with
difficulty or sadness or loneliness, just think of your father's
love.*

*Daughter, if that seems a small thing, then remember what I
have just told you, and know that it is truly the most glorious!
And if I might ask you for one small kindness, it would be
word that you are safe and well. Until then, I will persist in
believing you are.*

Med Kjærlighet Fra Din Hengivene Far

Before folding the letter and putting it in the envelope, I reread it
twice. My intention had merely been to tell my daughter that she'd
been on my mind, and that my love for her was undeterred. Why
then so much else? I thought of dashing the whole thing, but opted
instead for a simple postscript:

*P.S. A great storm is passing through Tromsø even as I sit at
a window writing you this letter. It has reminded me of the
hurricanes that came to Hammerfest when you were a young
child. I doubt you remember them, having been back then
only two and a half years old, but I do. I held you sometimes*

for whole nights and sang you every song I knew. Which I mention only because the weight of you in my arms tethered me to the ground while the world all around us blew into the sky. I think about that often.

May the winds be but a breeze where you are. And may you remember how I held you as a child. I hope against all odds to be able to see you again someday.

Now better satisfied, I folded the letter and stuffed it in the envelope and sealed it shut. I addressed it to my daughter and stood for a last look out onto the harbor. Outside the window, snow blew up the Storgata and I pondered briefly, as I often did while it stormed, the nature of wind, and where it went once it blew by. Did it simply disappear? Or did it persist, blowing onto other streets and mountaintops and seas? Did it whorl around the world and come back weeks or months or years later? Were the gales out on that street remnants of the same hurricanes that had recently held so much of my attention? Would they blow forever? Would they take my hat as I walked back to the Grand Hotel like the hurricane had taken my faering?

Unlike the previous day's guesses on Inger's whereabouts, this one found her sitting in the hotel's lobby as if she expected me just then, a cup of tea on the table beside her, a newspaper spread on her lap as though she were an aristocrat. She glanced at me, but otherwise made no effort to greet me. As I walked toward her, she might even have started reading again the news of the day.

"Hello, Inger," I said, standing before her. I could see that her hair had been recently washed and braided. She smelled wondrous.

"Hello, Odd Einar."

"It must be lunchtime, or thereabouts."

Now she did look at me. "I was hoping you'd return in time to dine with me."

I cannot say why she sounded so formal, but I had the strange sensation of our taking lunch together being compulsory. She picked up her teacup and saw it was almost full. "Would you like a tea before we eat? While I finish mine?"

"That sounds fine," I said, and looked around for the provenance of her cup, which was a tray across the hotel lobby. I went and got one and stirred in a lump of sugar and thought of how badly the next hour or two with my wife might go. We had not yet spoken of the night before, and though I had done my duty to Marius Granerud it would be a lie to say that I hadn't been preoccupied about her behavior. In all my married years with her, I'd hardly ever felt she had a secret from me. Until now.

The thought soured me, so I stirred another lump of sugar in my cup before I went and sat down beside her.

She folded the newspaper and set it on the table next to her and fixed the sleeves of her dress and finally turned to me. "I owe you an explanation, Odd Einar. So much has happened in the last few days. I've been altogether out of sorts." Her eyes were a study in uncertainty, and for the first time since we'd made love upon my return, I believed her.

"Do you wish I'd perished up there, Inger? Would you be happier if I had?"

"Of course not."

"Do you no longer love me?"

"Oh, Odd Einar. You know I do."

"Are you not content to be here? To have me earning these kroner?"

"We need the money, you know as well as I."

"Have I failed you?"

"You've never failed me."

"Is there some question I ought to ask but haven't? Is there something I'm missing?"

Now I could see a tear spring from the corner of her lovely eye. Inger seldom wept, and for a moment I paused in my questioning, which had been spontaneous and even seemed out of my control.

After she dabbed her eye with a handkerchief and collected herself, she said, "You've done nothing wrong, Husband. Nothing at all."

"I only ask because ever since I stepped off that mailboat, ever since old Magnus brought me ashore, ever since I laid eyes on our empty room and then you standing there over my grave with Bengt Bjornsen, why, I've felt a stranger in my own life."

"Oh, Odd Einar—"

"Or—pardon me, Inger—worse still: like a man sentenced for a crime he didn't commit."

"You've committed no crime. You know that. If I've been aloof, it's because I was already mourning you. When you appeared in the graveyard, you might as well have been Lazarus."

I reached over and took her hand. "Inger, you've already told me this. And I can well believe what a shock it would be to see me rise from the dead. Nearly every day up on Spitzbergen I felt like I was doing just that. But I'm here." I pointed to my feet on the carpet. "I'm no Lazarus. I'm no damn draugen or ghost. I'm alive, even if just barely. And I'm not"—and here I felt in my pocket, and knew the risk of invoking our daughter—"some unanswered letter." I waited for a reaction to play across her face, but none came so I went on. "When the going was hardest up there, when I wondered why it wouldn't be better to use my last bullet in my own ear than suffer another bitter night, it was you who were my answer. You and Thea both. You might as well have been calling to me through that damn darkness."

She looked at me again, and another tear came to her eye.

"I can wait patiently for your love, Inger. I truly can. But if it's not coming"—and now I lowered my eyes—"then you have to tell me so I'm not made a fool yet again. Ever since I got on board the *Lofoten,* ever since those conversations with Otto Sverdrup, I've proven over and over again that I should've just stayed by your side. Should have worked on our life from home. Should have proven my love to you. If I've lost you because I left, well, I couldn't bear that."

When I summoned the courage to look at her again, it was kindness that met me—of a sort I hadn't seen since Thea still woke each morning in our home. And so it was my turn to shed a tear.

She tightened her hold on my hand. "Of course I love you, Odd Einar. You needn't wait to know that." She held my gaze until her grip loosened, then she sat back in her chair and sighed. A gust of wind shrieked past the window, and we both looked out to see the snow blowing sideways.

"This wind has put me in mind of the hurricanes," she said.

"I spoke of them this morning. With Herr Granerud. And the same boat that came ashore in Hammerfest was docking this morning here in Tromsø."

"I saw it too. The schooner with the Danish flag. I'm sure that's what reminded me."

"Those storms were the beginning of our troubles, do you remember that?"

"Your boat blew out to Håja. Half the sod blew off our roof. It stole our pots and pans, that wind did." She gave me a discerning glance. "But we weren't the only family to lose a little. How many people lost their loved ones? How many lost their homes altogether?"

"Surely others had it far worse."

"You built us back up, Odd Einar. Your strength and conviction."

We both peered out the window at the blowing snow. A man walked past, the tails of his coat trailing him like his own ensign at half-mast. The tea had gone cool, and I drank it down in two long gulps and turned back to Inger. "Well, this day's wind is no match for those storms. But maybe it's a harbinger of change for the better, Inger. Maybe it will blow in good luck."

If I'd not known my wife so well, I'd have said a smirk rose from her lips. Certainly her eyes shimmered, and she set her empty cup down and took hold of my hand again and leaned across the space between us to whisper, "When's the last time we made love in the daytime?"

"Why, Inger!"

Now she grinned.

"Daytime or day*light*? The sun will set before we finish lunch."

"Then we shall skip lunch."

I might reasonably have wondered where this appetite came from. My wife had almost never tried to seduce me. But my mind went quickly to that first night back in Hammerfest, when the feel of her soft skin did much more to restore me than the coffee and kanelbolle.

Now, sweetening her offer, she put her wet lips to my ear and said, "I want to take you to our fancy hotel room, Odd Einar." Then she sat back and crossed her legs and I swear she was twenty years old again, and I the first and only man she'd ever loved.

"I remember that look as well as I remember the hurricane winds, Inger," I said.

"Then you know what's in store."

What sort of fool presses his luck in such an instance? When his wife, in all her loveliness, makes an overture so promising? I could nigh feel her suppleness already beneath my hands. I could feel, too, the sweetness of her kisses, one of which still lingered on my ear. But there was one thing still plaguing my mind: I would not be a cuckold, especially not to Bengt Bjornsen, whom even Marius Granerud saw fit to call out.

I sat back myself. Looked into my teacup and spoke into its emptiness. "There's one more thing I need to ask you. Our whole life Gerd Bjornsen has taunted us. How is it you and she have become friendly? She's a miserable woman."

"She is indeed. But not like you mean."

"Oh?"

"Behind most women whose lives are a misery are miserable husbands."

"It's no news to me that Bengt is a wretched man."

Now she looked at me as though I were a simpleton. I could tell I had taxed the long patience that she possessed in such abundance. Could see her calculating her thoughts. Weighing what to say and what not to. "These mornings, you go to Marius Granerud's office and tell him of your time stranded on the ice, yes?"

"You know the answer to that."

"You tell him about the agony you endured, the coldness, the isolation, how it will likely haunt you for many years. Maybe for as many more as you live, yes?"

"I suppose it will."

"And I suspect there will be many times when, as you contemplate your ordeal, your mood will turn inward. When you become melancholy, or worse. Perhaps even angry. Or dour."

"Or I may feel joy at having survived. At having returned to you."

A knowing look spread across her face. "All the better, then. So now imagine there never being a slim prospect of that joy. Your life being an endless and frigid snowstorm. This one with no hope of relief."

She may as well have been describing the Fonn! It wasn't the first occasion in our marriage that Inger had demonstrated the ability to own my most private thoughts. Ofttimes, those moments of intuition troubled or even spooked me. But on that afternoon in the Grand Hotel lobby, it gave me a feeling of great tenderness to have her back in the realm of my consciousness, sorry though it could be.

"You look pleased. Like you know of what I speak. The loneliness of such a prospect, that's what Gerd faces every second of her marriage."

"So you are her warmth? You come as relief to the everlasting coldness of this blighted life?"

"I am her friend, Odd Einar."

"And Bengt?"

"What about him?"

"Are you his friend, too?" I knew it was a simpleton's question.

She smoothed the pleats of her skirt and crossed her ankles under the chair and I watched the kindness of her expression waver before she gathered and held it forth again. "I will grant you this single instance of doubting my faithfulness, and answer you one time only: I am your wife, Odd Einar. I have been for more than twenty years. In all that time—indeed in all my *life*—I have never loved another man. Never even given such a thing any consideration. To suggest I might be capable of such a betrayal—with a man like Bengt Bjornsen, of all people—is an affront. When we wed, I stood on the altar of our church and made a vow to you before God. And even if your faith in Him has been tested, mine has not. In fact, it has never been so steady." She closed her eyes and raised her head and her hands found each other as though she were about to offer a prayer. But what she gave me instead was the last apology I would ever receive on the matter of my coming back from the dead. "I know I have seemed unkind and irritable. Or muddled. I know I have been slow to open my heart to you. And if I have failed to explain the reasons for my behavior, then I apologize. I have told you I will return to you, and every day brings me a step nearer. For this I am happy. And for this I thank God."

"Inger—"

"Please, Odd Einar. I'm not finished." Now it was her chance to pick up and study an empty teacup. When she spoke again, it was little more than a whisper. "For all that God has tested us, we find ourselves sitting here together. Is that not a miracle?"

These were not questions meant to be answered, so I sat still, listening attentively, while she did speak into the empty cup, her voice now came out of its whisper. "When I see things in this light, I am filled with hope." And then she did look up, but not at me. No, she turned her gaze to the onset of twilight, and it only just past lunchtime. "But when I look away from His kindness—when I look out into the world we live in, Odd Einar—I see darkness. And I see our trials are not yet finished." Finally she looked at me. "I will continue my toil. To honor the vows I made. And in truth I can see the hardships of our life becoming less fierce. I welcome this, of course. But on the matter of my fidelity, you need know that even if we were still penniless, even if we were still living in that dismal and isolated hut on Muolkot, chewing our fingernails off to boil into soup, I would still be true to you. Because I made that exact vow so many years ago. But"—and now she reached to take my hand in hers—"also because I love you from the bottom of the cold sea to the height of the distant heavens."

There was only one thing to do: I slunk to the floor and knelt before my wife and held her hand to my face wet with happy tears and said, "Thank you, Inger. I promise you I will earn that love every day. And I will give it back a hundredfold."

How long did I kneel there at my wife's lap, holding her hand? How long did I revel in this reward for having clawed myself off that mountainous island of ice and snow? How long did I hang my every hope on Inger's steadfast kindness? How long did I relish what I had not believed in many years: that we would rise from our privation together, and be better for having suffered it? Long enough that the voice that eventually called from across the lobby did not abolish my hope. Nor did the sight of Bengt's rotund belly and nose. Nor, even, did the smell of his rummy breath as he stood before me, offering his hand and a genial greeting as if we were old business partners.

For, when I looked back at Inger, she was smiling at *me*. She stood and took *my* arm. And when Bengt Bjornsen, his own wife nowhere to be seen, told Inger that he wished to know of a place to take his midday repast, she didn't so much as meet his eyes, and only told him that he perhaps ought to ask *me*, who had come to know this town far better than herself.

I told him they poured a delicious draft of Mack's brygge in the basement tavern, and that he might find a bowl of mutton or plate of fried fish to go with it, but that my wife and I had already had an early lunch and would be retiring to our chamber for a long rest. And so we walked, Inger and I did, up the open staircase, and turned to our passageway, and at the end of it, we walked into our room like young lovers. Hungrier for each other than for fish and potatoes.

Part Three

—

VANNHIMMEL

Friday morning, three days before Christmas. She sat at the kitchen counter, her hands wrapped around a mug of coffee, the laptop open before her, every one of her senses attuned to the life of her house: she heard footsteps in Liv's bedroom above, the dog's sigh and the whump of his tail as Liv came down the stairs; she could smell, below the coffee and the Christmas tree in the living room, the faintness of anise from the glass that'd held her aquavit the evening before, a drink she had alone in the living room, gazing out on the city's darkness with thoughts of Stig keeping her awake. Greta had a new awareness of things happening around her, almost like an animal. It was as if the reawakening of her sexual desire had revived other primal instincts. She heard and smelled and even sensed things that for years had eluded her. There the front door, the screeching hinge of the mailbox lid, the almost pneumatic hiss of the door being closed and the weather stripping sealing back up. But most of all, she had a clairvoyance about Frans: where he was, what he was doing, what thoughts possessed him. She knew, for example, that he'd just gone to get the morning's mail, and that in a moment he would bring it to the kitchen counter, and sheepishly refill his coffee, and offer to top hers.

She turned from the counter to look at the stairs, waiting to see Liv. The house was trimmed in garlands and holly berries. The tree was decorated and strung with cranberries, a stack of presents already wrapped beneath it. Outside, the lights Greta hung each year—to the height of the turreted entryway and the tops of the Tudor-style peaks—went on at dusk and stayed lit until midnight. To any passerby—and down here by Lake Harriet, even on these frigid days before Christmas, the city was busy with walkers and fat-tire cyclists and even skiers out on the frozen and snow-covered lake—the house would have appeared a bastion of cheeriness and affluence. Certainly the bank statement, which was pulled up on her computer screen, attested to the latter. Even with profligate Christmas spending, their checking account was flush with over thirty thousand dollars. She'd lately become fixated on their finances, figuring out, as she was, how to survive on her own.

The bulk of their money came from Frans, a combination of his work and his family fortune. Greta still wrote features for magazines and newspapers, but her income accounted for merely a fraction of their wealth, and she had lately begun obsessing about how she could ever make the financial ends meet. She even kept a page in her pocket notebook with a running tally of their accounts. She would have to work. To make more money than she was. But there was no danger of her being broke, not by a long shot. Still, how many times had she sat at the kitchen counter thinking how much of their money she'd trade to want to be under the mistletoe hanging in the archway between the living and dining rooms? The one that hadn't been commemorated except by Liv and Frans.

She closed the computer and walked through the dining room and under that mistletoe and into the living room. She looked out at the snow-crusted lawn and then the lake before turning around and running her hand across the back of the couch. At the piano she stopped and lost herself for a moment in thoughts of Stig. She could rest there, with the memory of him playing.

She walked back into the kitchen with him, picked up her coffee, and sat back down at the counter. She heard Lasse running upstairs, probably to brush his teeth before leaving with his father for some last-minute shopping, while Frans and Liv walked into the kitchen from opposite ends at the same time, her sleepy face such an antidote to his creeping gait as he paused behind Greta for a moment before setting a package on the counter next to a bowl of bananas and pears.

It was a padded manila envelope stamped with a return address from the Hammerfest Biblioteket, the crown-and-polar-bear town seal making it look official. It was addressed to her in penmanship so fine, she at first thought it was a printed label.

"What's that?" Frans asked. He'd rarely shown much attentiveness to the ordinary details of her life, not unless they had some direct connection to his own. But since she'd returned from Norway three weeks ago and told him she thought their marriage was over, since she'd isolated herself even further, to his great alarm, he'd been trying to demonstrate a little interest, which came across as nosiness.

"It's from the library in Hammerfest," he said.

She gave him a scolding stare—*obviously it is!*—and pushed the package aside and turned to the newspaper. Now she heard him move to the bread box, take the loaf from it, untwist the tie, and pop two slices into the toaster. She knew he would go to the fridge and get the jam, and she could smell the raspberries as soon as he opened the jar. A moment later, he was at her side with the coffeepot. He filled her cup and poured cream into it, and put the pot back in the machine. Then the toast popped up and she heard him spreading butter and jam on it, heard him take a plate from the cupboard, saw it appear at her elbow.

"I'm taking Lasse to buy Grandpa's Christmas present," he said, holding his own cup of coffee.

"I know."

"Do you need anything?"

"Take Liv, too. I have some things to do around here."

"Okay," he said, then turned to Liv. "When you finish your banana, brush your teeth, okay? You can come shopping with us."

There'd been a time, a month ago, in fact, when Liv might have protested or begged off to stay with Greta, but all of the tension in the house after Thanksgiving had left her timid, sometimes even cowering, so she stuffed the rest of the banana in her mouth and shot upstairs to get ready. That left only Greta and Frans in the kitchen. Both with their coffee and toast.

"Can you at least be civil over the holidays?" he asked. "For the kids?"

She folded the newspaper, put it aside, and picked up her cup. "Do you realize this is the first time you've ever taken the kids Christmas shopping? Your son's thirteen years old, for God's sake, and so far he's been made to understand that Christmas shopping's for girls."

"Is that true?"

That deference was new, too, and even less tolerable than his cocksureness. "Well, you're taking them now. If you can manage it without their knowing, you should also have them get each other something. I usually let them spend twenty dollars."

"Okay."

"They do have ideas for each other."

"Okay," he said again.

Now she heard one of the kids zipping their coat in the mudroom. She heard the familiar gurgling of the pipes in the bathroom off the kitchen, and another sigh from Axel. She felt the kitchen floor's slightest vibration as the furnace turned on right below her in the basement. She heard Liv's light step on the staircase, and then she was back in the kitchen. And she saw how deflated Frans was. Not by the task, but by the tension in their home. She sensed his total bewilderment.

Liv had put on the sweater Frans had brought home from Norway. Apparently he'd come bearing armfuls of gifts, including a jewelry box for Greta, which still sat in the packaging on her dresser upstairs.

"Are you ready to roll?" she asked Liv. "Your new sweater looks nice."

"I thought Grandpa would like it. It's woolly."

"You're a beauty," Frans said. "Can you put your coat on? It's cold this morning."

"I told my dad we'd be there for dinner tonight," Greta said.

Frans nodded before reaching into the mudroom for his own coat. As he buttoned it up and tied a scarf around his neck he said, "Have a nice morning," loud enough for the kids to hear. This was perhaps the most egregious of his new habits, making sure the kids could see his kindness and gentleness.

Greta got up, brusqued by him, and kissed Lasse and Liv on the tops of their heads. "Have fun," she said, then went back to the counter, where she grabbed the package and her coffee before heading upstairs.

In the bathroom, she locked the door and then peeked through the blinds, watching as the kids stumbled through the snowbanks toward Frans's Land Rover. She heard Axel get up to look out the window downstairs. She heard the back door close and the dead bolt slide into place as Frans locked it behind him. He would put his sunglasses on before opening the back door for Liv, slide each of his hands into the cashmere linings of his gloves, clap his hands twice, then get behind the wheel. Even from upstairs she could smell the winter air wafting through the house.

In a basket at the back of the linen closet, beneath cast-off makeup and toiletries and years-old tampons, Greta kept a pack of cigarettes. She fished them out, went to the window and opened it a crack, sat on the toilet, and lit one, blowing the smoke out the side of her mouth toward the window. The package sat on her lap for as long as it took her to smoke the cigarette, the butt of which she dropped into the toilet along with the ashes she'd tapped into the palm of her open hand.

When last they'd spoken, five days ago, Stig said he'd sent her something—a gift, he called it. Each day since, she'd stalked the mailman and the UPS and FedEx drivers. She even canceled a coffee date with a friend so she could be home, waiting. But now that she held his gift, she could hardly bring herself to look at it, much less open it. And for all she'd imagined it might be, for all she *hoped* it would be, she found herself now more fearful than excited.

She closed her eyes, traced the package with her fingertips, and then pulled the strip that opened the envelope. There were two books—or what she assumed were books—wrapped in brown paper, and an envelope with her name written across it and the admonition to OPEN THIS CARD FIRST, which she did.

On the outside of the card was a photograph of northern lights and starry skies above Håja and Sørø Sound. The picture might have been taken from where they sat on their first night together.

Dear Greta,

God Jul—Merry Christmas. When I was a child we gave presents on Christmas Eve. I hope you will find some quiet place to open my gift for you then (open the smaller package first). Until then, Nordvinden er for deg.

~ Stig

She read the note three times, then lit another cigarette from the crumpled pack in the basket and read it a fourth. Was this really all he had to say? It felt like a handshake, not the ardent kiss she'd hoped for. Had she misunderstood his intentions so badly? And did he honestly expect her to wait until Christmas Eve to open it? Did he not understand that she was *subsisting* on thoughts of him? On her *desire* for him? And that to ask her even for a *day* of patience was untenable? And what the hell did *Nordvinden er for deg* mean?

She took a package in each hand, weighing them, wondering. Clearly these were books, small ones. Her mind went to the poets she'd loved so much in college and suddenly understood that what she'd learned from them—from Frost and Whitman and Dickinson—had stayed with her, and was only now returning to her consciousness. A heart gone wild was *everything,* and to tame it was cowardly. What a pleasure, this realization. This rediscovery.

But from the library? Why would he send anything from *there*? She balanced the wrapped books on a knee and picked the envelope off the floor to study the return address again. She'd passed by the library several times on her walks through Hammerfest. It could've been a library in any town. For that matter, it could have been the firehouse.

Never mind all that, she thought, and took the smaller of the packages and tore the paper off. It was a book indeed, covered in pebbled black leather, and very old. A polar bear, forepaws raised before its snarling face, was embossed beneath the title, *Isbjørn i Nordligste Natt.* She flipped it open and the pages inside were almost brittle to the touch. She turned them carefully, one at a time, the Norwegian words coming up off the pages like the scent of him.

There were also eight engravings, each covered with a slip of bound parchment, and it was from these that she gleaned the story. Some old schooner among floes of ice. Two men killing seals. A polar bear mauling a man. A glacier in the valley of towering mountains. A desolate, snow-covered plain with a rock cairn in the middle of it. A stumpy-legged reindeer. Another polar bear looking back over its shoulder. And, last, the portrait of a man who was a perfect cross between her father and grandfather, had they been, she gathered, seal hunters at the top of the world a century ago.

If the first of his gifts left her dumbstruck, the second changed her life. She removed the wrapping and saw another leather-bound book, this one brand-new and handwritten by Stig. On the first page, it read: *The Polar Bear in the Northernmost Night.* She turned the page and started at the beginning:

Owing to its treacherous latitude and everlasting remoteness, most men left for dead on Spitzbergen might seek forgiveness from their Maker. Others might find only the darkness of their wayward souls. But what sort of man would abandon his faith in God and worship the snow instead?

I know one such fellow. I sat with him a week long, listening to his tale of survival. His name is Odd Einar Eide, of Hammerfest, a fishing village in Finnmark. A more unassuming gentleman you've never met. But when it came time to brave the polar winds and ice bears, when the choice between living and dying was hardly distinguishable, our man made bold decisions that kept him alive. He insists he's not a hero. But, dear reader, I'll tell you of his travails, and let you decide about that for yourself.

Allow me this observation about our fisherman from Finnmark, though, as you ponder whether he is hero or heathen: The land he tamed is strewn with the bones of men unsmiled upon by God, men whose last steps did nothing to provide a pathway to salvation. Yet there he sat in my office in Tromsø, alive to tell his tale.

She flipped again to the engraving at the back of the first book—the man who was her father and grandfather had they been one and the same—and froze. It would take a while for her to learn this, but what Stig had offered her was not simply this extraordinary gift. As she sat there on the toilet, looking at the picture of Odd Einar Eide, she had a glimpse of who she herself might have been. Of who she might yet become. Stig had given her the gift of possibility, after years in which only her children and her dear father had. He offered a new and different future.

As if the revelation of the rest of her life weren't enough, Greta noticed then another letter, in the crumpled wrapping of the second book. She took a last long drag from her cigarette and dropped it in the toilet, flushed, and picked up the note.

Dear Greta,

I think the man in this story is from your family. His name, as you told me, was Odd Einar Eide. The exact date of his birth I do not know, but I believe it was in the year 1854. In the Hammerfest cemetery there is a grave marking his life, but the date of death is false, I know this with certainty after a conversation with the sexton, who told me, based on the church records, that this same man appeared at his own funeral looking "every bit the Draugen." The story told in this book confirms that part of the parish record.

His wife was Inger Astrid Eide. She was born on November 6, 1855, and died on April 30, 1900. According to Jarle Berg-Hansen at the Hammerfest library, records show they had a daughter named Thea Eide, who left Hammerfest in August 1895 at the age of sixteen. In the registry, her final destination is listed as "Gunflint, Minnesota, America." If this is not the story of your family, then there must be two of you.

If you take the time to read this account, you might understand what I told you about this man being a legend in my part of the world. In fact, after Adolf Lindstrøm, who took part in two expeditions aboard the Fram and one aboard the equally famed Gjøa, Odd Einar Eide is probably our most celebrated character. Most anyone who lives in Hammerfest or the Rypefjord learns of him, like we learn of trolls or Vikings.

The man who wrote and published this account is also famous. His name was Marius Granerud, from Tromsø. For thirty years or more he was the principal newspaperman in Arctic Norway. He was the first man to talk to Fridtjof Nansen when he landed in Hammerfest in August 1896 after his renowned maiden voyage aboard the Fram. In his later years, Granerud wrote many biographies of notable Norwegians, including one of a man from Hammerfest named Bengt Bjornsen, who employed Odd Einar and Inger Astrid Eide for many years. I will try to find that book to send to you also.

I tell you all of this aware of how crazy it must seem. But after you left I made a discovery myself, that I had to know you better. Since I could not speak with you often, this is how I spent time with you. At least in my imagination. I hope that you will accept it in the spirit it is offered.

I want to tell you also that while I was making this translation, I thought of sailing to Svalbard with you. I will take you, if you will let me.

God jul, *again. I will go to the bowsprit of my humble boat on* julaften *and look for you in the Christmas Star. Will you look back?*
~ Stig

Now, instead of the sounds filtering through her home, she heard the *Vannhimmel*'s sails filling with the north wind, and the call of the terns as they came out to sea to meet them. She didn't feel the tears that fell from her eyes as she swore she would absolutely meet him under the heavens on Christmas Eve, but only the gift of his hand resting on her back.

I f I have made my whole ordeal sound like an exercise in spiritual awakening, I assure you there was more to it than that." Odd Einar studied the last bite of the jubileumsbolle Granerud's wife had sent with him. "My thanks to Fru Granerud," he added.

"She saw you on the quay yesterday and thought you could use some fattening up."

"On that account there's little to argue."

"I expect that by now, on the... what"—he glanced at his notes—"your fourth day without a meal, you'd found yourself riotously hungry."

"I've begun to think I'll spend the rest of my days with a gnawing in my gut. I can't quite get to the bottom of my hunger."

"My Heidi, she can see what I don't."

"Your wife?"

"Just last night I spoke to her of my fondness for you. I hope that's fine?"

"Fondness?"

"Naturally! It would take a special lout to fail to see your generosity of spirit."

The only thing that seemed generous to me were my failings, but I was determined to blaze a straight line through the rest of his inquiry, so rather than digress I returned to the subject of hunger. "The truth is, it took until that night on yonder side of the first glacier for my hunger to rise up. I suppose it was terror keeping it at bay, but with the small victory of crossing that glacier and the specter of another sleep-starved night, I realized that slumber was not the only thing wanting. As I moved snow into a berm around me and my thirst welled up and started scratching at my throat, I began shoveling handfuls into my mouth, trying to trick myself into believing these were whipped potatoes.

"Of course I knew it was only snow. For three full days I had supped on one mouthful after another—a fact that startled me almost as much as the bear had leaping up onto that berg. I wondered how long a man could live without food. What wretched state would this sort of dying entail?

"Let me tell you, Herr Granerud, the answers came swiftly and easily, and they were hardly those of a man thinking clearly. I suspected as much even in my desperation. So do you know what I did?"

Granerud didn't even look up from his notes, just gestured with his hand to keep talking.

"Well, inspired by my friend the krykkje, and understanding at least that I was a man with no resources, I saw in the darkness of that night an opportunity to catch one of those birds with my own hands."

"You mean to say you imagined it, friend."

"That doesn't suggest strongly enough the certainty which overcame me. I as much as saw the design of it drawn in the starry sky.

"You see, I knew there were cliffs along those shores, and that on those cliffs nested the krykkje and gulls. And I surely knew those birds were unfamiliar with the likes of me or any other man. If they saw me lying faceup to the afternoon light, why, they might think me some strangely shaped walrus or seal, dead to be picked at. Their curiosity, in any case, would be aroused. And when they came to peck at me with their golden beaks, I would need only grab one around the neck and wring it well.

"And since I practically had one of those fat birds already in my hand, I spent the rest of that night thinking of how Inger might prepare it for me. I tell you, sir, I ate that bird braised in butter and covered with herbs. I had it stewed with potatoes and rutabagas and ripe onions. Also breaded and fried in duck fat with a tablespoon of pepper. I even wrapped it in bacon and served it with bread pudding."

Marius made a playful show of removing his pocket watch to check the hour. "I say, is it time for lunch yet?"

"Oh, how many times did I ask myself that same question!"

He put his watch back in his pocket. "In*deed*, Herr Eide."

I felt a faraway expression wash over my face as the memory of starvation came back to life inside me. I closed my eyes, the better to see. "I would learn, the following day, that around the next headland was a veritable bird hotel. But except for one lone krykkje whirling on some gyre, my cliff was vacant. A month before there might've been a thousand birds nesting up there and flying all about the surrounding fjords. Certainly, it would not have been impossible to play dead for one and wring its curious neck. But when the sun rose over the mountain behind me, it shone on no birds but that single winged friend a hundred feet up."

"Is there a lonesomer place on earth?"

I finally opened my eyes and was almost surprised at being in his office, with its bookcases and cabinets and newspapers stacked around like battlements. "Oh, believe me, it would grow more lonesome yet."

He wrote that one down, then looked back across his desk at me. "What *did* you eat, Odd Einar?"

"Not much on that morning, though I did chance upon a patch of windblown ledge rock covered in mountain sorrel still clinging to its last greenness. Those are right bitter leaves on the stems of those plants, and by the time I finished with them my lips were puckered and my stomach churning. But by God, the edge was off."

"I believe I'd rather eat nothing at all."

"All those days without nourishment might convince you otherwise. In fact, for all the trouble those plants gave my bowels, I would indeed have been better off not eating them. Especially given the feast I would later that day chance upon."

Granerud raised his eyebrows in question.

"Not bacon-wrapped goose, but not damn far from it."

He sat back in his chair and folded his hands across his lap. "This I am most curious to hear about."

"As I am anxious to tell, for it was a stroke of enormous luck. My second of four such bits of good fortune."

"The first being?"

"Why, the ice bear deciding Birger Mikkelsen would make better fare than myself."

He nodded, a sly smile plain on his face.

"If that sounds ungenerous or unkind, I beg Mikkelsen's spirit for forgiveness. But how could I not see it so?"

"I think it neither ungenerous nor unkind. I've not seen an ice bear but through the lens of your description. And from that alone, it's plain that to be spared by such a toothy beast is far preferable to becoming its mincemeat."

"Trust me, there were times I wondered if that were true."

"You've not mentioned the bear in some time. Was it out of your mind?"

"Not often. But though it was the first threat—and indeed the last—I hope I've made it clear that countless other hazards held my attention in turn." I gestured at his pile of notes on the blotter. "I doubt I need recount any of which I've already spoken, but let me tell you about the second stroke of good fortune, which began as a conundrum of mighty power."

He sat forward now, and readied his pen, and then I told him about the reindeer.

During the months I'd spent on the seas around Spitzbergen, I'd seen countless of those furry creatures. I call them reindeer as though they have much in common with the herds that make their home in the fjelds and rocky hills around Hammerfest. In truth, they share about as much in common with each other as Bengt Bjornsen and I do.

The Spitzbergen variety had shorter legs and longer coats, which were brown across the back and blending to white like the snow on their bellies. It was the season of their rut, and I'd seen an awful lot of lonely bachelors on that island. While watching them, their heads bowed, seemingly feeding on pebbles from the rocky ground, I wondered what in creation they were eating. It turns out they were great fans of the mountain sorrel, same as me that morning.

After my bitter breakfast, I went back to my bivouac made of snow and mountainside. As my stomach kept growling, I feared I might have a bout of the runs, but after a while it settled and I actually felt revived. It was then I sat up and looked out over the sunny slope down to the ledge rock. One of those lonely bucks was grazing where I so lately had, his squat legs fixed on the scree, his towering antlers like birch branches above his hidden face.

As quick as I saw him, I shouldered the Krag-Jørgensen and sighted him. An easy shot, not fifty yards, without wind, his heavy left shoulder broad as a barn door. I levered my last bullet into the barrel. But the sound of it clicking into place brought with it a sudden and grave qualm: if I fired into the shoulder of that reindeer, I would be left without defense against the ice bear, should he make his inevitable return to devour me as he had Mikkelsen. But if I saved the bullet, by needs I would subsist on those sour leaves and whatever other vegetation could be scrounged from the rocks and snow.

I lowered the rifle and thought further across the expanse. I remembered the stink of seal blood in the killing boat and how that must've drawn the bear to our berg. Surely the blood of a healthy reindeer might work similarly, then I would not only have wasted my bullet, but also forfeited my kill. I might get only a single bellyful of that tender meat, as well as an hour of being elbows-deep in the warmth of its guts. Would that be worth it?

The reindeer lifted his face to the sunlight, his jaw working, before stepping a few paces farther on and resuming his lunch. From this angle I had a full profile of his majestic girth. Those creatures are generally smaller than the mainland reindeer I knew so well, but this one had twice the bulk of most I'd seen. He would reasonably have given me fifty or sixty pounds of raw meat, a bounty, but this led to the concern of how I could carry it all. I'd be soaked in blood from mittens to boots, with straps of tender venison like a coat over my back. Given my physical condition, already weak with hunger and exhaustion, I might reap but a third of it, and how long would that sustain me? I sighted him again, and this time he lifted his head and sniffed in my direction, his heavy neck now a perfect target. I'd not have missed him from twice as far.

I could have spent another hour deliberating, but then something struck me. I noticed the shadow of the reindeer long behind it. I noticed, too, that the sun, which had been so gracious all morning long, was falling toward the southern mountains. Reckoning another two hours of daylight, I felt the cold and sleepless night creeping toward me in the form of that blasted reindeer's shadow, and suffered then and there the gnawing of my hunger through a long, cold night. Would I even make it through another, without something proper to eat? Did I want to?

The answers were easy, and so I steadied my gun and aimed for that spot right behind his shoulder. He dropped where he'd stood before the report of the rifle bounced off the mountain beside me.

I had decided that the certainty of one more night alive outweighed the prospects of the rest of my life.

Granerud sat there with a conspiring expression on his face, his head shaking in solemn agreement. "And this reindeer you felled with your last bullet, you fed off its raw flesh? Flesh you cut open with Mikkelsen's stuorraniibi? The very same blade you found at the site of his dismembered body?"

"I fed off it for the next eight days."

"And your bear, he left you alone?"

"Until the ninth day, if I count them rightly."

Granerud stood, his potbelly packed under his waistcoat, and walked over to a cabinet in the corner of his office. His gait was clumsy, and when he returned to his desk with a white cloth sack that fit in the palm of his hand, I thought I detected a grimace on his ruddy face. He sat with effort, but motioned me closer and held up the bag.

"What is it?" I asked.

"I believe I told you I was the first man from the press to interview Fridtjof Nansen when he emerged from farthest north? Well, he gave me a small gift I would like to pass on to you."

"Whatever for?"

He loosened the strings and shoved his papers aside before dropping three bullets onto his blotter. He handed two of them to me, and held the third between his thumb and forefinger and regarded it in the lamplight. "The closest I have ever come to holding a gun—never mind *firing* one—is with this bullet right here. And I don't foresee needing to start hunting anytime soon." He handed me the third bullet and the cloth sack and sat back, comfortable again in his leather chair.

It occurred to me that Marius Granerud had the same aspect in that seat as the reindeer had had on the plains of Spitzbergen. I felt a pang of jealousy that my lot had been cast with the fishermen and hunters of the world, rather than with newspapermen or civil servants. I doubted Granerud's arms were pocked with scars, that his hands and feet ached with every shift in the weather, that when he woke in the morning his first thoughts concerned the luck of the sea. Instead, he had only to wait for some poor sap like me.

I noticed the gentleness with which he regarded me. "I was just thinking," he said, "how much I envy men like you, Herr Eide."

"Why should that be?"

"I suppose it's for the same reasons men always envy other men. Because I suspect my aches and sorrows are nothing next to yours; because I wish I knew what it was like to experience the type of fear you have; because I wish that I could pull the trigger on a Krag-Jørgensen and watch my target fall, then go to my prey and make it my dinner.

"Isn't it often true that our lives are but pale reflections of our aspirations, Herr Eide? Unless you are as heroic as Nansen—whose family will live on his accomplishments for generations—you're a man much like you and I are. Dissatisfied. Envious. Untrue. And lest you feel too sorry for us, think of our poor wives and daughters, who aren't even allowed to dwell on their own happiness or sadness, busy as they are attending our every pathetic need."

"I'll have to ponder that, Herr Granerud."

"Do you mean to tell me you weren't thinking, just now, that my life seemed easier than yours? That my rotund belly and fine clothes and warm office seem preferable to your own circumstances?"

"How do you know that?"

"For more than four decades, I've sat with men like you and asked of their woe or triumph. I believe I've paid attention. I think I understand the nature of men like you. Some wish to own or conquer the world. But you, you don't strike me as the sort of man who desires so very much. It's a quality I wish I possessed myself."

It felt otherworldly, to have this man gleaning my thoughts as though I'd already spoken them plainly. I wasn't irked, as you might expect. Rather, I found his understanding quite comforting. I put the bullets back in the pouch and drew the strings into a knot. "A very kind gesture," I said, holding it up before putting it in my pocket. "I thank you. And you're right, there's not much I wish for. Only a little peace and prosperity. These desires, they're the reason I signed on with Sverdrup. They're the reason I went with Svene Solvang."

"And I suppose they're the reason you're sitting here with me."

"At the outset they were."

"How was it that you ended up with Solvang?"

"I was occupied by that question for many hours on Spitzbergen. So much so that I believe I lost the thread of how it really happened.

"I recall with certainty that the *Lofoten* was anchored at Hotellneset, on the Isfjorden. There was a hotel and saloon there, full of trappers and tourists and hunters like Svene. He made an impression even in that assemblage of hard men and charlatans.

"Sverdrup introduced us. He recommended me for a spot on board the *Sindigstjerna,* which was bound for Nordaustlandet the next day, and when Solvang offered I found myself intrigued."

"And why was that?"

"I suppose I was flattered by Sverdrup's confidence. And Solvang's compliments. He said he could see in my eyes a marksman and a seal spotter, both of which proved to be true enough. I might add I relished the chance to see the icy side of the islands. The prospect of true adventure appealed to me greatly. And perhaps most important, I imagined it would be less thrilling to spend my days coiling hawsers on the deck of the *Lofoten.*"

"Solvang's offer, did it mean more pay than your work with Sverdrup?"

"I was to be paid a share on Solvang's boat, same as the others."

"So the chance was there? Boom or bust?"

"Precisely. But there was much promise, and we'd done well in the two months I was aboard. We had a hold full of sealskins." It occurred to me that my share of our slaughtering, as I understood it, would have been about what Granerud was paying me to relive this experience.

"Would you sign on with Solvang again? Knowing what you now do?"

The question had not crossed my mind, and I considered it earnestly. Surely, by now, I knew better than to fantasize about revising my life. The last few years, ever since we sent Thea to America, had been one notable misstep after another. At a glance, signing on with Svene Solvang had the same aura of failure. Yet here I was, sitting with this gracious man, Fridtjof Nansen's last three bullets in my pocket, a hundred kroner in my purse. And prospects with Inger more hopeful and promising after the previous night's conversation than they'd been since before Thea set sail. Though it's true I had survived an outrageous ordeal, I had lived after all. Perhaps that was all that mattered in the end.

"I believe I would," I said. "But I suspect the answer to that question would be different had I not got that reindeer. Otherwise, I

might very well have perished. From hunger or from lack of will."
As soon as I said it, I knew I was wrong. Lying or mistaken, who
could say?

"You've never suffered a lack of will, Herr Eide. That much about
you is perfectly obvious."

Now it was my turn to smile. "I feel great esteem for you. And I
marvel at your intuition. I must say, when I met you I was doubtful."

"Of what?"

"I thought, *Any friend of Bengt Bjornsen...*"

He let out a guffaw as he nodded. "I keep company with Bengt
because he plays no small role in shaping what happens in our
corner of the world, not because he's a friend. Though, in truth, I
believe he's more troubled than most, and so I reserve some sympathy for him."

"I know you do."

"And I know of your contempt for him."

"I've made it no secret. In actual fact, I'd rather not speak of him.
Not where our business is concerned."

"A reasonable request, to be sure."

"Let me finish telling of the reindeer, and the night that came
after, and my first true slumber."

He smoothed a fresh sheet of onionskin paper, dipped his pen in
the inkwell, and nodded.

I spoke of my walk across the plain, the ice coming up the fjord
from the same direction as the sun, which remained glorious, and
the kindly wind that followed third in line. I spoke of my hesita-
tion standing over the reindeer's antlers, his eyes open and blood-
rimmed, and how I reminded myself of the pungent smell his guts
would unleash, of the stain its blood would leave. I spoke of the
sweet sound the blade made cutting into its hide, of the care I
took in eviscerating it, of the hour I spent sawing off the choicest
meat. Of my first meal, gnawing on its ribs, my tongue slapping
on its flesh, my gut at first recoiling but soon growing fuller and
demanding more. A half hour I spent at my feast, packing meat
into my pockets, stacking it on the ledge rock as though it were
kindling to start the fires I dreamt of cooking it over. I spoke of the

falling light and the turn of sky and the weariness that followed from a full belly. Finally, I spoke of skinning the beast, and of using his hide as my market sack, and of traversing the plain once more, back to the igloo I'd built on the mountainside, and of the choice to bring my bounty into my home, risking the ice bear's visiting.

"And do you know what?"

He looked up and asked mutely, with his arched eyes, for me to answer my own question.

"I slept that night as though full of Inger's cooking, snug in our old home on Muolkot. She might as well have been keeping me warm beneath our eiderdown, promising coffee and kanelbolle come the morning. I slept through all eighteen hours of darkness and woke to a new day."

"Your fifth, yes?"

I don't know why I was compelled to say, "The day the good book tells us God brought forth fowl and fishes."

"The good book you've abandoned? The one you no longer believe in."

He meant this benignly, I'm sure of that. "The very one. But of His creatures I was never more grateful. For that morning brought back the birds, dozens of them pecking at the carrion that had come back up with the tide going out. The same tide that also left the ice dotted with enough seals to fill Solvang's hold all over again."

"Food for another day."

"Or for my friend the ice bear, so that I and my venison might be spared."

Granerud checked his watch, then set his pen down. "Unlike you, my faith in the Lord God has never wavered. But my faith in my fellow man? Well, this has been tested many times, and more so of late than ever before. But you, Odd Einar, are helping to restore it."

I'm sure his compliment turned me scarlet. Even as the morning's interview had awakened in me some small modicum of pride, I was still loath to think of myself as other than a dupe.

"May I give you some advice?" he continued.

"Of course."

"I do not offer this lightly, and beg your pardon if I'm overstepping, but I beseech you: look upon the crucible of your experience as evidence of your strength of character. The world is full of ordinary men who inflate themselves. Men such as Bengt. But there are just as many men like you. Men of substance. Of integrity." He looked into his folded hands and paused. When he spoke again, his voice was softer, almost apologetic. "Men who honor their women and children. *Right* men." Now he nodded as though he had solved some long-posed riddle. "You could be their spokesman." He sighed, clapped his blotter, and pushed himself up. "Tomorrow you can tell me more."

"Yes," I said. "Of course I will." And then, almost as an afterthought, I stood myself.

I waited while Granerud gathered his notes into his valise and crossed the room to don his inverness and hat. I buttoned my coat and together we walked from his office, past Herr Rudd, who was busy at his desk. Outside, on the Storgata, Granerud paused again and took hold of my shoulder.

"I believe Bengt Bjornsen will be taking his lunch at the Grand Hotel today. He and his wife both." He reached into his pocket and removed a two-kroner piece, which he pressed into my hand. "Perhaps you and your wife ought to have your lunch there as well."

He looked up at the sky and nodded, whether to its new softness or to God I could not say, then turned up the street and shouted, "Same time tomorrow!" over his shoulder.

"You can't eat it with your eyes, Odd Einar," she said, her voice teasing.

We were sitting at a table beside a window in the hotel's café. In one hand I held my spoon, churning the bowl of venison stew, and with the other I traced the three bullets pouched in my pocket. I looked up at Inger, who had her own bowl of stew, hers half gone.

"I was thinking about my conversation with Marius Granerud this morning."

"I figured such."

"I killed a reindeer up in Spitzbergen. Except for a few leaves and flowers, I ate nothing else. And here I am sitting in this fine café by candlelight, eating from porcelain bowls as though we were part of the bourgeoisie."

"That's God's good grace."

I nearly suggested that it was Granerud's good grace, but instead said, "I started to tell him something else, but we got sidetracked. I was explaining how I went from Sverdrup's to Solvang's employ. The *Lofoten* lay at anchor on an inlet on the Isfjorden. You'd not believe it, but there's a hotel up there—established by Vesteraalens, of course. A place for the sportsmen to wet their tongues before they go shooting. This is where I met Solvang.

"How did I end up at a table with Otto Sverdrup and Svene Solvang? In fact, it's quite unremarkable: I wanted to get my land legs back under me, if only for an hour, so after the tender had run our passengers ashore, the crew was offered passage. Only Sverdrup and I took that tender ride, perhaps owing to the nasty sleet cutting from the sky. In any case, he told me he was going to meet an old friend of his, whose boat—the *Sindigsterna*, you see?—was also at anchor. As we made the shore, he asked if I'd like to accompany him. Can you imagine that, Inger? Me keeping company with Otto Sverdrup?"

Again she squeezed my hand.

"Well, his friend was there at the hotel, sitting in the corner with a pot of tea and a big ledger before him. I tell you, he was a handsome, fearsome man. He wore a fur coat and hat, and when standing to greet Sverdrup he towered above us. His hand was more like a bear's paw, and had the strength of one as well. His beard a foot long, his hair blossoming out from beneath his hat.

"My goodness, he made an impression on me. I felt almost helpless against the magnetism of his eyes. And when he spoke, why, I lost myself in his voice. It was as if he'd uttered his words a hundred years ago, but they were coming out loud only just then.

"'Otto Sverdrup,' he announced. 'I heard you were a consignor now, running bankers and politicians and their well-fed wives up to our hallowed island. Tell me, how do you sleep at night?'

"He meant it in good fun, you see, but this was Solvang's manner, even with a man commanding such respect as Otto Sverdrup. Of course Sverdrup knew many men like Solvang. And he knew how to humor them. 'You should count me among your great allies, Svene. I've got a ship full of men here to kill all the ice bears. That's more seals for you.'

"'Otto, you know as well as I do that your cargo of slothful louts shouldn't even be here. This place will make a mockery of them. And then a mockery of these sainted precincts. You also know we need the bears, to keep us alert. To remind us of our mortality.' I kid you not, Inger. That's how Svene Solvang spoke. Whether buttering his bread or waiting out gales he was like a preacher. And he wasn't above striking fear into his crew. But on that first meeting, he seemed almost impish when he asked Sverdrup and me to join him."

I finally took a bite of my lunch, which even if tepid was peppery and delicious.

Inger had finished her bowl, and took the opportunity of my mouth being full to interject. "Why did you go with him? With Solvang, I mean."

The faraway look in her eyes told me she had more in mind than this simple question. "I went with him because he offered me a golden chance, and because Otto Sverdrup encouraged me. I went because I thought you might be impressed."

"Impressed? You've always impressed me. And here I'd wondered if you'd left because of the hard woman I've become."

"Inger—"

"If the prospect of all that desolation was more appealing than living with me."

"You can't believe that."

"Yes, ever since Thea left. Since we moved off the island. Since Bengt—"

"We're done with Bengt! You'll never have to speak with him

again. I promise you. I went because I thought it would help us get out from under him. That as soon as I got home we'd make a fresh start." I sat up in my chair and pushed my lunch aside and took both of her hands. "I went with Sverdrup because it was the first opportunity I'd had in years. That venture itself was plain enough. But I went also to see if the world was just too big for me. I thought it might be. And though you won't like this, I went because I wanted some evidence of God, even a trace of it."

Her eyes, in deep consideration of our joined hands, darted to meet my gaze, at once admonishing me for such blasphemy and asking what I'd found.

"I've learned things, Inger. I've learned the folly of pride. And how big the world really is." Now I looked away. "And if you're going to love me again, and stay with me, and remake our lives together—you're going to do it with a man who found no hint of God, and who departed that island bone-thin and weary but also resolute and free."

Her voice came sweet and quiet across the table. "I know that already, Odd Einar. And because I believe—in both God and you—I trust your skepticism will run its course, and that in time you'll come back to your faith."

"And if I don't?"

"Well, you have at least come back to me."

I hadn't realized how much I needed that affirmation until I'd received it. This was almost as if she'd forgiven me some transgression, in the wake of which I felt more emboldened than ever. A good thing, because in the next few minutes my strength of character would be tested even more severely.

First, I lifted her hands to my lips and kissed them. She blushed, naturally. Next, I ate the venison stew in bearish bites, with the thought of that raw reindeer flesh on Spitzbergen never entering my mind. After I buttered the last morsel of bread and finished it off, I looked down at my taut belly and rubbed it as though I were a jolly old fellow used to such repasts. All this time Inger sat sipping her tea, chatting about ordinary things like her knitting, her aunt, the village gossip. And the satisfaction I felt from witnessing her ease? Well, it gave me strength.

She even touched on the subject of the Tromsø museum, where earlier that morning she'd seen an exhibition about whales, their migrations and appetites and mating songs and reproductive practices. We'd seen them often enough in the spring and fall, their spouts rising up in the sound like bursts of smoke from a chimney. Inger was reminding me of the time a humpback breached just twenty feet off the bow of our faering, its tail exposed long enough to watch the seawater sluice back into the sound as we rowed out to Håja, and at that moment the expression on her face shifted as if that humpback's brother had just surfaced in the café.

By chance I then turned, and walking toward us, arm in arm, were Bengt and Gerd Bjornsen, him with a cane and patent-leather shoes and her on his arm in a fox coat, looking for all the world like half of her dread husband's shadow. With puckered lips, and her hands folded sternly before her, she held her gaze on Inger even as I wished her a good afternoon.

"I was beginning to wonder if we'd cross paths, Odd Einar," Bengt said. "Inger, good to see you here again."

"Herr Bjornsen," I said.

"How was your lunch, Odd Einar? The prices in this café are quite steep, are they not?" He shifted his rotten eyes between Inger and me. "I expect there are better uses for your hard-earned kroner."

"I beg your pardon," I said.

"I imagine your lovely wife, whose lot has for so long been cast in doubt, has a few requirements you might fulfill now that you've finally come into an honest bit of capital." He fixed now on Inger and raised his eyebrows as if to say, *Well?* And then slowly swiveled his ponderous neck toward me again. "And if her every wish has been fulfilled, then I think you ought to consider the great debt you owe your creditor before spending frivolously on fare such as this, which is no doubt well beyond your taste." He swayed forward, rising onto his toes, and tapped his cane twice on the wooden floor.

Since he'd imposed on our table, I'd regarded him only from the corner of my eye but now looked him straight in his satisfied face. "You have been a generous landlord, Herr Bjornsen. A landlord and employer, both. And I thank you for looking after my wife."

He breathed in deeply, and with his exhale a sinister leer unwound from the folds of his face. "It has been my great *pleasure* to take care of Inger in your absence."

"I have kept a tally of my debt to you," I said, "and I wonder how it squares with your own accounting."

As though awaiting precisely this statement, he pulled from his coat pocket a small notebook, which he opened to a page whose corner he'd already turned. "Since the bag of pears you bought for your comely daughter back in the summer of 'ninety-five—"

"That bag of pears was paid for outright," I told him.

"The pears themselves were paid for, yes, but the cloth sack in which I sold them to you was not. That's the first øre you owe me." He flipped to the next page in his ledger and scanned it with the tip of his finger, then turned to the following notes. "And of course your last debt is for the gravestone we laid in the cemetery back home. By my calculation, it appears you are just over one hundred kroner in arrears."

I felt in one pocket for the bullets Fridtjof Nansen had never fired, counting as quickly as I could the cost of getting me and Inger back on solid ground. Then I stood up and removed from my other pocket the purse containing most of the advance Marius Granerud had paid me upon our arrival in Tromsø. I uncinched it and reached in to pinch out several coins. As I dropped the first two-kroner onto the tabletop, I said, "I would appreciate a current invoice of my debt." I dropped a second silver and another and another until I dropped a fifth and said, "I hope you'll accept this as a token of my intention to pay you off in full." I then took more coins from my purse, and scattered a further forty kroner on the table, including a gold ten-kroner coin that I held up to the light before letting it fall. "I'll pay you the remaining debt on install-ment. We can devise this schedule after we've returned to Ham-merfest and I've seen a full accounting from you."

"All of this is rather presumptuous."

"I'm in your debt, and I conjecture you'd like to be paid. This is what I'm doing, and arranging to do so in full."

"What makes you think I'll accept these terms?"

"They're the only terms on offer. I've just paid half at the very least. That ought to demonstrate my good faith."

He eyed the money before resting his cane on the edge of the table and scooping the coins into his hand.

"I understand, then, that you accept this arrangement, sir." Now I turned to Inger and offered her my hand, which she accepted before standing and taking her place beside me.

Yet Bengt then said, "Inger, Gerd will require your assistance before our dinner this evening."

My wife—my fierce, true wife—glanced at me and then at Gerd before aiming her gaze on Bjornsen. "I happen to be spoken for this evening."

She might as well have cleaved his foot with an ax, given the astonishment on his face. He stuttered twice but was unable to form a thought.

"When my business here is finished, we'll go home. In Ham-merfest, our first task will be to retrieve our things from the room you've provided for us. Again, I thank you for the kindness you've offered my wife."

From their arrival Gerd had stood at Bengt's side, her arm looped through his, her expression as severe as the mountains across the sound. But when I looked at her just then, I saw panic. She almost seemed as if she wanted to join our side, leaning as she was toward Inger, resisting the urge, it seemed to me, to reach out for her hand.

"Inger, I could use a rest after that fine lunch. What say we adjourn to our chamber for a respite?"

She hooked her arm in mine, just as Gerd's was hooked in Bengt's.

"Good day, Fru Bjornsen, Herr Bjornsen." I nodded, and we started out of the dining room.

"Inger!" Gerd called, her voice hoarse and weak.

Inger only held my arm more tightly, and we walked on into the hotel lobby and headed up the staircase to our room.

Greta had gone hunting only once. Back in her junior or senior year of high school, the week before Thanksgiving, she and her mother had driven down to Greta's aunt's place in northern Wisconsin. The plan was to pluck their holiday dinner from the pine stands near Iron River. She'd gone against her will, but Sarah was determined that Tom—Greta's brother—would not be the only one of her children who knew how to aim and shoot.

Sarah herself could hunt and fish and cook and clean. She could play waltzes on the piano as beautifully as she could move around the dance floor at a wedding reception. She could change the oil in her car before breakfast and then discuss Rølvaag or Frida Kahlo while washing the dishes. She split wood like a lumberjack, and with the same ease she crocheted baby blankets for her friends' newborns. And though she had a decorated career—thirty years as a judge on Minnesota's Sixth District bench—she never let it infringe on her larger purpose, which was to raise her children well. She never missed a school play or ski race, she volunteered for the PTA, she stayed up late helping with homework. She taught Greta to be independent and physically strong. She taught Tom to treat women as equals, but also to hold doors open for them. Everyone found her generous and sweet. She loved her husband. They laughed together all the time.

As a girl Greta had aspired to be like her mother, so she, too, knew how to chop wood and make mushroom soup and sing as easily along with Gordon Lightfoot as with Maria Callas. But no matter how hard she tried to, Greta could not measure up, and by the time they took that hunting trip, she was well past trying to impress Sarah. On the contrary, she had entered that pubescent phase of wanting her mother to know that she hated her. Tramping through the duff while carrying a heavy Remington shotgun for two days had been a perfect theater for such a performance. She overslept, complained about the itchy wool blankets, whined about missing her friends, and dismissed all of Sarah's invitations to join her and her sister over the cribbage board in the evening.

On the second morning, Greta made a spectacle of misplacing her socks and the camouflage jacket she hated. She dabbled endlessly over her coffee and toast. And, when the time came to head out, she pretended to have a headache and cramps and begged to stay behind. But Sarah remained steadfast and firm, and before the sun rose through the pines Greta was perched near a clearing they'd spotted the previous afternoon. Her mother had arranged decoys along the perimeter before they took their places in a natural blind. And they sat there for hours before the toms finally came.

Greta could still remember kneeling for a shot as a turkey stepped toward a decoy, Sarah whispering instructions over her shoulder. *Get it sighted, then shoot.* But Greta would not shoot, and the bird strutted off into a tangle of pines. Knowing better than to press her, Sarah took the next shot herself.

She was the only one of them to bag a bird. Not once had Greta even pulled the trigger. And now, whenever taking inventory of her regrets, she'd think back to that day in the Wisconsin woods and count not firing as one of them. Over the last ten years or so, memories like this had come to her often enough, but it had become her habit to greet them indifferently. The frequency and urgency with which she'd been calling up her regrets now, however, was alarming. It was as if they were all linked together, like some chain stretching into the dark, murky waters of her past. Whatever was lying down there in the depths had the weight of an anchor, but was impossible to see.

This particular regret—not pulling the trigger on the turkey—

she thought maybe she finally understood. And if she could fathom one of the links in the chain, might the others follow? Could she find the strength to hoist up that goddamn anchor?

On this Christmas morning, Greta woke before the rest of her family. By the time Frans and the kids were up and scarfing down oatmeal, three pies—apple, pecan, and pumpkin—were cooling on the counter and she was cubing bread to stuff a turkey from Johnsen's Market in Gunflint. All the while she'd been thinking about her mother and how gracefully she'd managed her life.

It seemed to Greta that Sarah never faltered, not even when she had a teenager on her hands who made sport of being impossible. Not when, some twenty-five years ago, she had to care for her father-in-law as he slid into dementia in the guest room of her house. Not while her husband sorted out that same man's disappearance over an everlasting winter, his moods then as mercurial and dire as the season. It seemed to Greta that her mother had been made of different thread. She didn't contend with regrets, gave everyone the benefit of the doubt, and never looked back at anything except with the confidence of a life well lived. She'd even died well, which is to say unexpectedly and painlessly in her sleep. But best of all, she'd passed on knowing that her crowning achievement had been the love of her children.

For all of her failings as a mother, and these were countless, Greta knew that loving her children had been the easiest thing in her life. But since she returned from Norway almost a month ago, even the simplest things seemed compromised, and she could hardly look at Liv and Lasse without tears clouding what she saw. They were so beautiful and vulnerable. So attuned to her unhappiness and their father's befuddlement. They were still trusting but their innocence would not protect them from the decisions she was making.

The counsel she was keeping with her mother's memory? The late-night, fireside conversations with her father? The book she was reading after Gus went to bed, *Young Children and Divorce:*

A Guide? She was searching for protection for Lasse and Liv. This Christmas—the bounteous presents under the tree, the pies cooling on the counter, the turkey ready to be stuffed, the carols being practiced on the piano, the stockings hung from the mantel—was her offer of one last holiday all together. And she was determined to make it perfect in every respect.

She'd already drunk half a pot of coffee before anyone else stirred. She heard padded footsteps up in the loft, but couldn't tell whose feet they were. At home in Minneapolis, she would've known from the first step whether it was Lasse or Liv or Frans, but here at her father's house, even after all these years, the sturdiness of the timber frame disguised the early riser. Probably it was Liv, still excitable about Santa, even if she no longer quite believed in him. She'd written a letter to the North Pole asking for ice skates, and they sat there under the tree wrapped in paper emblazoned with St. Nick's cherubic face.

Finally, Axel lifted his head and gazed up the staircase. He would've uncurled himself from the carpet if it had been one of the kids, but when he rested his chin back on his forepaws and closed his eyes again Greta knew it was Frans who'd be coming down. His present lay under the tree, too, a new novel by his favorite writer about a man who runs a movie house on the North Shore. She'd only remembered to get him a gift while shopping at Northstar Books just the day before.

When she heard him coming down the stairs, she turned on the radio and tuned it to the WTIP Christmas marathon. The ringing of sleigh bells, even over the warbled signal, calmed her down a little. She took a mug from the cupboard, poured the coffee, and handed it to him as he walked into the kitchen.

"Merry Christmas," he said.

"Merry Christmas."

He gestured at the cutting board—half-heaped with bread surrounded by rosemary, sage, onion, celery, a jar of chicken stock, the hefty chef's knife—and said, "It smells great. You've been up for a while."

"I want to make a really nice meal for everybody."

He nodded, sipped his coffee. They'd had a few knock-down fights in the weeks since she returned, but now were both honoring the armistice they'd declared for the holidays. He broke off a small piece of warm crust from the pecan pie and dunked it in his coffee before popping it in his mouth. "Delicious," he said, then stepped around her to the window and looked out at the snow-covered woods and the ice-choked river. "The kids will be up soon," he said. "After the presents I'll take them skiing."

"Frans—"

"That snow from Thanksgiving stuck, didn't it? And plenty more after. It's already been one of those winters."

"I guess it's like most other winters," she said.

"No, it's not," he said, and took another drink of his coffee, his face unperturbed.

Greta began cutting up the second loaf of bread, which Gus had baked a week ago for this exact purpose. Now stale, it was perfect for the dressing. "Well, don't be late for dinner. We'll eat at three. Dad's rules."

When Frans didn't respond, Greta glanced over her shoulder. She could see the left side of his face and the steeliness of his eye. The episode in the fish house at Thanksgiving had been the only time she'd seen him cry. Even since they'd returned from Norway, after she said she was leaving him and he begged her to reconsider, imploring her to think of the kids, swearing a new kind of faithfulness and devotion, he hadn't betrayed himself with tears. She had little doubt that it was anything less than his own contract: to remain stoic no matter what pain they visited on each other. She turned back to the bread and drew the serrated knife across the crust.

"What does Gus have to say about all this?" Frans said.

She pressed the tip of the knife into the cutting board, hard enough that it stuck, and she let go of the handle. "My dad's really fond of you. You know that."

He nodded slowly, his gaze still out on the snow. "But he has to take a side."

"He's not taking a side. He cares about all of us. He wishes we weren't going through it."

"We have to tell the kids," Frans said. "It's not fair to me. It's not fair for him or the kids."

Now Greta stepped closer, and whispered through clenched teeth. "We're *not* going to talk to the kids about anything until after the holidays. I thought we'd agreed on that."

Frans slowly turned, his expression gone from apathetic to scolding. Even mean. Now he whispered, "Remind me what we agreed on?" He shook his head and looked back out the window. "Merry Christmas, here's your ice skates. Here's your iPad. What, it's New Year's? Your mom and I are divorcing. Happy goddamn holidays."

"I'm sure you can do better than that. Certain of it."

He waved his hand at the kitchen counter. "Eat your turkey. Have some pie. Be jolly and wait for you to call the shots."

"For crying out loud, I'm not calling any shots. I'm just asking you to hold it together for the holidays. For the kids. You want them to associate Christmas and our separating for the rest of their lives?"

He tossed his coffee into the sink, set his cup on the counter. "Okay," he said. Then went to the door, took his coat off a hook on the wall, and slid his boots on as he was stepping outside.

Greta went back to work, turning the radio a little louder and chopping up the rest of the bread. By the time Lasse and Liv woke up half an hour later, Frans had returned. He sat in front of the fire Gus had built and watched them open their gifts. iPads and skates, yes, but also books and clothes and computer games, remote-control cars and stuffed animals, Legos and tchotchke jewelry. Their delight was pure. They opened boxes and inserted batteries and tried on new sweaters while they ate cookies for breakfast.

When it was time for the adults to exchange gifts, Frans peeled the paper from Greta's, visibly bristled, and tossed the novel on the coffee table.

Liv looked up from a bracelet with blue dolphins on it. "Don't forget to say thank you, Daddy," she said, mimicking Frans's own gentle reminders.

Frans said, "You're right," then turned to Greta and said, "Thank you, honey. For everything."

"I know you like his books."

Gus stayed out of the fray, sipping coffee in his big leather chair, whistling at the kids' discoveries, relishing the stack of books he himself received. To any passerby, it would've been a picture of your normal Minnesota Christmas morning. Bounteous and peaceful. But of course Gus knew of the rot. Knew of his daughter's imminent departure, and that she wanted to keep it from the children until after the holidays. That Frans was angry and sad, that he thought it best to act like he didn't know anything at all. Or so Greta presumed.

After all the gifts were shared, all the coffee finished, the two of them gathered the gift wrapping off the floor and stuffed it into garbage bags. Instead of going skiing, the kids had settled into reading books in front of the fire, and Frans disappeared into the guest room down the hall.

"Quite a haul, you two," Gus said, shaking Liv by the toe. "Those are some awfully handsome skates Santa brought you."

Liv looked up from her book. "You look like Santa with your white beard, Grandpa."

Gus patted his belly and said, "Ho, ho, ho."

When Greta and Gus both made it to the kitchen, he went straight to the cabinet above the refrigerator, slid the Maker's Mark aside, and reached into the recess of his stash. When he turned back to her, he held another bottle: Stagg bourbon, which he knew was her favorite.

Greta looked at her watch.

Gus said, "It's Christmas, and you're still my daughter. You ought to cut your old man some slack."

He rinsed two coffee mugs and poured them each a finger's worth, then raised his in a toast. "Merry Christmas, kid."

"Merry Christmas, Dad."

They each took a sip, and Gus winced but took another sip. "It's been since I was a much younger man that I had a belt before lunch."

"I wish I could say the same."

"I'll spare you the back-when-I-was-running-the-Christmas-pageant speech and just say you deserve it."

"Deserve it. Right."

"You do. You're in heavy seas right now. I admire your courage."

"Courage?"

"You're a woman, Greta, and you'll get judged differently than Frans. Unjust as it may be, that's a fact." He swallowed the rest of his drink and his shoulders shook. "Whew," he said. "Good morning, Christmas Day." He put his mug in the kitchen sink, held up the bottle as though to offer her another ounce and, when she shook her head, corked it and put it back in the cupboard. "What I meant to say is that I can't imagine feeling like you do and having the will to upend everything. You're brave. And strong. And I admire your fierceness. All of that reminds me of courage."

"I'm sorry for bringing such a mess to the party."

"Don't apologize. All I care about is your company. Life can't be perfect all the time."

"You and mom always had perfect Christmases."

"Your memory's different from mine there," he said, smiling. "But I'm glad that's how you remember it. Your mom, she always had a knack for making it a special time of year."

"I've been thinking about her so much lately."

"Thinking what about her?"

"Mostly how disappointed she'd be. Earlier this morning, when I was getting the stuffing ready, I was remembering when she took me turkey hunting. I was so mean to her. Such a brat. I'm surprised she could stand to be with me."

"I heard stories about that weekend for years."

Greta covered her face in embarrassment, and spoke through her fingers. "I don't know how she did it. I don't know how she stayed so calm and so put together. Not just that weekend, but all through her life."

"Well, your mother had a pretty good grip on what was important." Now a forlorn look came over his face. "I miss her like hell this time of year. I mean, I miss her all the time, but especially at Christmas. Do you know what the last gift she ever gave me was?"

Greta shook her head.

"A toaster. That one right there." He pointed at it on the counter. "I don't know if I ever used it until she passed, but not a day goes by now I don't put a slice of bread in there for breakfast. Hell, sometimes I even have toast for dinner." He cast that long view of his out the window. "What I mean to say is that your mother wouldn't be disappointed in you. She might be sad for you, like I am. But not disappointed. What an unhappy thing, to realize you don't love your spouse anymore." He turned back to her. "I hope it's okay I say that?"

She nodded, and finished her whiskey.

With his eyes back on the window, he said, "You two will take care of my grandkids. That's the important thing now. And if you need money, let me know."

"I have money. And I can pick up more freelance work if it comes to that."

"Well, keep it in mind."

Now he turned to her, put his arms around her, and hugged her close. She thought she might cry, but the feeling passed and instead she felt rejuvenated by her father's love. "I have something I want to show you, Dad."

He stepped back but still held her by the shoulders. "Before you do, there's something I want to give you."

"What?"

"We'll have to get in the car. Can all this wait an hour?" He was talking about the turkey and stuffing and the rest of the dinner.

"I suppose," she said. "I don't even know where Frans went off to."

"I think Frans has worries beyond what time we eat dinner."

"He probably does."

"Get dressed, then. Let's leave in five minutes."

It took twenty minutes to get from her father's house to town, and they hadn't seen a single other car on the road. Arrowhead County was twice the size of Rhode Island, with only five thousand people living in it. Greta figured those who hadn't gone off to visit their families were sitting inside beside warm fires. She could've used a fire herself, since the heater in Gus's antique Subaru hardly staved off the cold. Earlier that morning, while Greta stood over the kitchen sink washing the mixing bowls she'd used for the pies, the thermometer read zero.

"Maybe it's time for a new car, Dad."

Gus took his right hand off the wheel to check the odometer. "I told your mom when we bought this car that I'd drive it until I turned seventy-five. I need to get two more years out of it."

"You've had it since I was in college."

"Twenty-five years." He checked the dash again. "There's a special club when you reach half a million miles. We'll have to see which comes first, another two years or twenty thousand more miles."

This effort at normal conversation felt unnatural to Greta, like she was lying or something. "The next two years will be the longest of my life," she said, intent on being honest.

"Your mom used to say time made the poor people rich, and the rich people poor."

"Mom sure had her sayings, didn't she?"

"Because she knew whereof she spoke."

Greta couldn't argue with that, so they rode on in silence and were about to crest the ridge overlooking Lake Superior. Even for all the places she'd seen, both here and abroad, that view remained her favorite sight. On this Christmas Day, the water settled beneath a suffocating sky as white as the snowbanks along the road, and its surface shimmered, the color of blueberries beneath its gray glitter. That lake, it had as many moods as Greta herself did, and in the silence of the car with her father she was experiencing a new one. Or, if not new, very old, recalling her childhood, when the lake inspired awe and anxiety in equal measure. Probably because of the toll it had taken on her family. Those stories were known well. She felt the pocket of her coat, where she'd put the book Stig had sent. She wanted to be able to tell her father everything, should the urge to come clean overwhelm her.

"I want you to know I've already talked to Tom about this," Gus said.

"About what?" She hadn't even wondered where they were headed until now, just as Gunflint and the harbor came into sight below. The streetlights were on. Two lonely cars drove east out of town, a mile between them.

"You'll see. But just know that your brother's fine with this. More than fine."

Greta looked over at her father. "You're being so coy." Just as she said it, the calm expression on his face snapped, and he slammed on the brakes. The car fishtailed, heading briefly toward the deep roadside snow before it straightened and lurched to a stop.

"Are you all right?" he asked.

Greta glanced up just in time to see the whitetail swerve around a tall pine and disappear into the woods. Then she looked at her father, who'd held his right arm out in front of her, as if to protect her. She took his hand in her own. "I'm fine, Dad. Are you?"

"Every day for over fifty years I've been driving this road, and that's the closest I've come to hitting one of those damn things."

"The luck of the Subaru," Greta said.

Gus pinched the key again and restarted the car. "Only twenty-five years of luck. The rest has just been good driving." He brought the car back up to speed.

"Where are we going, anyway?"

"You'll see," he said.

It was another ten minutes before they turned onto Eide Cove Road. It hadn't been plowed since the last snowfall, but the Subaru didn't have any trouble moving along under the weighed-down tree branches. Greta remembered the last time she'd been here, at Thanksgiving with Frans. A thought that brought with it a deeper chill.

Gus parked and turned the car off, then reached over and opened the tidy glovebox for the key. "Come with me, kid," he said, opening his door and stepping out into the cold.

Greta followed him through the doorway, the gray light spilling in behind them. It was exactly as she'd left it. The lantern on the hook by the door, the fish boxes moved aside on the counter, even the cigarette she'd stubbed out after that shameful fuck. She watched Gus scan the room.

"What are we doing here, Dad?"

He ushered her a few more steps inside and closed the door. He lit the lantern with matches from the box beside it on the little shelf, then walked to the windows on both sides of the barn door and pulled back the curtains. He turned and took in the whole place as though seeing it for the first time.

"I'm not a rich man. Not moneywise, leastways." He nodded at the window on the south side of the door, and then faced the window on the north.

Greta stood at the other window and peered out at the lake, which hadn't frozen yet but lay in the cove as still as if it had. The curve of shoreline heading out to the point was blanketed by snow.

"Not rich," he said, "but we have places important to our lives, don't we?" he said.

"We sure do," she said. She was lost in another favorite view, and thinking of Stig, as she so often did now. She wanted to share everything with him. This would be a good place to start.

To her father she explained, "I haven't done as much work down here as I wanted to, but I still intend to tidy it up. I hope that's okay."

"Well," he said, "I guess it's more than okay. And none of my business. It's all yours now."

"What's mine?"

"This." He spread his arms.

"What are you talking about?"

Now he put the lantern on the counter and pulled out the old three-legged stool beneath it and sat down. "All of this. The fish house. The three hundred feet of shoreline. The acre of land back to Old Shore Road. I figured you're going to need a place of your own. A place big enough for Lasse and Liv. A good place."

Greta was not herself quick to cry, and she felt the tears before she realized they were falling.

Gus looked up at her, his demeanor steady as the winter is long.

"I'm sure you've got some argument against this. I'm sure you're going to invoke Tom. But just hear me out, okay?"

She stepped to the counter and leaned against it, rubbing her eyes again.

"Tom will get the house up on the river when the time comes. You get this. Not quite a wash, so you also get the money. There's not much of it, and I can't give all of it to you now, but you'll get it eventually. It's a hell of a piece of property, as I'm sure you know. Larry Schmidt just sold his lot a mile west of town for two hundred grand." He shook his head. "That sounds damn near like a boast, which isn't what I mean."

"I know, Dad."

"In any case, I have but one request. It's actually your mother's request as much as it is mine. That you not tear the fish house down. Don't build one of those monstrosities all around us nowadays. See through some renovations of this place, okay? It's as much a part of our family as anything."

"I would never—"

"I know you wouldn't, but I had to say it, so there." He clapped his hands on his knees. "It feels good to make it yours."

Greta took a fresh look around and was overcome at once by the failure of her imagination before now. Where lately she'd thought this might make a nice three-season studio, she now saw it as a home to live in. She could add a loft, a full kitchen, a fireplace on the west wall. She'd replace the barn door with a huge window overlooking the shoreline. While rebuilding her life, she would rebuild the fish house. She would make each her own.

"I never thought of it as something to be passed down," Greta said. "It was just, I don't know, *our place.*"

"I might not've either, if not for your mother. When we used to talk about it, she'd say things like 'Greta's the one with the imagination, maybe she could make something of the old fish house.' Your mother, she knew you. And she loved you."

Greta looked around again, and saw the place with new eyes. She remembered her grandpa Harry bringing her down here when she was a kid. He'd find some little thing to give her. An old pocketknife or a fishing lure or a Coke bottle from fifty years before. And while he puttered around, looking for who knew what, he'd tell her stories about his father, the second Odd Einar, who'd drowned right off the shore, and who, as far as Grandpa Harry was concerned, was the single best man the world had ever known.

The thought of her great-grandfather reminded her of the book Stig had sent her. She touched the pocket of her coat and felt it there and wanted to tell her father about it, but in order to tell him about that—and about the first Odd Einar too—she'd also need to tell him about Stig.

"What is it, kid?" Gus asked. "You look like you've seen a ghost."

"Aren't you always saying this place is full of them?"

He nodded.

"I was thinking about Grandpa Harry, and how he used to talk about his father whenever he took me down here."

"Those two lived in this damn shack, if you can believe that. Pissed in a wooden box outside. Must've eaten beans from a can most nights, warmed up over a hot plate. But oh my, was my father a devotee. Yes sir, he was true to his old man. Who I think must have been pretty special. A single father until the day he died."

"I guess our family's full of special men."

"And women," Gus added quickly.

"Do you ever think about the misfortune? How bizarre your father's and grandfather's deaths were?"

"Sure," Gus said, as though he'd been doing so just then. "But both of them lived lives that might allow for it. Neither one was a retired schoolteacher."

"I learned something while I was in Norway. I learned lots of things, actually. But one in particular I want to tell you about."

"Okay." He seemed eager to listen.

"Your grandpa Odd Einar was preceded by another Odd Einar in Hammerfest."

"No kidding?"

"And that Odd Einar, he was described to me as something like a folk hero."

"What does that mean? And described to you by who?"

"He was a poor man, Odd Einar. His wife was Inger. A beautiful name, don't you think? Anyway, I gather Hammerfest in the 1890s was a hard place to make a living, because Odd Einar worked on a seal-hunting boat in the Arctic Circle. Up in Spitzbergen, which they call Svalbard now. One day, he and his hunting partner were attacked by a polar bear and presumed dead. He survived on his own for two weeks."

"Attacked by a polar bear? In Spitzbergen?"

Greta nodded.

"How do you know all this? Why was he a folk hero?"

"I read about it. In this." She withdrew *Isbjørn i Nordligste Natt* and offered it to him, as though it were a codebook. A sacred text.

He took the book from her with much the same reverence that she herself had bestowed upon it.

"That's the story of what happened to him. It's pretty remarkable."

"But it's all in Norwegian," he said. "How do you know what it says?"

"The local guy who sent it also sent a translation."

"And where's that?"

"Back at the house."

Gus stared at the book in his hands. "Who translated it for you? I'm having trouble tracking all this."

"I met someone."

"A translator?" he said, still looking at it. When, after a moment, she didn't answer, he looked up at her. "Oh," he said, "I see. In Norway?"

She observed in him the perfect expression of how she'd felt on Stig's boat, when she realized how much larger her world had just become by virtue of another's. "Yes, in Hammerfest. This man translated it. He told me about Odd Einar being a folk hero."

"What's his name?"

Again she thought of Stig, who'd asked the same question, in a similar tone, about her children. "His name's Stig Hjalmarson."

"Okay," he said, as though answering a question himself.

"I've known I was going to leave Frans since last Christmas, Dad."

"And how did you know that?"

For as much as she'd thought about it, she couldn't articulate an answer, at least not to her befuddled father. It would've been no less a lie to say she'd known their marriage was doomed from the time she'd accepted his proposal than to say she'd known it only since the night she heard Stig playing the church organ. "Isn't it funny," she said, thinking up the words only as they came out, "that it's so easy to tell people about falling in love, and so hard to describe falling out?"

"You really *don't* love Frans?"

"I haven't for a long time. Maybe I never did. Not like I was sup-posed to, anyway. I've been so sad for so long. A hundred times over the last ten years, I've seen how we're not right for each other. But the kids, you know? Last Christmas morning we had the most awful fight. I don't even remember what it was about, but I was making Lasse and Liv pancakes while he was in the living room playing with them, and I cried and cried because I knew that it was going to end. It was just that plain to see. Isn't that terrible?"

"For both of you, it really is. I'm sorry, Greta."

"Sorry for what?"

"That I hadn't actually *noticed*. That I didn't help you."

"You help more than anyone, Dad."

"What a hell of a Christmas."

Gus flipped carefully through a few pages until he came to the first engraving, the one of the schooner trapped in ice floes. Greta could well imagine the range of thoughts running through his head, and she was positive that at least one of them had to do with the boat he was studying, the cut of the sails and the rigging criss-crossing the decks. Even now, meeting this ancestral link for the first time, his mind would've been drawn to these practical mat-ters. Something for which she loved him all the more.

He paged through the whole book, stopping to study each pic-ture, lingering over the text as if he'd suddenly been gifted with the ability to read Norwegian. When, at the end, he came to the portrait of Odd Einar Eide, she studied his face for any changes.

She might've expected surprise or dismay, but instead she saw that famous smile come to her father's mouth.

"Well, I guess I used to be an old seal hunter," he said.

Now Greta could feel, for the first time ever, how enduring familial love really could be. "I guess so, Dad."

He glanced again at the portrait and handed the book back to her. "You say there's a translation of all this?"

"Handwritten. A private one, I suppose."

"What are the chances you'd let your old pops read it?"

"Pretty darn good."

Now he stood up and brushed the butt of his pants, and appraised the fish house like it was the last time he'd ever see it. "I always thought there should be a window where the barn door is. It seems silly, to be this close to the lake and only have those little portholes to look out."

"I already thought the same thing. And a fireplace along the west wall. A kitchen over here. Maybe even a loft with a couple bedrooms in the back."

Gus beamed, and Greta hugged him.

"I'll have the window put in before the steelhead run this spring," she said.

Now even more joy sprang onto his face. "You know, those fish return to spawn in the same river they were born in."

"You could've been a great poet, Dad."

"Who's to say I'm not?"

She slipped on her gloves and walked to the door beside her father. "How could I ever thank you enough for this?"

"Just find some happiness here. That's all I want for you. And for this place."

When they stepped outside, he handed her the key to lock the door behind them.

Over the next two days I met with Granerud in the mornings, our routine now not unlike the daybreaks of my former life, when I'd wake on Muolkot with Thea and Inger and take porridge and tea with them and head out before dawn to draw in my nets. Except now I woke up later, and in the extravagant Grand Hotel, then dressed in a respectable shirt and coat, walked along the quay to his offices and, instead of stepping aboard my boat and taking my spot on the stern sheets, I sat in a captain's chair to sail the rest of my story across the sound of my memory.

I told him about the ubiquitous fog, which rose from the mountains and glaciers each morning as sure as the steam from Inger's teapot did back home. I told him about how, on the fifth morning from my last, it drew down the fjord like a second dawn. Some days the fog settled onto the plain where I lived those last mornings, there to smother what little warmth the sun might offer. But I told him also about how darkness drew the fog away, and how the starlight then seemed like lanterns to light my dreams.

Twice I decided I'd rather work toward Kapp Guissez under those stars than in the soupy fog, and so many hours I might have been asleep passed walking through the night instead. Toward the next inevitable glacier, blooming beneath the night sky like a great milky river. I spoke of how I walked with my sack of meat slung over my shoulder, using my gun as a shovel or a cane, my hakapik in the other hand, my steps purely rote. As though plodding ever onward had been my sole adult occupation, and I was now a master cragsman.

I told him about the snow again too. The melodies of its falling and blowing. How it erased distance and time and shone the same under the daytime fog and nighttime stars and moon. It consoled me, and not only because the shelters I built with it provided some semblance of warmth. It was as if the snow spoke to me and eased what I knew to be my imminent death. So my reverence for it grew, and I spoke to it in turn as I had once prayed to God.

I told him how the cold had become the principal condition of my life. And how my reveries had gone from sumptuous feasts or sensuous nights with Inger, or evenings of song with my daughter after she'd returned home, to the much simpler desire for warmth. Every time my vision clouded with a gust of wind or a shift in fog, I'd conjure from the blurriness a great blaze toward which I'd hurry with fresh hope. Those hopes, of course, were dashed by the next shift in the breeze, and I would raise my voice to the snow once more, imploring it. Even, sometimes, asking for its forgiveness.

So I was rightly surprised on the same fifth-from-the-last morning—after all fantasies of a warm fire had been abandoned, same as any feast, or night of song with my daughter, or long slumber with my wife—when I drew my vision back across the plain and saw, a half mile distant, what at first glance appeared to be a whale's ancient skeleton, its ribs and spine scrubbed clean by time and wind and pecking birds, leaving only dried bones that glimmered there for my curiosity and pleasure. I wondered if I might be able to set them ablaze. To hang my sodden clothes to dry in the heat of that fire. Or to signal a distant ship.

But as I hurried toward it, I had the sobering realization that the beast would have suffered a terrible death, drowning on the same air that I myself breathed in such abundance. I wondered whether he had a whale wife or whale daughter who had swum off across cold northern seas and up into the bowels of a faraway continent. I wondered, too, whether in her memory he was loved or scorned. Or whether some whale landlord kept his corner of the sea in splendor, while this poor brute was made to beach himself, as I had done, on these sacrilegious shores.

And then, the closer I got, the more those bones seemed instead a bridge spanning a creek or small ravine, which thought put an extra quickness in my step. How many bridges had I wished for? Over crevasses high upon the second and third glaciers that I'd already crossed. Through this darkness of foggy days. Into peaceful sleep. Back to the poverty of my previous life. Back to my home.

If it seems unlikely that I'd recall such specific thoughts, I begged Marius Granerud to understand that my sentience in those days was drifting like the ice floes. It might as well have been subject to the same tides and winds, to the same ocean currents and distant calving glaciers. But for all of my mind's aimless wandering, I was aware more than ever of my *insignificance*, so I judged my thinking up against *that*. To say this was the great lesson of my time on Spitzbergen would be to underestimate the many others, so many of which cost me dearly. But I do believe that if I'd stood amidst the Fonn and failed to see my slightness, I would have perished that night, or the next, or at least before I heard the bell of a ghostly boat some days later.

But back to that whale's bones. I now stood nigh a hundred paces from it, wisps of fog breathing through me, the paltry sunlight low and straight into my eyes. I learned well in those days how distance collapsed with time, and at that spot on the beach I turned and contemplated the earth I had already trod. Perhaps fifteen miles lay behind me, a third of those across three glaciers, some by day, some by night. I could not have known that the last hundred paces separating me and the whale would be the last I'd cover, but I did know my exhaustion had reached its zenith. I felt the tightness in my stomach. I reached for it, and then let my hands travel up my own ribs. And there, on the beach, I realized how sick I was. If this understanding had come to me without that new destination before me, I might've laid myself out on the rocks and slept forever. I was disappearing. Dying, like the whale. I shivered and felt the flush of my fever. My own bones grew closer to my touch. The flesh on my face was drawn, so tight that it felt thin enough to tear like paper, should the right wind come off the fjord. As I stood taking that paltry inventory of my flesh, feverish even as I trembled with whatever sickness had taken root, I bargained with myself. I would walk to the whale, at least, and die in its company. And in ten or twenty or fifty years, or whenever the next lost soul should find himself wandering those plains without a boat to get home in, and then chance upon that bridge of bones, he would find my own ribs beside the whale's. And thus might have a foreshadowing of his own doom.

"They were lonely steps, Herr Granerud." I spoke those words on the second to last of our meetings, in the quiet of his office. To recall them was to summon again that feeling of certain death, and my face must have displayed it.

"And without God to walk with you," he whispered, with dire solemnity across his face. As though he were in fact mourning the loss of me.

"Halfway there, I looked up. Maybe I wanted to delay what I knew would come. Maybe I only wanted to take solace in my decision to give up. I felt a calm I'd not known since I'd last sat in Inger's sweet company. I laid the Krag-Jørgensen on the rocks and slid the makeshift sack of meat from my weary shoulders. Ten paces on, I dropped the hakapik. There were patches of fog still, and they continued to pass through me."

"Your face is serene, Odd Einar. Is it because you did not lie down and die? Is it because you lived to see your wife? To lie down instead in a warm bed with her?"

"I cannot think of those minutes on the plain without thinking of the warmth that came after."

"What warmth?"

"Why, the warmth of fires."

He appeared confused. As confused as I myself had been when I got close enough to see these weren't bones at all, only the ancient and upturned hull of a wrecked nordlandsbåt.

"This, then, it must have been another of your turns of good fortune? The third of four?"

"Can you imagine it? After all that cold? All that darkness? *Indeed,* to have, sitting there right before me, as though a treasure left behind by some earlier explorer, enough wood to build a bridge?"

"A royal find."

"Yes, Marius, given my sack of meat, I'd rather have had that wood than a tin of cookies."

He shook his head. "I've asked you a dozen times to call me by my given name, Odd Einar. And now you have."

"If I'm anything, it's slow to learn."

"We're all that, friend."

"May I ask you a question?"

"Of course," he said, and sat up in his chair.

"Having heard all this, do I strike you as a stooge?"

"Of course not—"

"Will the man or woman who reads of me think I'm a fool?" I pointed to the papers spread across his desk. "It's one thing to have lived through my ordeal, and to have suffered its indignities. But quite another, it occurs to me, to think about living it over and over and over again in the minds of people I'll never know. It's as if my woe will live on forever. Or for as long as people care to even pick up this story. Should I want that?"

He appeared speechless, a pose uncommon for him, and he looked between my wondering face and his notes on the blotter and said nothing at all. When finally he spoke, the strength of his voice had abandoned him and he sounded like an old man who wasn't used to speaking. "I don't know what to say, except it is my intention that anyone reading of your plight will know the man who came out of it alive did more than survive with dignity. I will want these readers to know he *redefined* dignity." He glanced again at his pile of notes, rearranged a few, and dipped his pen in his inkwell as if pressed to record his own thoughts. But he merely held the nib of his pen in the air. "I marvel at you, and not only because of what you survived. Not only because of your intuition and your will and your *instincts*. Odd Einar, I marvel at you for your humility, too.

"And though I cannot account for my own abilities, or for the sensibilities of whatever audience my work might gain, I can say with some confidence that my portrayal of you and your misadventure will reflect my great admiration, and that others will see what I do."

He now regarded me, maybe in hopes that his words did soothe me, and then dipped his nib once more, hardly removing his gaze from mine. He appeared to reformulate his thoughts twice, his lips parting and twisting as if to speak, before he said simply, "Tell me about how that fire felt, Odd Einar. Tell me about those last five days."

As soon as I kindled, with the help of Mikkelsen's flint and steel, the first fire on the shore of the Krossfjorden and felt its resplendent warmth and my shivering body found reprieve, I began to think of the new offerings that dreadscape might have for me. For as sure as I knew I was dead before discovering that ancient hull, I knew then with equal certainty that those old planks would prolong my stay and give me time to complete my inventory of memories. The ones I wanted to take to my death with me. For this I was deeply grateful.

The first memory was of my daughter on a morning in eighteen and ninety, her eleventh year. I had been working by lantern light one morning in the boathouse, carving a new rudder gudgeon for my faering, when Inger came hurrying in with Thea at her side.

"Odd Einar," she said, and from the tone of her voice I knew something gravely wrong was nigh.

"Papa!" Thea shrieked. "Come see the morning. Why's the sun all smoky?"

I looked at Inger, who nodded. "You'd best take a look," she said.

So the three of us tromped to the shore and gazed out across the water at the towering plumes of smoke rising from the village.

"It doesn't smell good, Papa," Thea said, pinching her nose and squinting. Inger put her arm around her daughter and held her close.

"You ought to go see if you can help, Odd Einar."

She was right, and I would, but I stood there for another minute positive I could be of no use and we were witnessing the end of our village, that it would never recover from the ashes of destruction. I cannot even say this thought was undesirous, forcing us, as it would, to move to a less hostile place.

If I was wrong about our fortitude in the face of ruin, I was right about my being able to help. By the time I rounded Skansen, the scope of the fire shocked me. From Gávpotjávri to the churchyard, a great conflagration seized the town. I could hear, even from across the harbor, the sizzle and hiss of the heat beneath the roaring exhalation of the flames. Smoke billowed and mushroomed and soot rained down. I thought of my friends and the people I'd known all my life. I thought of Inger's sister and her husband, Rune, and of their apartment on the Grønnevoldsgaden, next to Lundby's grocery store. All of it now char. Sitting there on the harbor I knew that forever after, whenever my eyes alighted on another fire, my memory would return to Hammerfest as it burned.

The fire smoldered for four days, and by the time its last cinders were doused, two-thirds of our village had burned. It surprised no one to learn that the spark that ignited it all came from the new electric ovens in Bengt's bakery, the ones he'd boastfully brought home from the World's Fair in Paris only the previous year. As with so many of his ventures, he trumpeted the innovation and progress of the idea as though loaves of bread were a new invention, and all his own.

Well, we were all in need of bread in the days that followed. Inger and Thea spent mornings at the kneading board while I rowed to the village to sift through the ashes, reclaiming as much as could be found. Have you ever seen the better part of a village charred and in ruins? Have you ever axed what was once your neighbor's front door, only to have the dormant fire flare up at your feet? Have you searched for your aunt's walking cane, and found instead the missing pastor's thighbone? For that is some of what awaited me in the rubble.

I told this story because I had an ardent belief that I would never see flames so intense again, but as I set the first of those boards afire on the beach in Spitzbergen, and as the smoke wafted around me, its warmth reaching into every part of me, as my shivering slowed and then stopped altogether, I realized that that fire, even in its containment, was just as wondrous.

I sat with the burning bones of that old nordlandsbåt for hours, divining the rest of my life from the shifting and dancing flames. For the first time since killing the reindeer I cooked its flesh rather than eating it raw, and the warmth of that meat settling in my bowels settled me. I undressed to my skivvies and hung my clothes to dry, and that night I slept like a cat on the hearth, my face toward the fire, waking only to stoke its flames.

The next morning I luxuriated further by roasting another hunk of brisket, toasted my feet, and then used several planks to build a lean-to beside the growing heap of ashes. I dismantled more of the hull and stacked the wood into three different piles. By my uncertain calculus, I estimated that I had enough to keep a fire going for nigh three weeks. Twice that long if I stoked them only half the night. At first thought, this seemed a boon. But then I started counting up the days before the ice might clear and men like Svene Solvang and his crew would be able to return for more seals. That would be six months, perhaps even longer. And no matter how I moved the wood around, there were sure to be four or five months without anything to burn at all. And it getting colder.

So the tide of my hope was pulled by those fires, same as the seas being pulled by the sun and moon. And like the ocean level, my mood changed incrementally, and then enormously. One moment I would bask in the warmth, and the next remember how my piddling stock of wood stood against the season to come. If I hadn't already been down with my neap tide, in those despairing hours before finding the hull, I might have panicked. But I was learning that this place gave as often as it took and here found fortitude, if not peace.

And with that in hand, I spent the next two days weathering my time. I had food. Dry clothes. Wood to burn. And time to consider every possibility. I gave thought to trying to paddle down the fjord. I might load a berg with my belongings and use a plank to steer with. But the problem was ice. Mountains of it had amassed, too much to navigate in a boat, never mind a floe. And so it made no sense to leave my lean-to and the copious fresh water I had to drink from the melting glacier. Even if Kapp Guissez was only ten miles hence, it might as well have been fifty. For I could no sooner cross the flooded moraine than I could navigate the congested ice. I was as good as encamped there, and fine with this fate.

At night, as I wandered into sleep, I contemplated that my fires were likely the first in human history to ever warm that shore. I found this beautiful, and for flickering seconds tricked myself into believing that my misadventure had some larger purpose. Like Nansen or Sverdrup or Andrée. Men whose ambition drove them to inhabit these wild places, and whose reward came with riches as well as respect. If such thoughts strike you as grandiose, you're not mistaken. But there was no vanity in my thinking, only delusion. And delusion was a remarkable aid to sleep.

On the second morning from the last, I woke to a dramatic change in my circumstances. Since I'd set up camp there, my practice had been to cache the venison under a mound of stones gathered for just that reason. I arranged the depot about two hundred yards behind me. Back where I'd first seen what I mistook for a whale's bones. My plan was not complicated. I wanted to protect my stores but also keep them some distance from camp. Though I hadn't seen my ice bear—or even any sign of him—since the day he killed Mikkelsen, I seldom went long without fearing that he lurked right beyond the next hummock of snow, or barely below the landkall clinging to the shore. In those last days, I admit a part of me desired to see that beast. To look him in his narrow black eyes and commune with him. To feel his isolation as I now understood it, after nearly two weeks in his territory. I also wanted to test my revised boundaries of fear, for though I knew well my vulnerability when stepping aboard one of Svene's killing boats half a season ago, and though my first few nights on that barren island were a lesson in abject horror, I found myself now almost amused by my old weaknesses. And surely this fellow's curiosity would best him. I had often sensed since last seeing him that he sat waiting at some distance, in darkness or snow, regarding me as I now wished to regard him. A not small part of me had fashioned for us a kind of brotherhood. As though the ice bear understood my plight and was watching over me.

Of course, I now judge these as sentiments from a taxed and snow-blind mind beset by great loneliness. The true reasons he might've had for avoiding me until then are much plainer to see in retrospect. There was an abundance of seals, and he knew how to hunt them a hundred years before he ever set foot on the ice. Why would he trouble with some creature who might plug him with another round from the Krag-Jørgensen? He had no idea that gun was as useless to me now as the planks it was leaning against. Or maybe his taste for filthy human flesh had been cured by devouring my comrade. Perhaps the blood of man tasted of corruption and compromise, neither of which settled well in his bear belly. Or, most likely, he'd merely wandered off into the expanse of that infinite snow, happier in his isolation than in my pitiful company.

In any case, whatever compulsion kept him at bay had been either forgotten or forsaken, and when I woke on the second to last morning, it was to a perfectly clear view across the distance that separated me from my cache, where the bear was making a breakfast of my remaining venison.

Oh, he was a picture of aloofness, sitting back on his haunches, gnawing on the meat like he'd been invited to a picnic. I had endowed him with vengeance and rage, given the lead lodged in his shoulder. But even through the wisps of fog—it came every day now—I saw a simpler beast, one who only wanted enough to eat. I was of no more interest to him than I was to the King of Norway. The ice bear knew I sat there studying him. Likely he found my fire curious. He may even have had a notion about the hull of the ancient boat being dismantled and gone from his lifelong view. But until he got hungry again, or unless the seals were all killed, he wouldn't need my flesh any sooner than I needed his.

This came as a relief. And that night I quit trying to devise plans to make the wood and meat last. That night, when snow again began to fall, and the heavens darkened and then swirled violently, when I shifted the position of my lean-to to protect me from the wind and lay in the crook of it, my face warm from the fire, I replaced my thoughts of rescue with a long remembrance of my daughter and wife.

Christmas morning of her twelfth year, Thea woke me without waking Inger. Together she and I went to the stove, and while I rekindled it she got water for tea and placed the krumkake she'd filled with sweet cream onto the platter adorned with holly berries. I still don't know if Inger truly slept through our preparations that morning—it's hard to believe she did—but when Thea brought her a cup of tea, she at least feigned waking.

All through Advent, Thea and I had been working on a surprise for her. A song we'd perform. My fiddle, accompanied by Thea's haunting contralto. She still had a child's heart, and she loved to sing. At church. While doing her chores. While readying herself for bed as well as first thing in the morning. Earlier that autumn, she told me that as long as she was free to sing, she could be happy. And indeed she was. Despite our beggary, which by then had grown serious. We ate more of the fish I caught, and so had less to sell. Our garden yield that summer was scant. Our clothes getting shabbier despite Inger's fine sewing ability. And perhaps worst of all, we lost one of our sheep. The winter ahead would be a struggle unlike any we'd known before.

But on that Christmas morning, as I bowed the simple cords from my hardingfele while Thea sang so beautifully, Inger rose from her slumber on our notes, with joyful tears burnishing her sweet cheeks, and we none of us wanted for anything.

The song was about a troll living on the rocky shore of Muolkot, who seined little nissefisk from the shallow waters. They were made into delicious soup that filled you right up, but also gave you hope and courage. One day—Christmas Eve, as it turned out—the troll went to his nets and found them empty. Naturally there was much fretting, because the family had planned its holiday feast around those bountiful bowls of creamy broth. Yet they ought not to have fretted, for the soup also nourished their faith and that belief brought them a cornucopia for their Christmas feast. Which of course was topped off with krumkake filled with sweet cream.

After we finished the performance, Thea made a great show of presenting Inger with the cookies she'd made and together we sat on the bed, laughing as each of us cupped a hand below our mouth to keep crumbs from falling under the eiderdown. Of all the memories of my daughter, this was perhaps the most enduring. I can still see the glint in her eyes, put there by pride and by love. And I can still taste the sweet cream, it being the last I'd had.

Recalling that scene on the wastes of Spitzbergen—my venison pilfered by the ice bear, the winds shifting around from the north as more snow fell—was enough to buoy me and to give me peace all through the night. What a strange thing, for this one day to resound in me so strongly in that place, removed by so many years and miles. And how strange that each memory holds many others. Like the nesting dolls we gave to Thea on that same Christmas morning.

I conjured up many such memories that night, basking in the warmth of the fire, fearless and without care, less sleeping than dreaming my life all over again. But always coming back to Thea and Inger, with the eager hope they were thinking of me too. I was readier than ever to pass into the Fonn, and for the next twenty-four hours I braced myself against that north wind, as dead as I was alive.

And so I might be forgiven for my behavior on the last morning on that island. For thinking that the sails I saw unfurled and moving with the north breeze in the sunlit fog belonged to some vessel from my past. Or for mistaking the clambering bell on her deck

for my sjeleringing, and for believing that the pervasive feeling
of lightness was last-minute proof of God taking my soul heavenward, and not, as it would turn out, my fever breaking. In the crack-
ling fire, and through the whispers of that cold wind, I heard voices
too. And no chorus of angels, either, but a searching and inharmonious gaggle speaking in Russian and Swedish and my own
tongue. I rose on an elbow and silently admonished the flames for
their clamor, so that I might hear better what was being said over
the water: *"Zdravstvuyte? Vems eld är det? Er noen I live der borte?
Det lukter som brann."* "It *is* fire," I whispered back. "Who's there?"
I said, struggling up and waving my arms. *"Obrezh'te Parusa.
Davayte posmotrim."*

Though I knew a few Russian words from a fisherman friend
from Linhammar, who used to bring his catch to the Hammerfest
market, I couldn't understand that last expression. When things
went quiet, I feared they had given up and were continuing on. So
I whooped and bawled and stoked the fire with armfuls of wood.
By then the boat had moved past me and I could see the broad
transom dark as the water against the glowing fog.

"No! No! Come back! I'm here! Please!" It's no noble thing to
beg, but I certainly did. And though in my mind I recall a thousand
shouts, it must've only been a few, because the next shift in the
image of that boat was a darkening around the masts as the sails
lowered and the boat came about. The last thing I heard from the
Pobeg was her engines turning on and the call *"Du er i live! God
Gud, du er i live…"* Behind that voice I saw a man, his hand raised
as though we were old friends.

After stepping off the dinghy and scrambling up the landkall, he
introduced himself as Vladamir Doltskavich. He wore a coat of ice
bear pelage with buttons of yellow teeth. Any beast with lesser fur
would not have covered him, for here stood a man taller even than
Svene Solvang, his beaverskin hat festooned with the feathers of a
hundred different birds. As he righted himself before me, the tip of
my nose was hardly above the belt on his coat.

"Which one are you?" he asked in clear Norwegian.

"What?"

"Mikkelsen or Eide?"

"I'm Odd Einar Eide. Of Hammerfest. I last served Svene Solvang on the sealing vessel *Sindigstjerna*. This is my fourteenth day alone in the Fonn."

"What the fuck is the Fonn? You're wandering Spitzbergen, my friend. And lucky not to be dead four different times and ways." He turned back to his boat, some twenty yards offshore, cupped his hands round his mouth, and shouted, "Butter up some bread and brew some coffee." He turned back to me, took off his mitten, and laid his massive hand on my shoulder. "Was it Mikkelsen's legs, then? And those his boots?" He pointed down at the komagers on my feet.

"Yes."

He shook his head and gripped my shoulder tightly. "No doubt you've got some stories to tell. But first, what say we get you off this fucking wasteland?"

Can you imagine fortunes so shifted by the wind's direction? For that, I would learn, is what happened. About the time the ice bear looted my stocks, and on the night I lay down to die while those north winds brought such a bitter chill, they also cleared the Kross-fjorden of ice, or at least enough of it that Vladamir Doltskavich was able to sail windward from his weather station on the Kongs-fjorden to find me on the Kross.

I gathered my few belongings and was taken on board the *Pobeg*, which was little more than a yawl outfitted for polar climes that Doltskavich used to sail along the west coast between Danskøya and Hotellneset. He'd been based on the Krossfjorden for a year, I learned, filling his days with the mundane tasks of reading instruments and measuring temperatures and precipitation for a purpose he was not quite clear about but that was deemed urgent under the reign of Tsar Nicholas II. Mostly, as it happened, he spent his time fishing and hunting and playing chess with the Norwegian trapper who'd pulled me aboard the *Pobeg* and now was cooking seal meat for his Swedish assistant, a man named Ludvig Bokløv, who was as diminutive as Doltskavich was imposing.

It turns out that Solvang had steered the *Sindigstjerna* for Doltskavich's weather station before motoring south for Vardø to bring the seals to market. Solvang told his old friend about the two men he'd lost to the ice bear on the Kross, their dismembered and disappeared bodies, and that he would telegraph their next of kin when he reached Norway. Doltskavich, impressed by the gruesome details, was determined to sail up the middle finger of the Kross before the deep freeze set in, should the ice permit. For a while those prospects looked grim, but that night—the second of northerly winds—showed bright the ice coming down from the Krossfjorden and on out the Kongsfjorden, and with little fore-thought Doltskavich summoned his assistant and the two of them embarked to the trapper's cabin on Kapp Mitra, where he'd lived for some ten years, winter and summer both.

On his deck, I asked what force had sent him to me, and he replied casually that something about Solvang's story left him uneasy. When he went on to say he'd scried a disturbance on his island, he added that, ice permitting, he'd go and have a look. The wind changed directions, the ice blew down the fjord, and he raised his sails to find my fire on the shore. He explained all this as if it were the most natural occurrence.

"What will happen to me now?" I asked. We still hadn't even gone belowdecks, though I could smell the strong coffee brewing.

"I'll bring you to Hotellneset. I was hoping to make one more trip for supplies, and anyway, my trapper friend Fredrik offered me a krone to bring him down and back. From there you'd best hope for a whaler or sealer to be making one last run. But for now I'll get you that coffee and bread, then we'll hoist our sails and catch this tailing breeze down Forlandsundet."

All of this happened before the fire still burning on shore receded from my view. I had been rescued from that place as swiftly and unexpectedly as I'd been stranded there. Two weeks earlier I had watched our killing boat drift down the Krossfjorden laden with seal meat, ferrying my hopes of survival. And yet, here I was, in the company of an eccentric Russian, bound for the place my Spitzber-gen trial began: Hotellneset. In the worst-case scenario, I would need to winter there and await the first ships of spring. But I was saved, that much was clear, and as Fredrik brought a pot of warm coffee on deck, I saw the final wisp of my fire burn behind me.

I turned to Doltskavich and said, "I should thank you, but before I do I must say I haven't an øre to give you, much less a krone."

Again, he put his hand on my shoulder and said, "I can't imagine how much you've paid already." He took the coffee from Fredrik and handed it to me. "Drink this. If you like, you can go down into the cabin for some rest and a bite to eat. Or you can stand beside me. With this wind, we're a day from Hotellneset. You'll be warm tonight. I'll have Bokløv find you a dry shirt and coat." He took a deep swig of his own cup of coffee and wiped his lips on his bearskin sleeve. "But for fucksakes, don't worry about a krone."

So I stood beside Doltskavich drinking hot coffee, eating buttered bread and sardines, and watching that great northern silence recede. It was interrupted only once, half an hour into our sail, when all the fog lifted and a krykkje alighted from the brume above onto the masthead. It cocked its head and called three times and then lifted off again.

"This was how I was brought to Hotellneset, where, after one day, I boarded that season's last downbound ship," I told Marius.

"Your fourth bit of fortune."

"If being made to shovel coal for three days with hardly a sip of water can be called fortune, then yes. But that sounds bitter. It was good fortune indeed. For here I am now. With Inger awaiting me for one more supper at the Grand Hotel."

"Before you go, I'll have you sit for a portrait that we'll print beside your story. I'll have other drawings made, too. Normally, I'd have a subject approve such pictures, but your descriptions of that place leave me quite certain of the images we'll include. I might say, we'll run the story in six parts, to equal the number of days you've spent here in Tromsø."

"A portrait?" I asked.

"Naturally. So the world can see the man. It won't take long. An hour, at most. We can even do it before lunch. I can have Herr Rudd summon our portraitist now, in fact, and he'll be finished before we're done."

And thus a man arrived to sketch me. He sat at Marius's shoulder with paper and charcoals and explained that he would make the sketch into an engraving, which would then be used in the newspaper.

"There's been some talk of making your story into a book, Odd Einar," Granerud interrupted. "Of course, should that come to pass, we'll send you a copy when it's printed. You'll have to let me know where you land when up in Hammerfest. I mean, to what address I might send such a thing."

To learn, in the space of two off-the-cuff comments, that I and my story would be memorialized in a portrait as well as a book seemed an awful lot to take for granted, but what did I know anymore?

In that last half hour, Marius confirmed details for the record. Matters of dates and time, weather, landscape, materials, grief, despair, belief. He had a list and went down it as though quizzing me on my own life. I'd already found reason to suspect a few things I'd told him that seemed, even according to my own sensibilities, to be refutable or even impossible. But as I sat there answering his questions, I realized this was how memory worked. And so, I cast aside my doubts as I had once cast aside my hope.

The portraitist finished and gathered his materials and left without a goodbye. Then Marius took a last look at his list of questions and said he had one more. "Is there anything you have not told me that you wish to?"

I considered the realization that had just crossed my mind, and almost admitted it. But in answer simply shook my head.

He stood and pressed the small of his back with both of his hands, a look of sincere fondness on his face. I stood there across his desk.

"Then our time together is drawing to a close."

"I'll miss your company, Marius."

The sound of his name on my voice brought a smile to his face. "For now, Odd Einar. Only for now. Indeed, our paths will cross again. Of this I'll make certain. I hope you'd look forward to that as well?"

"This goes without saying."

"Excellent," he said, then came around to my side of the desk and offered his hand. "I promise to do my damnedest by you and your story."

"I believe you."

"I hope it's not too much to say, but from now on please count me among your friends and admirers. If there's anything I can ever do to help, simply send word."

"Thank you, I will. And once Inger and I find a new home, I'll let you know the address."

"Very good."

I let go of his hand and stepped to the door, where I put on my coat and buttoned it up. "I never meant for any of this to happen, you know? I only wanted to provide for Inger. Only wanted our happiness back. I went to work for that."

"Any man would do the same."

"I guess I mean to say thank you. Just as Doltskavich rescued me from that island, you have rescued me from my drudgery. I intend to honor you by staying above it."

"I've no doubt you will," he said.

I shook his hand once more before turning to leave. But after one step I paused and turned back for a final look about his office. "Make sure you put in your story how much I love my daughter. Would you do that for me?"

"It's already a part of it. There'll be no mistaking that."

That evening Inger and I stood on the deck watching as Tromsø grew distant behind us. Our boat would stop first at Skjervø and then Alta before docking in Hammerfest, and we watched intently and for a long while with the night fair and waters smooth all around us. The boat passed the town's outskirts and then the first farms until all that stood before us was a distant landscape.

Inger hadn't said much, but she'd hooked her hand in my arm

while the boat was still tied to the wharf and hadn't let go since. Her hair smelled of lavender, her breath of sugar. Twenty minutes up the sound, she nudged me and said, "We'll be all right, won't we, Odd Einar?"

"As long as we're together," I said.

I could feel her body slackening beside me, and her grip tightening on my arm. "I love you."

I turned to face her. "You are all I've ever loved. You and Thea."

She sighed and turned back to look out over the water. "I'll miss the Grand Hotel."

"A fine, fine place."

"What will we do now? When we get home?" The resignation in her voice was plain to hear. Like she knew our lark had ended, and now the business of becoming ourselves again commenced.

My every third thought had returned lately to this same question, and though I knew it also weighed on Inger we had so far neglected to discuss it. Simply put, I didn't know what we'd do. Altogether we had probably seventy kroner to our name. We still owned my boat and Inger's spinning wheel and a few remnants of furniture and household goods. Not much to rebuild a life on, to be sure, but I had the serene feeling that the boat bringing us home was bringing us also to happiness. I would ready my faering, Inger would find other work. We would be frugal. And as long as we had each other, we would make ends meet. I doubted she shared my sanguinity, but something had changed in her during our time in Tromsø. A softening. A warming. And I knew, or at least believed, that even if she still saw rough seas ahead of us, she was also on board the boat with me.

"I guess we step ashore," I said. "We walk up the Grønnevolds-gaden and see about someplace to live. We gather our things. We start over again." I wanted to say, *We find Thea. We bring her home.* But the pull of Inger beside me was too strong, so I only thought it for fear she might have a change of heart.

"Okay," she said, and then a second later pointed off the star-board side of the boat. "What's that?"

I might've thought I was dreaming or hallucinating had Inger not pointed it out: a great blazing fire onshore. It must have been a farmer's slash pile, or some unlucky fisherman's boat house, for the fire reached halfway to the moon.

"Odd Einar?"

"I reckon someone's had a bit of bad luck."

"What's wrong?" she said, and I knew she was asking not about the fire, but the wistfulness in my voice.

I turned to her. "I never told you about the fire I was lucky enough to find on Spitzbergen. A venerable old boat hull upturned on the shore of the spot I spent my last five nights. I burned almost all of it to keep myself from freezing. The flames from my fire brought the Russian to me. It saved my life."

"A fire so great as that?" Again she pointed out across the water.

"Not nearly, no. The timbers of the hull of that boat were so large I could hardly lift them, let alone take them apart. But I kept a bed of hot coals and fed timbers into the flames a foot at a time. When awake, I would chip the embers off with the hakapik to stoke the bed of cinders. I'd built a pit of stones around it, so I could shift the vents according to the wind. I tell you, Inger, I tended that fire with the care I gave our newborn daughter. I swear I did."

"You were such a good father, Odd Einar. Your daughter adored you."

"I'm still a good father, Inger."

I expected her to recoil, but she simply squeezed my arm again.

We both watched the fire grow fainter over our shoulders.

"Without that hull on the beach I would've died, Inger. I wouldn't be here now. That fire, it saved me. And I can't help wondering if I deserve it. That skeletal hull meant that others had perished before me. I was the heir of their misfortune. Is this how things forever must go?"

"Every night I pray for God to enlighten me."

Now I held her more closely, and we stood there without speaking until the fire disappeared altogether.

"Shall we go to our quarters?" she asked. "I'm ready to lie down with you."

Without waiting for my response, she ushered me down the gangway to our berth on the second deck.

"If I'm honest with you, my faith has wavered too, Odd Einar. So many of my prayers have gone unanswered. I've been tested and tried." She stopped at the bottom of the gangway, moved her hands to my chest, and looked up at my eyes. "But I was wrong to doubt. I was wrong to fear. For here you are. Don't you see?"

I held her in my arms and closed my eyes. "I do," I said. "I do."

On weekends when Frans had the kids, Greta went up to Gunflint to work on her projects. The first order of business had been to replace the stovepipe and flue on the old potbelly. She knew the stove would eventually head to the dump, but didn't want to spend all winter shivering. So she brought one of her father's old splitting mauls and his chain saw down from his place, and cut and split herself a cord of wood from the overgrowth around the fish house.

During the last three months, she'd gutted the place from floor to ceiling, culling both the detritus of her family's life there and materials she didn't expect to use in the renovation. Gone was the counter that had once been used to clean and salt the herring, and where she'd last fucked her husband. Gone the old fish boxes, all but three, which she kept for posterity and to use as she moved things around. Gone the half wall near the entry door, the old whiskey barrels, the floorboards that had rotted, the net rollers and buoys and scrap wood, some of which she added to her woodpile. Gone the strongback on which her father had built his canoe so many years before. But the canoe itself she kept, along with the tools in the wooden toolbox, the old Coleman lantern, two pairs of sawhorses, and a picture she'd never seen before, painted by Grandma Lisbet. It was a large canvas of a frozen Eide Cove at sunrise, though the light was blotted by the grayness of fog or snow or clouds, it was hard to tell which. The trees out on the point were mere shadows, bent southerly as though the morning brought with it a north wind. It was a striking and somber painting, but also beautiful. Greta hung it on the barn door, which would eventually become a large window overlooking the lake. She thought she might find a few additional treasures, too, but other than an old Skippy peanut butter jar full of antique coins and the sketches and blueprints for her great-grandfather's boat, which she planned to frame, the place offered nothing of value.

In toto, she'd scrapped two dumpsters' worth of junk. And now, in March, except for a folding card table and pair of chairs, the stove, a tiny refrigerator like the one she'd had in her dorm room at the University of Minnesota, and the old bunk, atop which she'd put a new mattress, the place was a blank canvas. And though she'd had plans drawn for the loft addition, fireplace, kitchen, and new lake-facing south wall, she felt the freedom to change anything at any time, and so kept a notebook of her own drawings, designs she might incorporate or not. A landing on the staircase, dormers on the loft windows, a deck or patio, anything was possible. This weekend she intended to start framing the kitchen island and counter.

All winter she'd worked for ten or twelve hours a day, and at the end of them, after she called the kids to say good night and say she loved them, and after she talked to Stig, something she did almost every day now, she'd sit down to a dinner of summer sausage and cheese and her dad's homemade bread. Those fifteen minutes were often the only rest she gave herself all day, and even then she'd look around the fish house—*her* house—and raise the stories it held invisibly. This in itself was another kind of work.

After supper, she would open her notebooks and spread them about the card table and continue imaginary conversations she'd been carrying on all day. It started with the book that Stig had sent, *Nordligste*, as she now thought of it. She must've read it ten times by then, so often that parts were fully memorized. Sometimes she read it out loud, and when doing so, she'd attribute to her three-times-great-grandfather a voice plaintive and sweet. She tried to capture that quality when she wrote.

But what began with Odd Einar Eide and his ordeal at Spitzbergen soon became more labyrinthine. Mere weeks into writing about him, she had created a hand-drawn family tree in one of her notebooks, and jottings for everything she knew about any of them. Thea and the other Odd Einar, Rebekah, Harry, her grandpa and grandma, Gus and Liv and Lasse and Frans and Stig.

When her father saw the notebook left open on the card table one day in February—he dropped by often, whether to help or just to pass some time with her—he picked it up and studied her drawing and said, "What've you got here?"

The simple answer was that she didn't know. "Am I right remembering that when you taught high school, you told everybody that history did not abide acts of the imagination?"

A doubtful look spread up to his eyes. "I'm afraid I used to say plenty of things that I'd be wary of standing behind now."

"That memory and imagination are two different things? Didn't you used to say that?"

"I think I used to talk about that one in English class. When we'd talk about Emily Dickinson."

"I recall you used to say it pretty often. Especially after Grandpa Harry died."

"You were in grad school when Grandpa Harry died."

"And you'd call me to talk about him. His death seemed to be the only thing on your mind for about two years."

He appeared humbled, as if those years in the nineties had been some mark against him. As though grieving your father was somehow a sign of weakness.

"It's okay, Dad."

"I know it is. I was just thinking about the years after Grandpa Harry died. A lot of what I once held to be true was proven wrong by his disappearance. Well, that and the fact I spent the next couple years reviewing my life with him over and over again in my head. I about drove your mother batty."

"Well, the story of our family isn't exactly paved with straight roads, that's for sure."

"And that's what this is? You're straightening out the roads?"

"I'm getting to know them a little, maybe that's how I should put it. I'm trying to learn how I got here." She closed her eyes and saw the parade of Eides passing through the darkness. When she opened her eyes, and noticed the searching look on her father's sweet face, she knew that his grief was her own, and that the notebooks spread out before her, and the hundreds of sleepless hours spent dreaming about her entire genealogy, and her devotion to a past that depended equally on her memory and her imagination, all of it was a gift. To her father and to her son and daughter and to the man she was planning a new life with.

"I've not been very good at letting the people closest to me know how much I love them. You included. Maybe what I'm doing is trying to tell you all."

"I've always known how much you love me, Greta."

"Well, maybe that's because you knew me back when I was pretty good at loving people." And here she picked up one of the notebooks on the table and thumbed through the scribbled pages. "And maybe now I'm trying to get better at it."

"At love?"

"Yes."

He looked so lonesome, then, this beautiful old man with the white hair and beard. He was still trim and fit, still dressed each day like he was going to teach his classes, still went down to the Blue Sky Café to play cribbage with some of the Gunflint folks on Tuesday afternoons. But aside from those games and an occasional fishing date with Eddie Riverfish on the Burnt Wood, and chance encounters he had with old colleagues at the co-op or donut shop, he spent his days alone. And all of that time seemed to have gathered in his gaze, which he kept on her now.

"I could use your help tomorrow," Greta said. "The windows and doors I ordered from Buck's came in. I have to pick them up."

"You got it," he said.

The next morning, he arrived at seven-thirty and came in without knocking, as was his habit. But because she hadn't heard his car rolling up the drive, she jumped when he shouted hello.

"You scared me," she said. She'd been standing in front of the painting of Eide Cove, drinking her coffee, and some of it splashed onto her hand, which she wiped on her jeans.

"Sorry about that," he said. "I've got some things for you." He raised both hands, holding four of the canvas bags he often carried around. They were stuffed to bursting, and when he set them down next to the card table, they thumped. He hurried back out to his car and came in next with an old number-four Duluth Pack and put it beside the other bags.

"Cleaning out your closets?" she asked.

"I'm sure you don't want to keep all this here while you're building the place out, but you'll definitely want to see what I've got." He took his coat and hat and gloves off and laid them across the back of a chair, then removed from one of the canvas bags a paper sack from the donut shop. He spread two napkins on the table and put a chocolate knot on each, then went to the stove, got himself a cup of coffee, and came back to sit at the table. He wore an expression she remembered from when he was her teacher, too, the one that said: *All right, today we're going to talk about "The Buck in the Snow"* or some other such lesson, hundreds of which she'd heard in Arrowhead High classrooms and at their own kitchen table alike.

The first bag he lifted from the floor was capped with Grandpa Harry's red wool hat. The only trace they ever found of him after he wandered off into the woods and never came out, drowned in the Devil's Maw, if what everyone believed was true. Greta had seen it, naturally, sitting on her father's dresser in his bedroom as though it were a souvenir from a trip to Canada. And she knew what it was. But in all her life she couldn't remember ever holding it. When Gus handed it to her, it was as if she'd been visited by Grandpa Harry's kind and distant eyes, and she felt tears welling in her own.

"You know about that, eh?"

"Grandpa's hat."

"He wore it every day that winter we went up onto the borderlands."

Here, too, was a shock. Because after the summer of 1997, Greta never once heard her father mention that misadventure, and if someone else dared to, he was quick to say he was done talking about it. As though it were a terrible secret that he alone must bear, instead of the only thing the people of Gunflint talked about for ten years after. Greta knew the story better as hearsay—or myth—than as the most trying experience of Gustav Eide's life.

"There's more about that," he said, and reached down to unbuckle two straps on the Duluth Pack, then pulled out a black bear pelt and laid it across the floor like a rug.

"I've never seen that," Greta said. "That's the bear you killed?"

"It's like Odd Einar put our destinies in motion up there on Spitzbergen, isn't it? And my grandpa after him. This bear was my birthright."

"I'm happy these bear confrontations seem to skip a generation."

"I don't really think anything skips a generation, do you?"

"Maybe not. I'll let you know when I'm finished with this," she said, and gestured at her notebooks.

For an hour Gus regaled her. Photographs and newspaper articles, a couple of her grandma Lisbet's sketchbooks, the stack of letters that had never been sent or delivered between Thea and her parents back in Norway, the ones Berit Lovig found in an old safe during renovations on the apothecary. The ones Gus believed had been stolen by Rebekah Grimm. There was Thea's Bible. And Berit Lovig's diary, which had been willed to Gus, along with dozens of love letters that she and Harry had sent to each other. And the book of maps Harry had drawn and that for years had stood on the mantel at Gus's house, untouched, as though they were the Dead Sea Scrolls or something equally valuable. He also had the maps Gus drew in a composition book while they were up there; the ones that got them out of that wilderness.

And there were other things too: invitations to weddings and high school and college graduations, the bulletin from Sarah's funeral, as well as the obituary that Greta herself had written. There were several leather-bound ledgers that had once belonged to Hosea

Grimm, the town apothecary and would-be doctor who more or less raised Odd after Thea died. These accounted for everything from the births and deaths in Gunflint—excepting Thea's own—to the levels of the Burnt Wood River for over twenty years.

He had given her a trove of information and artifacts, and just when Greta thought he'd finished he gave her two more things. The first was the handwritten account of what happened to Odd and Harry on the day the father drowned while ice fishing with his son. Written by Berit Lovig, Harry's great love, this had been stored all these years in a wooden box with nothing else in it. Greta sat there and read it, and when she was done she folded the stationery it had been written on and put it back in the box. "It's like a little coffin," she said, holding it up.

"I thought it was a beautiful letter. It meant more to me than any story or poem I ever read. And it inspired me to forgive my father. How about that?"

"Your father needed forgiveness?"

"Sweetheart, we all do."

The last thing he pulled from the bag was the most magnificent, though—a three-ring binder that must've dated from his earliest teaching days, three inches thick and as overflowing as the canvas bag he'd pulled it from had been. "No making fun of me," he said, sliding it across the card table. She opened it and first saw a typewritten poem called "Née Bergan," whose dedication read, *For my bride on her wedding day*. There were hundreds and hundreds of poems.

"You come by it honestly," he said, as Greta quietly wept. "I thought to bring my mandolin too, but I still play it all the time. You can have it when I'm done. But all this"—and now he gestured at the things scattered across the table—"I thought it might be of some use."

And so it was.

Now, toward the end of April, three weeks after her father had given her that bounty, she was back up for another weekend in

Gunflint, Lasse and Liv with Frans at his new condo in the Minneapolis warehouse district. Her project was to install the kitchen sink. The house had already been plumbed for it, and a bathroom as well. It would be a relief to have running water, and she had everything she needed to get the sink in. The tools and parts and faucet and the sink itself, all of it was sitting right there. But as often happened, she instead found herself hunched over the card table for most of Saturday morning. Despite everything her father had given her, and all the stories the artifacts told, she'd lately found herself frustrated by the lack of completeness in them. She might read a page from Berit Lovig's diaries, about the first time she saw Lisbet Johansson sail into Gunflint harbor, for example. She could see the boat arrive, and was privy to Berit's thoughts, and how her grandpa acted when he saw her. She could see all of that, and begin from it, but the stories usually wandered into unknown territory, and it was there that she found the deepest pleasure in her writing.

That morning, the trail that led her under the sink to finally get it installed had begun with an *Ax & Beacon* story from March of 1910: "Boy Mauled by Bear on Frozen Burnt Wood River." She of course already knew about her great-grandpa's encounter with the bear, which lost him an eye. But it had lived in her consciousness all these years as family legend, and here was something different: the reported facts. So how should *she* write about it? This was the question she came up against almost daily, one that frustrated her away from one kind of work into an urgent other.

As she lay on her back under the kitchen sink, attaching the trap to the PVC pipe, part of her mind was still back with that young boy on the Burnt Wood River, and on how his story had lived through all these years—more than a century of them. She was there on the river as a boy, and wrapping Teflon tape around a locknut, when she heard a car door slam outside. She heard another one open and then close and she figured it was her father, bringing her something, another loaf of bread or sushi from the co-op. She heard the fish house door open and boots kicked against each other and she shouted, "I'm down here!"

Her reading glasses were steaming up from the sweat on her

brow, and she could feel her hair sticking to her neck. She tightened the trap and set the washer and the drain elbow in place and tightened them. Since her father hadn't answered yet she called, "Dad?" and when he still didn't answer she pulled herself out from under the sink and straightened up and saw Stig standing in the doorway with a handful of plastic-wrapped flowers.

She put the Channellock she was holding in the sink and looked at him again. They stood like that for a long time, his face expressionless, her breath short and her hands shaking. Finally, he looked at the flowers and then held them out as though to say, *Here.*

"Say something to me," Greta said.

"I'm in love with you."

She leaned back against the frame of the counter and put her hand on the edge of the sink.

"I had to come tell you," he said.

All the hours they'd spent on the phone and FaceTiming, all the texting, it had begun to seem that he wasn't real. That he only existed as a fantasy on her iPhone and as the fulfillment of the spiritual void she'd long felt. But here he was. He'd cut his hair and was wearing a dark gray ski jacket and jeans and leather boots and he still had the flowers in his hand.

"You came to tell me?" she said.

He looked at his watch and said, "I landed in Minneapolis at nine. I came straight here. Yes, to tell you I love you."

"So when I talked to you this morning, you were in Minneapolis?"

"Yes."

"And when you asked if I'd be working at the fish house, you wanted to know where to go?"

He only grinned.

"And you knew how to get here because I sent you the Google Map?"

"Well, I had to ask. There's no sign for Eide Cove Road."

"Who did you ask?"

"At the co-op. Where I got these." Again he held the flowers up. "You are even more beautiful than I remember."

Now she looked down at herself, jeans and a flannel shirt and running shoes. She felt her neck and the hair still stuck to it, even though the sweat had dried. "I'm a mess. I've been installing this sink."

"You are not a mess."

"You should've told me you were coming. I could've made myself presentable." She glanced around in the glaring light, at the chaos on and around the card table, at her sleeping bag on the bunk, at the empty coffee cups on the windowsill. "And cleaned up around here."

"I love you," he said again, and now he unrooted himself from that spot by the door, he walked across the room, and handed her the flowers, which she set aside and in the same motion, as though it had been choreographed, took ahold of him, her hands beneath his jacket, her body pressing into his, her lips finding his. That kiss, it felt as if it had been happening since their last at the Hammerfest airport, when he said goodbye now more than four months ago.

When he stepped back and looked at her again, she was grateful that her hands were still on his waist to help steady herself. She'd wanted this for so long. Through so many conversations, some of which lasted all night. Through so many other sleepless nights. She'd imagined him walking back into her life a thousand times, and in many different scenarios, including this one. But now that he stood before her, it was as if they were on the *Vannhimmel* and in each other's embrace again for the first time. She put her cheek to his chest and said, "I've been waiting for you. I didn't think you'd ever get here."

"I promised you."

She tilted her head back to look up at him. "We promised each other."

"Yes, we did." And he pulled her close again, his big hands covering her back.

The past four months had been a master class in desperate thinking. The choice to meet him. The choice to stay in Hammerfest.

The choice to go to his boat. The choice to tell Frans, and to leave him, and to give herself the chance to start over. And the choice to have faith Lasse and Liv would be all right. And to trust that this man now in her arms would be as true as she believed he was. All of this choosing had been done without the conviction that things would work out. Hope, yes, in abundance. But she'd come to think of herself like Odd Einar on Spitzbergen, wandering through the Fonn, beseeching some force she couldn't name. Yet she knew that she'd rescued herself.

This thought inflamed her and she reached her hands up to his face and brought it down to hers. If the first kiss had felt like a continuation of their last in Hammerfest, this one felt like it would last the rest of their lives. And it was thanks to this that she had the confidence to step back and drop her hands from his face to the buttons of her flannel shirt, to step again so he could see her as she slowly undid them there in the brilliant afternoon light, exposing herself one inch at a time. If she'd had the ability to step outside of herself, she might've felt shy or hesitant. It'd been some twenty years since a man other than Frans had seen her naked in the full light of day. She was not, she knew with both certainty and pride, the same woman she'd been then. She had the wisdom of two children written on her flesh. That experience could be hidden in the darkness of a boat's berth, but not here. Had she been outside herself, this next step might've given her pause. But she had never felt as bold as she did when sliding the shirt off her shoulders, reaching behind to unclasp her bra as she took those backward steps toward her bunk. She pulled her hair over to one side and laid it across her shoulder, then unbuttoned her jeans and put her hands to the waistband before he said, "Wait. Don't move, please." He took off his jacket and dropped it to the floor as he covered the space between them, the eagerness of his expression as plain as the sun pouring through the windows.

Once in front of her, he dropped to his knees. Still his head came up to her chin, which she rested in his hair as he put his face into her neck and inhaled. Three, four, five breaths before he sat on his heels and put his hands on the waistband of her jeans. She looked down at him and knew how water felt when plunging over the falls. Then, instead of pulling her jeans down, he spread his hands across her stomach, his thumbs in her belly button and the tips of his pinkies on her ribs, and ran them up her body, rising from his heels until he could touch her neck so gently, and then finally through her hair, which he brushed off her shoulders so they both were bare and absorbing the light, and when he'd done all of this and then run all eight of his fingertips down the river of her spine before resting them again where he'd first put them, she realized she hadn't taken a breath since he knelt before her. She took a gulping one now.

"You," he whispered. "I am here with you."

She took another deep breath and as he tugged her jeans down she felt an even deeper kinship with those waterfalls. She kicked her shoes off and peeled her jeans from her feet.

"Here," she said, stepping backward until she reached the bunk and the bunched-up sleeping bag.

When he began unlatching his belt, she reached for him. "I've wanted to do this for so long," she said. "Let me undress you." And she did. He raised his arms and bent at the waist and she pulled his shirt over his head. He'd lost a bit of his paunch and when she ran her fingertips down his chest and belly, his stomach rippled like a little wave. She put her mouth on his navel and kissed him while she pushed his jeans and underwear down. His boots were still on and he tried to kick them free, but she had to help untangle his pants. Finally, they got them off and looked at each other and laughed.

Stig looked around as though someone besides her might see him there, naked in the sunlight, which seemed aimed directly on them through all six windows.

"No one's coming," Greta said, leaning back on the bunk. "It's just us." She unzipped the sleeping bag so it covered the whole mattress and fluffed the pillow and took her underwear off before lying down, her knees joined and lying to the left, her arms, she hadn't realized until just then, covering her breasts.

He sat down and slowly moved one of her hands and then the

other until they rested above her head. Here he paused and gazed at her and she nodded her head in permission and he ran his hand down the length of her, from wrist to waist to knee, all the while staring into her eyes.

Now she put a hand on his knee. "Your skin feels so nice," she said. "I can't believe you're here. I've never been so surprised or so happy." She was whispering, she noticed. "You came here for me," she said.

"Yes, I did. Of course I did."

Now she moved her hand up his body and sat up a little herself and when her hand retraced its line she ended on his cock. He closed his eyes and groaned just barely and because he was stunned and because she couldn't wait a second longer she sat up and grabbed his shoulders and shifted her left leg over his lap and as if they'd made love a thousand times she sat astride him, easily guided him inside of her, and locked her arms behind his head. With each slow and almost imperceptible gyration of her hips, she felt a pressure both releasing and mounting that rolled out over her entire body and increased with every movement of his hands, with each brush of his lips against her neck, with each whiff of his hair and skin. But she also felt an exhalation, again from her entire body. As though the blizzard within was finally releasing its snow.

She dozed after they made love and woke to the icicles dripping from the eaves outside in the afternoon sun. Stig was up and standing at one of the small windows overlooking the lake, his wild hair like a filigree between her and the light. He was naked except for his socks and his hands were slightly raised, his fingers playing imaginary keys in the air. When she leaned up on her elbow and pulled the sleeping bag over her, he turned in place.

"Why are you covering yourself?" he said.

She glanced down and shrugged and then pushed the sleeping bag aside. "What are you looking at out there?"

"The lake looks like home," he said. "*You* look like home," he said, and then walked to the bed. He lay down next to her and put his left hand on her hip and kissed her.

"Were you playing a song you know or composing a new one?"

"Another new one."

"Another?"

He kissed her again. "I have written one hundred songs since I met you."

"I swear I know them already. The songs."

"Know them?"

She nodded. "I've laid awake so many nights after we talked. I swear I could hear them across the night. They're beautiful."

He glanced around and into the corners filled with the falling light. "Will there be room for a piano?"

"Right there," she said, pointing to the spot she'd pictured him playing. "Tell me about the songs?"

"I would rather just play them for you."

The thought of it made her shiver.

"Are you cold?" he said, offering to pull the sleeping bag up.

"No. I'm ecstatic."

"Me too."

They kissed again and pressed their naked bodies together and the thought they might make love again so soon, well, that such a thing was even possible baffled her. Like hearing a foreign language for the first time and understanding it at once. She reached for him and pulled his cock into her and then she was holding on to him, this time lying side by side, their lips less kissing than feeling for each other, their legs in an odd, desperate tangle. But she reached down between them and pressed her clit and they made love until she came, her body shaking, one hand holding on to him, the other letting herself go.

"Jesus," she whispered, her voice slow and languid. "I've never made love twice in the same day, never mind the same hour. I mean, it's been years since I made love twice in the same *month*."

"Me too. Are you all right?"

Their bodies had already started slipping apart, and in answer she pushed her hips back into him. She reached around his back and pulled him closer.

"It is okay, then?" he said.

"Fuck yes," she said.

For the first time she saw a sort of arrogant grin come across his face. If it hinted at pridefulness, she'd never before now found this attractive in a man.

He shook his head and sighed and lay back, now offering his right arm for a pillow. She nestled into him and they rested in the silence long enough to hear the waves rising out on the shore.

"I thought the lake would be frozen," he said.

"It was a month ago. It rarely freezes over completely."

"In Duluth I saw a big ship coming to harbor."

She looked at her watch, at the date. "It's early for that."

"A lastebåt. A long ship, yes?"

"Freighters, we call them. Or boats. Not ships. We call them boats."

"What is the cargo?"

"Taconite, coal, other things. It depends on the boat."

"Taconite?" he pronounced it awkwardly.

"Iron ore. For making steel. It's mined on the range and sent down to Chicago and Gary and Detroit and places in Ohio."

His eyes lit up and he started humming the Gordon Lightfoot song about the *Edmund Fitzgerald*.

"Yes, exactly," she said, laughed and patted his bare chest. "That wreck's the most famous, but around here we also remember a boat called the *Ragnarøk* that went down not far away."

"When was this?"

"Oh, fifty years ago? Maybe longer?"

"It is a very rocky coast. All the way from Duluth. I imagine the lake is very deep?"

"Thirteen hundred feet at its deepest."

He shook his head and kissed her and said, "Did I really come here to ask you how deep is the lake?"

"I know why you came," she said, and they laughed together.

His stomach gurgled, and he glanced at her and smiled.

"You're hungry," she said. "Me too. All I've got to eat here is cheese and bread."

"That's enough for me."

Now she sat up on her elbow again, her body still pressed against his. "No, let's go get something. There's a good restaurant only five minutes from here." She checked her watch. "It won't be busy now."

"I am not sure about leaving this place," he said, running his hand over the slope of her shoulder and down her ribs and resting it on the small of her back.

"If I'm going to make love to you again, I'll need some fuel."

Now he held her more firmly and gave her a playful spanking.

"After we eat," she said, and stood up and stretched and then looked at him lying on the bunk. The arm he'd had around her was folded under his head and the other across his chest, which was hairless and broad, his hand splayed there and relaxed. His stomach was sunken, the bottom of it rising back up to his pelvis. His cock, still half-hard, lay in the tangle of blond hair. She stared at it, even though she knew he was looking into her eyes. It twitched and she turned slowly to look at his impish face. His stomach growled again. "After we eat," she said again, but now with less conviction.

He took a deep breath and scratched his belly and then his pelvis and said, "Okay, Greta."

Her clothes were strewn across the wood floor, and she went from spot to spot picking them up and putting them on. By the time she was buttoning her shirt Stig finally got up, too, and from across the room she could see the shape of his back, the skin she knew to be so soft, the firmness beneath his flesh. She'd never looked at a man like this. Never seen in his nakedness the perfect expression of her desire.

When he finished dressing he joined her at the door, took her by the elbows, and looked at her without saying anything. She put her hands up to his hair and flattened it and then rested them on his cheeks. For a long time they just stood there, taking contented breaths until she whispered, "I'm in love with you too. I am." She pulled his face toward her and with their lips touching, she said, "How did this happen?"

———

How did it always happen? Slowly, and then all at once.

For ten or twelve years, she had spent each day in a loneliness complete, not even knowing enough to say that it possessed her like an illness. Her children suffered for it. Her father suffered for it. Her friends suffered for it. And of course Frans did too. When she'd finally boarded the plane in Hammerfest two mornings after she'd first tried to leave, Stig's scent still on her jacket, his shadow behind her like the longest day, she panicked. She would miss him like she couldn't even imagine. What's more, she didn't know if she ever would see him again. That vulnerability was appalling, but only for as long as it took her to get on the plane. She sat down. She fastened her seat belt. She was crying, but didn't notice until tears fell onto her folded hands.

As the plane left the gate, she looked out at the terminal. Snow blew down and the window blurred from it and she watched as the sharp lights from the fuel truck and the baggage cart faded and the plane stopped in the halo of floodlights from the roof. And then she saw Stig standing in the parking lot. His hands up and poking through the chain-link fence. His eyes, even through the smudgy darkness, were visibly frantic. And just as she saw him, and reached her own tear-streaked hand up to wave, the cabin lights went out and the plane taxied onto the runway.

She closed her eyes and wiped them dry and saw him, there in the light of her mind, coming to her again. She would miss him until then, but already the loneliness of her destination was replaced by the promise of him standing out there in the snow. The promise of the things they'd said. By the time she landed—first in Oslo, then in Newark, then in Minneapolis—she knew that she'd traveled not only a great many hours over thousands of miles but also very far back, to a place where she could begin again to try to become herself. She would learn what that meant, in an extremely difficult course. But even once she was in the taxi from the airport heading home, she knew that it had much less to do with distancing herself from her husband than it did with moving forward herself. With Stig. After only a few days in Hammerfest, she could see a future she'd never had with Frans.

Another surge of resoluteness swirled through her as that taxi had exited on Diamond Lake Road. There at the stoplight she resolved to make a future for herself. With Lasse and Liv and Stig. She knew it wouldn't be easy, but also that she was fierce and determined enough to do it. She would be a more attentive mother. She'd be happier with them, would scold them less, and love them more simply, without her resentment of Frans muddying her affection. She had to. She fucking would. Stig had cracked the ice in her, and now she would finish busting it up.

That was how falling in love with Stig began: by looking ahead. Or she might have said that's where she felt the first possibility of it. Certainly, during their time in Hammerfest, Greta had glimpsed it. But that had been like remembering a song instead of listening to it, like nodding her head to a rhythm she hadn't heard in years. When the plane from Newark to Minneapolis touched down, she opened her e-mail, and saw that he'd sent her a note. They were the first words in a conversation that lasted until he'd arrived at the fish house, whether through the ether or in the quiet of her own mind.

Now, as they turned onto the highway toward town, all of this had become clear to her, thanks to his being here. "I do know how this happened," she said, reaching over to him in the passenger seat and taking his hand in hers.

He'd been looking out the window, up at the patches of snow still in the hills above Gunflint. "How what happened?"

"How we happened. How falling in love happened."

"You can tell me?"

She stared out the windshield at the blacktop glistening with snowmelt, both hands back on the wheel. "When I left you in Hammerfest, for the whole trip home I thought about how meeting you had changed me. It was as if the part of me that had been frozen like ice was now starting to melt. By the time I got home I felt like a different person. I felt like I could do anything. Even things that seemed impossible. Like navigating my kids through what I knew I'd have to. Like disentangling myself from the cold person I'd become. Like waiting for you." She again took his hand. "How did I know all that with such certainty?"

"Like you say, because we were falling in love."

"And now we have all our lives for that."

"Yes we do," he agreed.

When they turned in to town on Wisconsin Street, her father's Subaru was parked in front of the historical society with the rear hatch open, and as she slowed at the intersection for a pedestrian, Gus looked up and saw her and waved. She had no choice but to stop.

"Holy shit," she whispered, pulling into a parking spot.

"What is it?"

"That's my father." She pointed at him, as if several men on the street were waving.

Stig sat up straighter, like he'd been called to attention. Greta put a hand on his leg and said, "This is fine. This is good. My dad is wonderful."

"You will introduce me?"

"It would be strange if I didn't. So come on, then."

Gus had started walking toward them, with a big white bucket in his left hand. When Greta and Stig opened their doors and stepped out, his tall body unfolded from the passenger side like a sail filling with wind. He came around to Greta's side, she hooked her arm in his, and they walked over to Gus.

"Hi, Dad."

He smiled. "Hey, kid." He stepped closer, held out his hand, and said, "You must be Stig."

"Hello," he answered.

Greta said, "Stig, this is my dad, Gus."

Gus eyed him like Greta had never once seen him do before. Up and down, almost like he was about to challenge him. Her eyes widened in surprise. But then he said, "So, you're the man who pointed my daughter home?"

"I think she pointed herself, yes?"

"Well, you might've had something to do with it." He turned to Greta. "I didn't know you were expecting company."

"I wasn't. A surprise visit."

"I like your style, Mr. Hjalmarson."

"What's with the bucket?" Greta asked.

"Oh, time to swab out the *Odd Einar.*"

"The Odd Einar?" Stig asked, doing a verbal double take.

"There," Greta said, pointing at the boat sitting in front of the historical society.

"My own father's boat. And his father's before him. Our Odd Einar built it, in Greta's fish house. That was when?" He looked at her as though he didn't know for sure. "Back in nineteen what?"

"Nineteen twenty," she said. And then, to Stig, "Every spring he comes down and cleans it up, and every fall he repaints it."

"I can see it would look beautiful on the water," Stig said.

During their few conversations about Stig, Greta had not told Gus that he was a sailor. And though Gus hadn't been on the water himself for a long while, he still loved to watch the boats come in and out of the harbor. Countless poems he'd written had been about exactly that.

"Come on over," Gus said, ushering them along the sidewalk and saying, "She was a very fine boat. And gorgeous on the water, you're right. I can remember from when I was a boy. Very smooth. Very steady. She's got a hell of a keel."

Greta watched the two of them amble around the boat, each of them pointing and nodding and smiling. At one point they both squatted and Gus ran his hand between the keel and the skeg and Stig shook his head as though in disbelief. They made a full circumnavigation of the *Odd Einar* and then stood looking up into the bulkhead, Gus pointing and then miming waves coming over the portside. They spoke too softly for her to hear, but she could see by the expression on her father's face that he was listening. Impressed. Curious. It was not a look he often had when listening to Frans, and though Greta had long ago made up her mind about the future of her life, that look on her father's face struck her as a fine confirmation of her choices.

After a few minutes more, Stig caught her eye and she walked over to them. "I was telling Gus about the *Vannhimmel*. He says I should take you sailing around the northern seas."

"I agree," Greta said.

"But not until summer," Gus said. "We've heard what happens up there in winter."

Now Stig stepped around the boat and ran his fingers over the escutcheon, a scroll famously carved by a boatwright in Duluth that had finalized the reclamation of their family vessel. He looked up at Greta and her father and said, "Who would think that some-day I am standing in this place with you, looking at this boat. I have known about this man"—here he pointed at two words on the stern—"for so many years. For my whole life, really. And now I hear about his grandson and meet his great-great-grandson and already know his great-great-great-granddaughter." He shook his head and beamed. "It is a strange life we all live, yes?"

Gus picked the bucket off the sidewalk and tilted his chin up to look at Stig through the bottoms of his bifocals. Through the lenses, Greta could see her father's eyes blooming. "Welcome to God's country, Stig. I hope you two have a nice lunch." He glanced at his watch. "Or supper, whatever it is you're eating."

Greta and Stig watched him mosey up to the historical society, unlock the door, and go inside. Greta knew he'd fetch a bucket of warm water and spend the next hour with a mop and scrub brush, shining everything up, and that when they came out of the Burnt Wood Tavern, Stig would want to look at the boat again. She also knew that someday he would sail her off to wherever she wanted to go.

After they ate—fish stew for Greta and a bowl of chili for Stig—she called Lasse and Liv to say good night. She talked to Frans, too, and said she planned on staying a couple extra days if he could manage to take care of the kids. She was midstream in a project, she told him, and wanted to wrap it up. He didn't ask what it was, just said it was fine if she needed a few days. That was how Greta and Stig ended up staying together at the fish house for three nights.

On the last, they made sandwiches and washed them down with a growler of the local brewery's Devil's Maw IPA and, as they had on the previous nights, built a roaring fire out on the shore and pulled up the Adirondack chairs and talked and planned and finished falling in love. Nothing had ever been so easy. They took their phones out and checked their calendars and made plans to meet in New York in June. She would visit him again later in the summer, when Frans was taking the kids to see his parents in Oslo. He would go to Bodø and take care of his own divorce. He would sell his mother's house or get it ready to rent. He would either put his boat up or sail it over here.

She couldn't help thinking, as she sat there with him, that *this* is what a future looks like. Their chairs were arranged arm to arm and they held hands looking up at the brilliant sky. Excepting the births of Lasse and Liv, she could not recall a single instance of greater happiness in her entire life. But a kind of gloom sat with her too, knowing as she did that after this night she wouldn't see him again for almost two months, in New York. She took a sip of beer, and turned to him at the same moment he was turning to her.

"I have something for you," he said. "I meant to give it to you first thing."

"What?"

He sprang up and hurried around the fish house and then she heard the car door open and shut, and just like that he was back at her side holding out a paper bag.

She set her glass on the arm of the chair and took it. "I didn't get you anything," she said.

"You didn't know I was coming!" he protested.

"What is it?"

"Open it. See for yourself."

So she did, tearing the paper aside.

"It's not so romantic," he said. "But I hope you will like it."

She held the book toward the firelight so she could read the cover. "*Viktige Liv i Norsk Historie,*" she stammered, then held it at a slightly different angle. "Marius Granerud?" she said. "This is a book about Granerud?"

"*Important Lives in Norsk History.* Yes, Granerud."

"This is incredible," she said. "Is Odd Einar mentioned in here?"

"Yes, of course. And Fridtjof Nansen. Otto Sverdrup. Bengt Bjornsen. Gerd Bjornsen. All of them."

Greta flipped through several pages. "But it's all in Norwegian."

"You are lucky to have a translator who isn't very ugly."

She set the book down and straddled him in the chair, their jackets bulky between them. She unzipped his and took off her mittens and slipped her hands under his shirt.

"You are happy for the book?"

"Very much."

"And glad that I come here?"

She kissed him, her hands now up in his untamed hair. When she leaned back again, he appeared distant.

"What will we do now?" he said. "What is next?"

"Everything," she said. "We do everything. Just like we said."

Later, in the middle of that night, after they'd made love and dozed and made love again and should've been asleep, Greta got up and went to the window overlooking the lake. The same one Stig had stood at, playing his imaginary piano, on the day he arrived. The fire had burned out and the night shone darkly luminous as she watched the waves come in slowly while the cove, now free of ice, returned its darkness to the night. She stared out into the distance, the future and past both.

Stig rolled over behind her. "What is it, Greta?"

"Since I've met you, from the first moment I allowed myself to imagine us, you've felt like safe harbor. But that's not quite right." She shut her eyes against the darkness, then faced him again, walked to the bed, and lay down beside him. "You're the whole wide sea. Every drop of it."

I t never failed to please me, seeing my faering there with the other boats in the harbor that had welcomed us home. The harbor we saw each morning, living as we did in a second-story room on the church end of town. Yes, the harbor that had taken but also given. After more than two years, I finally understood what it was: a place to dock my boat and sell my fish. And I'd sold plenty, at a price fair to all, from my first catch back in 'ninety and seven until this winter day. So many fish had I sold that I could have afforded a new boat, one for larger waters. But my faering had been true to me, so I would be true in turn.

Inger had also been true. My elskede, there every morning and again each evening. We had weathered so much together, and though time had schooled me not to speak for her I could hazard a guess she'd found happiness with me again. Just this last Christmas, after our plates of pork and cabbage and potatoes, after we sipped our tea and rested in the warmth of our stove, she with her Bible, I with my trusty copy of *Mysterier,* she looked up and said, "That book again?" as though I hadn't been sitting there all evening with her. "About the man with the viola?"

"Yes, Inger. My good friend Johan Nagel and his fiddle."

She gave me a coy look and made a show of turning her attention back to Deuteronomy—Moses being preferable to Nagel—before she sighed and said, as she had on many such occasions, "We can't all be characters in the stories of our own lives, can we?"

Indeed, she had read *Isbjørn i Nordligste Natt* three Christmases past, and while the burden of that yarn hung heavy between us then, it was now almost a thing to tease about. And tease she did, often speaking of the man lost on Spitzbergen as though he were a fiction. As though he were Johan Nagel.

She closed her Bible and set it aside. "That fellow up on Spitzbergen, he would've been better off with a hardingfele, don't you think?"

"I don't know, Inger. I've not read his story."

She got up and went to our small shelf of books and took my story down, with its black leather cover, the ice bear with his growl. I remember stopping to marvel, seeing it for the first time in the window at G. Hagen Bokhandel. I might even have gone in and held it. But something stopped me, some force I could not name. I remember people passing me on the Kirkegata, whispering and glancing away when they met my eyes. It wasn't until Herr Hagen himself stepped out of the shop and shook my hand and gave his thanks that I was able to move. And so it was with his handshake and word of gratitude that my reputation was restored. From then on, there were no shifty looks, no whispers. In fact I became something like a curiosity, and folks might stop me to ask of some profundity, as though I had wisdom to spare.

In any case, it was Inger who brought our copy of that book home, a complimentary one from our friend Marius in Tromsø. And on that Christmas three years back, she paged through it again and said, "Yes, this part here where he sleeps under a cairn of rocks, I believe a fiddle would have done him well."

"That's clever," I said, and turned back to Knut Hamsun.

"Honestly, can you not see when your wife wants to play? Put that book down please and go look on the bureau."

Ever dutiful, I marked my page and set down my pipe and went to the chest of drawers on which sat a brown leather case. I couldn't fathom by what sleight of hand it had arrived there, but I picked it up and brought it back to my chair and held it on my lap.

Inger's patience was then extinguished by nervous excitement. "Well?" she said.

I unclasped the buckles, slowly opened the lid, and withdrew from its velvet lining a hardingfele and bow and also a block of rosin. I held it as though it were a newborn child. For a long time, I did.

When I at last looked up at my wife, she said, "Play me a song?"

I had hardly stopped playing since. On this February morning, walking past the church with my hardingfele in one hand and my wife in the other, I went to play once more with the town band. On the Kirkegata we were hardly alone, with nigh everyone making the pilgrimage out to the Jannebakken, where for a week the ski club had been shoveling and packing snow to make the jump. Rumor had it skiers were coming from as far south as Christiania, and that the best of them might soar one hundred feet or more on the kicker they'd built.

"Are you looking forward to the festival, Inger?"

She turned her face up to the pleasant sun. "It's a perfect day for it."

"We should stop by Lundby's and check the post," I said.

"Maybe the Queen herself has written!"

Since *Isbjørn i Nordligste Natt* was published, I often received letters. At first Inger teased that I was more famous than Fridtjof Nansen, but when one letter turned out to be a proposal from a wealthy heiress in Trondheim she began to insist that all such missives go unanswered.

"Don't you remember?" I joked. "She came in person."

Inger laughed, and on we walked.

At Lundby's, while she bought a jar of preserves and a block of cheese and crackers for our picnic, I asked Lundby's son to check our post. Indeed, there was a small stack of letters, one of which stood out conspicuously. Postmarked GUNFLINT, MINN. JANUARY 29, 1900, it had a certain heft. Setting my hardingfele case and the other letters on the counter, I studied that envelope and the fine penmanship that addressed me and my wife. I heard her across the store, wishing a good day to Fru Klykken, whose son Ove would that afternoon be competing at the skihopp.

"Odd Einar, you look like you've seen a ghost." It was Lundby himself, standing behind the counter in place of his son.

I looked up at him.

"I noticed the postmark," he said, and put his hands together in a prayerful gesture. "Here," he said, giving me the kerchief from his pocket. "God bless you." Then he called to Inger, and gestured for her to come over.

She walked toward me, the basket of goods hooked in her arm. "What is it?"

I handed her the letter, which she, too, studied before placing the basket on the counter and stumbling to a straight-backed chair in the corner. I went and knelt at her side and there passed a period of time that might have been two minutes or twenty.

It was Inger who next spoke. "I can't open it. I don't want to." She handed it back to me.

I looked around as though I had in my hands not the letter I'd dreamt of for so long but a stick of dynamite, so wide was the berth Lundby and his customers had given us.

"Please, Odd Einar, open it." She touched the letter and then closed her eyes and turned her head heavenward.

Standing up, I removed my pocketknife, unfolded the blade, and carefully sliced the top of the envelope. There was a letter indeed, two pages covered with impeccable penmanship not my daughter's and not in Norwegian. There was also a smaller, unsealed envelope holding two photographs. In the first, my daughter gazed down on the babe in her arms in a bed, her legs covered by an eiderdown and her head resting on a pile of pillows. The child was sleeping, swaddled in a white gown, a tuft of hair on the top of his head. And my daughter was every bit a woman, her own hair pulled off her face and into a little cap, her shoulders draped by the puffed sleeves of a nightgown.

As I gazed down on the photographic paper, all the distance and time that had separated us the previous five years vanished. All of my suffering, gone with it. I was with her again.

"Well?" Inger said.

I gave her the first photograph without a word and looked intently at the second: a boy in a sailor suit holding a toy boat, all of three or four years old, sitting with a young woman decidedly not my daughter. She had about her a doubtful countenance and a rigid posture. She looked posed, whereas Thea, in her photograph, appeared wholly at ease and in the middle of a blessed moment with her newborn. This other woman was beautiful, too, and clearly a woman of means, but she also looked *unhappy*. I flipped the photograph over and on the back was written: REBEKAH AND ODD, CHRISTMAS 1899. Christmas. Jul. But *Odd*? Was the boy's name Odd? Was this the same boy as in the first photograph? I looked down at the photograph Inger held, turned it over, and read, THEA AND ODD, DECEMBER 1896.

Now I knelt beside my wife and showed her the second photograph. When I glanced up, many of the marketgoers were staring at us. If by instinct I felt defensive of our privacy, I then realized that they weren't gawking, merely readying their kindness and sympathy should it be required.

"This is our Thea," Inger whispered. "And our grandson."

"I think so."

"What does the letter say?" She appeared so doubtful.

"It's in English."

"Is it written by Thea?"

I looked at the signature on the second page. "No. Someone named Hosea Grimm."

"Who is that?" she asked, as though this man and I were old acquaintances.

"I don't know."

"Let me see," she said, taking the letter from my hand. She studied it for some time, as though actually reading it, before looking up at me. "What does it say, Odd Einar?"

"Gerd Bjornsen knows English. Will Gerd be at the skihopp?" I watched Inger struggle to catch up, could see her wanting relief in this moment even as the part of her that for five years had grieved the loss of her daughter was keeping its guard up. "Or perhaps we should skip the skihopp, Inger. We can go home and catch our breath from this."

"Gerd does know English." And now her faraway gaze grew sharper and sharper. "She *will* be there today, Odd Einar." She stood and took the letter and second picture from me and slipped it all gently back in the envelope, then handed it to me and nodded at her provisions. "Go pay Lundby for this."

When I took the basket and started for the other end of the counter, she said, "Here, Odd Einar." She held out my hardingfele case. "You can't play without this. And the band can't play without you."

We were speechless when we arrived at the Jannebakken, even as the stream of townsfolk sang and danced and reveled together. The crowd funneled onto the path up to Gávpotjávri, but all had to wait there a few minutes until Ábo Somby and his reindeer herd came down from the fjeld. The people shook their bells and whistled; their merriment was made still livelier by this delay. Even Ábo got in on the ruckus, tossing back a swig of aquavit offered by one of the bachelors in the crowd.

The Jannebakken was decorated with bunting and seats for the press and even a pair of saunas at the bottom of the skihopp. There was a stand selling beer and glogg, and another roasting sides of venison. A third sold sweets and cookies from Bjornsen's bakery, and Gerd stood behind that table. When she saw Inger hurrying toward her, Gerd's whole aspect changed, and she quickly came around the table to greet us.

Before she could even say a word, Inger took the letter out of my hand and told her that our daughter was alive and handed her the first photograph. "What's more, we have a grandson. Just look at him!"

"And look at Thea," Gerd said. "A grown woman and the spitting image of her mother." Then she looked at the other photograph. "And such a handsome boy. What's his name?"

"He's Odd. Can you believe that? Just like his grandpapa."

Now Gerd looked at me as friendly as she often had since Bengt passed. "Congratulations, Odd Einar." She clutched Inger's arm, and the affection passing between them was obvious. "Tell me, what has Thea written?"

"That's just the thing," Inger said. "The letter isn't from her, it's from a man named Hosea Grimm. I've never so much as heard of him."

"Well, what does his letter say?"

Inger unfolded and handed it to Gerd, who glanced at it knowingly and then turned to her girl. "Ruth, you'll be fine for a few minutes. Remember, two øre for the candies, three for the cookies." Then, to Inger and me: "Let's step behind the tent there. It's quieter."

So we moved through the crowd and stood huddled in the shadow of the tent.

Gerd nodded. "Would you like me to just read it to you, the best I can?"

We put our four hands in a knot as Gerd took a deep breath and began:

Dear Mr. and Mrs. Eide,

May I present to you my son, and your grandson. His name is Odd, and as I write this on New Year's Day, 1900, he is just recently turned three years old. A boy so doted on the world has never known until now. I believe he is ready to command the new century!

His mother, my wife, sends her regards, and thanks you both for your eager correspondence. A true thing about your daughter: Since she arrived in Gunflint she has been without her voice. The reasons why are most confounding, but from her first steps on the Lighthouse Road—that being our main thoroughfare—she has been almost mute, and so seems ever to be more and more inward looking. It is only thanks to Odd and myself that she communicates with the world at all. If this sounds glum, you needn't worry. She is otherwise healthy, and loved beyond measure by both her husband and son. And indeed, each day finds her more and more open, which you shall see proof of anon.

But first, about the boy! He is taken care of mostly by our governess, a very capable woman called Rebekah. I tell you, your grandson has a fondness for her that he shares with none other. And what else? He has a great curiosity for the natural world, and a love of boats. A lucky thing, given our remoteness here in Gunflint. Our hope is that when the time comes for him to sail on or sail home, he'll choose home. Starting in three years he will be tutored in the arts and sciences, and if all goes well, he will study to become a surgeon like his papa. He is handsome—as you can surely see, thanks entirely to his mother's great beauty—and witty and playful all day long. He already shows a great aptitude for kindness and empathy. And, above all, he loves his parents truly.

If, as you read this, you are wondering why it has taken us so long to return your own letters, I will provide this in answer, as well as in confidence: Thea, my sweet, sweet wife, suffered a great deal upon arriving here with no one to greet her. If I may be so bold, I would tell you both that the horrible loss of her aunt and uncle, and the tragic, even ruinous nature of their deaths, was a grave blow to her. So great that until recently she has been keen to forget who she was before her arrival.

It was neither animus nor a grudge she felt toward you, rather simply shock at her present condition. I doubt I could explain to you in clear enough language the wilderness in which she found herself. Lesser souls than hers have taken but one look at our outpost and turned tail. But not our Thea. She bore down, and worked hard, and now she has our son. The good news—indeed the great news!—is that she has asked me to extend to you an invitation to make the journey to America, to meet your grandson and to stay with us. She would have written herself, but she fears the length of her silence might have caused you pain enough to doubt her abiding love. In any *case, it is my pleasure to offer the invitation on her behalf, and to note that I share in her enthusiasm for you to join us.*

I send this letter in good cheer, for it warms my heart to see my wife in such peace and tranquillity. I might be quick to add that throughout her ordeal here in Minnesota she has remained true to her faith, a fact she wished for me to convey. Nightly she reads from the good book, and her prayers, why, they echo across our great lake.

But lo! Here comes Odd, with another of his toy boats, asking Papa to play with him.

I do hope the New Year finds you in good health and prosperity.

Ever yours,
Hosea Grimm

Inger had tears in her eyes as she took the letter from Gerd, folded it, and replaced it in the envelope, then again pulled out both photographs. She kept the one of the toddler boy and handed me the picture of Thea and her babe. I took it and walked out of the shadow of the tent, into the sun shining down on the Jannebakken, holding it up before me and regarding it as intently as I had the sails of the *Pobeg* on that final morning up in Spitzbergen.

There at the bottom of the hill, I stumbled into the throng. My boyhood friend Rolf Arne Buskum was using his speaking trumpet to shout, "... First up, here from Bergen and one of the favorites this afternoon, the world record holder with a leap of more than one hundred feet just last year at the Solbergbakken, Eivind Torr! Show him a warm Hammerfest welcome!"

The clamber of cowbells called my attention, and I looked up to see this man speeding down the inrun, then disappear for an instant before he rose into the air, backlit by the sun, his arms spread like wings. He seemed to hang there, the image of grace, and I saw *myself* in him. I felt Inger's touch on my elbow. I knew she, too, was watching Eivind Torr.

After he landed his perfect telemark, and as the crowd raised a mighty cheer, Inger took the photograph of our daughter from me and slipped it back in the envelope, folded it shut, then unbuttoned my coat and put it inside my pocket. "You were right," she said.

I shook my head, felt the contagion of her tears, and patted the envelope inside my coat.

"You believed in her. You never stopped."

"I only hoped, Inger. I hoped and I loved."

"It's no small thing. To hope."

"Or to love," I said. "You've taught me that."

The crowd huzzahed again and we turned to see another skihopper, this one spinning on his back toward the bottom of the hill, a cloud of snow rising around him like a waterspout. After sliding to a stop, he sprang right up and waved his arms. The crowd cheered louder, and Rolf Arne's voice rose above the noise: "That's Torjus Hemmestveit, folks. Let's see if his brother can stay off his rump! He's next up."

Above the din, I heard the band's accordion rising, then the bass, and the people gathered around the tents started waltzing. Inger's smile sent me off. I trotted over, unpacking my hardingfele, and joined them midsong.

We played all afternoon, the songs in me like my love for my daughter, while one skier after another leapt into flight. All I wanted was to live with this joy forever.

The story of her family, for as far back as she knows, has been lived in snow and ice. They were fishermen and judges, dowagers and orphans, boatbuilders and schoolteachers, weekend poets and fine artists. They were Norwegians and Minnesotans, immigrants and townfolks, travelers and stayers. But whoever they were, they lived against a tide of frozen water, measuring time's passage not only by their love for one another but also and often against the winter to come, or the winter just gone. Or, in the case of Greta on this night, winter at its most cruel. She can't help staring out into the blackness of the storm and remembering her grandfather's and great-grandfather's tragic ends.

To distract herself, she looks over at her daughter asleep by the fire and thinks of her son up at his grandpa's house. Of all the things being a mother requires, nothing is more important than keeping Lasse and Liv safe. Is this true, or has winter's rapacious hunger only made it seem so?

As if the dog knows what she's thinking, he gets up and walks across the puncheon floor and coils his huge body under her desk. She reaches down and scratches Axel's ears and then opens her computer and clicks on the file marked ANOTHER KRYKKJE ON ANOTHER MASTHEAD. She's going to finish Odd Einar's story. It's going to end in the brilliant Arctic summer, a thought that gives her no small relief. She's known this to be true from the first time she saw him, there in the Hammerfest cemetery. *How* she knew, she can't describe. But it's been certain all along. And if he appeared first like a ghost, he's by now become like flesh and blood and she loves him in much the same way.

Greta wonders about the dreams that visit her. There were times, especially on nights such as this, when Greta thought she could plainly see them. As though they projected from the aura of her daughter's slumber. Similar to how Odd Einar appears to her each time she sits down to visit with him.

Her phone rings, loud and shrill against the quiet of her house. She turns quickly and answers it before she even looks at the caller ID, figuring it's Stig calling to say good night.

But in fact it's Frans. "Hi," he says. "How are you?"

"Oh," she said.

"Can you hear me?"

"Yes. Hi."

"We just touched down in Ushuaia. In Argentina. What a strange flight. We're already a day behind schedule. There was a storm . . ." The phone crackles and then goes silent and Greta says "Hello?" before his voice comes back across the line "—the day after tomorrow, I think. I hope that's okay."

"You'll be a day late?" Greta asks.

"If I can get the first flight to Buenos Aires."

"I hope you can, Liv's pretty excited about seeing you."

No response. She can't tell if they've lost the connection again or he's merely resigned to another of his silences, then his voice reemerges from the static "—on Monday at about five. Tell her and Lasse I can't wait to see them?"

"Of course."

"Okay. Well."

"Frans?"

"What?"

"How was it down there?"

As though he's rehearsed the answer many times, he says, "The ice is the same at the bottom of the world as it is on the top. Or what's left of it is."

Then the call does disconnect, and when Greta looks at her phone the red dying-battery image blinks twice and the screen goes black.

The divorce had been made final in July. She and Frans went to the same Minneapolis courthouse where they'd applied for their marriage license twenty years before, this time sitting on benches across the hall from each other, not standing hand in hand. Despite all that had happened, for all the enormous changes those years had brought, she felt very much the same woman now that she believed she'd been then. She remembers looking across the hall-way at Frans and wanting to ask if *he* felt different. But his faraway gaze told her that in this respect, as in every other one, they were moving apart now. It was up to her to figure things out. Twenty years ago, as they'd stood before the judge, she'd had no idea who she was. Regardless of all her confidence and intelligence. But on that next trip to the courthouse? She knew exactly.

This wisdom had come at a steep cost, though, and from across the cold concrete floor she said, "I'm sorry we're here."

Frans looked up slowly. "I know you are. Me too." He buttoned and unbuttoned his coat and ran his long fingers through his hair. "Me too."

The mediator told them, at the end, after everything had been tal-lied and divided, that she'd rarely seen a divorcing couple so decent to each other, and their agreement reflected that. They would share time with the kids. She'd keep the house and he the bulk of their considerable savings. Their investments would be split. The household property and cars would be divided fairly. She kept her truck, he kept his Land Rover. He'd bought a condo downtown in the warehouse district. He planned on spending more time in Norway. She was going to do so in Gunflint. It still surprised her, even six months into their separation, that their lives could absorb so much upheaval. But of course they did.

"Oh, I forgot to mention," he said, "that trip has come through. I'll be in Antarctica for two weeks in February. Remember? We talked about it."

"That's great."

His face flickered alive, and she could almost hear what he

was going to say next. But as quickly as that, he merely shrugged and looked back down. That was something else she'd have to get used to.

The last night he stayed in the house with her—months earlier, he'd been sleeping in his office in the basement—he'd come upstairs after the kids went to bed. He poured himself a glass of wine and asked if she wanted one. She said yes and he poured it for her and they sat at the kitchen counter and he told her about the Antarctica trip. Asking, more or less, for her permission, a thing he'd never done before. "It'll only be two or three weeks. And maybe another trip a couple months later. Real meaningful work again. At the Troll Station."

"Of course," she said. "It's a dream come true for you." He'd wanted to go for so many years.

He sighed, then got up and went to the bathroom, and when he wasn't back ten minutes later she tiptoed to the door and held her ear close and listened to his breath catching as he sobbed. Then she went back to her stool at the counter and pretended to read the newspaper. Five minutes later, he returned and sat down. She could see him mustering up courage before he said, "Will you ever tell me why? *Really* why?"

"I'll try."

"Was it all because of Alena?" He said her name more and more these days. "Or what else?"

"I wish I could explain," she said. And that was true. He'd asked some version of this question many times, her only answer always escaping further and further into the fog of her former self. She did know, with great clarity, that by leaving him she had saved herself, and that she would pay whatever the fates meant to collect. "But I'll try. Someday."

He drank his wine in a long gulp. "Can I ask you a favor?"

"Of course," she said.

"Can I hold your hand?"

Greta pushed their glasses aside and took his hand and he wept freely, silently. What could she say? What was left to say?

But it was Frans who spoke, just barely above a whisper. "I'm sorry."

Now she cried too. From sadness and happiness both. For the regrets and mistakes. For all she had gained, and all she had lost. For herself and for him. For Lasse and for Liv. For all the memories of nights like this last, there at the kitchen counter. After a while, Frans got up and hooked the dog on a leash. He stood at the back door zipping up his jacket, putting on his hat and gloves, then turned back to her. "Thanks," he said, and took Axel out for a walk.

"Frans," Greta said. A group of photographers and journalists was crossing between them, a boom mic and bright lights and television cameras shining on the face of some notable litigant, she didn't know or care who. "Frans," she said again.

When the crowd passed and the courthouse floor settled between them like a narrows on a still river, he looked across to her.

"Which one of us will take Axel?"

"Did we not talk about that?"

She shook her head.

"You keep him," he said. "Okay? He's your dog. He loves you the best."

Axel rests his chin on her foot and she reaches down to scratch him. Above and below his sweet bellows she can hear the wind changing directions, an easterly blow now. She dims the lantern and steps to the window and cups her hands close to the glass to look outside. That's the Fonn, she thinks.

She goes over and adds a log to the fire and returns to her desk. She opens her computer and plugs in her headphones and opens the file Stig had e-mailed her on Valentine's Day, his recording of "Vannhimmel" made on board the *Vannhimmel*. Five hundred times she's listened to it. So many times that she imagines she can play it herself, though never once has she sat down at the piano she bought him and tried. The song was his gift to her, after all, as the piano is hers to him. She will wait for him to play it.

She clicks the cursor on the line beneath the title and closes her eyes. Before commencing her other work she listens to Stig's performance, all seven minutes of it, then opens her eyes and plays it again. The music is also an invocation, and there with the lantern light and wind, with Axel under her desk and Liv asleep by the fire, she's visited by Odd Einar one final time. He's on his way to the cemetery, two cloudberry stems pinched between his thumb and forefinger, flowers picked on his walk down from the Gammelveinen, where he and Inger have lived for the past two and a half years.

If Greta has worried from time to time that her communion with Odd Einar is peculiar, in these last days together she's learned she was wrong about that. He's taught her as much about love as her grandfather ever did. He's taught her as much about perseverance and determination as her father, who's no slouch in those departments. He's taught her about patience. About forgiveness. About faith.

When she sees Odd Einar reach the Kirkegata with those flowers in his hand and he turns back to face her and says, "I'm going one more time to say goodbye," Greta bows and says, "I know."

"Then I'm going to see Skjeggestad about some sails."

"I know that, too."

"Inger would think me a fool. Anyone would. But Thea is all I have left."

This time he doesn't wait for Greta to answer back. He just hums that old Christmas song his daughter wrote for her mother so long ago. Greta doesn't have the heart to call after him. She can't bring herself to tell him that his daughter died in 1896, less than a month after giving birth to her son, that the fever consuming her took three nights to do its work, that the last thing she saw was the empty cradle beside her own bed and the last thing she heard was her son cooing in the next room. How could she tell him any of these things? Or that this moment in her story is as close as he's ever going to come to knowing what happened to Thea?

Or is it? Maybe some part of him has known for a long time.

Maybe he's not going looking for her, but for the end of his sorrow. In any case, he's walking away from Greta now and it's too late to ask him anything else, so she watches instead.

At the cemetery gate I paused, as I did every time I visited Inger, and recalled the morning two and a half years ago when the pastor offered a prayer over my grave. Life between then and now had made me into a different man many times over, but none so absolutely as an evening this April when I returned from a day on the water. The kanelbolle Inger had baked the night before still lay under the cheesecloth on the board by the oven. The socks she was knitting were heaped in the basket beside her chair. A basin of bathwater sat beneath the window, cold. Since we'd lived in those rooms, I had come to know just by the quality of the air whether my sweet wife was home or not, and when I called for her that day the rebounding silence told me all.

I found Inger in bed, her book in her hands, her eyes open and unblinking, her cup of tea on the bedside table every bit as cold as the water in the basin. She must have gotten up and readied her bath and made her tea. Must have felt unwell and returned to bed. And though it was not uncommon for her to pick up her Bible, she rarely did so of a morning, when much work beckoned.

I stood there looking down at my wife and wondering had she known what was happening? Did she call my name? Or think of me at all? For the first time since Spitzbergen, I missed my faith. I wanted to pray for her. That she'd felt no pain. But how could I pray she had not suffered? Or was now at peace? How could I even consider raising my voice to heaven?

Instead I went to her side and knelt. I touched her eyes shut and ran my hand down her hair. I folded my hands in hers and rested my forehead on her lap. And what I did instead of pray was hope. I hoped that her faith was a comfort to her until the end. I hoped that her last thought was of her daughter. And as I wept there beside her, I hoped that when all her thinking was over she had passed with the surety of my love, along with God's, lighting the path to darkness.

When I got to her grave on this last day, I stood above it in the brilliant shine of midmorning and took the sun's warm grace to be her permission. I told her I would come back. That I would think of her every minute. That her love would light my path as I hoped mine had lit hers. And then I lay the two small flowers on her grave, and put my lips there too.

I walked out of the cemetery gates and on down the Kirkegata and through the village and out past the stream and around the harbor. I went up the road to Skjeggestad's and helloed into the darkness of his shop and when he emerged he was holding the new sail he'd sewn for me. He set it down on the workbench between us and took out his pipe and pouch, offering me a pinch.

"May this one always catch a fair breeze," he said, patting the rolled-up canvas. He struck a match and lit our pipes, then went back into his shop and came out with another roll of canvas that he set beside the sail. He showed me the brass grommets around the edge and the larger eyelet for the handle end of the extra oar I'd use to pitch this sheet like a tent.

"It looks just fine," I said.

"You'll be the driest fisherman ever to sail out of Hammerfest."

"Someday I'm going to build a new boat, with a pilothouse. But for now this will do."

"You've about remade that boat from tiller to tip, Odd Einar."

"She was in need of it."

He turned and gestured into the shop. "I can't think of another thing you'd need."

"Have you got a good bail bucket in there?" I patted the canvas. "And I suppose I'll need a rope for this."

"Ja, of course," he said, then disappeared once more and came out with a braid of his fine line sitting in a two-gallon bucket that he plopped on the counter.

"How much?"

He took the pencil from behind his ear and the pad of paper from his apron pocket and ciphered out my invoice. "With the bucket and line, make it twelve."

I put my pipe between my lips and counted out the silver from my coin purse.

"I thank you," he said. "Could you use a hand with all this?"

"You've helped more than enough." I took a last puff on my pipe and emptied the bowl and put it back in my pocket. Then I shouldered the canvas, lifted the bucket handle, and said goodbye.

"I'll look for her full of wind," he said, pointing at the sail.

Down on the quay, I loaded my new supplies on board. She'd never been so well appointed and I was anxious to embark, but there was one more stop I had to make. I walked back up to the Strandgaden and into the bakery. A bell chimed as I entered, and Gerd was there behind the counter.

"How are you, Fru Bjornsen?"

"All ready for you." She busied herself loading the baskets, stacking the bread and crackers carefully before closing the lids and lifting them from the wood counter behind her to the glass case between us. "Six loaves of rye, six dozen crackers, two pounds of butter, two jars of preserves, and enough cookies to finally fatten you up," she said. "All of it in separate tins."

"I'll be well fed, at least."

She came out from behind the counter and held the door open for me and we stood there outside, me with my baskets, Gerd shielding her eyes against the sun. "It's a fine day for getting started. Have you said your goodbyes?"

"Ja."

"Well, then," she said. "I'll keep you in my prayers, Odd Einar."

I put my finger to my lips as if to say "Shhhh," said goodbye again, and went back to my boat. I stepped aboard, stowed the baskets, untied her from the dockside cleat, and took my seat at the oars. The only person in the village who knew where I was going had just supplied my larder. Free of charge, I should mention. She and I having come to an agreement after Inger passed, by which she kept me in bread while I helped with the heavy lifting in her life. That *we had damn near become friends was proof that my allotment of miracles hadn't ended when the* Pobeg *emerged from the fog on the Krossfjorden.*

And I was not fool enough to think that what I now endeavored would require anything less than another miracle. I would go north around Sørø and hope for an easterly breeze to push me across the Norwegian Sea and on to Jan Mayen. If the wind blew kindly, I might expect to pass that island in four or five days' time. If I made it that far, I would consider the next thousand miles. And the thousand after that.

Ah, but first I had to leave the Hammerfest harbor. I pulled on the starboard oar, steering the bow of my faering around to lead. With all my cargo, she went heavy in the water, but I'd never trusted another boat as well. So I rowed out past Skansen and on up Sørøsundet toward Muolkot. Before the church tower fell out of sight I stood against the mast, hooking an arm around it to steady myself against the gentle chop. I raised my hand in a final goodbye, and whispered my love across the water, then I sat and took the oars again, closed my eyes to quell my tears, and tilted my face up for the warm sun. I opened them at the sound of a krykkje landing on the masthead. Its yellow beak parted, but it whispered, too, and all I could hear—all I would ever hear again—was my daughter's voice, beckoning me.

She wakes with her head on the desk, her arms folded across her thighs. The lantern is out and the fish house wracked in darkness. Axel must have gone back to sleep by Liv, and when Greta stands up, she expects to see them asleep in the hearth's glow. But the fire has burned to embers and she can't see anything there, so she looks outside instead. The snow's blowing with a ferocity she's not seen since she installed the window. The Fonn in a rage.

She picks her phone up to use its flashlight, but it's dead and she opens her computer. The bright blue of the screen casts shadows across her desk and onto her legs. It's 3:22 in the morning.

My God, can she ever lose the hours. She closes the computer, and goes over to stoke the fire. There's a chill in the air, and the house sounds like it used to, back when the wind howled in off the lake and through the interstices of the bowing boards with impunity.

She throws a log on the bed of coals and stirs it with the poker and before she turns around the blaze is back up. She studies the flames' lick, Odd Einar still on her mind as he so often is after she's spent time with him. She can't wait to tell Stig that she's finished his story. That she's set him on a course they themselves will be taking together in three short months, aboard the *Vannhimmel* instead of Odd Einar's old faering. Stig is bringing his boat to her. Bringing himself too.

One of the logs snaps and an ember flies out of the fireplace onto the hearth. She kicks it back toward the grate. Has all of her work telling Odd Einar's story been frivolous? An exercise in wishful thinking? Does she await the same fate he found, or one similarly cruel? Of course she'll never know, fate being unkind in the way of warnings. But she hopes not. Indeed, with this warm fire and this beautiful house, the story now finished on her desk, with Stig coming to her and Liv sleeping peacefully behind her and Lasse sleeping just as warmly up at Gus's house, she realizes that even though Odd Einar's life was difficult and beset by tragedy, the act of writing it down has restored to his memory a rightful dignity. But it's brought her some dignity too. After all, his story has helped her through some of the longest hours. Hours she misses Stig with an indescribable fervency. Odd Einar's been a companion during those lonesome times. Someone to walk with in Stig's absence. Someone to show her how to love with fierceness. She's getting good at it.

Greta turns to Liv, the covers up around her head, and she almost lets her be. But she wants to see her innocent face, so she pulls back the heavy comforter and Liv isn't there.

Greta jerks the comforter right off the chair, where only the stuffed polar bear and pillow remain. But Liv is definitely gone. Turning to run upstairs, she passes the door at the bottom of the stairwell and notices it's slightly ajar. She hadn't registered the wind now inside, and snow has drifted over the threshold, the cold filling up the house. She pushes the door shut, and hurries upstairs to see if Liv has climbed into bed.

But she's not there, either, and Greta rumbles back to the great room and checks beneath the comforter she laid out on the chair. No, Liv and Axel are both gone. She feels along the wall for his leash, but the only thing hanging there is her own jacket. She puts it on in a frenzy and slides her stocking feet into her shoes and pulls the door open and strains to see footprints in the snow. But it's dark and the snow blown smooth. She screams her daughter's name yet can hardly even hear it herself. Not above the wind shrieking off the lake. Running straight into it and the darkness, all she can see is her daughter lost in the immensity of the night, in the blackness of the storm out on the cruel ice.

At the shoreline, she pauses to holler for both Liv and Axel, cupping her hands around her mouth and screaming until her throat hurts and then bursting into sobs. Since her eyes are gaining on the night, she scans the snow on the ice for any sign of their tracks, but this snow might as well be the dust on the moon.

Just as she's about to head for the woods behind the house, Axel comes gamboling out of the pitch-black darkness, his leash trailing his long tail. He stops the second he sees her and sits immediately, like he's been caught misbehaving.

She drops to her knees and grabs his ears and shouts, "Where's Liv?"

Axel squirms free and tilts his chin into the night and lets out a howl unlike any she's ever heard from him, one very much like those of the wolves she often hears at night. He howls again and then stands and shakes the snow from his coat. Greta jumps up and starts after him out onto the lake, still hollering. Pleading with the night.

And at last there's a light, faint but true and unmistakable. It stops her where she stands, then she turns and sees, from thirty paces away, that it's coming from the lamp on her desk through the fish house window. This confuses and disorients her, as sudden light often can, and for a second she thinks to go toward it. Back to the house. But then she remembers and turns toward the lake.

Liv's tripping through the snow there, the hood on her jacket pulled up. She's wearing a scarf and even has her snow pants on. Greta rushes to her and unwraps the scarf from Liv's chin, and what she sees in the faltering light from the fish house across the yard is her daughter's smile. What she hears is Liv's laughter, and her voice explaining below the wind that Axel had to go out and she knew she could take him out. That she was brave enough to do it.

Greta pulls Liv close and kisses her cold cheek, and together they turn and are blown back to the fish house holding hands, the light from the window summoning them home.

This novel features the historical figures of Fridtjof Nansen and Otto Sverdrup, whose first voyage aboard the *Fram*, which began in 1893, plays a small part in the story. With one exception, I have attempted to be faithful to true events, most of which I've gleaned from Nansen's own book, *Farthest North*, and Roland Huntford's essential biography of him.

When Nansen returned to the Norwegian mainland with Frederik Johansen in the late summer of 1896, having been farther north than any man in history, they landed first in Vardø aboard a vessel called *Windward*. The following day, they sailed on to Hammerfest, where they were given their heroes' welcome and where Nansen saw his wife, Eva, after a nearly three-year separation. While there, the Nansens stayed aboard a yacht called *Otaria*, which was anchored in Hammerfest harbor. All of this is true to the best of my knowledge.

The fictional liberty I've taken comes in the story of Nansen and Johansen reuniting with Otto Sverdrup, who captained the *Fram* and was the leader of the expedition while Nansen and Johansen made their run for the North Pole. In fact this reunion occurred in Tromsø, whereas in this novel it happens in Hammerfest. Though the time line reflects the historical record, and though my imagining of their personalities was based on extensive research, as characters in this book they are purely fictional.

Three other historical figures are mentioned in this novel: Christian Skredsvig, Adolf Lindstrøm, and Svend Foyn. Their lives have been fictionalized as well. The real-life vessels I've included are the *Fram, Gjøa, Otaria,* and *Lofoten,* which Otto Sverdrup himself captained in the summer of 1897 for the steamship company Vesteraalen, which owned it.

With respect to Norwegian place names and words, I have employed—for simplicity's sake—the spellings and diacritics of contemporary usage.

One final note: Though there are graves in the Hammerfest cemetery with the surname Eide inscribed on them, they're not related to the Eide family of this novel, which is wholly fictional.

ACKNOWLEDGMENTS

THANKS:

First, to Jesseca Salky, for her tirelessness and excellent counsel, and to Rachel Altemose.

To Gary Fisketjon, friend and magic man, you've charmed every one of these pages.

To the crew at Knopf: Sarah New, Suzanne Smith, Jason Gobble, John Gall, Pei Koay, Kathleen Fridella, Susan Brown, Zachary Lutz, Emily Wilkerson, Kathy Hourigan, and Sonny Mehta. And especially to Tim O'Connell and Anna Kaufman for stepping in when the going got tough.

To Matt Batt, Steph Opitz Lanford, and Chris Cander, fair readers all.

To Beckett and Augie, for letting me turn the playroom into an office.

To Finn, Cormac, Eisa, you guys inspire and amaze me.

And to Emily, whose love not only made writing this book possible, but helped make it better too. You are the whole wide sea, every drop of it.

WINTERING

One day, elderly, demented Harry Eide steps out of his sick-bed and disappears into the brutal, unforgiving Minnesota wilderness that surrounds his hometown of Gunflint. It's not the first time Harry has vanished. Thirty-odd years earlier, in 1963, he'd fled his marriage with his eighteen-year-old-son Gustav in tow. He'd promised Gustav a rambunctious adventure, two men taking on the woods in winter. With Harry gone for the second (and last) time, unable to survive the woods he'd once braved, his son Gus, now grown, sets out to relate the story of their first disappearance—bears and ice floes and all—to Berit Lovig, an old woman who shares a special, if turbulent, bond with Harry. Wintering is a thrilling adventure story wrapped in the deep, dark history of a rural town. *Wintering* is a true epic: a love story that spans sixty years, generations' worth of feuds, and secrets withheld and revealed.

Fiction